also by c. c. hunter

WEDNESDAY BOOKS
NEW YORK

THIS HEART OF MINE. Copyright © 2018 by Christie Craig. All rights
reserved. Printed in the United States of America. For information,
address St. Martin's Press, 175 Fifth Avenue, New York, N.Y. 10010.

www.stmartins.com

Designed by Anna Gorovoy

Library of Congress Control Number: 2018931151

ISBN 978-1-250-13165-2 (hardcover)
ISBN 978-1-250-03589-9 (ebook)
ISBN 978-1-250-03590-5 (trade paperback)

Our books may be purchased in bulk for promotional, educational,
or business use. Please contact your local bookseller or the Macmillan
Corporate and Premium Sales Department at 1-800-221-7945, extension
5442, or by email at MacmillanSpecialMarkets@macmillan.com.

First Wednesday Books Paperback Edition: February 2019

10 9 8 7 6 5 4 3 2 1

To the donor and family of the donor from whom my husband received his kidney and his second chance at life: thank you for giving us the precious gift of time.

To Dr. Anna Kagan, my husband's transplant nephrologist, whose bedside manner and caring nature inspired the fictional Dr. Hughes in this novel. Thank you for your kindness, and for all the effort in keeping my husband alive and kicking. Thank you for the heartfelt hug you gave me and my daughter that scary day when they moved my husband into ICU; it warmed my soul and speaks not only to your ability as a doctor, but to the caring person you are beneath the white coat.

To Dr. Bree, my husband's cardiologist, who told us that if he got a kidney, his heart could improve. Your words gave us hope when others seemed to steal it from us.

To my husband, who went through it all and almost never complained. You set the bar of whining so high, I don't know if I can meet those standards, but I'm going to try. Thank you for being the man you are. The man I love.

ACKNOWLEDGMENTS

Writing a book requires such dedication that so often an author's ability to do it stems from the support of those around her. So thank you to my family, to my friends. To my agent, Kim Lionetti, who after listening to this idea said, "You are going to write this book!" To my new editor, Sara Goodman, who took over *This Heart of Mine* midproject and helped make it what it is today—thank you for all your work. And to Rose Hilliard, who got the book up and going and whose belief in me and my career never wavered.

this

of

mine

MAY 13TH

"It's over, Eric. Accept it. Let it go, would you?" The words echo from a cell phone into the dark night.

Eric Kenner sits at the patio table in his backyard, listening over and over again to Cassie's voicemail. Listening to the pool's pump vibrate. Listening to the pain vibrate in his chest.

"I can't let it go." Pain tumbles out of him. It is so damn wrong. He can't accept it.

Glancing back, he sees the light in his mom's bedroom go off. It's barely eight. She probably took another Xanax. His mom can't accept things either.

Why did life have to be so damn hard? Was he cursed?

He hits replay on his phone. Hoping to hear a crack in

Cassie's voice, something that tells him she doesn't mean it. There's no crack in her voice, just the one in his heart.

He bolts up, sending the patio chair crashing into the concrete. Snatching the piece of furniture, he hurls it into the pool. The chair floats on top of the water. While he feels as if he's sinking, drowning.

He swings around and shoots inside. Moving through the kitchen, then the living room, he stops in front of the forgotten space that was his father's study.

His dad would have known what to do.

Eric walks in. The door clicking shut shatters the silence. The room smells dusty, musty, like old books. The streetlight from the front yard spills silver light through the window. The beige walls look aged. The space feels lonely and abandoned.

The huge clock on the wall no longer moves. In here, time has stopped—just like his dad's life.

Eric's gaze lands on the flag, the one the military handed him at his father's funeral. The thing sits on the worn leather sofa, still folded, as if waiting for someone to put it away.

They called his dad a hero—as if remembering him that way would make his death easier. It hasn't.

It would have been his dad's last mission. The day he left, he'd doled out promises—camping trips, redoing the engine of the old Mustang in the garage. Promises that died with him.

Moving behind the mahogany desk, Eric drops into his dad's chair. It creaks as if complaining he isn't the man his dad was. Leaning forward, Eric opens the top drawer.

Swallowing a lump that feels like a piece of his broken heart, his eyes zoom in on one item. He reaches in and pulls it out. It's heavy and cold against his palm.

He stares at the gun. Maybe he does know how to fix this.

If he can find the courage.

1

ONE MONTH EARLIER
APRIL 13TH

"You lucky bitch!" I drop back down on my pink bedspread, phone to ear, knowing Brandy is dancing on cloud nine and I'm dancing with her. I glance at the door to make sure Mom isn't hovering and about to freak over my language. Again.

She isn't there.

Lately, I can't seem to control what comes out of my mouth. Mom blames it on too much daytime who's-the-baby-daddy television. She could be right. But hey, a girl's gotta have some fun.

"Where he's taking you?" I ask.

"Pablo's Pizza." Brandy's tone lost the oh-God shriek quality. "Why . . . why don't you come with us?"

"On your date? Are you freaking nuts?"

4

C.C. HUNTER

"You go to the doctor's office, you could—"

"No. That's *hell* no!" I even hate going to the doctor's office. If people stare long enough they see the tube. But this isn't even about me. "I'd die before I get between you—"

"Don't say that!" Brandy's emotional reprimand rings too loud. Too painful.

"It's just a figure of speech," I say, but in so many ways it's not. I'm dying. I've accepted that. The people in my life haven't. So, for them, I pretend. Or try to.

"But if you—"

"Stop. I'm not going."

There's a gulp of silence. That's when I realize my "lucky bitch" comment brought on the pity invite. Brandy's worried I'm jealous. And okay, maybe I am, a little. But my grandmother used to say it was okay to see someone in a beautiful red dress and think, I want a dress like hers. But it wasn't okay to think, I want a dress like hers and I want her to have a wart on her nose.

I don't wish Brandy warts. She's had the hots for Brian for years. She deserves Brian.

Do I deserve something besides the lousy card fate dealt to me? Hell yeah. But what am I going to do? Cry? I tried that. I've moved on.

Now I've got my bucket list. And my books.

The books are part of my bucket list. I want to read a hundred. At least a hundred. I started counting after I got out of the hospital the first time I survived an infection from my artificial heart. I'm at book twenty-eight now. I won't mention how many of them were romance novels.

"Leah," Brandy starts in again.

The chime of the doorbell has me glancing at the pink clock on my bedside table.

It's study time. Algebra. I hate it. But I kind of like hating it. Because I hated it before I got sick. Hating the same things as before makes me feel more like the old me.

"Gotta go. Ms. Strong is here." I bounce my heels on the bed. The beaks on my Donald Duck slippers bob up and down. Lately, I've been into cartoon-character slippers. They make my feet look happy. Mom's bought me three pairs: Mickey, Donald, and Dumbo.

"But—" Brandy tries again.

"No. But you're gonna tell me everything. All the sexy details. How good he kisses. How good he smells. How many times you catch him staring at your boobs."

Yep, I'm jealous all right. But I'm not a heartless bitch. Well, maybe I am. Heartless, really *heart*less, but not so much a bitch. I carry an artificial heart around in a backpack. It's keeping me alive.

"I always tell you everything," Brandy says.

No, but you used to. I stare up at my whirling polka-dot ceiling fan. Even Brandy's walking on eggshells, scared she'll say something to remind me that I got a raw deal, something that will make me feel sorry for myself. I'm done doing that. But I hate hearing that crunch as people tiptoe around the truth.

"Leah." Mom calls me.

"Gotta go." I hang up, grab my heart, and get ready to face algebra.

I really hate it, but it's number one on my bucket list—my last hurrah. Well, not algebra, but graduating high school. And I don't want a diploma handed to me. I want to earn it.

I spot Mom standing in the entrance of the dining room turned study. She's rubbing her palms over her hips. A nervous habit, though I have no idea what's got her jittery now. I survived the last infection and the one before that. She hears my footsteps, looks at me. Her brow puckers—another sign of serious mama fret.

I stop. Why's she so nervous? "What?"

"Ms. Strong couldn't make it." She's rushes off faster than her hurried words.

I hear someone shuffling in the dining room. I'm leery. Hesitant. I move in. My Donald Duck slippers skid to a quick stop when I see the dark-haired boy at the table.

"Shit." I suck my lips into my mouth in hopes I didn't say it loud enough for him to hear.

He grins. He heard me. That smile is as good as the ones I read about in romance novels. Smiles described as crooked, mind-stopping, or coming with a melt-me-now quality. I swear my artificial heart skips two beats.

He's one of the Kenner twins, either Eric or Matt, the two hottest boys in school. I used to be able to tell them apart, but now I'm not sure of anything. If I combed my hair today. If I brushed my teeth. If I have on a bra?

I close my mouth, run my tongue over my fuzzy-feeling teeth, trying to quietly suck them clean.

Glancing down, away from his eyes, I rock back and forth on my heels, my Donald Ducks' bills rocking with me. Should I run back to my room? But how pathetic will I look then? And if I do, he'll leave. Lifting my gaze, I realize I'm not sure I want him to go. I kinda like looking at him.

"Hey," he says.

"Hey," I mimic and realize I'm hiding the backpack behind my leg. I give my bright red tank top a tug down to cover the tube that extends from the backpack and pokes into me under my left ribcage. A hole that kinda looks like a second belly button. Yup, I'm hiding the very thing that's keeping me alive.

"Ms. Strong couldn't make it," he says as if reading my mood and realizing he needs to justify his being here. "She asked me to sub."

"For how many extra credit points?" I wait for him to tell me he did it just out of kindness. And, if true, it would mean he did it out of pity. I'm not sure I'd enjoy looking at him anymore. I'd rather be someone's means to a better grade. Brandy told me that everyone in school knows about my dead heart.

"Fifteen. I got lazy and didn't turn in some homework. You'll pump me up to a B."

"You should have held out for twenty."

He smiles again. "I don't think it was negotiable."

Moving in, I try to guess which twin he is. I try to figure out how to ask, but everything I think of sounds lame. *Let him be Matt.*

I had a thing for Matt since seventh grade. It might have been wishful thinking, but in tenth grade I thought he liked me too. Not that it ever went anywhere. He was football, I was book club. He was popular, I was . . . not. Then I started dating Trent. A guy in book club. A guy I let off the hook as soon as I found out my heart was dying.

"Your books?" he asks.

I don't understand the question, until I see he's pointing to my backpack.

Crap! I freak a little. I have several pat answers in my head that I came up with when Mom, afraid I was turning into an agoraphobe, insisted I get out of the house. But I can't remember them. The silence reeks of awkwardness.

So I go with the truth. "No. It's my . . . heart."

"Shit." He spills my favorite word.

I laugh.

His eyes meet mine and he smiles again. Yup, it's kinda crooked. My mind's not working. And I'm melting.

"Oh, you're joking," he says. "Right?"

I nod yes then shake my head no as if I don't know the answer.

His smile fades like a light on a dimmer switch. "Seriously?"

"Seriously." I move to the desk in the corner. One-handed,

I pull my math book from a drawer and drop down in the chair across from him. My heart lands in the chair beside me, so he can't see my tube.

When I glance up, he's doing exactly what I expect. Looking at the books so he doesn't have to look at me. People have a hard time facing me, facing my death, maybe even facing their own mortality. I understand, but it still bothers me.

He turns a page. The silence is so loud, I can almost hear the page float down to find its place. "Ms. Strong said we should start on chapter six."

"Yeah." Disappointed, I flip my book open and consider letting him off the hook, telling him I've got this, assuring him I won't mention it to Ms. Strong. But I look up, and I'm suddenly feeling selfish.

Hey, he's getting extra credit.

He glances up, and before I can look away, our eyes meet and lock. And hold. Longer than they should, because it feels . . . too. Too much. Too intimate. As if we've passed some invisible barrier. Like when a stranger stands too close to you in line.

We both look away.

He smacks the book closed. He flinches.

"What happened?" He whispers the question. His tone sad, sweet, and somehow still sexy.

I admire that he asked. Most people don't.

"A virus. It killed my heart." I hate the haunted look I see in his eyes. The sexiness vanishes. "It's highly contagious."

The oh-poor-you look on his face flips right to fear. Joking with him feels right.

I lose it. A laugh bubbles out of me and I feel instantly lighter.

"Real funny." He chuckles.

A crazy thought hits, one that says there's something almost . . . rusty about his laugh. And bam, I remember. I feel like the heartless bitch I swear I'm not for forgetting.

Not quite a year ago, his dad, a soldier, was killed. I'd been in the hospital, right after my condition had been diagnosed. His dad had been on the news, where they showed the pictures of soldiers and asked for a moment of silence.

I feel my smile slip from my eyes, my lips, and fall completely off my face. I know the look he sees in my eyes is probably the same pity-filled expression I saw in his seconds ago.

"I'm sorry," I say. "About your dad. I just remembered."

Ah, hell. Now I made his smile fall off his face. I should've kept my mouth shut.

"Yeah." He looks back at the book. "It sucks."

"Sort of like this." I motion to my backpack.

He glances again at the chair holding my heart. "Was it really a virus?"

"Yeah. The virus caused myocarditis."

His gaze sticks to my backpack. "How does it work?"

It's a question no one has ever asked. "Just like a heart. It's a pump. Sends my blood through my veins and throughout my body." I summarize the surgery to connect the pump that's in my backpack and the batteries I have to carry.

He makes a face, even rubs his chest as if feeling empathetic pain. "So you have a tube going inside you?"

I touch my shirt, right under my left rib, where the tube goes in. "Gross, huh?"

"Yeah, but it's keeping you alive, so . . . not really."

I agree. The hesitant footsteps easing down the hall pull my gaze from his.

Mom stops at the door. "Do you guys need something to drink or eat?"

She's rubbing her palms on her jeans again. Her pinched maternal concern locks on me. She's worried I'm mad about his being here. It's odd that I'm not.

The only person from my old life I've allowed to be close to "Dying Leah" is Brandy. And the only reason I allowed it was because she wouldn't go away. Both Mom and Dad have been pushing me to get out some. Socialize. There was even mention of my going back to school. I nixed that idea really fast. I want to graduate, but facing my peers while carrying my heart . . . Unh, uhh. Not doing it.

I have good reasons too. In seventh grade, Shelly Black had leukemia. She came to school bald, wearing a scarf. Everyone tried not to show her how difficult it was to see her that way. She wasn't even my close friend. But my heart hurt for her. I'd rather be alone than put people through that. Then I look at the dark-haired hottie sitting across from me and wonder if that's what he feels now.

Then again, he chose to come here. He's asking me questions and seems interested in my answers. And it feels good talking to him. Like I'm a normal high school kid talking to a friend. An extremely hot friend.

I'm still not going back to school, but why not take advantage of this?

"I have sodas and chips." Mom's voice drags me back to reality.

I wait for him to answer. He declines with a thank-you.

Mom leaves, and we dive into algebra. We spend the next twenty minutes reading examples; then I do problems for him to check and see if I understand. It's not really awkward, but it's tougher than it is with Ms. Strong. I can't concentrate on math, because I'm concentrating on him. About which twin he is. Matt? Eric? Eric? Matt?

I recheck my answers before I push him the notebook. While he's reviewing my problems, I'm studying him. The shape of his lips. The cut of his jaw. The slight five o'clock shadow that tells me he's shaving.

I rub my index fingers against my thumbs and peer up at him through my lashes.

"You got it." Pride sounds in his voice. His smile reflects the same emotion. He pushes the notebook back. "You want to do some more?"

I want to say no, but I'm afraid he'll leave. And I'm feeling greedier than ever. I want my forty-five minutes. "Sure."

Then without thinking, I blurt out, "Instead, can I just ask you something?"

We stare across at each other again. "If I can ask you something," he counters.

"Okay." I rub the soles of my slippers on the wood floor under the table. "Me first." How to ask it? "I . . . I used to be able to tell you and your brother apart. But now . . ."

He grins, but almost looks disappointed. "Now you can't? You don't know who I am?"

"Guilty." Frowning, I flatten my palms, now slick from nerves, on the table. "So which one are you?"

He shoulders back in the chair. His posture's crooked. One shoulder is higher than the other. Didn't Matt used to sit like that? "How did you tell us apart before?"

"You mean physically or your personality?" Now I'm thinking I should have kept my mouth shut.

"Both." Anticipation brightens his eyes.

It's as if my answer matters. As if I need to be careful what I say.

"Uh, Eric wore his hair a little longer. Matt's hair was a little curlier." Unable to stop myself, I look at his hair, remembering sitting behind Matt in English, studying how it would curl up, and wondering if it was as soft as it looked. A lot of girls, bolder than I, would play with his curls. I always wished I had the guts to do it. But I was gutless. The bravest thing I ever did in school was start a book club.

My gaze shifts away from his hair. "And one of you is a little broader in the shoulders."

"Which one?" He sits straighter, his chest lifts, his shoulders stretch out.

I'm scared to answer, but that would be awkward.

"Eric?" I try to read his expression, but he seems to purposely keep it blank. "Not that both of you aren't . . . buff," I say for a lack of another word and feel myself blushing, because buff sounds . . . sexy or something.

He grins. "And?"

"Personality wise, Matt's quieter, more of a thinker. Eric's more outspoken."

He picks up his pencil and rolls it between his two palms leaving me to think he's rolling my answers around in his head.

The pencil slows down. I swear my heart speeds up like my old one would have.

"So which one am I? Buff and outspoken or thin and quiet."

"I didn't say thin or quiet. I said less buff and quieter." The desire to say I preferred Matt over Eric tap dances on my tongue, but if he's Eric?

He laughs and that sound is like magic, less rusty, more melting.

I'm sure he's Matt. Eric didn't have the same effect on me. Maybe I imagined it, but I could swear that Matt actually . . . noticed me. I don't think I hit Eric's radar. He had too many cheerleaders falling all over him. Not that Matt didn't have the girls flashing him smiles and playing with his curls. He just didn't seem like it went to his head as much. Sometimes, it even looked like it embarrassed him.

My backpack beeps, shattering that comfortable silence that we'd finally found. The dreaded chirp lets me know that I have less than thirty minutes of battery life left. Panic flashes in Matt eyes. Or is he Eric?

"It's normal," I say, but because of that noise, of that damn tube, of my own dead heart, I feel anything but normal.

"So is this like forever?" he asks.

I shake my head. "No, it's supposed to be until I get a transplant."

"Supposed to be?" His gaze sweeps over me.

I look toward the hall to make sure Mom isn't around. So far, the truth has worked with him, and I decide not to waver from my approach. "I have a kind of rare blood type. AB. The odds aren't great."

"AB?" His brow wrinkles. "It's not that rare. I have it. If it was a kidney, I'd give you one."

I laugh, but this one's forced. I hate thinking about a transplant. Not just because I don't think it'll happen, but because someone having to die to give me life is all kinds of wrong. And that's what my parents and even Brandy are doing. Sitting around hoping someone will die.

That's even worse than wishing warts on someone.

"But . . ." The pause seems to mean something. "You . . . you just stay on this until a heart's available."

Okay. The truth didn't work. "Yeah," I say what he wants to hear. What everyone wants to hear. Never mind I've had two infections due to the artificial heart and each one nearly killed me. Never mind that no one has lived more than four years with an artificial heart. Never mind that hundreds of AB-blood-type people are waiting for a new heart, a new life, a miracle.

He frowns. "The way you say it sounds as if you don't believe . . ."

I need to work on that. "I'm sure it'll happen," I lie, and then suddenly I don't want to. I don't have to. Not with him. I sit up taller. "Look, it takes a lot more energy to hope than to accept. I'd rather spend my energy enjoying what I've got now."

"That really sucks." His frown deepens.

"Yeah, it does. But I'm okay with it." And for the most part, I really am. At first I kept telling myself that I had to hope, that a heart would come. But the more I read about statistics, the more I came to realize that the odds of getting a heart were slim to none. And rather than fooling myself or sitting around being miserable, I decided to make the most of the time I have left. Hence the bucket list. And I'm happier now. Really.

He looks up at the clock. "I guess I should be going."

I want to tell him he doesn't have to rush off. How sad is it that this is the most fun and the most alive I've felt all year?

He stands up. I do the same, then slip on the backpack, always hiding the tube.

He moves down the hall. I follow. I'm staring at his hair, the way it flips up. Again hoping he's Matt. I'm so into his hair, I don't notice him swing around.

We run smack-dab into each other.

"Shit." He grabs me by my shoulders and pulls me against him. "Are you okay?"

His hands are on my upper arms. My breasts are against his chest.

Then bam! I feel something I haven't felt in a long time. Excitement. My very own I'm-a-girl-and-you're-a-boy excitement. Not the borrowed thrill I get from reading romances.

I can smell him. Like men's soap, or deodorant; a little spicy, a lot masculine. The desire to lean in and bury my nose in his shoulder is so strong I have to fist my hands.

"I'm fine," I say. *Don't pull away. Don't pull away. Please don't pull away.*

He doesn't pull away. He gazes down at me. This close I can see he has gold and green flecks in his brown eyes. A voice inside of me says I should step back, but you couldn't pay me to move. I'm dying. Is it wrong of me to want this?

"I . . . I forgot my books." The words fall from his lips in an uncertain tone. The pads of his thumbs rubs the insides of my arm. Just the tiniest, softest friction that feels so damn good.

I run my tongue over my bottom lip. "Oh, I . . . I thought you were going to kiss me." I hear my own words and wonder where I got the balls to say that.

His eyes widen. Not in an oh-crap way, but in a surprised kind of way. "Do you want me to kiss you?"

I grin. "If you're Matt, I've wanted you to kiss me since seventh grade."

His gaze lowers to my mouth and lingers. "Is your heart strong enough?"

I burst out laughing. "Are you that good of a kisser?"

"Maybe." A smile crinkles the corners of his eyes. He leans down. His lips are against mine, soft and sweet. I slip into sensory overload. I lean in and open my mouth and ease my tongue between his lips. Yeah, it's bold, but it's not like I'll live long enough to regret it.

His tongue brushes against mine. One hand moves to my waist, the other slides back behind my neck. He gently angles my face to deepen the kiss. I feel it, every contact that is his skin against mine. I feel awesome. So freaking alive.

I get even ballsier and reach up and run my fingers through his hair. It's even softer than I thought it'd be.

When he pulls back, we're breathing hard, and we stare at each other. The dazed look in his eyes tells me that this wasn't a pity kiss. We start inching closer. His lips are almost on mine again when the sound of the front door opening shatters the moment.

We jerk apart and walk back down the hall to the dining room. He picks up his books.

My dad calls out to my mom.

I ignore it.

All of my attention is on the guy standing in front of me, his lips still wet from our kiss. I grab a pen off the table, scribble my number on a notebook paper, rip it out, and hand it to him.

"If you ever want to talk. About everything that sucks," I add. Then I worry that sounded stupid.

He takes the paper. Our fingers meet and I feel that magic

spark and I don't care if it sounded stupid. I vow not to regret this. If he calls. If he doesn't. This was too good to ever regret.

We stare at each other again. I want to kiss him again so badly, I'm shaking. The sound of my parents talking in the kitchen echoes and invades this magical moment. I wish we were somewhere different. I wish . . . I wish . . . But before I stumble down that dangerous path of wishing for the impossible, I push it away.

He starts down the hall and I follow him to the door. He reaches for the knob then turns. We don't say anything, but we exchange smiles. In his eyes, I see a whisper of embarrassment, a touch of uncertainty, and a hint of something raw. I hope desire. He glances over my shoulder, as if making sure we're alone, then brushes a finger over my lips. Soft. Slow. Sensual.

I tell myself to memorize how it feels. This is the good stuff.

He turns and leaves, way before I'm ready for him to go.

I bolt to the side window, not too close in case he looks back, but close enough so I can watch him walking down my sidewalk. I watch him get in his car. I watch him drive off. I watch his car disappear down the road.

I lick my lips, still tasting his kiss. If I died right now, I'd go happy.

Mom and Dad's footsteps echo behind me. They say something, but I ignore them. I'm in that moment, reliving it. How his kiss felt. How his kiss tasted. How his hair felt. How sweet life is. It doesn't even matter that I'm dying.

I move in and press my forehead to the glass. It's cool, the April weather still holds a hint of chill in the air. Then I frown when I realize he never told me if he was Eric or Matt. I remember what I said about wanting Matt to kiss me since seventh grade. If he hadn't been Matt, he'd have told me, right?

My heart says it was Matt, but my heart isn't real. Can I believe it? Damn, I don't know who I kissed.

"Leah?"

I turn. Dad and Mom are staring at me, all happy like.

"That seemed to go well." Mom offers up a real smile. The kind that wrinkles the sides of her nose. It hits me then that I can't remember the last time her nose wrinkled like that. I put that on my bucket list. Give mom more nose wrinkles.

They look at me all goofy like. Part of me wonders if Mom saw us kissing. I don't care. If it makes her happy, I'd kiss him again. It wouldn't be a hardship.

"Yeah. It went well." Moving in, I hug her, then Dad. It becomes one of those group hugs. I hear my mom's breath shake, but it's not the bad kind of shake.

"I love you both." Emotion laces my words. Happy emotion. Then I break free and me and my Donald Ducks bounce back to my bedroom to plug in my heart.

While it's not supposed to work like that, I'm sure that kiss ate up a lot of battery life.

Once I plug in, I pick up the phone to call Brandy to tell her my boy news. Then I stop. Knowing Brandy, she'd feel obligated to find out whom I'd kissed, and even try to push him to come back. Maybe I'll just keep this to myself. My secret. The one I'll take with me to the grave.

2

The pizza's cold, the consistency of cardboard. For a moment, Matt Kenner thinks he's cut into the box, but he eats it anyway. It fills the hole in his stomach, but not his heart. He wants to call Leah. Wants to see her again. Wants to kiss her again.

Wants to freaking pound his fist into the kitchen table. Death had already robbed him of his dad.

The thump of a car door shutting has Matt sitting straighter. The swish and thud of the front door opening and closing adds to the late-night murmurs of the house. His brother's footsteps clip across the wood floors as he no doubt follows the one light on in the kitchen.

Matt looks over. Eric stands in the doorway. Eric, the buffer, more outspoken twin.

Matt's mind rolls that around for a second. It bumps into his ego. But Leah had wanted to kiss him—not Eric. Most girls Matt dated came to him by the way of Eric. When they couldn't catch the eye of the more popular twin, they set their sights on him. He never blamed his brother, but who wanted to be someone's second choice?

"Hey." Eric's keys hit the table. He sees the pizza, goes to the kitchen candy drawer and pulls out a handful of M&Ms, then drops into a chair. Snatching a piece of pizza, he takes a bite, then drops three M&Ms into his mouth. He swears chocolate and pizza were meant to be eaten together.

Right then, stale beer and another unpleasant smell mingle with the cold-pizza aroma. If his mom were up, and aware, she'd give Eric hell for drinking and driving. She isn't up. Isn't aware.

She'd been like this ever since their dad died. Going to sleep by eight after crashing from Xanax, only to get up the next morning and load up all over again.

"Should you be driving?" Matt fills in for his mom.

"I had two beers." Matt's disapproving expression is one more reserved for a parent than a brother, but the look doesn't hang on. His brother has done his share of filling in when it came to Matt too.

Eric rears his chair back on two legs. "I thought you were going with Ted to stay at his dad's lake house."

"I changed my mind."

"Why?"

Matt's only answer is a shoulder shrug. After he'd left Leah's, he'd just wanted to feed his stomach and be alone.

"Were you talking to someone?" Eric eyes the phone in Matt's hand.

"No. Just thinking." Matt sits his phone down on top of Leah's number.

His brother, pizza balanced on his fingertips in front of his face, studies Matt as if picking up on his mood. "About what?"

"Leah McKenzie." No real reason not to tell Eric.

"Who?" Eric shoves the pizza into his mouth, tosses in three candies, chews, then swallows. "Wait, isn't she that girl who's sick? The pretty one, dark hair and light blue eyes, but too shy."

Matt swipes his phone, pretends to read it, but his mind's on Leah. *Oh, I . . . thought you were going to kiss me.* She isn't shy anymore.

"You had a thing for her. Wasn't she the one you were trying to get the nerve to ask out but she started dating someone else?"

Matt feels Eric staring. "Yeah."

His brother takes another bite. Matt's ego feels dinged again. The day he'd been about to ask Leah out, he saw her in the school hall, standing shoulder to shoulder with Trent Becker. Matt had lost his chance. Which was the real reason he'd jumped at the opportunity to go to her house today. Yeah, he needed the extra credit, but he'd already resigned himself to getting a C.

"Why are you thinking about her?" Eric lowers the front chair legs, gets up, and pulls a soda from the fridge. "You want one?" he mumbles around a mouthful of pizza.

"Yeah." Matt takes the can, puts it on the table, palms it, and feels the cold burn on the inside of his hands. "I went to see her today."

"Why?" Eric pops the top on the soda, downs the fizzy noise, and drops back in the chair.

"Ms. Strong tutors her and couldn't make it today. She offered me extra credit to do it."

Eric's brow wrinkles. "Is she like dying sick, or just sick-sick?"

Leah appears in his mind, soft, smiling, and for some reason happy. "She doesn't look sick, but . . . she's got an artificial heart."

"Really? Like connected to a machine?"

"It's small, like a backpack. But . . ."

"But what?"

Matt spills, hoping it will lighten the weight in his chest. "She doesn't think she's gonna make it." Which is why he can't get how she could be happy.

"Damn." Empathy laces Eric's voice. He sips his soda and studies Matt over the rim as if he knows there's more to the story.

"I kissed her," Matt confesses. Keeping something from Eric is impossible. Identical twins know each other's secrets. That weird twin-connection thing. Mom used to tell the story of how Eric, only three, had broken his arm playing at a friend's house and Matt had come to her crying that his arm hurt before she'd even been notified. Matt couldn't remember it, so he wasn't a 100 percent certain it was true.

"Why?" Eric nearly chokes on the soda.

"She wanted me to. I wanted to."

Eric sets the can on the table with a half-full clunk. "No. You can't do this. Don't go there."

Matt stares at his unopened can. He wants to pick the damn thing up and throw it. "It's just—"

"No!" His brother's sharp tone brings Matt's gaze up. "Look at us. We haven't . . . We haven't gotten over losing Dad. Mom can't handle another loss. You can't handle another loss. We gotta heal, damn it. No more death around here."

Matt stops short of taking his anger out on Eric. Hadn't he just said the exact thing to himself? Wasn't that why he hadn't already called Leah? "I know."

"Seriously," Eric says. "We can't take on more grief."

"I said I know!" Matt closes his eyes, then opens them, wishing he didn't see Leah's smile, didn't see her dreamy expression after he'd kissed her. Silence fills the yellow kitchen. The color reminds him of Leah's Donald Duck house shoes.

Eric finishes off the slice of pizza and then licks his fingers. Matt feels the slice he'd eaten, a lump in his stomach. The silence stretches out for too many long seconds.

"Where've you been?" Matt asks, before the silence gives away just how hard this is for him.

"Nowhere, really."

The vague nonanswer smells like a lie. Matt raises an eyebrow.

Eric shrugs.

Just like that, Matt knows where Eric's been. "You're seeing Cassie again?"

"Get out of my head." His brother drops the chair down on four legs with a clunk.

"Like you don't stay in mine!" Matt picked up his soda then slams it down. "What did you just tell me? That we need to heal. Cassie isn't what I call healing."

His brother squeezes his can. The crunch of aluminum sounds tense. "First, this thing with Cassie isn't what you think. Second, getting involved with someone who's dying isn't in the same category as Cassie."

Dying. Matt flinches. "Maybe not, and nothing against Cassie, but she dumped you twice, and you went into a funk both times."

"I told you, I'm not dating Cassie. It's not like that."

"Then what's it like?" Matt hears his mom's tone in his voice.

"She's dealing with something." Eric exhales as if he's been carrying around old air, or old pain. Matt feels it too.

"What kind of something?"

"Will you stop it!" Eric belts out, then closes his eyes in regret. "She won't tell me. She won't tell anyone." His jaw clenches. "Everyone's saying she's been acting weird, so I talked to her, and something's definitely going on."

"Can't she turn to one of her friends for help?"

Eric's posture hardens. "I'm not going back to Cassie."

Yeah, you are. Matt can see it, even if Eric can't.

The *whoosh* of a toilet flushing from his mom's bathroom brings their eyes up and the tension takes an emotional U-turn. Not that it lessens, it just changes lanes.

Matt hates this lane.

His dad's death still hurts, but the way they're losing their mom is almost as bad. Instead of moving past the hole in her heart that their dad's death had brought on, she's curled up inside it. Lives and breathes the grief.

Matt exhales. "Did you call Aunt Karen?"

"Yeah." Eric shakes his head. "She going to call, but she can't come down. She's working some big case." He pauses. "She came down twice last month. We can't expect her to do more."

Matt stares at his hands cupping the cold soda. "Then we have to do more."

Eric nods.

"Maybe we could get Mom out of the house tomorrow," Matt says. "Go see a movie and eat dinner out. I'll see if I can get her to go jogging with me. She used to all the time."

Eric runs a hand down his face. "We could take her to the plant store. She used to love working in the yard."

"Yeah." Matt closes the pizza box. "You want another piece?"

"Nah. I'm out of M&Ms. Besides, I went by Desai Diner and ate the food of the gods."

"That's what I smell." Matt's brother's love for anything curry, and chocolate and pizza, are probably the only two differences in their tastes. Well, that and girls.

Standing, Matt sticks the leftover pizza back in the fridge, then snags his soda and phone. His gaze falls to the scrap of paper with Leah's number that he'd hidden under his cell. He picks it up, wads it up, feeling the same crumpled sensation in his chest, and tosses it in the garbage.

Eric is right. When one person in this family hurts, they all hurt. He can't do that to them.

3

MAY 15TH

Matt wakes up gasping for air. He blinks, trying to make out the images flashing in his head—images of running in the woods. Of fear. From what, he doesn't know. *Just a dream.*

Swiping a hand over his eyes, he sits up. Sharp stabbing pains explode in his head. He pushes his palm over his temple. Agony pulses in his head with each irate thump of his heart.

Though he's not certain why he's angry. He goes to get up, feels dizzy. Feels himself falling. But he's not falling. He still grabs for the dresser.

When able to walk, he heads to the bathroom in search of some painkillers. Swallowing two bitter pills without water, he stares at himself in the mirror. For one second he swears he sees Eric standing behind him; then he's gone.

Confused, he splashes cold water on his face. The pain fades but leaves a numb sensation.

He heads back to his room, stopping when he notices Eric's bedroom door is open. His brother sleeps with it shut. Matt peers in the room. The bed's unmade, empty. The clock on the bedside table flashes the time. Three A.M.

He walks to the kitchen thinking his brother is probably eating a bowl of cereal. The kitchen's as empty as the bed. The ice maker spews out a few chunks of ice. The air conditioner hums cool air through the house. Matt feels cold.

Frowning, he goes to peer out the living room window. His brother's car isn't here. Where the hell is he at three in the morning?

Damn him, he knows better than to stay out past midnight. Sure, his mom's no longer enforcing curfews, but they'd agreed to stick by the rules.

He shoots back to his room to call his brother. Eric's probably hanging with Cassie again. The 'not going back with her' promise hadn't lasted two weeks. This last month he's spent more time with Cassie than at home. And Matt sees the effect it's having on his brother. That girl isn't good for Eric.

He snatches up his phone already practicing the hell he'll give his brother, but then he notices he has a new text. From Eric.

When did that come in? Two fifty-three. Right before Matt woke up.

He reads the text. *I need . . .* Nothing more. Almost as if Eric had been interrupted and accidentally hit SEND.

What did Eric need?

Matt hits the call button. One ring. Two. Three. It goes to voicemail.

Hey, leave a message.

"Shit!" Matt mutters. At the beep he says, "Where are you, Eric? Call me. Now."

Right then he feels his brother behind him. Relief washes over him.

"Why are you late?" He swings around. Eric's not here.

Not here.

Not. Here.

The pain in Matt's temple starts throbbing again. His stomach churns. He recalls the nightmare of running in the woods and, just like that, he knows. It hadn't been him in the dream. Eric.

Chills crawl up Matt's spine, his neck, all the way up his head. He can't breathe. His brother's in trouble. He knows it like his lungs know how to take air. Like his eyes know how to blink. Like his heart knows how to beat.

His grip on his phone tightens, and he considers dialing 911. But to say what? *My brother's not home?* Eric's only three hours late.

How can Matt explain this feeling? This emptiness, the not-here feeling that is spreading through him like a virus. His stomach lurches. He rushes to the bathroom, barely making it to the toilet before he pukes. The retching sound echoes in the dark house.

He wipes his mouth with the back of his hand. Tears fill his eyes. No!

How can he explain to the police the god-awful feeling that's telling him Eric isn't just missing? He's gone.

"Are you okay?"

Matt keeps his head over the toilet but glances at his mom. Perched at the door, she's wearing the sweats she wore yesterday. Her blond hair is a mess—she's a mess. "Are you sick, hon?"

He tries to find his voice, but can't. His throat isn't working. Not for talking. He pukes again.

Hands on his knees, his heart thumping in his head, he sees

her move to the cabinet. She pulls out a washcloth, runs water over it, then steps closer.

She brushes the cold wet cloth over his forehead, then lovingly swipes his wet bangs from his brow. Her green eyes meet his. For the first time in forever, he sees a hint of his old mom. And yet he knows he'll be losing her again.

"What's wrong, Matt?"

"I'm sorry," Dr. Bernard says. To her credit she looks sincerely remorseful.

Thirty-six hours. That's how long it had been since Matt woke up knowing. That's how long it took for the doctors to tell Matt and his mom what he already knew.

"All of the tests confirmed my fears. There's no brain activity."

His brother's dead. Brain death they called it.

He and his mom had called the police. They didn't seem to take it seriously. That changed at six this morning. The cops showed up on their doorstep with news that Eric had been found at a roadside park. A gunshot to the head. They life-flighted him to a hospital in Houston, where the best doctors work. But not even the best could save him. He was gone.

The police had found the gun next to his body. The Glock had belonged to their father. Gunpowder residue had been found on Eric's right hand. One of the cops used the words "possible attempted suicide."

Now they'd change it to "suicide."

Matt couldn't wrap his brain around that. He didn't have the stamina to fight it yet. Fighting didn't come nearly as naturally to him as to Eric. But as soon as he could breathe right, he planned on correcting the police.

Yeah, Eric got into funks, and he'd been acting off with the whole Cassie problem, but to kill himself? Not Eric.

His brother fought and won at everything. School, girls, sports. He didn't know how to say quit, much less do it. Eric never gave up.

More important, he'd never leave Matt and his mom like this. He knew what it would do to them.

His mom lets out a soulful groan that sounds like a wounded animal. Aunt Karen wraps her arm around his mom. Matt had called his aunt first thing and told her they were going to need her. He didn't need her, but he needed someone to take care of his mom, because he couldn't. He couldn't console himself, how the hell was he going to console her?

Breathing hurt. Blinking hurt. Being alive hurt.

The doctor leaves. His mom and aunt stand in the middle of the room holding on to each other. There are still three cops hanging around. He wishes they'd go find out what happened instead of just standing here, watching their pain as if they feed on it.

His mom makes sad noises, and his aunt says, "I know. I know. I know."

All that Matt knows is his brother is dead. Gone. He drops into the chair, drops his elbows on his knees, and tries to get his lungs to accept air.

He stays like that. Eyes closed. Trying to shut everything out, but he can't. He hears his mom crying, he hears his aunt soothing, he hears his heart breaking. And in the distance he can almost hear the beeping of the machine that forces air into Eric's lungs.

Matt breathes in.

Matt breathes out.

With the rhythm of the machine.

That's all he can do. Breathe. And that doesn't feel normal.

He closes his eyes and almost goes to sleep for the first time since it happened. Waking him up are voices. He looks up. There's a lady in a suit telling his mom something. He doesn't want to listen, but his mom cries harder. What could they say now that would hurt more than what's already been said?

His aunt's gaze beckons him to come over. Her green eyes, eyes that look just like his mom's, have more soul, more life. She hadn't lost her husband and her son.

He stands and goes to stand by his mother.

"No," his mom says. "No."

"What?" he says.

The woman focuses on him. "I'm with the transplant center. I know this is very difficult, and your loss is so great, but you have a chance to save—"

"Yes," he says before the woman finishes.

In the back of his mind, he remembers Leah and others who would get a second chance at life. But his heart hurts too much to think about her; he just knows that this is what Eric wanted.

"But I can't live with the thought of them taking . . ."

"Stop it, Mom!" Matt says. "Eric wanted this. You can't deny him that."

"I will not let them do this," his mom snaps.

He tries to find patience. Digs deep, but he doesn't find much. He curls his hands up. "Eric and I registered when we signed up for our licenses. He told me he wanted to do this. I'm not going to let you stop it."

"He never told me."

He might have if you'd ever come out of your bedroom. Thank God he finds the thread of strength not to say what he feels. Deep down he knows this isn't his mom's fault. It's not Eric's fault either.

"Well, he told me. It's on his license." He looks at the woman and sees she has Eric's license on her clipboard. He takes the board from her hand and shows it to his mom. Then he looks back at the woman. "Yes. The answer's yes."

The woman looks at his mom. Tears run down her cheeks.

She nods, turns around, buries herself in her sister's arms and sobs.

I'm reading a romance novel. The first kiss is about to happen. The phone rings. It's not him, I tell myself.

It rings again. I frown, now completely pulled out of the story. Not so much from the ring, but from hope that won't die. It's been a month.

It's not even my phone. He wouldn't call my home number.

Then I start ticking off every reason he would. He lost my cell number. He wanted to make sure that it was okay with my parents if he called me. Yup, sadly even after all this time, every time a phone rings, I hold my breath and wait for my mother to call my name and tell me it's for me. I allow myself to wish for something that I shouldn't.

"Leah!" My mom's voice rings all the way down the hall to my room. I suck in a quick breath, slap my romance novel closed, and look up as mom stops in my door. Mom with a phone in her hand. Mom with a strange look on her face. Hope flutters in my stomach like a butterfly beating its wings for the first time.

"Is it for me?"

She nods.

I smile. I stand up. That smile curls up inside my chest. I hold my hand out for the phone. I'm trembling inside. I try to think of what to say. I don't want to sound too eager, but . . .

Mom doesn't move. "Give it to me."

She blinks. "We . . . You. There's a heart available." Her voice sounds like she's inhaled helium.

It's not Matt, or Eric. It's . . . I digest what she said. Then it's like time stops. The air from my pink polka-dot ceiling fan whispers across my bare skin, and I feel the tiny hairs on my arms stand up. "You sure?" I shake my head, certain she's mistaken.

She nods. "Yes."

"Shit," I say, and hear it like it's too loud. My knees start to give, and I lock them. My plans hadn't included . . . living. It's not that it's an unwelcome change; it's just a huge change. One that includes . . . getting my chest cracked back open.

I drop back onto the mattress. The memory foam sucks me down. I'm stunned. I'm numb. Oh, shit! I'm scared.

My hands shake.

Mom smiles and cries at the same time. "Come on." She rubs her hands down the side of her pants. Up. Down. Up. Down.

I'm getting dizzy watching them, but I can't look away. I can't . . .

"We have to go. They want you there in an hour and a half. I'm calling your dad. Grab your bag from the closet. You're getting a heart, baby! You're getting a heart."

Standing, I feel numb and yet top heavy, as if I have too much emotion in my chest. I grab my extra battery that's charged and ready to go. I stick it in my backpack. I slip my shoes on. They feel too tight. Like they belong to someone else.

In less than five minutes we are out of the house. Dad works close to Houston. He's meeting us there. Mom keeps talking. I stop listening. I stare out the side window and watch the world pass by. Cars. Trees. Houses. People.

I wish I'd have remembered to bring a book. Something to help me forget this fear.

"It's gonna be fine," Mama says when we're a mile from the hospital, and I'm almost certain she's said it around a hundred times by now.

I want to believe her. I really try. I try not to remember the statistics of how many don't make it through the surgery. I try not to think about the person who just died. The person whose heart is going to be put into my chest.

I wonder how old they are? I wonder if someone is crying for them. Then my vision blurs and I realize I'm crying. Crying for them. Crying because I'm scared. Crying because if something goes wrong, I'll die. Today. I could die. Today.

I'm not ready. Maybe I've been fooling myself about accepting it. Or maybe it's just because I haven't completed my bucket list. I haven't graduated yet. I haven't read a hundred books. Haven't figured out if it was Matt or Eric who I kissed.

I haven't lived enough.

Matt stands in the hall, leaning against the wall. He ignores the nurses, doctors, the hospital sounds, and the smells. His mom and his aunt have gone into the room to say goodbye. They come out, looking older than when they went in. He tells them to go on back to the hotel. He wants to say goodbye alone. His mom argues. Then her sad eyes meet his, and she relents.

They start out, but his aunt swings around and hugs him. "You sure you're okay?"

There is nothing okay about this. But he forces the lie out. "Yeah."

He watches them walk down the long hall, getting smaller and smaller. Only when they turn does he walk into his brother's room. His lungs feel like they have liquid in them. He sits in a chair next to his brother's bed. He can't look at him.

The machine beeps, beeps, beeps and makes swishing sounds. Finally, he forces himself to watch his brother's chest go up and down. "Hey," he says. Not that he believes his brother is there. Or maybe he does.

He looks at his brother's face, almost completely bandaged. "A lot of damage," they'd said earlier.

Closing his eyes, Matt sits there, his heart beats with the

machine. Thu . . . thump. Thu . . . thump. He closes his eyes. After a minute, or maybe ten, he opens them.

He looks again at his brother. It's him, but it isn't. His personality, his essence is gone.

Seeing the clock on the wall, he realizes his time is up.

"What happened, Eric?" The damn knot crawls up higher in Matt's throat. Tears fill his eyes. He touches his brother's hand. Matt's breath catches when it feels cold.

He glances back to make sure no one is standing outside the door. Then he stands up and moves closer to his brother's side. "You know, you told me when Dad died that we just had to live for him. Well, now I've got to live for the both of you. That's hard to do."

Matt runs a hand over his face. His chest feels so tight he's sure it's gonna break. "I don't know how to be me without you."

His voice shakes. "I'm gonna try. I'll do right by Mom." He pauses. "But I'm pissed at her right now. If she hadn't . . . I know you didn't do this. I won't stop trying to find out who did. I promise you. Now go hang out with Dad. Tell him I love him."

He hears a slight shuffle and looks back. A nurse is in the doorway. Her eyes are wet. She walks up to him as if to hug him, but he holds out his hand.

He hurries out of the ICU and finds an empty family room. Dropping into a chair, he wipes the tears from his cheeks and tries to piece together what's left of his broken soul.

He leans back in the chair, closes his eyes, and attempts to smooth the emotional wrinkles from his head. Staring at the blackness of his eyelids, he lets his thoughts float away, feeling so damn tired. Maybe if he could sleep a few minutes . . .

Maybe.

He lets his shoulders relax. He's almost asleep when he sees it and feels it again. Sees Eric running through the trees. Fear swells in his chest, his brother's fear. He senses someone is giving chase. He can almost hear the thud of footsteps following. Who? Who would want to hurt Eric?

Matt shoots up from the chair. Runs a hand over his face. He feels Eric. Feels him here. "You trying to tell me something?" He waits for an answer and then . . . worries he's losing it.

Unsure what he believes, he heads to his car. The heat claws at his skin. The air feels thick. Sweat runs down his brow. He sticks his hands in his jeans and thinks about Eric's cold hand.

He stops walking, realizing he doesn't even know where he is. He looks around. His car isn't where he thought it was. He stands there, fisting his hands in his pockets. Then he remembers parking in front of the emergency room. He starts that way, through a maze of cars, hurrying to get out of the smothering air.

He rounds the corner of another building. Nearby voices float above the sound of traffic. Something familiar about the voices causes him to look up. He sees the dark-haired girl with a backpack about two rows over. Leah and her parents. His knees almost buckle.

His gaze stays on her, on the way she walks, a little slow, her shoulders slumped over as if she's carrying too much. And not all of it physical weight, but emotional.

Air, with the weight of cement, catches between his Adam's apple and tonsils. They're walking into the hospital.

Just like that he knows. Leah McKenzie is getting Eric's heart.

Eric wanted this. Matt wanted this. Yet an emotion he can't quite name pushes its way into his already crowded and clutching chest. Leah gets to live. Eric gets to die. That feels so unfair.

He waits for the three of them to get inside before he dares to take a step. Then he bolts to his car.

Climbing behind the wheel, he fists his hands onto the steering wheel, as if by hanging on to it, he's hanging on to his sanity. Five. Ten minutes later, he's still there.

Still hanging on.

He's not in a hurry to leave. Instead, he sits there trying to fit everything he feels in a nice, neat little package.

It won't fit.

It's not nice. It's not neat.

Even his father's death didn't hurt this bad.

4

I don't want to do this!

Tears. Hugs. Kisses. Then reminders from a nurse of what I can expect when I wake up from the surgery.

If I wake up.

My mom holds my hands. Her grip is tight. But not tight enough.

"You'll have the tube down your throat, just like with the other surgery," the transplant nurse continues. "Do you remember?"

As if I could forget waking up gagging, unable to swallow, or the ache in my chest bone that had been sawed in half and pulled apart. I still force a brave face for my parents' sake. I see the pain in their faces. It's worse than mine.

"Just a few more minutes." The nurse starts doing things to my gurney.

They are about to wheel me back, and the smidgen of bravado I had is gone. I swallow my tears. I don't think I can let go of Mom's hand.

I start shaking. I need to tell them things. Things I've been putting off. I start talking, fast. "I love you and I know all you've done for me. None of your sacrifices have gone unnoticed. If—"

"Stop," Mom screams, tears chasing tears down her pale cheeks. Her green eyes look too large, too much pain. "You are going to be fine."

"I know that," I lie. Now my dad has tears in his eyes. Great, now I'm gonna cry.

"We need to go," the nurse says. But right then an anesthesiologist steps into the room and moves close to the bed. He's already introduced himself. He smiles at me. "You ready for a new life?"

I nod, but I'm still not sure. "I'm going to give you something to help you relax," he says in a comforting voice. He has dark hair and soft brown eyes. He reminds me of . . . Matt.

The man pushes a needle in my IV. The cold tingly current runs up my arm, and I feel as if someone is dropping a warm blanket over me. My fears float off me like steam.

Mom kisses me. Dad leans down and whispers, "I love you, sweet pea."

His words are the last thing I hear. Then the last thing I see is Mom and Dad looking at me as they roll me off. Mom is crying and wiping her hands on her jeans. Dad is smiling, but he, too, has tears in his eyes.

The last thing I feel is a tear gliding down my cheek. The last thing I think is, *I don't want to die.* I want to live. Not even for me, but for them.

Pain. Pain. Pain. I feel as if someone sawed me in half, but then again, they have. I almost welcome the pain, because I know it means I'm alive.

Almost. Almost welcome the pain. It hurts like hell. And I wish it'd go away.

I try to swallow. I can't. I gag. I remember it's the oxygen tube. I tell myself not to fight it. To relax my throat. They won't take it out until they know I can breathe on my own.

Relax. Relax. Relax.

A deep voice, a faraway voice, fills my ears. I'm not sure if it's someone far away, or me mentally far away. But I think he's angry. I can't make out what he's saying. But I just had surgery. Why would someone be mad at me?

I try to open my eyes. At first, I can't.

Finally, I manage it, but my lids feel fat and heavy. I expect to see the white walls of the recovery room, a nurse hovering over me. I expect to hear the beeping of monitors. I expect the air to smell of bitter astringent.

Nothing is like I expect.

I see trees, spring-colored leaves, flying past me.

I smell damp earth and night. I smell fear.

I'm running. In the woods. My heart is thudding in my chest. I fall. The coppery flavor of sheer terror explodes in my mouth.

Pain. Pain. Pain.

Not in my chest now. My head. All I see is light. White light. Bright light. Oh, shit. I'm dying?

I try to scream. Can't. Then it's gone. The raw panic. The pain in my head. And suddenly I'm not there. I'm here.

I smell the hospital. I see the white walls. I feel the pain . . . in my chest. The beeps of the monitor fill my ears.

The nurse is standing over me.

She smiles. "It's okay. Just relax. You're doing fine."

Closing my eyes, I let myself go away. Not back to the woods, but back to nothing. I don't feel pain there.

Hours later, I don't know if it's two or twenty, I wake up in the woods again. Running, scared. Someone says my name. I blink. I'm back in the hospital. Someone has my hand. I recognize that touch. Mom.

I glance to the side. I can hardly turn my head, I have tubes coming and going into me everywhere.

My mom and dad sit in chairs by my bed.

They look like shit. Tired. Scared. But happy. They smile. I can't smile, but then I know how much it will mean for them, so I try. Hoping they at least can see it in my eyes.

I hear the beeping of the monitor marking my heartbeat. *Correction.* Not my heart.

But it thumps in my chest. It's keeping me alive.

Is it at home there? Does it miss its donor? Will it somehow change me? Will I feel the same? Love the same?

I recall some of this being covered in the transplant classes I had to attend to be on the list. Unfortunately, I didn't retain the information. Didn't think this would happen.

Through the pain and uncertainty of my whole freaking life, a thought hits. I'm going to live.

I'm not just going to graduate from high school. I'm going to read way more than one hundred books. I'm going to date boys again. I'm going to experience more toe-curling, blow-my-mind kisses.

I can stop accepting and start hoping. It's allowed now.

Suddenly, I'm past ready for the healing to be over. I want to start living.

I'm tired of dying.

"I brought you flowers too, but they took them away from me," Brandy says. "I was going to fight if they tried to take this." She hands me a book.

It's by a paranormal author we both love. "Wow, when did this come out?"

"Last week."

"Thank you. I'll start it today. I could use some vampire love." I look up smiling.

"Are you allergic to flowers now?"

"It's a mold thing, but thank you anyway."

This is the first time I've seen her since the surgery, but Mom said she was up here the day I had it. She also told me they hugged each other and that Brandy cried. She's that kind of friend. Like a good Band-Aid, she sticks.

I watch her tuck her blond hair behind her ear. She must be growing it out. I realize she's wearing the purple T-shirt I gave her for her birthday that says BORN TO READ. She's a purple lover and just as big of a book geek as I am.

All of a sudden, Brandy stops and stares at me. "You look so good. I was worried you would . . . look sick."

"You look good too. You're growing out your hair."

She makes her duh face. "Brian wants to see how I'd look with it long. I told him I'd grow it out, but then I'm cutting it off again. No boyfriend is going to dictate how I wear my hair."

I laugh.

She continues to stare. "I don't know if it's your coloring or just . . . you look like you again. Not connected to anything. But . . . I have to tell you something. Don't take it the wrong way, but you gotta lose the pink. It's not your color."

I laugh. "Yeah, Mom's got a pink fetish."

One of these days I'm going to have to tell my mom that I'm not into pink. The dozen helium balloons, pink and pink polka-dotted, are tied to a chair in the corner of the too-small, too-white, too-sterile room. Mom even bought me a new pink throw in case I get cold. And the new PJs she brought me match perfectly with the balloons.

And that's not even counting what she did to my bedroom at home the last time I was in the hospital. It looks like a bottle of Pepto-Bismol exploded in there.

One of the masks from a dispenser connected to my door hangs around Brandy's neck. I assured her she didn't have to wear it if she wasn't sick. Which the doctor told me I could do, but I know if Mom walks in, she'll have a shit fit. Thankfully, Mom's not due for a while.

"I feel pretty good," I tell her. And it's not really a lie. The meds are messing me up a little, and I still have pain, but it's only been nine days since the surgery. I might even get to go home in a couple of days.

Mom already talked about me going back to school. The doctor recommended I wait until January. I agree I should wait. Not because I'm afraid I won't feel healthy enough, but honestly I'm scared. I haven't gone to school in over a year. When I go back, I really want to feel like me again.

"Trent asked me to tell you hello," Brandy says, her good-news smile brightening her green eyes.

"Did he?" I ask. The only reason I broke up with him was because I was dying. Trent made me happy. I liked him. I liked his personality. I liked his smile. I liked his kisses. But not how I liked my last kiss. Crazy how, even after over a month, I can't forget it.

The hospital door swishes open. Dr. Hughes, my cardiologist, walks in.

"How's my favorite patient doing?" She pulls her stethoscope out of her white coat pocket. She's tall and lean. I like her. How could I not? She'd actually pulled her shirt up and showed me the scar on her chest where she'd had heart-valve surgery fifteen years ago.

"Fine." I smile. "Brandy," I say and motion to Dr. Hughes, "this is my favorite doctor."

"Do I need to go?" Brandy asks, her tone tight, fear riding each word.

"No," the doctor says. "I'm just listening to her and going to peek at her incision."

"I don't do incisions." Brandy runs out of the room as if something is chasing her.

The doctor stares after her and makes a disapproving sound. "Teenagers," she says, as if I'm not one.

"She's super squeamish, but she's stuck by me," I say, defending Brandy. "Came to see me three or four times a week."

"Then I'll forgive her." The doctor points to my feet covered by a sheet. "What is it today?"

"I think Dumbo." I push the sheet off, exposing my slippers and wiggling my feet.

"Love 'em." She grins. "You are one of a kind." She moves closer. "How's the breathing?"

"Fine." I do the routine of breathing deep, breathing normal.

She asks me to unbutton my top. I almost don't care that I'm flashing my boobs. I think everyone in the hospital has seen them. They try to cover them up with the sides of my pajama top when they examine me, but it never fails, something slips. Boobs are slippery like that.

I almost flashed the janitor the other day. He walked in and thinking he was someone who needed to check out the incision, I started unbuttoning my shirt. Hell, if this was Mardi Gras I would have a fortune in beads.

"It looks really good," Dr. Hughes says. "Did your mom get you the cream I told her to? You can use it in another week or so and it should help with scarring."

"Yeah. She told me she did." I look down at the red line running between my boobs, then there's the scar where the drainage tube came out and another one where my artificial heart was connected. I look like a scarecrow. All patched up. They aren't pretty, but it's a small price to pay for having a future. And if my scars fade as much as Dr. Hughes's did, they really won't be that noticeable.

The doctor closes my top. "Are the dreams and headaches going away?"

Buttoning my PJs, I look up and frown. The dream I woke up with after the transplant has hung on. Not a night's gone by that I haven't woken up with it. Each time, I see a little more. I'm sure there's a voice there in the background too. I can almost make it out. Almost.

"No," I answer. "But the transplant nurse said it'll probably go away after I get moved down to a lower-dose steroid." Unusual dreams can be a side effect of the steroids I'm taking to help me from rejecting the heart.

"Yeah. We can lower it after two weeks." She repockets her stethoscope. "Other than that, any complaints or compliments? And I prefer compliments."

I chuckle. "Everyone's so nice. My only complaint is I want to go home. Oh, and the food. Are they trying to kill me?"

"I've had worse. Except for their meatloaf . . ." She makes a funny face. "We'll see your blood work, and if everything is good, maybe Wednesday."

"That's three days. I thought we were talking two."

"That's what you get for being nice to the nurses. They want to keep you."

"Okay, I'm taking the gloves off now. I can be a bitch." I'm joking, but disappointment echoes in my voice.

"You? A bitch? Bitches don't wear Dumbo slippers."

I half-ass smile. She leaves. Brandy, in slow motion, walks back in. She's sucked into her phone and frowning as if she's reading something bad.

"Everything okay?"

She keeps reading.

"What's wrong?"

She finally glances up, her expression troubled. "Someone posted something else about Eric Kenner."

"What?" Just hearing the name makes my brain spin. My shoulders snap back. I want to believe it was Matt I kissed, but what do I know?

"What about him?" I ask, hoping it sounds casual, but I hear the quaver in my voice and it seems to come from my heart.

Her eyes widen. "Crap. That's right. You don't know?"

"Know what?" The words spill out of my mouth with impatience.

"He killed himself."

I pop up off my pillow. I feel the crack in my chest. My heart, my new fragile heart, skips a beat. And that's not good. I pull in air, but it seems too thick to swallow. "Wh . . . ? Wait. What?"

She sits on the edge of my bed. She gets that look, the look that says she has something juicy to tell me. I hate juicy. Or maybe it's death I hate.

"Everyone says Cassie Chambers broke his heart and he couldn't handle it. But Matt swears his brother wouldn't kill himself. He's on a campaign to prove that to the police. He asked everyone on Facebook who knew Eric and believes he wouldn't kill himself to go to see the detective on the case."

I'm trying to get everything she says, but my mind wants to reject it. "How did . . . What happened? Jeeezus, they just lost their dad."

"I know." Brandy makes her sad face.

I sit there feeling numb, but not numb enough. This hurts. "When . . . ?"

"Like a couple of weeks ago. They found him at the edge of the woods off of 2920. He shot himself in the head with his dad's gun. He was still alive. One of those helicopters brought him . . . I think to this hospital, but they said he was brain-dead. They pulled the plug a little bit after that. Everyone is leaving flowers where they found him."

My chest tightens so much that my lungs leak air. My new organ is trying to handle its first piece of heartbreaking news.

I wonder if this is bad for my condition. If there should be a warning sign on my door, DON'T GIVE LEAH BAD NEWS. But my thoughts move past that, move past me.

"How's Matt doing?" The thought marching through my befuddled brain is so loud, I flinch. What if it was Eric and not Matt? What if the guy I kissed and dreamed about all this time is dead?

"He's taking it hard. I mean, they were identical twins. So, like, they were even together in the womb."

Another wave of hurt shatters over me like shards of glass. The pain pulls at the seams of my new heart. At the stitches that holds the organ inside me. I feel it thump and thump against my sore breastbone. I sit there and try to breathe, using the techniques they taught me to control pain and panic.

"You okay?" I hear Brandy ask.

"Yeah." I lie. "Just tired."

"Should I get the doctor?" She jumps off the bed.

"No." Somehow, I fake that I'm not torn up inside.

Brandy leaves. Mom and Dad are due here any minute. I grab my phone and google Eric's name.

The first link is to his funeral announcement. My chest tightens again. It wasn't that I didn't believe Brandy, but . . . "Damn! Shit." I say.

How could this happen? I put my finger on the link to open it, my hands are shaking. Everything inside me is shaking.

I read his name and the dates below. June 5th, 2001– May 15th, 2018.

My eyes start to read on, but I stop. My eyes shoot back to the date. To the last date. To the date Eric died.

It's the same day I got my heart. In my mind, I hear the words, *"AB isn't that rare. I have it. If it was a kidney, I'd give you one."* Chills run down my spine, down my arms, up my legs, and meet together like they're magnetically charged. Then they pool together to form a tingling mass right over my incision.

It couldn't be, could it?

I put my hand over my chest. I feel the knock against my palm as if the organ is trying to tell me something, or as if it wants out.

"Please, please don't be Eric's heart."

5

TUESDAY, DECEMBER 31ST

It's Eric's heart.

I stare at my reflection in the bathroom mirror and put my hand over my scar that's still red and angry-looking even though I've been using the cream for seven and a half months.

I know its Eric's heart. And not just because of the blood type or the date of his death. It's the dreams.

It's been months, and the amount of steroids I'm taking is almost nothing compared with before. Not only are the dreams just as vivid, but they've expanded, gotten more detailed. I feel more. See more. I get them at least twice a week, sometimes more.

I've seen the shoes on my feet while running. Only they aren't my feet. They're male tennis shoes . . . and big. Last night I saw my hand. Saw what I had in my hand. A gun.

I didn't see what happens with the gun. The dream ended with me seeing light, and feeling pain in my right temple. Then there's always the angry voice. I hear it yet still can't make out the words, but my gut instinct says it isn't Eric's voice. That leads me to believe that Eric wasn't alone.

And that leads me to believe that maybe Matt's right. Maybe Eric didn't kill himself.

I'm not a fool. I've read the paper. There's been a lot of pieces on teen suicide. I know it happens. I also know other people believe that's what happened. But my heart, Eric's heart, seems to know different. As bat-shit bizarre as it seems, it's as if he's showing me what happened in the last few minutes of his life.

Do I really believe that? Yeah, I do. And believing it scares the hell out of me.

The only thing that scares me more is figuring out how I'm going to tell Matt. How I'm going to tell him that I have Eric's heart. How I'm going to ask if he was who I kissed. How I'm going to feel if he hates me because I'm alive and Eric's dead.

Would Matt believe me if I told him that a part of me hates myself for it too? That knowing Eric died and I'm alive feels wrong?

But none of that matters. I still need to tell him.

He's desperate to prove his brother didn't shoot himself. I know because I read his Facebook posts every day. Not that he knows it's me. I made up a fake Facebook account. I'm Jenny Hamilton from Dallas. Brandy, a computer wizard, helped me. She asked me why I didn't just friend him.

I told her about Matt, or perhaps Eric, coming to tutor me that day. She got mad at me for not telling her earlier, but she got over it. Thing is, I'm still not telling her things. Not about the kiss. Or the dreams. Especially not about having Eric's heart. She'd think I'm crazy.

And maybe I am?

I comb my hair, decide to leave it down. Let the dark strands ride my shoulders. Then I put on makeup, but I almost don't remember how to do it. Looking cover-girl pretty isn't a top priority when you're dying.

Dressed, with makeup applied, I stand in front of the mirror to check my reflection. Am I ready? Ready for tonight and school that starts in six days? I don't have a freaking clue.

But I square my shoulders, stare myself in the eyes, and say, "Ready or not, here I come."

I'm going to Brandy's New Year's Eve get-together.

The red long-sleeve stretchy T-shirt fits snug, but not too snug. The round neckline is high. High enough to hide my scars. The jeans softly hug my hips. The small sterling silver hoop earrings are about as much bling as I ever wear. Part of me wishes I was more into bling, but when I put on bigger earrings or chunky necklaces, I feel like a little girl playing dress up.

I continue to stare at the mirror. I look pretty good for a girl who is working on her third heart. Yeah, I count the artificial one. I feel good too. Well, as good as someone who's taking immune-suppressant drugs can feel.

Sometimes they make me feel blah. But I can handle blah when my life doesn't come with an expiration date.

I grab my purse, my nighttime meds, check to make sure I haven't left any out. I put them in my purse. Zip them along with my shitload of fears in the inside pocket.

The doctors and the transplant team preached to me about taking the pills on time and never, ever forgetting them. Like it's life or death. And it is. Just one missed dose and my body will see the heart as a foreign object and start rejecting it.

I walk out of my room, knowing Mom's waiting in the living room in a full-blown panic. This is only the fifth time I've driven since the heart transplant.

Right now, it's not driving that's gnawing on my nerves.

I want to do this, I want my old life back, but . . . Mom and Dad have been my touchstones, and I'm feeling a little separation anxiety.

But I've got to learn to live again. To learn to be around

people. Other than my parents, Brandy, and the doctors, I've been a hermit. Not all by choice—it was the whole germ thing too.

But now they say my immune system is as strong as it will ever be.

It's time. Leah McKenzie needs to face the world.

To face Matt.

I put my hand on my stomach and try to calm the nervous flutters in my gut.

When I enter the living room, Mom and Dad walk in from the kitchen. Immediately, I feel guilty that I'm lying to them. I tell myself it's not a whole lie. I *am* going to Brandy's party, but I'm making a detour first.

"You look beautiful," Dad says.

"More than beautiful," Mom says. "Where are your pills?"

I pull the plastic pill carrier out of my purse. I knew she'd want to check.

She clicks them open, studies them. Counts them. "Okay." She hands them back to me and holds out her hand. "Your phone?"

"I set the alarm for eight fifty-five and I'll take them right when it goes off," I say, but she still wants to check. I'm not mad, but this might get annoying.

After seeing the alarm is set, she returns my phone. "Drive carefully. No hugging. No kissing. You can't get germs. And I know it's a party, but you can't eat—"

"No raw vegetables, no fresh fruit, no lunch meat. And no rare meat. I got it," I tell her. Because of my compromised immune system, I'm susceptible to getting food poisoning, and certain foods are big no-nos. Like a it-could-kill-you no-no.

"Let her go." My dad's voice deepens. "She's seventeen, not seven."

I tell myself the same thing. Yet the little girl inside of me says differently. Mentally, I pull out the big girl scissors and cut the apron strings. But then I get this image of me just floating off. Having nothing to hold on to.

I blink, tell myself to snap out of it.

Mom sighs. "Call me when you get to Brandy's."

"I'll text you," I say. "And please don't be calling every few minutes. It'll be embarrassing. I haven't seen my friends in a year and a half. I don't want them to think my mama's hovering."

Mom frowns and starts to give me the speech. The one where she tells me she loves me and I just have to accept that she's going to be overprotective for a while.

"She won't call," my dad says. He wraps an arm around my mom as if he knows how much my leaving is hurting her. And me. "But text her, especially when you take your meds, so she isn't driving me crazy. And be home by one. Not a minute later."

"One?" my mom squeals, and her eyes grow unbelievably large.

"Katherine," my dad says in that deep don't-argue-with-me voice.

She slams her mouth shut, but I can hear her mama motor muttering in discontent.

"Happy New Year." I hug them, whisper I-love-yous that come from the most honest part of my soul. Squaring my shoulders, determined to go find me again—the old me—I leave my touchstones.

"Take a mask," Mom says as I walk by the entryway table where she keeps them for most people visiting. Yeah, it's overkill, but it's because she loves me. "If anyone even sneezes . . ."

"Have fun," Dad cuts her off.

I don't look back, because I know it'll hurt. I slip a mask in my purse. Oh, I don't plan on wearing it. If someone is sick, I'll leave.

Lingering on the porch taking a few minutes to breathe, I collect myself. The fuzzy, buzzy feeling circles my heart. Yup, separation anxiety.

I could turn around. Stay. And I could be forever stuck here.

It only takes a minute to find my courage, and with it comes a longing for independence.

Soaking up a sense of freedom, I head to the car. The sun is bright as I walk to the street where Dad has already pulled my car out. The temperature isn't as cold as I thought it would be, and I take my sweater off before I get in the Honda. The sky's blue; the calm breeze carries the scent of Christmas. And bam, suddenly I'm exhilarated. *I'm alive.*

I'm scared shitless.

Not just about being alive, but about what I'm going to do: see Matt.

I start driving toward his neighborhood. But I see the exit to the highway. To the place where Eric was found.

I don't know why I feel as if I need to see it, but I do. I start that way. It's as if this has been my plan all along, but I hadn't known it.

I come to the little roadside park, with the white cross sticking up. My heart's beating too fast. I seriously consider just driving past. But at the last minute, I pull over. My hands are sweating and the steering wheel feels slick. Sitting there, gazing over my shoulder, I try to visualize parts of the dream.

Never turning off the car's ignition, I just stare. Then I see a figure walking out of the woods. My first thought is that it might be Matt. It's not. It's Cassie. Cassie Chambers, Eric's girlfriend. She's crying and doesn't notice me lurking.

My heart picks up its already breakneck speed. As crazy as it seems, I wonder if Eric is seeing her through my eyes. If it's Eric making my/his heart beat to the tune of crazy. If it's him suddenly making me feel overwhelmingly sad.

Freaked out, feeling as if I'm spying on Cassie, and worried I shouldn't have come here, I speed off, hoping she didn't recognize me or my car. Then again, why would she? I'm not in her league. She probably doesn't even know my name.

I drive to the Kenner home and park on the street. When I first got my car, and before I was sick, I would drive by here every now and then hoping to get a peek at Matt. A few times, he and Eric were playing basketball with friends in his driveway. One time I know he saw me, because he waved. He mentioned it the next day at school. I lied and said I was dropping something off at my mom's friend's house.

I was so damn embarrassed. It's not embarrassment I feel now. My hands white-knuckle the steering wheel as if refusing to let me get out of the car. My pulse hums to something close to a horror-movie theme.

Why am I afraid? Why am I feeling the same sensation I get from the dream? Fear, which somehow doesn't seem to even belong to me.

Is Eric making me feel this?

Forcing myself to release the steering wheel, I turn on the radio and let the music calm me.

I do a breathing technique that a nurse taught me in the hospital for pain and stress. My fear lessens. Five minutes pass.

I see the time on the dashboard and panic a little. I text my mom and say I'm at Brandy's. The written message zips through cyberspace, but still manages to sit on my conscience.

Then the truth hits. It's not just the lie spreading liquid guilt through my veins.

It's that Eric is dead and I'm alive.

I'm so damn tempted to drive off, but my gut says if I do, I'll never do this. The secret will stay inside me. It'll slowly poison me.

I get out of my car and make my way to his front door. I hear voices. There's a large window. I'm too scared to look in it. Instead, I just hit the doorbell. I drag my palms over the sides of my jeans and stop when I realize I've acquired Mom's nervous habit.

Voices echo louder from behind the door. No, not just voices.

Laughter. I didn't expect that. From Matt's Facebook posts, he's bordering on depression.

I lean to the side to peer through the window. I can see a living room, and into the kitchen. A woman, who I think is Mrs. Kenner, is there.

Barking, yappy-puppy type of barking, reaches my ears, followed by footsteps. I'm suddenly unsure if coming here unannounced was the best idea. *Oh, shit! What the hell was I thinking?*

The door starts to open. My mind begs me to hotfoot it back to the car, but my shoes feel superglued to the porch.

The door moves the rest of the way open. Matt appears. He has a smile on his face as if someone has just said something funny, but it slips right off. I feel it crash at his feet. Then surprise, and not the good kind, rounds his brown eyes.

His posture gets rock hard, as if he's playing defense on a football team. He glances back inside, and the barking starts again. He hurriedly steps out on the porch and shuts the door.

I don't know if it's to keep the dog in or me out.

I take a few steps back. *This is such a bad idea!* My . . . Eric's heart thumps against my rib cage as if I've been running.

"Hey," Matt manages to say.

"Hey," I repeat his greeting, because I can't think of one. I can't think of shit.

We stare at each other for one second, two, but it gets so uncomfortable that we both look away. Leaving seems like a good idea, but I have to do this. I glance up.

There are so many emotions flickering in his eyes, I can't read them.

I can't decide if I think he somehow knows about Eric's heart, or if he's just upset because he kissed me and didn't call. Or maybe he doesn't even know about the kiss because it was Eric who'd come to my house that day.

The silence happening around us surpasses awkward and heads straight toward freaking weird.

Someone needs to say something, and that would probably be me. But for the life of me I don't know how to start. Yes, I practiced, practically memorized my speech, but it's gone.

Finally, I open my mouth and push out words. "I just wanted—"

"It's not a good time," Matt blurts out.

Embarrassment and fury, at myself, for being here, heats my face.

"Okay." Turning on my heels so fast it's almost a whirl, I rush toward my car. *I tried. I tried. I really tried.* Guilt's off my shoulders. But why do I still feel guilty? Oh, yeah, I'm alive and his brother's dead.

"Leah?" His voice sounds behind me. The option to pretend I didn't hear is tickling my brain. But I can't. I stop.

Before I turn around he's beside me. The breeze picks up. It's getting colder, but I'm not cold. I'm numb.

"Can I come by your house in a couple of hours?" he asks.

"Yes." Then I realize what I just said. "No."

"Yes or no?" He looks baffled.

I feel baffled. "No," I say.

He looks as if he's worried I'm two eggs short of a dozen.

"Yes." Sooner or later, I'm going to get control of my mouth. The explanation hangs on my lips. "I'm . . . not going to be at home. I'm going to a party at Brandy's house."

"Brandy Hasting?" he asks. "Does she still live across the street from Austin Walker? In Oak Woods subdivision?"

I nod, surprised he knows where Brandy lives. But then I remember him and Austin being friends.

"Can I come there? Not to the party, just to talk. In my car or something." His words sound rushed. The wind yanks them away and scatters his hair across his forehead. It's longer than he usually wears it. The ends curl up. I remember how soft it is. I remember our kiss. I remember he didn't call me. Or *was* it him?

The wind catches my hair now and whips it around my face. I gather and grab the long brown strands and hold them.

Our gazes meet again. His soft brown eyes still flash with emotion that I can't read. But I've found one answer I came looking for. I kissed Matt Kenner. How I know, I'm not exactly sure, but I'd bet anything it was him.

The urge to look at his mouth hits strong, but I didn't come here for that. So I glance back to the street.

The next gust of wind brings his scent, male spicy soap. I turn to him. He's looking at me.

Worry tightens his eyes. "I'll see you in a couple of hours." He slips his hands into his pockets and then out. He's nervous. Why?

"Okay." I hurry to my car.

When I look back in my rearview mirror, he's watching me drive off. Not smiling. Not frowning. Not blinking.

My wheels hum on the pavement, and riding shotgun with me is the question, does he know? Does Matt know I have Eric's heart?

6

Matt watches her go. He's almost dizzy before he realizes he's not breathing. Does she know? Does Leah know she has Eric's heart? Is that why she came?

Or did she come to give him shit for not calling her. *I deserve shit.*

Not calling Leah back had been a selfish act. Sure Eric had

said not to, but Matt had already made up his mind when Eric came home that night.

No doubt Matt had hurt her.

He'd hurt a girl who was dying. How much of a selfish jerk could he be?

And he'd probably hurt her again now. Shutting the door so fast, as if he was ashamed she was on his doorstep. But he'd panicked. Mom had been against donating Eric's organs. And for the first time in forever she's finally crawling out of her depression.

Would learning Leah got Eric's heart knock her back there?

Matt doesn't know, but he can't chance it.

Watching until Leah's car turns the corner, he stays there, feeling his own heart dodge blows of guilt.

Is it wrong to want Leah to know she has the heart of a champion in her chest? Is it wrong that from the second he opened that door he hasn't stopped thinking about their kiss and thinking about doing it again?

"Matt?" His mom's voice has him turning around.

She's standing in the door with a wiggling puppy in her hands. "What are you doing?"

"Just giving directions to someone who was lost." On the scale of bad lies, ten meaning piss-poor bad, he rates that one a twenty. Lying has never been his specialty. Until recently. Now he's been making a habit of it.

He hasn't told his mom about his campaign to prove Eric's death wasn't a suicide.

He starts up the sidewalk, dragging his guilt with him.

"I got her to sit," his mom says.

"That's good." He walks into the house and shuts the door. Mom sets Lady down. She squats right in front of them and, with pride, proceeds to pee on the beige carpet.

His mom laughs. And damn if it isn't a nice sound. He could use more laughter in his life. His mind goes to Leah and how much they'd laughed that day he'd helped her study. How could a girl who thought she was dying find it in herself to laugh?

He grabs some paper towels, squats down beside the dog, blots the spot, slaps the floor, and tells Lady a firm no. Then he picks the puppy up and heads out to the backyard.

His mom moves with him. As he walks outside, he's lifting his chin this way and that trying to avoid being French-kissed by his dog. His mom chuckles.

They got the puppy for Christmas. Their other dog, Flops, also a yellow lab, had passed right before his dad died.

Matt's pretty sure getting the puppy was Aunt Karen's idea. She's been coming down almost every weekend now. He's also certain that his aunt is behind his mom's crawling out of her hole. About a month ago he heard them talking in the kitchen. Or rather heard his aunt talking and his mom crying. "*I know you're hurting, Sis. But the thing you're not seeing is that you're not the only one. You haven't lost everything. You still have Matt, and he needs you, damn it!*"

He hadn't liked hearing that. But if it helped his mom, he supposed he could tolerate it. Besides, it was the truth. He needed his mom to be okay.

And since then he'd slowly seen her change. She's sleeping less. Seeing a therapist. Probably taking fewer of the pills too. She's started making him go running with her every morning.

"Oh," his mom says. "Ted called when you were outside. He said there was a bunch of your friends going to see the fireworks. He wants you to go with them."

"He called our home phone?" Matt asks.

"He said he called your cell, but you didn't answer."

"Yeah, I was going to call him back." Not really.

"Why don't you go? It would be good to bring in the New Year."

"Nah, I'd rather just stay here with you."

She frowns. "I'm half considering going out with some friends."

Wow. That would be a first. "You should. Go," he says.

"I will if you will." She looks at him. He knows she's dead serious. If he says no, she won't go. He doesn't like this, but . . . hell.

He needs to go see Leah, but the fireworks don't start until ten. "Okay. But if you don't go, I'm going to be pissed."

"I'll go. I promise." She smiles. A real smile. Or he thinks so. Even if this is her faking it, it's still nice. What's that saying? "Fake it until you make it." Maybe Mom's going to make it.

Maybe he'll make it too. But not until he finds out who killed Eric and gets them locked up in prison.

And that might be soon. Cassie, Eric's girlfriend who left to go live with her father in California after Eric's funeral, is supposed to be home soon to finish school here. She's avoided every one of his calls. Then he was told to stop calling her. But now that she's back in town, he's going to get answers.

His gut says Cassie knows a hell of a lot more than she told the police. He's pretty sure she knows who's responsible for his brother's murder.

I'm sitting on Brandy's bed, in her bedroom that, by the way, is not pink. I'm here about ten minutes before I casually drop that Matt's stopping by.

"Holy bat shit!" Brandy isn't taking it very casually. Which is upping the amount of butterflies playing follow the leader in my stomach.

"I'm just going to sit in his car and talk for a few minutes."

She smiles and rubs her hands together so fast I can almost see sparks. "This is going to be crazy interesting."

"Not interesting. Please don't make anything out of this." I say the words like I mean them, but freaking hell if I'm not making plenty out of it.

My insides are quaking. What's Matt gonna say when I tell him about the dreams, about having Eric's heart?

The picture of Brandy and Brian on her bedside table draws my attention, and, needing a distraction, I pick it up. They look happy. Brandy deserves happy.

We've been friends since third grade. She'd been the new girl at school and I agreed to share the gummy bears from my lunchbox with her.

She ate every one of them. But I couldn't have picked a better friend. In spite of being totally and completely disgusted by anything medical, she stuck by me during my heart issues. Even after she'd fainted when she saw the blood on my hospital gown after my first surgery.

Brandy lets out a giggle. "I'm just wondering what Trent is going to think."

"Trent?" The name falls off my lips as if I'd just said "toe fungus." I sit the picture down. "Why did you invite him?"

"Because I invited everyone in the book club. Because he still likes you and because—your words not mine—'he's really nice and I only broke up with him because I was dying.' Now you're not dying."

Yeah, I'm not dying and Trent's nice. And he was . . . part of my old life. But since Matt showed up at my house, I learned that there was more than . . . nice. There was awesome and toe-curling, practically break-Donald-Duck's-beak-off-my-house-shoes kind of kisses.

While I'm human and want to put the blame on Brandy for inviting Trent, I can't. I Facebook messaged Trent twice—because he messaged me—but I still did it. But I never hinted that we'd pick up where we dropped off.

I was just trying to ease back into my old life. Dip my toe back into the water.

Now I wish I'd kept my toes dry. And not because I think Matt and I have something. I know better.

But . . . shit shit shit! Is Brandy right? Does Trent still like me? I don't want to hurt Trent. I don't want to hurt anyone. I fall back on Brandy's bed and stare up at the ceiling.

I lay there for several insignificant seconds searching for an out. I find nothing. I'm so screwed. Moaning, I pop back up.

"What are we going to do?" I ask Brandy as if this is her problem. Not that she minds. She's that kind of friend. We tell each other everything. Almost everything.

She told me she slept with Brian. A rite of passage I haven't made, but I'm eager to since I've read fifty romance novels telling me how wonderful it can be. With the right person, of course.

"You don't have to do anything," Brandy says. "You aren't going out with either of them."

"But it'll hurt Trent."

"Okay, then lie? Tell Trent that Matt's tutoring you, which wouldn't be a complete untruth. Because he did." She scrunches up her mouth, the way she does when she makes a point. "Though you somehow forgot to tell your best friend."

"I didn't tell you because . . . I don't even know, but I can't lie to Trent. I already lied to my mom when I told her I was coming straight here." I drop back again on the mattress feeling answerless.

"Oh. So you have a one-lie-a-day quota?" Brandy's grin is so genuine I can't get mad.

"Sort of," I say.

"Wait," Brandy says. "What time did you say Matt is coming?"

"He said two hours so it would be five thirty."

"Problem solved. Party doesn't start until around six or six thirty."

I sit up and finger-comb my hair. Bed hair is so not becoming and I've worn that style for too long. New Leah wears makeup, not bedhead.

"So one lie a day, huh?" Brandy's question comes out loaded.

I nod, suspicious.

"Then let me ask you something. What's really going on between you and Matt Kenner? And don't say you're just still crushing over him, because I know it's more. I see it in your eyes every time you say his name."

I inhale and try to decide how much to tell, how much to keep to myself. "Okay, but you can't say anything."

"Can't say anything about what?"

I reach up and press my hand over my chest. "I'm pretty sure I have Eric's heart."

Running twenty minutes late, Matt parks in front of Austin's house, then hurries across the street to Brandy's front door.

There aren't any cars lining the street. Just Leah's. What time did Brandy's party start? It's almost dark as he walks up the sidewalk. The lights are on in the house. As he gets close to the porch, the front door opens.

Light beams out and Leah steps out in a glow, making her look almost surreal. He stops. The door shuts and now it's dark again. Then the porch light pops on. Spotlighting her. She keeps walking, toward him. She's so damn pretty, his breath catches in his throat.

She stops in front of him. "Did you say we could talk in your car?"

"Yeah." He starts back to his car. "Would you like to go grab a Coke or something?"

"In the car's fine." Her words spill out. That and the way she's rubbing her palms on her jeans tell him she's super nervous.

That makes two of them. "Okay."

They settle in, then look at each other. He's practiced his apology, but he can't remember it. Can't remember why he told himself kissing her again would be wrong. Can't remember why he's so damn sad when there's someone as perfect as her in the world.

He just blurts it out. "I'm sorry. I should've called. I just . . . was going through a rough time and . . ."

Something flashes in her eyes. It almost looks like relief. "I didn't come to see you about that." She rubs her palms down, then up her legs.

He holds his breath and waits for her to explain.

"I heard about Eric."

The light in the car isn't good, yet he can swear she has tears in her eyes. "I'm so damn sorry."

"Yeah." A thousand people have told him that, but she seems to mean it more. Perhaps because she has Eric's heart. Or perhaps that's not it at all. Her empathy just feels like more. Leah McKenzie *is* more.

"I . . . don't know how to say this," she continues, "but . . ." She folds her hands in her lap, unfolds them, then laces her fingers together. "Eric died the same day I got my heart."

She knows. His chest feels instantly empty, as if someone sucked all his emotions out. And he's waiting for her to put them back in.

"I . . . know we have the same blood type. You mentioned it when you came to my house. Well, you said we had the same. And identical twins . . ."

She knows.

His chest fills back up with so many emotions he can't decipher them.

"Did . . . Eric donate his organs?" She put a hand on her chest, over her heart. Over Eric's heart.

She knows.

"I saw you." The words slip out.

"Saw me?"

"At the hospital, when I was leaving. You were coming in with your parents."

She blinks. A tear, almost silver from the low hue of the streetlight, slips down her cheek. "So you knew?" Her lip trembles.

He nods. The desire to brush that tear off her cheek has him clenching his fist.

"Do you hate me?" She bites down on her bottom lip. He watches her straight teeth press deep into the tender pink flesh, and he has the strongest desire to tell her to stop. Instead, he runs a finger over her lower mouth.

She releases it. Her lip is soft and wet against his finger. He's lost in looking at her. Touching her. Wanting to keep touching her. Then, realizing how awkward this is, he pulls back his hand.

"Why would I hate you?"

She unfurls her fingers and brushes the tear away. "Because I'm alive and he's not."

He remembers feeling that way that day. He's embarrassed for feeling it too. But he knows it was his grief talking.

"You getting his heart had nothing to do with him dying." The honest words leak out of him.

She nods. Her hands shake.

Without thinking, he reaches over and folds his fingers around her hand. Her palm is warm. Small. Soft. "There is no one in this world I'd rather have gotten Eric's heart."

She stares at their hands, then hesitantly lifts her chin. Their gazes meet and there is something so right about it, it scares him.

She glances away. "I need . . . to tell you one more thing, but . . ."

"What?" He gives her hand an encouraging squeeze.

She inhales then lets out air. He can hear it. He hears the slightest tremble in her breath.

"I'm afraid."

"Afraid of what?" He shifts, so he's facing her more.

"That you'll think I'm crazy."

7

From the second Matt touches me, my fear becomes manageable. It's as if something inside me says, *Don't worry, this is Matt.*

I swallow. I can still feel his finger against my lip. Like when he kissed me, I long to memorize the feeling.

I look at him knowing I just need to get this out. But how?

Then I look into his eyes again and just say it. "When I woke up from the transplant, I started having dreams. The doctors say it's a side effect from my medication, but . . . I think they might have something to do with Eric."

His eyes widen. His jaw drops. I hear him inhale . . . then exhale.

He releases my hand and scrubs his palm over his face.

My fear comes tumbling back so fast I want to get out of the car. Run away. Be alone.

"I know how it sounds, but I swear, it's the only thing that makes sense."

"Leah, I—"

"I'm not lying."

"I know." He touches my hand again. "Eric's running in the woods, isn't he? He has a gun?"

Now it's my turn to be shocked. "How do you know?"

"Because I'm getting the same dreams. I woke up that Sunday night he was shot with the dream. My right temple was throbbing. I know how it looks. Everyone thinks he committed suicide and that I'm in denial, but I'm not. Eric didn't kill himself. Someone did this to him."

I absorb what he says, but my mental sponge is so dry it takes a minute.

"I believe you. In the dream, I hear a voice. A man's voice. He seems angry."

Matt's eyes widen. "What does he say? Who is it?"

"I don't know. It's distant, and I can't make it out."

"Will you tell this to Detective Henderson? Maybe he'd believe me." His eyes light up with hope, and until then I didn't realize how sad his eyes were.

Then the consequences of doing what he asks flash through my mind. *What will my parents say? I haven't told them.* I haven't even told my best friend.

"I . . . Won't he just think I'm crazy? Have you told him about your dreams?"

The hope in his eyes fades. I remember I'm alive because Eric's dead. "I'll do it." I blurt out.

"No. You're right. I haven't told him about my dreams because . . . He's not going to believe it."

He looks out the window as if collecting his thoughts. Then he focuses back on me. "Is it freaking you out?"

It is. "No." I really pass my lie quota for the day. "What about you? You're seeing it too."

"Yeah, but we're twins. We have a special . . . Had . . . Damn it!" He hits the steering wheel. "Someone murdered my brother. Everyone thinks he killed himself. And I don't know how to prove he didn't."

He keeps mixing up his tenses, some are present as if Eric is alive, some aren't.

I did that with my grandma.

Matt hasn't accepted his brother's death. I want to console him, hug him? Is it even my place?

"Maybe the dreams give us something more." I've been praying the dreams would go away. Not now.

"More?" he asks.

I swallow. "Yeah. Like I didn't see the gun at first. That came later. Maybe we'll see other stuff."

Matt passes a hand over his face as if trying to wipe away the hurt and grief. "All I see is he's running and carrying a gun—he's in different parts of woods." His voice catches. "He's so scared. I think he knows he's going to die."

The pain in Matt's eyes is so raw that it bleeds onto me. I feel it. The stickiness on my skin. The stain of it on my soul. "I'm sorry."

"If Cassie would get back, I might find answers."

"Back?" I ask.

"She left after the funeral. Went to her dad's in California. Even started school there, but she's supposed to return and graduate here."

"I saw her today . . . at the roadside park." Her image flashes in my head and the same lonely feeling from earlier echoes inside me.

"You sure?" Matt says.

I nod.

"I'll go to her house tomorrow. She's got to talk to me."

I sit there in the tense silence. "Do you really think she had something to do with this?"

"She knows something. She refuses to talk to me. Even before the funeral. She told the cops I was calling her, and the detective told me I had to stop. Now, she blocks my calls."

"Maybe she's just devastated. You and Eric were identical. That has to . . . hurt."

I recall how Cassie looked walking out of those woods, as if she'd lost her best friend. I don't think Cassie is behind it.

"I'm hurt," Matt spits out. "If she cared, she'd talk to me to try to help. And she told the cops that Eric hadn't been at her house that night. But he told me that's where he was going. Why would he lie?"

"Did you tell the detective this?" I ask.

"Over and over again. Even he's dodging my calls. They've made up their minds it's a suicide." Desperation leaks out with his voice and sinks inside me.

"Then you have to prove them wrong."

He stares at me, oddly, as if having an epiphany. "We." He reaches for my hand again. "*We* have to prove them wrong. Tell me you'll help me, Leah. Please."

His jaw clenches. "I know I don't deserve it, because I didn't call you back. I was an ass. Forgive me."

I've forgiven him. Haven't I? I mean, not for one second do I regret that kiss, but yeah, I guess I'm smarter for it. You don't wait for a call that never comes without learning to be careful what you wish for.

Still, how could he think I could refuse him anything? I have his brother's heart. Before I can answer, a knock hits the window. My butt bounces two inches off the seat and I squeal. I see the familiar face behind the glass. It's Sandy, and behind her are Jeremy, LeAnn, Carlos, and . . . Trent.

"Oh, my gawd, is that really you?" Sandy jumps up and down and screams. She motions for me to get out of the car.

Something happens then. Like a switch turning on. I realize I've missed these people. The reasons I'd shut them out of my life now seem stupid. As if dying wasn't a good enough excuse.

Still, a gooey feeling warms my chest. They are part of the Old Leah, and I want her back.

I reach for the door handle and look at Matt, who's also

gazing at my friends. People he knows, but doesn't. It's an in-your-face kind of reminder that we aren't in the same crowd.

Why is it that I suddenly feel farther apart from him? As if there's a line that divides us—the proverbial railroad track. Not the rich and nonrich divide, but the popular and not-so popular. His kind. And my kind.

I can't help wondering if our different worlds had something to do with his not calling. Or was it just about my dying?

"I should go," I say. "But yes. I'll help you."

Our eyes meet.

Lock.

As crazy as it seems, I feel as if my old life is outside the car, and I need to go to it.

Sandy knocks again.

"Bye." I get out. Sandy hugs me before I have a chance to tell her I can't hug. I shut Matt's car door. Trent is looking at me kind of funny. I smile.

They all start talking at the same time. I'm halfway across the street before it hits how rude I was. I should've said something like . . . *You guys know Matt Kenner, don't you?*

But that would've sounded silly. Everyone knows him. The polite thing would've been to ask Matt to come in. Oh, he'd have turned me down. He has his own friends and parties to go to on New Year's Eve.

A little voice echoes in my head. *Welcome back to high school.* It's the world of cliques, snobby chicks, and an occasional dick. But I still belong there. It's where I'll find Old Leah.

Matt watches Leah and her friends cross the street. He recognizes everyone, but doesn't know their names. Except Trent Becker. You didn't forget the name of the guy who stole the girl you liked before you had your chance.

Is Leah still with him?

"Doesn't matter," he says aloud. He's not looking for that.

Matt starts the car, but something keeps him from driving off. He can't quite put his finger on the emotion sitting on his chest. Loneliness, maybe? Since Eric's death he's mostly pulled away from his friends. Having fun seems wrong. When he finds out who killed Eric, he can start living again.

He looks back across the street. It's not just loneliness. He feels excluded. Had Leah been rude, or was he just being pathetic?

He sees Trent shoulder up next to Leah. Yup, it's more than loneliness.

He doesn't want her there. He wants her here.

What's up with that? Then he gets it. She's the only person he's told about the dreams. The only person he's able to talk to about this. And to find out she was having the same kind of dreams? It had to mean something. And, of course, he'd feel . . . connected to her after all that.

Another possibility hits. Hard. Could it be Eric's heart he feels connected to?

He pushes that aside, because he'd felt this before Eric's death. Leah's special. Looking back at her, Trent at her side, he takes off, maybe a little hard. His tires squeal.

A block away, he comes to the stop sign and just sits there. Batting back emotions, he forces himself to focus on what matters most.

Eric.

Instead of turning to go home, he heads toward Cassie Chambers's house. He has questions. It's been over six months. She'd better have answers.

An hour later, I'm sitting on the sofa in Brandy's game room. Half of my old friends are on the other side of the room; half of them are here. Yet I feel crowded. I feel . . . like I don't belong.

LeAnn is going on about reading *Great Expectations*.

"It was boring," I say. "I couldn't finish it."

LeAnn gasps. "It's a classic."

"Classically boring."

"You're too smart to say that," Sandy says.

I recall Sandy and LeAnn both being occasional book snobs.

"Intelligence doesn't have anything to do with it," I counter.

"That could get you kicked out of the book club," LeAnn says jokingly.

Or maybe it's not a joke. Maybe I'm no longer a good fit. But I started it. How could I not belong?

"I've been reading romances," I blurt out, and I don't know if I wanted to push their buttons or what. But there it is. Out there.

Sandy laughs. "You're joking, right?"

"No. I found a box of them that belonged to my grandma."

"Way to go, Grandma," Trent says. I sense he's trying to show he's on my side. A little too close to my side. The back of his hand touches mine and I think of Matt. His touch. His sad eyes. My rudeness.

I scoot over. Reclaim a few inches on the sofa.

"Don't worry," Sandy says. "We'll give you some good books to read and clean out that *love* trash."

Love trash? Since when is love trash? "I thought the book club was open to all genres."

Everyone looks at me oddly.

Trent speaks up, "LeAnn decided we needed to be educated more than entertained. But we read our own stuff on the side. We just don't tell her." He cuts LeAnn a smile.

"I think a book can be both entertaining and educational," I say.

"Of course." Sandy's tone is practically placating.

I sit there swimming in frustration and wondering when everyone changed. Then it occurs to me. They haven't. I have. First, I spoke up. I didn't used to do that. I kept my opinions to myself—if I had any.

I remember someone writing in one of my yearbooks: *To Leah McKenzie, a better listener than a talker.*

The next hour, I don't talk and force myself to listen. Trying to find . . . me.

But none of this feels like me. I pop up.

"You need anything?" Trent catches my arm.

Not unless you're going to pee for me. "Restroom," I say, tempering my less-than-polite response and pull away.

I take a few steps, surprised Trent doesn't follow. He's been stuck to me like new Velcro. I can hear the crackly *rrriiip* when I get a few feet from him.

The thought of being home snuggled up with a book appeals to me more than being here, snuggled up with him. But leaving would hurt Brandy. She threw this party for me. It's my welcome-back-to-the-living party, a chance to reconnect with my old life.

I was looking forward to it too.

What the hell happened?

I take a step, hit my toe on the coffee table. "Shit!" I belt out. Everyone stares at me. "It's just shit." Then I realize they haven't heard me say "shit." Old Leah didn't say "shit."

"Sorry," I mutter, then hate that I'm apologizing.

It's as if New Leah is walking on eggshells around Old Leah. Around Old Leah's friends.

I make it across the room. Brandy lets go of Brian for the first time and follows me.

"Nothing's wrong with her," I hear Trent say.

I look back knowing they are talking about me. In spite of being irritated by Trent's attention, I recall why I liked him.

He's smart, sweet, and stands up for people. He's even cuter than I remember. His shoulders are wider, his arms thicker, his face more chiseled. Any girl would be lucky to have him.

So why don't I feel lucky?

Why do I keep thinking about Matt?

Brandy follows me into the bathroom. She jumps up on the bathroom counter. Watching me pee isn't a problem. We gave up all sense of modesty between each other in seventh-grade gym class. We always took turns changing into our gym clothes. One of us would dress while the other held lookout for Lisa, the class bully, to keep her from yanking open our dressing room curtain so everyone could see us naked.

God, I haven't thought about Lisa in forever. The idea of seeing her again annoys me. But something tells me that I won't take her shit anymore. How sad is it that it takes almost dying to learn to stand up for yourself?

"Did you tell Matt you think you have Eric's heart?" Brandy rubs her hands together waiting for juicy news. She asks as if the whole thing is cool.

I don't think it's cool. Actually, now that I know Matt's having the same dreams, it's freaking scary. It's as if Eric is trying to talk to us. As if he wants justice. As if he wants *us* to *find* him justice.

But I don't believe in ghosts. Or I didn't. Not that I've seen one. But today when I saw Cassie, I think I felt one. I felt Eric inside me, even questioned if he had the power to make me do things. Like go to the roadside park.

Chills crawl up my neck like tiny spiders.

Then I realize what scares me more than a dead person living inside me is the thought of me trying to find the person who made Eric dead.

I'm sure this person doesn't want to be found. I'm sure if he killed once, he'd be up to killing again. I'm sure I don't want to be his next victim.

I let the possibilities roll around my mind. Then another scary thought pops up.

Matt and I have both been through hell. What if we're just reading into the dreams to help us cope?

What if none of this is real?

8

"Earth to Leah." Brandy's eye-rolling expression reminds me that her question still hangs in the Febreze-scented air. "Did you tell him what you suspect about the heart?"

"He knows," I say.

"He knows. You mean you really have his heart? Seriously?"

I nod. "He saw me and my parents walking in after . . . after they signed the papers."

"Holy crap! This is like movie-of-the-week stuff."

If only she knew everything. I want to tell her. About my dreams. About Matt's dreams. But I'm not ready. Wasn't I just questioning the possibility that the whole dream stuff wasn't real? Or maybe I just need time to wrap my head around the craziness of it before I can share it. But I shared it all with Matt. That seems odd.

Brandy's feet swing at an impatient pace, bumping against the bathroom cabinet. *Clunk. Thump. Clunk. Thump.* "And?"

"And nothing," I say.

"So he didn't like ask you out or say he'd call?"

That would be a big hell no. "I think we're going to talk, but it's not like that."

"What about that kiss?"

"He only kissed me because I told him I wanted him to."
I need to remember that too.

"And you don't want him to kiss you now? He's Matt Kenner, for God's sake. Who doesn't want to kiss him? I'm with Brian, I'm madly in love with Brian, but I still want Matt Kenner to kiss me."

Mulling over my answer, I finish my business, complete my paperwork, zip, and go to wash my hands. Brandy jumps off the counter.

I reach for soap.

"Don't go silent on me," she demands.

The soap slides out of my hands, and the suds get sucked down the drain along with my rational thought. I don't understand what I'm feeling. Being scared of a killer. Feeling as if Eric is partly alive inside me. Doubting that what I'm feeling is even real. "It's just not like that now."

"Because he didn't call you back?" Her smile fades. "It pissed you off, didn't it?"

But damn. Sometimes Brandy can read me better than I can.

"Maybe, or maybe I'm smarter now. Like you said, 'He's Matt Kenner.' And I'm . . ."

"You're awesome," Brandy says. "Seriously, every guy at this party is like drooling over you. I had to give Brian a jab with my elbow. You are rocking that outfit. I think your boobs got bigger."

"Yeah, right." I flick my wet hands at her.

She ducks, giggles, then asks, "Okay, so what gives with Trent?"

I look at her.

"You don't have to answer," she says between chuckles. "Your expression says it all."

"I didn't have an expression."

"Yes you did. The sour-milk expression." She unzips, pees, all the while grinning up at me. "Hey, I'm not judging. I'm just surprised."

"He's not sour milk. He's nice, but . . . I'm not ready." Maybe I wasn't ready to be here either. I almost tell her how I feel. That I don't fit in with everyone anymore.

But I can't. These are Brandy's friends. They were my friends.

What the hell is wrong with me?

She tilts her head and studies me. "You really like Matt."

"I don't know how I feel." Other than more overwhelmed than I've been in a year. Obviously, living takes much more mental energy than dying.

Later, everyone piles into three cars and drives to the Walmart to watch the fireworks. We bring lawn chairs, blankets, and hot chocolate.

The big fireworks don't start until ten, but to secure a spot we get there at eight. Some fireworks are already going off. Everyone is *oohing* and *ahhing* over the explosions of color in the sky. I try to ignore everything that's rolling around inside me. Everything about Eric. Everything about Matt. Everything about me. About the me who doesn't fit in.

Next to us is a family with a boy around three. He keeps rolling his ball toward me; I keep rolling it back. His smile is so big. His mother, who doesn't look much older than me, tries to stop him, but I tell her it's okay. It keeps me from feeling awkward sitting next to Trent, who is still Velcroed to my side.

As I watch the boy curl up in his mother's lap, I remember something. A crazy something.

I can't have kids. Before, it didn't matter. I'm not sure it matters now, but it's there. Like a piece of gum stuck under the desk, it's stuck to the bottom of my mind. One day I'm going to want to scrape it off. But I can't.

I push that thought away.

I notice it's almost nine. The hot chocolate's gone. I need something to take my meds with.

I get up, tap Brandy on the arm, or I hope it's her arm—she and Brian are so wrapped up with each other I'm not sure what limb belongs to who.

"I'm going to go buy some water."

"I'll come with you." She starts untangling herself from Brian.

"No, I'm fine."

"I'll go." Trent's words pipe up behind me.

Brandy shoots me a sorry-about-that glance. I force a smile, and then Trent and I head out. The cold weaves itself through my sweater. I wish I'd borrowed a jacket from Brandy. We skirt between the crowds of people and cars. Trent's shoulder brushes mine. He used to do that all the time. He never went for public affection. Shoulder bumps were his way of saying "I care."

I don't want him caring about me, not like that.

"You feeling okay?" he asks over the exploding firecrackers.

"Yeah." I glance up at the streaks of blue and red racing across the sky.

"The meds don't make you feel bad?"

"How do you know about the meds?"

"I asked my dad about transplants. He said the meds can mess you up."

I forgot about his dad being a doctor. But the fact Trent asks about my meds is another nice thing that makes me feel like shit. "It's not bad."

"You ready for school?" he asks.

"I think. I'll have to work to keep up."

"I'd be happy to help."

His pleading gaze tells me he's thinking about Matt tutoring me.

"Maybe." Another jab of guilt hits because I don't want Trent tutoring me. I don't want Trent. But I used to. Used to. Suddenly I realize how often those words have played in my head tonight. Why is this so hard?

We keep walking, following the scent of popcorn. I try to think of a way to set things straight between us, but I can't. Or I can, but they all sound too blunt, too mean to say to someone who is too nice.

The crowd noise around me is loud, but the silence between Trent and me is louder. "It's colder tonight than it was earlier." I feed the words to the silence.

"Take my jacket."

"No," I say. But it's too late. He drops his jacket on my shoulders. Even pulls it around my neck, a tender, caring gesture that makes me angry. I feel like a bitch.

His scent rises from his jacket. It stirs memories of us close. Making-out close. A couple of times we went to third base. When I thought I was dying, I reflected on it a lot.

I'd even wished we'd gone all the way. Probably due to all those romance novels I read, but now I'm glad we didn't. In fact, thinking about us touching each other so intimately feels weird.

Feels wrong. Embarrassingly wrong.

"Thanks," I say, when I want to say, *Stop. Stop being so nice.* We come to the concession stand and get in line.

"Do you want some popcorn?" His shoulder presses against mine again.

"No." I reach into my purse and reclaim my shoulder. "I'm just getting water."

I force the anger back because it's not fair to target Trent. He didn't do this. A virus did this. Myocarditis did this.

"Do you need anything?" I ask.

"No." He's too close again. "But I'm getting your water."

"No," I say sharply. "I've got it."

He looks at me all strange like, as if I'm acting different. And I am. Old Leah didn't argue. Old Leah was always accommodating.

I focus on the couple in front of the line being handed sodas and popcorn. They turn to leave. Recognition slaps me in the face.

"Matt?" His name falls out of me, taking my breath with it. He stops so fast kernels of popcorn float to the ground. He stares at me all swallowed up and warm in Trent's jacket.

Then I see the girl he's with, her shoulder brushing against his. She's pretty and reminds me of Cassie Chambers.

"Hey," Matt says.

"Hey," I repeat.

"This is Paula." He introduces the blonde. "And this is Leah." He shifts his popcorn at me. Another few butter-scented kernels fall off the top.

"Paula's friends with Ted's girlfriend. She's with them."

It's as if he's trying to explain why he's with her. Or maybe I'm just reading more into it.

I notice he doesn't try to explain me. But what could he say? *"Leah is no one important. She used to be the shy girl who started the book club in our school. And now she's the girl who has my brother's heart and we're having the same dreams about the last minutes of his life."* Yeah, that's not explainable.

Trent's shoulder shifts closer. Then closer.

I let Trent's sleeves fall past my hands, as if wanting to hide. "You know Trent?" I force myself to be polite.

Trent slips his arm around my shoulder. He seldom did that in public, even when we were dating. Without thinking, I lean into him.

Oh, hell! Why did I do that?

The reason plops itself down on my conscience.

I'm jealous. Then I'm angry that I'm jealous. Angry because I'm using Trent. Angry because I'm not a user. Angry because the blonde is so pretty.

The guys exchange nods. It gets too quiet too fast. Even the fireworks stop.

The tension makes the cold air feel dense, unbreathable. Matt shifts away from the blonde. A few more kernels of popcorn hit the ground. Trent's arm on my shoulders feels too heavy. His coat too hot.

It doesn't fit. Trent doesn't fit.

I don't fit. I don't fit me anymore.

"We should go." He shifts from foot to foot. "Talk to you later."

"Yeah."

Matt and the girl leave. When I step forward, Matt's popcorn crunches beneath my shoes, and I'm grateful that Trent's arm slips off my shoulder.

I don't say a word to Trent. If I didn't need the drink to take my pills, I'd leave. Just walk home.

I finally make the counter and ask for a water. I see Tootsie Rolls and add one to my order for the little boy who'd been watching fireworks next to me. Trent and I start back. Dogging our steps is the uncomfortable silence.

We're almost back to the others when I can't take it anymore. I stop and face Trent.

A voice in my head tells me not to do this, that I might regret it. That in a couple of weeks I'll feel more like myself, like Old Leah, and Trent will fit again. That New Leah will be lucky to have him.

I take his coat off. It's cold, but I feel free. "Here."

"You can wear it." He hands it back. I don't take it.

Words squirm around in my chest, then crawl up my throat. I'll choke if I don't say them. "I like you, Trent. But I just want to be friends right now."

He looks punched. Hurt. I feel like a bitch. Not a heartless one anymore, but with a heart that's not mine. A life that's not mine.

He tosses his coat over his shoulder. "Because of Matt Kenner?"

"I don't think so . . . but I don't know. I'm trying to figure this all out."

"Figure what out?" he asks.

"Me." My answer echoes in my head then crashes into my new heart. It's so true it hurts. Hurts because I don't fit into my old life any more than Trent fits in my new one. Or is it the heart that doesn't fit?

No, it's not just the new heart. It's me. I've changed.

I'm not sure who I am anymore. I'm not sure I can go back to being Old Leah. And who this New Leah is is a big freaking mystery.

9

Voices bounce around Matt. Fireworks light up the Texas sky.

Ted and the others are laughing. Matt's huddled in a lawn chair, wishing he wasn't here.

Then he gives up. "Hey, I'm cutting out early." It's only eleven, but so what?

He can't stop thinking about her. Her with Trent. Wearing his coat.

At least this time, she introduced him.

Instead of looking up at the fireworks, he's spent the last

hour looking out in the crowd—searching the faces for Leah. He wants to talk to her. To tell her about Cassie's mom lying to him, saying Cassie wasn't back in town yet. He wants . . . Eric to be alive.

But his reason for wanting to see Leah isn't all about Eric.

Earlier, he realized he never asked her how she was doing. How selfish is he?

He drives to his house, pulls in the driveway, but doesn't get out. His mom's car isn't there. She's still out.

The house is dark, looks abandoned. He feels abandoned.

The thought of walking into the empty house has him backing out of the driveway. He doesn't know where he's going until he turns into Leah's neighborhood.

He parks across the street. The garage door's open, as if waiting for someone to come home. Leah's car, the one he spotted at Brandy's house, isn't here. Which means she's still with Trent.

One of the drapes in Leah's front windows flutters back, and someone peers out. Feeling like a stalker, he drives off.

His heart leads the way again. Not to home. He pulls over at the roadside park where Eric was found. He doesn't turn the car off. He doesn't turn his lights off. He doesn't turn the pain off. Not that he knows how.

His headlights light up the white cross there for his brother.

He shoves the car in park. "What happened, Eric?"

Closing his eyes, time and his anger crawl past. Fireworks pop off overhead.

Then he starts to feel things. Emotions that don't feel like his own. Fear. Frustration. Fury.

He considers getting out and trying to walk it off, but a police car slows down as if checking on him.

Not wanting to explain to a cop why he's here, he starts the engine and pulls away.

His mom pulls up into the driveway at the same time he

does. He looks at the time as he gets out. Five minutes until midnight.

She meets him in the driveway. Both his dad's and Eric's cars are still parked in the garage. As is the old Mustang his dad had bought and they were supposed to rebuild together.

So now they park in the driveway.

"You're home early." His mom rests a warm hand on his shoulder.

"Didn't want to get caught in the traffic leaving the fireworks."

She studies him. Lately, he's noticed her doing that, as if she's looking for something. "Did you have a good time?"

"Yeah." He white-lies it. They walk into the house. Lady yelps from her kennel. He lets her out and heads toward the back door. His mom follows him. They stand in the dark and watch Lady sniff in circles. Frost forms on his breath in the cold night air.

"Did you have a good time?" he asks.

"Yeah. It's been a long time since I met up with my friends. We need friends," she says.

The fireworks start, and the puppy, tail tucked between her legs, races up to Matt and climbs his leg.

They chuckle. Matt picks up the animal. Lady buries her head under Matt's chin, hiding from the crackles and booms. Her breath is warm and puppy-scented.

Matt and his mom look up at the sky exploding with colors. She slips her hand in his and squeezes. He feels it all the way to his heart.

"Happy New Year," she says.

"Happy New Year." He squeezes her back. They walk inside, and he sets Lady down. She slips and slides to her puppy bowl to crunch on her leftover dinner.

"You want something to drink?" she asks.

"Nah," he says. "We still on for running in the morning?"

"Yeah, but a little later." She motions to the barstools. "Sit down. Chat time."

That means it's serious. She hasn't requested chat time since before his dad died. She used to do it all the time with him and Eric. She said it was her way to make sure her boys were following the right path. Then after their dad died, she didn't worry about paths.

He drops down. "Is everything okay?"

"Yeah." She sits beside him. He notices some new wrinkles around her eyes. She's not quite forty, but looks older. Losing people does that to you.

He bet he had a few wrinkles, if not on the outside, then surely on the inside.

"Have you thought more about seeing a therapist, like we talked about?"

"Not yet, Mom. I'll tell you when I'm ready."

"Then what would you think about a grief counseling group? Where we meet with other people who have lost someone and offer each other support. I'm thinking of joining one. It's for all ages. I thought maybe you'd come with me."

His mental brake is all the way to the floorboard. "I'm not sure that's . . . I think it's great for you, but I don't think it's for me."

The wrinkles around her eyes deepen. "We'll never be the same after what happened to your dad and Eric, and the way to healing is going to be a long road. But there are people who can help. It's a huge burden to carry alone, Matt. And you don't have to."

"I know, Mom. I'll think about it, okay?" He doesn't really intend to, but saying so will make his mom feel better.

Lady whines and he picks her up. She hides under his chin again. Her nose is cold. The firecrackers popping off sound too loud. Fractured light flashes in from a few windows.

His mom's gaze meets his. There are tears in her eyes, but he sees something else there too. Worry. Fret. A new kind. What the hell's wrong?

She finally speaks. "Detective Henderson called me."

Shit! This is what chat time is about. "I just want him to do his job."

"He has done his job, Matt. They investigated it."

"No!" Matt's tone comes out locked and loaded with emotion. He puts the puppy down and faces his mom. "You told me yourself you didn't think Eric did it."

Tears fall down her cheeks, and she wipes them away with her palm. "That was before we knew it was your dad's gun. God, I don't want to believe it." She chokes up, and he can hear the tears in her voice. "But Matt, why else would he have taken it?"

"I don't know. But I know it's not true."

"You don't know, Matt." She shakes her head.

"I do!" He hits the counter with his palm. "I know it like I knew Eric's arm was broken when he was three. I knew he was gone the minute it happened. Why do you think I was throwing up that night? And I know he didn't commit suicide."

Her tears continue to fall. She doesn't wipe them away now. She puts her palm on his cheek. It's warmer than his face. Her touch is so soft and motherly and it sends currents of emotion into him. Love, grief, sadness.

"I messed up with Eric." Her voice shakes. "I refuse to mess up with you. I don't want you . . ."

"I'm not going to kill myself." He grips his fist as his chest tightens. "That's not in me, no more than it was in Eric."

She blinks. "I know the truth is horrible, but we need to accept it so we can heal. So we can go on living."

"I can't. I'm going to prove that Eric didn't do it; then I'm going to make sure the person who did it rots in a jail for the rest of his life!"

He storms off to his bedroom, the storm inside him brewing harder than before.

My alarm chimes at 8:55 A.M. on Wednesday morning, the first day of the year. Eyes still shut, I slap the alarm off. Then I run my hands around the nightstand, palming the top of it to find the thermometer. I find it, press the button, and slip it in my mouth, still studying the backs of my eyelids.

Every morning and every night I have to check my temperature and take my blood pressure. When the thermometer beeps, I force one eye open. Seeing it's normal, I grab the blood pressure cuff, fit it on my arm, and hit START. When it beeps, I check the numbers, write them down, roll out of bed, and sleep-walk into the kitchen.

"Good morning, Sunshine," Mom says.

I half nod at the breakfast table.

My eyes are still at half-mast. I pour milk, snag my pills, down them, and start out of the kitchen.

"Did you have fun last night?" Dad asks.

They were awake when I came in. I heard them talking. Dad wouldn't let Mom come in and question me. I love that man. But I'd love him a lot more if he'd let me go back to bed.

I point to my face. "I'll tell you all about it when I wake up."

I got in at exactly one. Then couldn't sleep trying to figure out who New Leah is.

Failing at that mission, I told myself that I'd figure it out first thing in the morning.

But who wants to start a new year sleep deprived.

I step toward my room.

"Did you take your temperature and blood pressure?" Mom's motherly concern slows me down.

"Both normal." I make it to my bedroom and fall face-first on my mattress. I reach to fluff my pillow and see the notepad beside my bed. Last night I decided to keep a record. Every time I have a dream about Eric, I plan to write it down.

The pad's empty. I didn't dream last night. I fall back to sleep.

Later, Mom's touch, checking me for a fever, almost wakes me. She's afraid I'll reject my heart.

Honestly, I don't know why I'm not living in constant fear of it. Why I have so much faith that things are going to turn out this time, when I had zero before. Maybe I just can't let myself go there. Maybe it's because I refuse to believe Karma would give me Eric's heart and then let it fail.

I bury my face in the covers. Sweet slumber claims me, or it does until I'm stirred awake again. "Leah?" It's my father's voice.

"She's not here."

"It's eleven thirty," he says in his forever-patience voice.

"One mo' hour."

"Okay. But this is the second time he showed up this morning."

I hear him, but it takes like two seconds for me to get it. Sitting up like a loaded spring, I flip my hair, squinting to block out the sun that streams in from my window. "He? Who? Hewho? Hewho?" I sound like a bird belting out a mating call. I swallow too much air, too fast; my lungs feel like they might explode. I force myself to slow down. "He, who? Who is it?"

Before he answers, I think I know. I lose my *oomph*.

"Trent?" My memory foam mattress pulls my butt in, and I recall the memory of giving Trent the just-friend speech. The visual of the hurt in his eyes sucks on my conscience, and I start to suck on my teeth. Even New Leah doesn't like hurting people. New Leah also hates dirty teeth, but so did Old Leah. I keep sucking.

"Not Trent," Dad says. "Your mom said his name was Mark or Matt."

"Shit, shit, shit!" I scream and haphazardly swipe some more hair from my eyes.

Dad chuckles. My newly acquired language doesn't disturb him as much as Mom.

I bolt up and off the bed like a superhero. I stand in the middle of my room, trying to think. *I need . . . my bra, my jeans. I need to wake up.*

Finger-combing my hair, one of my slippers peers out at me from halfway under my bed. I snatch up Dumbo. Standing tall, still sleep dazed, I hold the slipper like the Statue of Liberty holds her flame. I'm not even sure why I picked it up. Then with my other hand, I start running my index finger over my front teeth to remove the morning fuzz.

I slow the back-and-forth motion long enough to focus on my dad perched at my door. A big grin widens his lips. He laughs. Deep, happy laughter. I have no idea what's funny.

"What?" I garble the question out around my makeshift toothbrush.

"You. Seeing you so . . . normal."

Since when is me panicking, finger-brushing my teeth, and holding up one Dumbo normal?

I toss down the shoe and pop my finger out of my mouth. "Ask him to give me a minute."

"Okay." Dad's footsteps tap-tapping down the hall are followed by his laughter. I'm never going to understand parents.

I blow into my hand and smell my breath. Ugg. Finger-brushing is not going to cut it.

"Make that like five or ten." I raise my arm, smell my pit. "Fifteen!"

I bolt into the bathroom, start the shower, and jump in before it's hot. Goose bumps chase bigger goose bumps over my skin. I don't care.

This feeling, the excitement racing, running through my blood tells me that this, this is going to be the first step to discovering who New Leah is. Who the hell knows how it's going to involve Matt.

Especially when he might have a girlfriend.

No! I tell myself. Like the time I kissed him, whatever happens, I vow not to regret it.

I realized if I've learned anything from almost dying it's that life's too short to spend a second of it regretting.

As the warm water finally flows, goose bumps die, steam rises. The glass door fogs up. The gotta-hurry feeling fades into a strange calm. I press my hand on the door. When I lift it, the condensation drips away. My print becomes nothing but a fuzzy smear.

I think about Eric. About him being gone and yet not really. I have his heart.

And my own is gone.

Is that why I don't feel like myself?

I wonder if Eric knows . . . knows I'm about to see his brother. I remember feeling sad when I saw Cassie yesterday. Was that Eric? Or am I losing it?

"Snap out of it!" I say aloud.

Then remembering Matt's waiting, I bolt out of the shower, brush my teeth as I hum the "Happy Birthday" song to keep time—old habits are hard to break.

I comb my hair, and because I don't have fifteen minutes to dry it, I clip it up. It's gonna be curly as hell later, but I'm choiceless. I take two seconds to swipe blush on my cheeks and gloss on my lips. Then I dress like a runway model on speed, eager to start the New Year and the New Me.

10

Matt gulps fear down his throat and stares at Leah's front door. Lady, on her leash, is trying to chew herself free. Matt can relate. With what happened last night, and not knowing what her parents know, it was hard to show up this morning. Even harder to come back the second time.

A phone rings behind the door.

Nerves gnaw on Matt's sanity.

If her father opens the door and says Leah's still asleep, Matt's gonna know the truth. Leah is refusing to see him.

And then what?

Damn it. She said she'd help. And with his mom riding his ass, he could really use some help.

Why would Leah turn her back on him? *Seeing him with Paula?*

Matt had explained that Paula wasn't . . . his girlfriend, hadn't he? Then again, how could she be upset about Paula when she was attached at the hip to Trent Becker, and all snug and warm wearing his coat?

Matt pushes that whole bitter thought aside. Leah and he are just friends.

Yeah, they kissed and it was awesome, but that was then.

An uncomfortable thought hits. What if Leah told her parents she has Eric's heart? Maybe it's her parents who don't want him here?

Footsteps sound behind the door. He stands straighter. The door swooshes open. Mr. McKenzie, holding a phone in his hand, in a flat-footed stance just stares.

"Sorry, I had a call."

Matt waits to be sent packing.

"She's getting ready," her dad says. "You want to come in?"

Not really. But does he have a choice?

Matt remembers Lady. Maybe he does have a choice.

"I'll wait. I have my dog."

Mr. McKenzie stares at Lady. A jolt of nerves skateboard down Matt's spine. The meeting-the-dad-of-the-girl-you-like kind of nerves. Not that this is a date. Does Leah's father know that?

"Is he housetrained?" Mr. McKenzie asks.

"She." Matt hesitates. "Sort of, but—"

"Then come in. The shower's going. She might be a while." He pushes open the door.

Matt barely crosses the threshold when Mr. McKenzie looks back at Lady and says, "But if she's the sort that poops and pees, you clean it up."

"Of course." He scoops up the squirming puppy. Her big yellow paws tread the air and her pink tongue is busy trying kiss his face.

Leah's dad leads Matt into the kitchen. "Have a seat."

Matt's unsure if the man is being nice or is about to interrogate him. Matt pulls the chair out from the table, leaving room for Lady in his lap, then drops in the seat. Mr. McKenzie remains standing and staring. The dog starts twisting and turning, right along with Matt's insides.

Her father finally speaks. "Want a Coke?"

"No, sir." He remembers his manners. "But thank you."

"How do you know Leah?" Mr. McKenzie settles in a chair.

Here comes the interrogation. "At school."

"You tutored her once, right?"

"Yes, sir." Lady barks, wanting down. She starts the howlish whimpering. Matt sits her on the ground, but holds her leash and hears her sniffing around for table crumbs.

"You're a senior, too?" Mr. McKenzie asks in a non-interrogation tone.

"Yes, sir." Matt wishes he could drop the "sir," but when you had a father in the army, "sir" is ingrained in you.

Her dad runs his hand over the edge of the table. "My wife mentioned you're a twin?"

Was a twin. Matt's nod is small.

"You two close?"

Matt nods again, this one slower. He'd done a lot of nodding with people who didn't know. It hurts less than explaining.

"It's Matt, right?" Mr. McKenzie asked.

"Yes, sir."

"What's the last name?"

"Kenner."

"Kenner?" Her dad tilts his head slightly to the right as if . . . His eyes round. Instant pity turns his blue eyes a shade darker.

"Your brother, he . . . passed away?"

Matt nods. This one hurts. *Thank God, he didn't say killed himself.*

"I'm sorry. My wife hasn't kept up with the news. And I didn't put the twin thing together."

"It's okay," Matt offers the hated pat answer and thinks *shit.*

Then he smells it. Shit. Dog shit.

He ducks his head down and moans. Lady's in full hunched mode doing her business.

Mr. McKenzie leans sideways and peers under the table. Their frowns meet.

Effing great! "I'll get it, sir." Matt loops the leash around the chair, bolts up. "Paper towels . . . ?"

"On the counter." Mr. McKenzie's voice is muffled from covering his nose.

Matt, paper towels in hand, crawls under the table. "Not ladylike," he scolds Lady, using his mother's words and tone. The puppy plops down in a poor-me pose. Matt scoops up the crap and is attempting to crawl on three limbs when he hears footsteps.

Still under the table, he glances out and up. Leah's standing in the kitchen doorway. She's wearing soft-to-touch-looking faded jeans that aren't tight but hug her every curve. The red sweater she's wearing does to her top what the jeans do to her bottom.

"Where is he? You told him to wait, didn't you?" Disappointment slides off her words. Matt almost smiles realizing she wants to see him.

Lady, past the pathetic mode, dashes from under the table, taking down a chair as she goes.

Leah squeals, jumps, then stares at Lady. "What . . ." She slaps a hand over her nose.

"He's . . . uh, under . . . there," Mr. McKenzie's tight voice echoes from above.

Leah squats down. Their gazes meet, hold, then her focus shifts to his hand holding . . .

Damn! Of all the ways a guy didn't want a hot girl to see him, down on his knees holding a towel of dog shit has to top that list.

Matt frowns. "Lady shi . . ."—he corrects himself—"had an accident."

Leah's surprise fades into something softer, sweeter. A sparkle lights up her blue eyes. They crinkle at the corners with humor, and her face transforms into one big, so-damn-beautiful smile. He's captivated.

She giggles—falls back on her butt. Lady rushes her with puppy excitement.

Leah's laughter is like a song you want to sing along with. One he hasn't sung in a long time. He wants that back. He wants to be able to let go of the pain he's felt since his father died, since his brother died, and laugh like that. Laugh so free—free of grief.

Then Mr. McKenzie's laughter roars above. Even Lady makes happy puppy sounds. Then it happens. A light feeling swells in his chest and his own laughter spills out. He can't remember the last time he's laughed so spontaneously. But for these few seconds, he doesn't want to think about it.

He just wants to enjoy it. He knows it won't last long, because in just a minute his heart is going to remember everything he's lost.

I rush to get the garbage can for Matt, who crawls out from under the table. I hope he knows I wasn't laughing at him but at the situation. He stands up. Our gazes meet. His eyes still hold the most amazing smile. No hard feelings, I assume.

Dropping the paper towels in the trash, he grabs a few more, dampens them in the sink, and climbs back under the table to finish the job.

"Looks like you're an expert," my dad says, leaning down to watch Matt.

"Unfortunately," Matt answers, from under the table. "Mom gave Lady to me for Christmas. But she didn't come with a cleaning service."

Dad chuckles. "It's the gift that keeps giving."

Leah hears Matt laugh, but it's there and gone. Not nearly as unencumbered as the last.

He crawls out and drops those paper towels in the trash I'm holding out. His gaze shifts to my dad. "I'll take this out for you, if you'd like."

"Sure." Dad's still smiling. He likes Matt, I think. For some reason I like that.

"Trash can's in the back." Dad points to the kitchen door.

Matt pulls the bag from the can. I grab Lady's leash and follow him out.

Hurrying to the trash can, I lift the lid for him.

I feel bad he's taking out our garbage. Feel bad that I took so long getting ready, which caused the accident. And I still feel bad I hadn't introduced him to my friends when they surrounded his car.

"Sorry," I say.

He drops the bag in the can. I drop the lid. Our eyes meet. Hold. The moment feels so special, perfect, I ignore the trashcan aroma permeating the air.

"Sorry?" he asks. "You didn't shit under the table."

I laugh.

He stands there; time freezes. He's looking at me all dreamy like—the kind of look that says he's really seeing me. That he likes what he sees. The kind of look that happens in romance novels. And I do love those novels. I don't give a damn what Sandy and LeAnn think.

"You . . . have a pretty smile." He shrugs then looks embarrassed for tossing out the compliment.

But I'm not sorry.

"Thanks." My smile widens, my chest fills with something light, airy, and oh-so good.

Lady tugs on the leash. Trash odor still hangs on. But I'm in the clouds. I'm floating. Then I notice his jacket, his school-issued letterman football jacket with his very own number. And bam, I crash back to garbage-scented reality.

I remember the girl last night. I remember Matt's here because of the dreams, to get justice for his brother. I remember who Matt is.

I realize that his liking my smile doesn't mean a whole hell of a lot.

Not in the big picture.

Not when school starts in a few days.

Not when he's still Matt Kenner. And I'm still . . .

I don't know who I am.

While I might be on a mission to discover answers, I'm

positive even New Leah isn't in the same league as the school's quarterback. And when we're in the world of cliques, snobby chicks, and dicks—in the world where guys like him don't really notice girls like me—he's going to realize that we don't match.

I need to remember that.

I might have lost the expiration date stamped on my ass, but I shouldn't let myself start wishing for impossible things.

Damn it, though . . . My spine tightens; my shoulders lock. It's not going to stop me from enjoying today. Or any of the time I get to spend with him.

The silence lingers a smidgeon too long. Matt must feel it too, because he starts talking.

"I . . . I was taking Lady for a walk in the park and thought you might come so we could talk."

"Yeah," I say, hoping I don't sound too eager. But I am eager. Unable to stop myself, I go right back to full-blown wishing.

Wishing that school didn't start in five days.

Wishing I could have a few months to enjoy this.

Wishing I had time to convince Matt that, out of his league or not, we could mean something to each other—mean more than just a method of finding justice for Eric.

Ten minutes later, Matt's driving to the park. Leah, riding shotgun, is quiet. But so is he. Lady's never quiet. She's in the backseat, bouncing from window to window, barking at every car on the road as if it's her job.

He recalls he still hasn't asked about Leah's health. He glances at her. "How are you?"

She looks confused.

"With the heart transplant, I mean?"

"Oh, I'm . . . good." The slight indecision in her voice gives him pause.

He keeps switching his focus to the road, to her. She's a better view. "Everything is like . . . before. You're like healed. Normal?"

"Yeah." She gazes out the window, and he can't help thinking she's not being completely honest. But maybe not.

"You look good." But he thinks *really* good.

That earns him a hesitant smile. "Thanks." She focuses back on the road. "Which park are we going to?"

Looking around, he gets his bearings. "The one we passed about a mile back. Sorry."

She smiles, and this one appears real.

"I do that sometimes. Especially when I'm in the good part of a book."

He chuckles. "You read while you drive?"

She laughs. "I mean, thinking about a book."

"Are you going to take charge of the book club again?"

"I don't know." She pauses. "Do you read?"

"Yeah. Probably not as much as you. Especially lately." He glances at her. "But I finished all the Harry Potter books. And I like James Dashner's books. What are you reading now?"

She hesitates. "Mostly girl books."

"By who?"

"Christie Craig, Lori Wilde, Susan C. Muller. Diane Kelly."

He doesn't recognize the names. "What kind of girl books do they write?"

She looks away. "Some have suspense, paranormal, humor, and relationships."

"Romances?"

She gives him a cute look. "Don't judge."

He bites back a smile. "Not judging. My mom reads them. Used to."

He recalls the day Eric brought one of his mom's books into Matt's bedroom and read some of the sex scenes. They laughed their asses off. Was Leah reading those kind?

"She doesn't read now?" Leah asks.

"No, she . . . gave up reading when . . . Dad died." *They all had.* "I should probably pick up a few books for her." *And maybe even see if Dashner has a new one out.*

Leah shifts in her seat. "I've got a stack that I was going to donate. You could take her those."

"Yeah. Thanks."

They don't talk again until he pulls into the park. He unbuckles his seat belt.

She doesn't. "Did you dream last night about Eric?"

"No. I don't dream about him every night. Sometimes it's not even a dream. It's like . . . I get this feeling and he pops in my mind."

He gazes out the window. The park is almost empty. The sun is bright, making it look warmer than it is. And right then a little bit of truth leaks out of him. "Sometimes I . . . start feeling a certain way, not so much how I would feel, but how Eric would feel. It sounds crazy but . . ."

He looks at her. She looks . . . scared. Really scared.

Matt's positive it's fear widening her eyes. "You've felt Eric, too, haven't you?"

She blinks. "When . . . I saw Cassie at the roadside park. I felt so sad. It didn't . . . It's like you said. It didn't feel like me feeling it."

Matt draws in air. "You have his heart."

She swallows. He hears the gulp. The scared sound becomes trapped in the car. "But you don't," she says.

"We have that . . . twin thing." He tells her the story about Eric breaking his arm and feeling the pain. "Even later," he continues. "We were so connected. Eric used to say, 'Get out of my head.' "

He runs a hand over the steering wheel. "I'd give anything to hear him say that again."

Lady starts barking.

"We should probably walk her," he says.

"Yeah." She unbuckles her seat belt. The click almost sounds too loud.

They walk down the path. A lot of the trees are winter naked, leafless, but a few still cling to their fall-colored leaves. The air is crisp and cold, but the sun is warm and bright. It feels good. Leah's wearing a light jean jacket on top of her sweater. He thinks about her in Trent's coat again. The temptation to ask her about him grinds at Matt's gut, but it doesn't feel right.

"I got a notebook," Leah speaks up. "I'm keeping it on my bedside table. When I have a dream, I'll write down what I saw and felt. It might help."

"Good idea," Matt says. "I'll do the same. Maybe we should also write down when we get those . . . feelings. We can meet up and share what we have."

"Yeah," she says.

So she doesn't mind seeing me again.

They keep walking. Lady tugs on the leash. Being with Leah tugs on his emotions. "I went to Cassie's. Her mom told me she wasn't back yet."

Leah stops. "But I saw her."

He nods. "I didn't believe her mom. It felt like she was lying to me." He tightens his hand around the leash. "And that makes me wonder. Does Cassie's mom know something about Eric? Are they both hiding something?"

Leah looks out at the woods, then back. "But . . ."

"But what?" he asks.

"When I saw Cassie, she was upset. And if our crazy theory is right, we're actually getting Eric's feelings, wouldn't he be furious if she was behind this? Why would he feel sad?"

Frustration bubbles inside Matt and leaks out like old air he'd been holding for too long. "Because Eric loved her. Knowing him, he'd love her even if she killed him. She'd already broken his heart once, and he went back to her anyway."

Leah doesn't look convinced.

"Fine," he says. "Maybe she's not behind it, but she's hiding something. Why else would she refuse to see me?"

"Because . . . like I said before, looking at you is like looking at Eric. That would . . . hurt."

Matt stops. "You're wrong. It feels like something more." Sighing, he massages his temples with his fingertips.

Leah rests her palm on his arm. He can feel the touch through his jacket and shirt. Feel it as if it's right against his skin.

"I'm on your side, Matt. I just think . . . we need to look at all angles."

Shit. Had he snapped at her? "Sorry. I'm . . ."

"You're hurting. It's understandable."

"Yeah. And now with my mom riding my ass, I . . . I want this solved." He grabs a dying leaf off a tree and twists it.

"What's your mom doing?" Leah stops by a bench on the side of the path and sits down.

He drops beside her, careful to not get too close. "Detective Henderson called her."

"And?"

"I hadn't told her I'm trying to get him to reopen the case."

"The case is closed?" She leans back against the bench.

He exhales a gulp of pain. "They said Eric had gunshot residue on his hands, and because it was my father's gun they . . . ruled it a suicide." He rakes a palm over his face then looks at her, suddenly scared she'll believe it. "He didn't do it, Leah."

She frowns. "Does your mom believe it?"

"She says she can't figure out why else he'd have taken the gun. She wants me to stop looking into it because she's afraid . . . I'll kill myself."

Her breath catches. "You wouldn't, would you?"

"No." He frowns.

She looks relieved.

He presses a palm to his forehead. "But I can't drop it. And Mom's finally getting better and I don't want this to set her back." He exhales. "When Dad died, she got so depressed. She wouldn't get dressed or comb her hair for days. I think she felt it was okay because Eric and I had each other. Now, with Eric gone, she's trying to take care of me."

He hesitates. "She's started running and getting grief counseling, and she's started pressing me to join a support group." He stares at Lady. "She even went out with friends last night."

"That's good." Leah's voice is soft, almost lyrical, caring. Not the kind of caring that sounds fake. She's genuine. Everything about her is genuine.

"Are you going to go?" Leah asks. "To the support group?"

"No."

"Why not?"

"I don't like talking to strangers." *I'd much rather talk to you.* She nods.

"I don't want to be what prevents my mom from getting better, but I have to find out who did this to Eric. He'd hate people thinking he did this to himself."

"We'll do it," she says. "We'll figure it out."

We. That one word works its way from his head to his heart.

He wants to take her hand, but he doesn't. Doesn't because he wants it too much. Or maybe because he wants more than just holding her hand. He wants to kiss her again.

God help him, but he wants to feel her soft breasts against his chest like when he kissed her before.

He wants.

He just wants.

For a beat of time, they don't talk. He tries to control his wants and let himself find peace in the fact she's here. She's helping him. Listening to him. That should be enough.

"Do you have any idea why Eric would have taken the gun?" Leah asks.

Her question bumps against raw nerves. How long has he tried to figure that out? "No. But I think Cassie knows." A thought hits and he looks back at Leah.

"Maybe if you call her or see her, she'll talk to you."

The tightness in Leah's eyes tells him she doesn't like his plan.

"I . . . I'll try, but she doesn't know me."

"You've gone to school with her since first grade."

"Yeah, but we . . . we've never been friends."

Something about her tone tells him there's more to it. "Have you two had problems?"

"No. We've just never . . . talked. But, I'll try." She looks down at her hands, then up. "Today being New Year's, I should wait. Tomorrow, I could go there. You'll have to tell me where she lives. And what you want me to ask."

He nods. A cool wind whooshes by, stirring a few tendrils of Leah's hair that have fallen out of the clip. He watches it brush across her face and neck.

He likes her hair better down.

"Did Eric have any problems with anyone?" Leah asks.

Lady jumps up on her leg, and Leah leans down to pet her. The scooped neck of her sweater falls open. Matt can't stop his eyes from going there. But what he sees isn't what he expects. Leah has a scar. A red scar.

His chest hurts. Aches for her.

He looks away before she notices. He hadn't thought about her having a scar. And a big one. But he should have. They had to put Eric's heart in her chest.

She sits up. "Did he?"

"What?" He's lost. He forces himself to look at her.

"Did Eric have any problems with anyone?" she repeats.

"Just Cassie."

"What kind of problems?"

He forces his mind away from her scar. Away from the pain she must have felt. "They had broken up like five months before. He was just getting over her. Marissa, Cassie's best friend, called him saying something was wrong with Cassie and asked him to call her."

"What was wrong?" Leah pulls her knee up and hugs it.

"He wouldn't tell me. Said it wasn't something he could talk about. But he was upset." Matt closes his eyes. "I should have made him tell me."

"You can't make someone open up," Leah offers.

Matt runs a hand through his hair. "Whatever was going on, it made him take Cassie back. He'd started dating Haley and he broke that off."

"Haley?"

"A girl from Southside High. They started dating a few months after he and Cassie broke up."

"Why did Cassie break up with him the first time?"

"She never told him. That's what drove him so crazy. He was still grieving over Dad and then she did that."

"Had Eric been depressed?"

"No! Okay, yeah, he was in a funk, but not bad." *Not as bad as I was.* Or am. "He acted worse after he got back with her. Not depressed, just worried." Matt looks at Leah. "Maybe you could ask Cassie about that."

Leah nods, but still appears unsure.

Tugging her knee closer, she pauses. "Marissa, Cassie's best friend, doesn't she go to our school, too?"

"Yeah."

"Have you asked her about Cassie or asked her to talk to Cassie?"

"She says she doesn't know anything, says she hasn't even spoken to Cassie since she left to live with her dad."

Leah goes quiet. Lady curls up at his feet and naps. The sounds playing around them are nothing but the breeze and fluttering bird wings echoing from the trees. The sun falls behind a cloud.

Leah pulls her jacket closer.

"You want my coat?" The second the words fall off his lips, he regrets saying them.

Their eyes meet, and he knows she's thinking about Trent. About Trent's coat. She probably knows he's thinking about it too. He wants to ask her what the deal is between them, but she might guess Matt's interested and then feel uncomfortable with him.

"No, I'm fine," she says. "When we walk, I'm not cold."

They stand up and amble along in silence. It's not uncomfortable, but it's too long, feels empty. He misses the sound of her voice.

When they get settled into his car, he faces her. "I need to run by the vet and grab Lady more puppy food. It's on the way to your house. Do you mind, or do you want me to take you home?"

"I don't mind."

He smiles. "Thank you."

"For what?"

"Being here. I really need someone right now." Then, damn, he regrets saying that too. The last thing he wants to come off as is weak and needy.

"I'm here." She sends him a soft look that chases away his regret and even some of the pain.

Starting the car, he puts it in reverse, then shoves it in park. "Leah, I know I've already said this, but . . . I'm sorry." He holds onto the wheel. "I didn't call you back after I came to tutor you. You probably needed me then, and I bailed on you."

She sinks her front teeth in her bottom lip again.

He feels even worse. "I was in a dark place. That doesn't make it right. I was a bastard."

"No, you weren't. I get it. I do." She sends a quiet smile.

It's the prettiest damn smile he's ever seen.

His chest tightens and releases at the same time. The hurt he feels, has felt for so long, eases a little more. Being with her is to this pain what an aspirin is to a headache.

Only he needs a bigger dose.

12

I watch Matt drive. I watch the world go past, and my mind juggles everything we've talked about. About his apology for bailing on me. It reminds me how much I wanted him to call.

I really don't blame him. I was sick. But it produces a wiggle of worry inside me. If he knew I wasn't completely out of the woods—that I'll never really be out of the woods—would he bail again?

Part of me says I'm getting in over my head, agreeing to talk to Cassie, but Matt needs someone.

I want to be that someone.

Who I don't want to be is the sick person in his mind. I've been her for too long.

He turns into the vet parking lot.

There are no cars here. I remember it's New Year's Day. "I think they're closed."

He frowns. "Yeah."

"There's a grocery store down the street. I think it's open."

He looks back at Lady, who's belly-up and sound asleep. "I guess it won't hurt her to eat a different food for a day."

The grocery store's parking lot is filled with cars. As soon as he parks, my phone rings in my purse.

"Excuse me." I reach for it. I check the number. I also see I have new texts and two missed calls. I'll deal with them later. But this call I can't ignore. "It's my mom."

I answer. "Hi, Mom."

"Hi, hon'. You still at the park?"

"Just left." I glance at him hoping he doesn't think it's rude to take the call. He doesn't look upset. "We stopped at the grocery store to buy his puppy some dog food."

When she doesn't reply, I ask, "Everything okay?" Which is my cue for goodbye.

"Yeah. I think your dad liked him."

I almost gasp. I can't believe she's saying this now. "I gotta—"

"I didn't realize Matt had lost his brother and father. Is Matt okay?"

"Fine." It hits me then. If Mom finds out I got Eric's heart, she might . . . well, she might feel uncomfortable about me hanging with Matt. "Can we talk later?"

"Oh, sorry." She finally realizes how inconvenient this is.

Matt's looking at me, and I hang up before I hear my mom say goodbye. "Sorry."

"It's fine." He sounds like he means it. Which means he didn't hear anything, right? "You want to come in?" he asks.

I look back at Lady. "I can wait in the car."

"No. I've left her in the car before. You can help me pick out a new collar. Mom says I need one that says she's a girl."

I grab my purse. The moment my feet hit the pavement, I'm hit with wind carrying the scent of something wonderful. Something spicy. Something that sets my stomach growling.

"What's that smell?" I'm taking in big sniffs of air, searching for a restaurant.

"Indian food." He studies me.

My stomach commences to chewing on my backbone. I spot Desai Diner beside the grocery store.

"Have you eaten there?" My mouth's watering.

He's still staring. "Yeah."

"Would you mind if we . . . grab something? I just realized I haven't eaten today."

"Sure." He doesn't sound sure.

I remember Lady and glance back. "Or . . . I could just get it to go."

"No, she's asleep. After her walks, she crashes for two or three hours. And I'll check on her."

The moment we walk into the restaurant, I'm in heaven. "It smells so good." We step to the counter. The menu's on the wall.

"What should I order?" I ask Matt.

His brow pinches. "What do you like?"

"I don't have a clue. I've never eaten Indian food. But if it tastes as good as it smells, this is going to be my favorite restaurant." I look around. "Is this place new?"

"No. Why?"

"It's just . . . Mom and I come here to grocery shop. I don't know why my nose hasn't already led me here."

"Can I help you?" an Indian woman walks up to the counter. She smiles. "Mr. Kenner, we miss you."

Matt nods, a strange faraway kind of nod. Right then the smell makes my stomach growl so loud Matt glances at me. "Sorry." I blush. "What should I get?"

He hesitates. "Try the butter chicken with lemon rice."

I pick up the takeout menu and study it to make sure I can eat it with my transplant restrictions. When all's clear, I glance up. "That's what I'll have."

"Same for you Mr. Kenner?"

My stomach grumbles again, even louder. I pull two twenties from my purse, but he holds up a hand.

"I got this."

"No." I recall not wanting Trent to pay for my water. "This was my idea."

"I got this," he repeats.

I open my mouth not sure what to say, then blurt out, "It's not like it's a date." The second I hear the words, I want to suck 'em back in.

Then I don't want to. What I want is for Matt to correct me. To tell me it's a date.

I study his expression, hoping . . . waiting.

He doesn't say a word, even glances back at the menu. "You're helping me."

I feel my stomach about to roar again. "Then I'll get the next one." I excuse myself and take off. When I get to the restroom, I move to the mirror and stare at my reflection. "Can you not embarrass me?"

My reflection doesn't answer. New Leah doesn't answer. My stomach does. It growls so loud, I worry it can be heard outside the bathroom.

I don't leave the restroom until my stomach stops bitching. Matt's sitting in a booth, looking at his phone.

As I approach, he looks up and smiles. I put on my best face.

He pushes his phone aside. A subtle way of saying I'm more important.

I'm still awed that I'm here. With him. Before I sit down, I ask, "Should I go check on Lady?"

"I just did. She's sleeping."

I slip into the booth. "I really don't mind paying."

He frowns. "I said I had this."

I nod. It occurs to me that I'm less upset with Matt paying for my lunch than I was with the idea of Trent paying for my water. I know why too. I wouldn't mind if this was a date. Not that I'm the type to let the guy pay for everything, but . . .

He pushes a glass over. "You didn't say what you wanted to drink. I had them bring you water, but we can order something else."

"Water is fine." I force a smile.

A man carrying a tray of steaming food walks over.

"Mr. Kenner." He grins at Matt. He's wearing a name tag that says Ojar. "I was afraid you were cheating on us and visiting the new Indian place across town. I haven't seen you here in months."

Matt gets a lost look on his face that I can't read.

"Just busy." He sips his water.

"Okay, let's see." The man looks at the tray and picks up a plate. "Your regular, sir."

He sets it down in front of Matt. Matt speaks up. "No. That's hers."

Ojar looks confused. "Wait. You're playing games with me. You are not Eric. You are Matt."

That's when I understand Matt's lost look. Ojar doesn't

know Eric's dead. And Matt doesn't want to tell him. My heart hurts for Matt.

I want to save him. "I'm so hungry." I even pat the table, hoping it'll distract the conversation. But the man's focus stays on Matt.

"You're a tricky guy," Ojar says.

Matt's brown eyes find mine; then he looks back at Ojar. "Yeah."

The waiter sets the plate in front of me—with a salad I can't eat—then sets a plate of what looks like fried rice in front of Matt.

Ojar focuses on me. "Your young man doesn't like my food."

I wish he was mine and I also wish this guy would leave and stop making Matt uncomfortable. "I'll make up for it. Thank you." I say the words as a send-off.

Ojar leaves. I look at Matt. "I'm sorry."

"I probably should've told him, but . . . I hate . . . I get tired of doing it. It happens all the time. You'd think no one in this town reads the paper or watches the news." Pain laces his voice, and I feel it all the way down in my empty stomach.

How hard it must be to have people mistaking him for Eric.

"I wouldn't worry about it." I set my fork down. "You want to get these to go?"

"No. Eat." I see him put up a front, and I know I've only gotten a glimpse of how much he's hurting.

I want to say something, but I feel my stomach about to speak up, so I dish a big bite of chicken and sauce into my mouth. The flavor dances on my tongue. It tastes even better than it smelled. How could I have gone this long without trying Indian food?

"This is . . . it's really good." I don't wait for him to reply, I'm already pushing another bite into my mouth.

When I look up, he's staring and not eating his lunch. "What?" I reach for my napkin, thinking I've spilled something on my chin. The napkin comes back clean.

"Nothing," he says.

"You want my salad?" I push the bowl to him. "I can't eat it."

"You're allergic to lettuce?" He smiles.

I start to tell him the truth, that I can't eat raw foods because they might have bacteria on them and it could kill me. That, because of the immune-suppressant drugs, which I have to take for the rest of my life, I can get sick at the drop of a hat. I stop myself from answering.

I gaze down and then up. He's still looking at me as if expecting an answer.

"I don't like salads," I say. "Eat it."

"I've got plenty." He picks up a fork and takes a bite of his food.

His expression makes me laugh and chases away the mini pity party I'm secretly having. I chuckle. "Ojar is right. You don't like his food."

He makes a face and leans in. "Even when I ask for no curry, it tastes like curry. I think their pots and pans are seasoned with it."

"Well, all I can say is that your tastes are off." I fork another bite, this time of the lemon rice. "Why am I just now discovering Indian food?"

Matt relents and pulls my salad over. He picks at it while I eat. At one point I notice him watching me, and I realize I've almost cleaned my plate. I probably look like a pig. I stop.

"I was in a hurry because of Lady," I say. Then add, "But that was really good."

"I'm glad *you* liked it."

"Not liked. I loved it. It's like . . . the food of the gods."

Matt's eyes widen.

"Do I have something . . ." I run my tongue over my teeth for fear I have something nasty caught right in front.

Matt shakes his head. "You're fine. It's just . . . weird."

"What's weird?"

He stabs my salad as if to kill an innocent cherry tomato. "What?" I ask.

"You liking it so much. Because . . . Eric did. He even described the food the exact same way. As 'food of the gods.'"

I take in a small gulp of air. "You think I like this because . . . because Eric liked it?"

"No, I didn't . . . I'm sure it's nothing. Just feels odd."

I digest what he's saying. It's not easy, because my body is busy digesting more food that I've eaten in one sitting in a year.

And just like that I'm back to wondering how many of New Leah's feelings aren't about me but about Eric.

When I get home, Mom asks me to help out in the kitchen. She and Dad have friends coming over tonight. I don't think she really needs the help as much as she wants to pick my brain about Matt.

I don't want my brain picked right now. It's too full of shit that I'm trying to rationalize.

"Did you have a good time?" she asks.

"Yeah." And I did. I just need some time to sort things out.

"I was hoping Matt would come in. I was going to ask him to stay for dinner."

"Don't do that," I say, remembering I don't want Mom putting the whole heart thing together.

"Why not?"

"He's not . . . my boyfriend or anything."

She lifts a brow, her green eyes tighten, and she gives me

that motherly you're-lying-to-me look. "That's not how it appeared when he came and tutored you."

Okay, so I'd suspected she saw us kissing. "That was a one-time thing."

"If you say so," she says, and grins suspiciously.

Dad walks in from the backyard. I smell the grill smoke on him.

"Did your boyfriend go home?" he asks.

I roll my eyes, and my heart rolls with it. "He's not my boy-friend."

Dad studies me. "Well, that's a shame. I liked him better than the last guy."

Mom laughs and waves him out of the kitchen.

I finish loading the dishwasher and start it up. Then I stand over the sink and stare out the kitchen window. At the garbage can where Matt and I had that moment.

I remember him not saying anything about my "it's not a date" comment. I remember Brandy looking shocked that Matt even kissed me. I remember school is going to start and he probably won't even speak to me because I'm not in the cool-kids club. I remember he already bailed on me once.

My throat tightens, crowding out my tonsils. I can taste my salty unshed tears in my mouth. "Can I go to my room now?"

"Yeah." Mom smiles. "I'm always here if you need to talk." I hear her just-spill-it tone and know she wants me to explain things.

I don't want to explain anything. More than that, I can't. Not only am I afraid I'm about to burst into tears. But . . . hell, I'm more confused than ever.

I snag my purse and run to my room. I feel a few of those salty tears roll down my cheek. Shutting the door, I don't even pull out my phone. Instead, I grab my laptop. I turn it on, pull up Google, then hesitate.

THIS HEART OF MINE   III

I'm not sure what to type. Part of me says this is ridiculous.

But then my fingers start moving.

Stories about transplant patients feeling their donors are haunting them.

I'm sure it'll take several tries to get the wording right. I probably won't even find anything at all.

Wrong.

The list of links on the page are so many, I feel attacked.

"Shit," I mutter. After a second, I start clicking the links.

It's all there.

Dreams.

Feeling unexplainable emotions.

Strange changes in a person's taste in food.

I might not have listened that well in those transplant classes, but I'm positive they never discussed this.

My heart races. No wonder I don't feel like myself.

13

When Matt pulls up at his house, he sees his mom dressed in sweats, cleaning out the flower garden in the front yard. He cuts off the engine and listens to Lady bark, eager to go greet his mom. But he still doesn't move. He just sits there, watching his mom, remembering Eric wanting to take her to the nursery.

She wouldn't go then.

Now she went.

She's getting better.

That thought lingers. It makes him happy, and yet it hurts too.

It reminds him of the things he's not doing. Of the things he used to enjoy. Hanging with his friends for longer than a few minutes. Reading. Sports. Working on cars.

He and Eric had dropped football after Dad died, but then Eric talked him into signing up for basketball with him. *We gotta start living again,* Eric had said. Matt had actually started. Then . . .

Mom waves. He forces a smile. For her. He's happy she's getting better—even if he's not.

Getting Lady back on her leash, they walk over. Lady is so happy to see his mom, she's whining and climbing all over her.

His mom looks up—smiling. They'd gone for a run this morning. His mom hadn't mentioned the detective, but a couple of times he'd thought she was going to.

"That was a long walk at the park."

"I . . . waited until a friend could go."

"Who?" She pulls her hand out of one glove to pet Lady.

"L . . . Lori," he says quickly, remembering he didn't want to bring up Leah in case his mom has heard she got a new heart. With his mom doing better, why tempt fate?

"Lori who?"

"MacDonald." The lie lands on his conscience.

"I didn't know you were seeing anyone." Her smile widens.

"I'm not. She's just a friend." *It's not like this is a date.* His ego takes another ding just thinking about it. "You need help?"

"Nah, I'm almost finished with this bed and I'm stopping. It's getting colder." She gives Lady a good scratch behind the ear. "One of my New Year's resolutions is to get this yard in shape." She swipes hair out of her eyes. "You got any resolutions?"

Find out who killed Eric. He doesn't say it. "Haven't given it much thought."

She looks at the dead plants she pulled out of the ground. "I went online and found the grief group counseling meeting is Friday night. I wish you'd change your mind."

He shakes his head. "I'm doing okay. I've been talking to . . . Lori."

She nods, but her eyes tell him he's disappointed her. But what can he do?

She dusts off her hands. "I've got some chili cooking for supper."

His mind moves to food, but not chili. *The food of the gods*, he remembers Leah saying. Then realizes his mom is still looking at him. "Chili sounds good. I'm going in."

"Yeah," she says. "If you're hungry, we can eat early. I skipped lunch."

"Sounds good." He snatches up Lady and carries her inside. The rich, hearty aroma reminds him how much he's missed his mom's cooking.

He lets Lady off her leash, then heads toward his bedroom.

He thinks of Leah. Of how much he wanted to kiss her before she got out of his car.

He makes it to his room, tosses his coat in a chair. He thinks of how he wishes she'd put on his jacket, so he could replace the image of her wearing Trent's in his mind.

Dropping on his bed, he laces his fingers behind his head and stares at the ceiling. Could he do that? Find a way of getting her into his jacket. Maybe even into his arms.

Then bam, he realizes something. A small something, but it doesn't feel so small.

He sits up on his bed. This is the first time he's walked past Eric's door without . . . without feeling as if he would drown in grief. Walked past like . . . like maybe one day he could find his way back to his own life.

He's not quite there. He's sure he won't be until he finds out who killed his brother. But he's closer now than he's ever been.

He knows why too.

"Because of you, Leah. Because of you."

He pulls out his phone, stares at it, and thinks about calling her. Then he closes his eyes. He told her he'd call her tomorrow and they could talk about her seeing Cassie. She even agreed to meet him at the park afterward.

He can't push her. If he does, she might push back. Push away. He can't let that happen.

"Damn!" Brandy sounds freaked as she reads the stuff I found on my computer. But not so freaked that she stops eating Dad's smoked chicken or my mom's black-eyed peas and cream potatoes. Both her parents are engineers, hardworking overachievers, and firm believers in takeout. At her house, frozen pizza is considered homemade.

I'd called her and bribed her to come over by inviting her for dinner. I need to talk to someone. Someone needs to talk me down from the ledge. Reading all this shit was scary. Life-altering, my-life's-not-my-own kind of scary.

When she got here, I asked Mom if we could eat in my room. She agreed too quickly. Probably because Ms. Frankly had sneezed. If they weren't about to sit down to dinner, she'd've asked her friend to wear a mask. Mom's still obsessed about germs and me catching them. Just build me a bubble already.

When Brandy and I first got to my bedroom, I poured my heart out to her. Told her everything: the dreams, Matt having the same dreams, the feeling that . . . I'm being taken over by Eric.

She listened to me ramble while she polished off a chicken leg.

Then I told her I wasn't the only one. I pulled up the links for her to read.

Now we're sitting here, TV trays on each side of my bed. Her plate's almost empty. My plate . . . untouched.

I'm not hungry. I don't know if it's because I was a glutton at lunch or if I'm just scared shitless.

Brandy finally closes my computer. Calmly. Like she'd just read Jane Austen and needed to absorb it.

She looks at me, but instead of talking, she picks up her last drumstick and takes a big bite and chews. And chews. She never stops studying me, and I can tell she's thinking.

What if she thinks I'm crazy?

No, she wouldn't. She's my best friend.

After a few seconds, she swallows and then says, "You really don't believe that crap, do you?"

Wow. Wow. That stings! "What . . . do you mean?"

"I mean it's . . . crazy."

I guess best friends can think you're crazy. "But what about the dreams and about the buttered chicken and lemon rice?"

"I like Indian food." She looks hesitant to continue, but she does. "And Eric has nothing to do with it. And didn't you tell me that the doctors blamed the dreams on the medicine?"

"Yeah, but . . . I'm only taking a small dosage of steroids now, and I'm still having them. And how can you explain that Matt and I are having the same dreams?"

"Everyone dreams about running away from something." She says it so calm, like it might not hurt me as much. "I'll bet it's the most common of dreams."

Hearing her say that none of what I've experienced is true just makes it feel *truer.* "I thought you'd believe me."

"I do . . . I mean . . . I don't. It's so weird." She lets go of a sigh, like she knows she's disappointing me. "You know, I like weird stuff. I love sci-fi and paranormal books, but . . . This isn't a book, Leah. This is your life."

And that's the freaking problem. I'm not sure it's all mine anymore. "You think I don't know that?" A lump, the size of a fat-ass frog, leaps into my throat.

"Did Matt put this stuff in your head?" Brandy frowns. "Everyone at school's saying he's losing it. I feel sorry for him, everyone does, but I don't want him to make you crazy."

"Stop." My chest tightens, emotion swells inside me, and I recognize it. I'm angry. Angry that my best friend thinks I've lost it. I probably shouldn't be, because I've considered it myself. Then I realize something. I'm pissed off not just because she doesn't believe me but because she doesn't believe Matt. And, as at the restaurant with Ojar, I want to protect him. He's been hurt enough.

I pop up and go stand at the window and pretend to stare out. All I'm really trying to do is stop myself from reminding Brandy of all the times I believed her. Like when she was sure she was adopted. Or when she thought she was Jane Austen reincarnated. Yeah, all of that was in sixth grade, but I still believed her.

Yet I keep my mouth shut, because I don't want to make her mad.

"Now I've pissed you off," she says.

I guess I can't fool Brandy.

I take a deep breath and turn around. She's sitting on the side of my bed. Her rust-colored pants and orange sweater clash with my pink bedspread. The doubt I see in her eyes clashes with what I want from her right now. I want understanding. Empathy. Advice.

Am I going to start feeling as if Brandy doesn't fit in my life, too? I can't lose Brandy.

"I just . . . I need you to believe me."

Her shoulders slump. "I believe that you believe it. Just like I believe Matt believes his brother didn't kill himself. But . . ."

"But what?" That's when I recall a flash of doubt I felt when

Matt told me the gun his brother used was his dad's. That there was gunpowder residue on his hands.

I've read enough mystery novels to know that's solid evidence. But I still believed him.

"Have you read all of the articles about it? About Eric's death?" she asks.

"Just the recent ones."

"Go online and read the old ones. They spell it out pretty clear." Brandy stands up. "Read them and be open-minded." She walks over. "Both you and Matt have been through hell. And it's totally freaky that you got his brother's heart. But I think you both might be . . . I don't know . . . not seeing things right . . . and then feeding into each other's ideas in an unhealthy way. It's not your fault. Your emotions are just really out of whack right now." She hugs me.

I let her, but only because I don't want to lose my best friend. I don't buy what she says, even though I hear the logic in it.

I hate hearing it too. Because I'm a logical kind of girl.

Or I used to be. I'm not sure what kind of girl I am now.

I feel my new heart pounding, faster, faster. I'm afraid. So afraid. The sound of my footfalls hitting the earth clamors in my ears. I look down and see the tennis shoes moving, running.

Immersed in fear. I feel the object I'm grasping in my hand. I glance down. My heart trips on the beats. It's a gun. It's heavy. It's cold. I don't like the gun.

But I need the gun.

I'm winded. Can't get enough air. My sides pinch. My legs cramp. I need to slow down. I can't. I can't. I'm going to die. Then I hear it. A gun explodes.

It's not the gun I'm carrying. Or is it? The footsteps are closer.

I wake up. A scream, lodged in my throat, is about to pour out of me. I roll over, smother it, so I don't wake my parents.

Then I roll back over on my back, trying to catch my breath. Gasping for air, the fear, the raw, ugly panic I felt in the dream, hangs on with sharp claws. My heart thuds against my rib cage. I can't breathe.

Then the fear twists and turns. It's not about Eric anymore. It's about not being able to breathe.

It's about those months that breathing was hard, before I got the artificial heart. It's about dying.

I force myself to draw in one shallow breath. Then another. I block out the terror enough to do my breathing techniques.

In. One, two, three. Out. One, two, three.

In. Out. In. Out.

My chest loosens. My lungs soften. I stop rejecting oxygen.

I don't move for several minutes. Just lay there. Breathing. Clearing the clingy cobwebs of fear from my sleep-dazed mind.

I'm not dying, I tell myself. I have a new heart. I have Eric's heart.

Then I remember. I sit up and turn on my bedside lamp and grab the pad and pen. I force myself to recall. Recall everything I saw. Everything I felt. I write it down. When I'm finished, I start back at the beginning.

I keep writing, not rereading, just writing until I have nothing else. I drop the pen and paper and cut off the light. I sit there. The red illuminated numbers on my clock seem to scream at me.

Four A.M.

Sleep. I need sleep. I fall back on my pillow. The things I dreamed, the things I wrote keep flashing in my mind. Then I hear it over and over again. The sound of the gun firing.

What did it mean? I didn't hear the voice this time. I didn't really feel I was being chased. Or did I?

I hear Brandy's voice from earlier. *You and Matt have both been through hell. I think you both might just be . . . I don't know . . . maybe not seeing things right.*

When she left, I went on the Internet and read every article I could find about Eric's case.

I hate to admit it, but she's right. Everything pointed to suicide.

But then how can I explain the dreams? I clutch my pillow.

"Is this you, Eric?" I whisper into the somber darkness of my pink bedroom. "Did someone kill you? Or did you kill yourself?"

Just asking the question makes me feel like a traitor to Matt.

And Leah Mallory McKenzie isn't a traitor.

At least, Old Leah wasn't.

My alarm yells me awake at 8:55 A.M. I slap it off. Eyes still closed, I palm my bedside tabletop looking for . . .

The dream rakes through my mind. I feel the buzz of fear shoot through me. I remember my doubts about how Eric died.

I brush the pad and pen off the nightstand. They *thud* to the wood floor. The sound of the pen rolling away echoes in the room.

Running my hand over the smooth tabletop surface, I don't stop until I find the thermometer. Opening my eyes, staring at the ceiling, I do my morning and nighttime ritual—temperature reading and blood pressure check.

My temperature is normal. The blood pressure is . . . ? I stare at it. It's . . . I blink, refocus, and stare harder as if that might change it. Nothing changes.

It's high. Too high. I remember the dream. I remember reliving the panic from the dream right before I took my blood pressure. I'm sure it's that.

I feel fine, don't I? Fear slices through my mind like a sharp knife. I remember not being able to breathe after the dream.

I remember hearing Mom cry all those nights when I was sick. Recall seeing her rubbing her hands up and down her jeans. So afraid.

I do a mental diagnostic workup.

Breathing fine. Check.

No pain. Check.

No lethargic feeling. Check.

Heart palpitations. Uhh? Only when I'm close to Matt or when I dream. I recall last night. I was scared, that's all.

I conclude I'm fine. I'm not a doctor, but with all I've been through, I should at least have earned a nursing degree.

I retake the blood pressure.

Lower, but still high. It's the dream.

Frowning, I start to write down my numbers. Then, knowing my mom will check, I fudge. But I put a dot beside it, so I'll remember. And if it's high tonight, I'll have to say something.

I pause and feel better remembering that tomorrow I'll see Dr. Hughes.

I push myself up to go get my pills. Mom won't allow me to keep them in my room because she wants to see me take them. No doubt she's sitting at the kitchen table already worrying that I'm thirty seconds late.

"Good morning, Sunshine." Mom smiles when I walk into the kitchen.

She always says that. I was born at 5 A.M. and Dad says that those were the first words she said to me. Sometimes it's annoying. But when I really got sick, before I got the artificial heart and was on oxygen and a huge heart machine, it was hearing those words first thing in the morning that convinced me I was still alive. I remember worrying that when I died and found myself in an afterlife, that it wouldn't feel right not hearing them.

I had even had a plan in place. I was telling my grandma she had to say them to me.

That thought gives my heart a quaky, achy feeling. I push it away and offer Mom a smile. I want to hug her, but I'm afraid she'll know I'm emotional.

"All good?" she asks.

She means my temperature and blood pressure. I turn to the fridge for milk so I don't have to look at her when I lie. "Yup."

"You want some cereal?" she asks. "I left it out."

"Sure." I set the milk on the table and grab a bowl and a glass.

"You look tired. You feeling okay?"

"Fine," I say with confidence that I don't feel bad.

"Did you stay up too late reading?"

She knows me well. "Yeah." And it's the truth. I had needed something to take my thoughts off Eric. And the book was amazing. Sexy, suspenseful, and seriously funny.

"Another romance novel?" Her tone says it all.

I nod and slug my pills down with milk. Like Sandy and LeAnn, Mom's a bit of a prude when it comes to her reading tastes. She doesn't really approve of my reading romances, but she hasn't told me to stop either.

Then again, she can't. Not when I caught her reading *Fifty Shades of Grey. Just to find out what all the hype is about,* she'd said. Right, Mom!

I reach for the cereal bowl. "Heart healthy" is printed in large letters on the package. And it shows a bowl of cereal topped with strawberries. Generally when they show fruit on top, it's because you're gonna need it.

And I can't eat fresh fruit. Well, I can if it's guaranteed clean. Mom doesn't want to take a chance. Me, either. I like this living thing.

I fill my bowl with the dry flakes, drown it with milk, and grab a spoon.

"I thought we could go shopping and pick up some school clothes," Mom says.

No, no, no. I'm going to Cassie's and meeting Matt afterward. I need to shoot this idea down, but I've just shoveled a bite of almost-not-sweet, almost-cardboard cereal in my mouth. I shake my head no, hold up one finger, and swallow.

It scratches my throat going down. While I try to get use of my mouth, I check the clock on the wall. Matt said he'd call around 9:15, and I left my phone in my room.

"I can't today." I move the last bits of cardboard off my tongue, then scramble to form another lie. "I . . . I promised Brandy I'd help her . . ." *With what? Shit shit shit.* "Help her organize her closet."

I stare down at the milk. *Seriously, organize her closet?* Is that the best I've got?

"Oh." Mom's disappointment hangs in the air, and I feel it. If I look up, I'll see it in her eyes and it's gonna sting.

I drop the spoon in the bowl, nudge it away, and face the music. "We have to go to the doctor tomorrow, right? We can do lunch. Make a day of it."

Her eyes light up. "Yeah, let's do that." She smiles, a real smile. I know it's real because her nose wrinkles. Then she glances down at my bowl, makes a funny face, and passes the sugar bowl. "Here."

"Mmm," I say. "Sweet cardboard is much better than plain cardboard."

She chuckles. I add sugar. Then, not wanting to miss Matt's call, I scarf down the cereal, but not so fast as to create suspicion.

Mom gets up to refill her cup of coffee. I used to drink it with her, but caffeine is sort of a no-go for me now.

"But we won't have too long to shop," Mom says.

"Why?" I ask.

"The Kellys invited us to their place in Fredericksburg, remember?" She adds a teaspoon of sugar to her cup.

I do now. And I'm so tempted to ask if I can just stay home, but the odds of that happening are zero, minus a couple more zeros. If I said I didn't want to go, Mom wouldn't go. And she's been looking forward to getting away.

"We could shop a bit while we're there too." She stirs her coffee, *clink, clink, clink.*

"Sure." I'm ready to bolt.

She picks up the cup, holds it up to her lips, and stands there looking at me over the steam. "I've got a good idea," she says. "Brandy should come here and help you organize your closet after you do hers. I've been asking you to do it for a month."

I think *shit!* but say, "Yeah." I reach for my cereal bowl and shovel one more bite in my mouth. "Gotta go." I talk around the food and suppose it's poetic justice that I get punished for lying. But how I'm going to get Brandy to share in the punishment is another question.

Guess I'll have to pull a girlfriend card. I'm almost certain she'll do it. She is my best friend. The fact that she doesn't believe me right now is just an inconvenience.

14

It's eleven o'clock when I turn onto Cassie Chambers's street. My cardboard cereal is heavy in the pit of my stomach. My wrist and the base of my neck flutter with a speeding pulse.

This is an older neighborhood, with a lot more trees than we have in ours. But some of the houses look a little worn, tired, begging for a fresh coat of paint.

I spot the number on the mailbox. The two-story house is brick that's been painted white. An orange cat sits guard on the front porch staring at my car easing past.

I don't pull into the driveway because . . . I don't feel like I belong there.

Cassie Chambers probably won't recognize me.

Matt doesn't believe that. He thinks because he's noticed me, everyone has.

It's not so.

It's not like I've been bullied. Just ignored.

Well, not *just* ignored. There was the day in science class in tenth grade when Tabitha, one of Cassie's friends, was asked to team up with me on a project. She turned to Cassie, who sat behind her, and said, "Why is he putting me with that book geek?"

Cassie glanced at me and looked embarrassed.

It stung, but not for long. Frankly, I was a blatant book geek.

I wasn't embarrassed about reading. If anything, it saddened me that some people were missing out. I smile, remembering that I'd been looking for a name for our book club. Blatant Book Geeks had a ring to it. I don't know if she ever realized it, but I was proud of it. Still am.

Even though I haven't been to a meeting in a year and a half, it was started by *moi*. *Moi* even turned some nonreaders into book junkies.

I'm glad I could do that for them because, holy smokes, it helped me cope with a lot of shit this last year and a half. Reading's my escape when I need one. And forget sex ed, I just read a romance. Yeah, I know it's fiction, and probably glorified, but since the whole world makes a big effing deal out of it, I'm betting there's truth to it.

The guard cat meows loud enough that I can hear it. I look back up at Cassie's house. She's not going to know me. I'm not sure if that will bother me or not.

A curtain in the front window flutters open. Someone knows I'm here.

I put the car in park. The heater blows. My palms are slick on the steering wheel.

Crap.

I don't want to do this.

But I'm gonna do it. "For Matt," I whisper. "And Eric," I say because right then I feel it again. Unexplained emotions.

Does he know I'm here? Does he miss Cassie?

I cut off the engine.

My mind races to recall the questions Matt wanted me to ask Cassie. I'll rephrase most of them. Matt's version sounds . . . accusing. I still don't think Cassie is behind Eric's murder.

For that matter, I'm still on the fence about whether I believe Eric was actually murdered.

And that bothers me, because until yesterday I hadn't questioned it. Had I been gullible because I just wanted to help Matt? Or—I swallow the unexpected lump down my throat—am I nervous about actually hunting down a killer?

With that thought skittering up my spine, I get out of my car and walk to the door.

The orange cat slinks against my calf. I reach down and give it a quick pass with my fingers. I don't let my fingers linger because, like uncooked food, cats can hurt me. They can carry a dangerous parasite that can affect both pregnant women and people with low immune systems.

I stand, take that last step to the door, square my shoulders, and knock.

I hear someone at the door. Suddenly my case of bad nerves is something more. Fear. No. Terror. And it's not just mine. Eric?

Shit. Crap. Shitcrap shitcrap shitcrap shitcrap!

Matt's phone beeps with an incoming text. He checks it immediately. From Leah. *On my way.*

He'd asked her to text when she left Cassie's so they could meet at the park—by the bench again. He's already here.

Lady is busy sniffing the ground. He's busy fretting over what Leah learned. Could it be this easy? Could Cassie have confessed?

Okay, maybe it's farfetched to think Cassie killed Eric, but Matt's gut tells him Cassie knows something. She holds a clue to the whole damn mystery.

He stands up, planning to meet Leah halfway.

He gives Lady a this-way tug, then takes one step.

And bam!

He's not here. He's not him. He's Eric. He's running.

He . . . drops the gun.

There are flashes. He feels as if he's falling. Then pain. Hot pain in his temple.

Then it's over.

Lady is biting her leash. Matt presses a hand to his head. He breathes in the scents of winter, of the dirt, of the cold.

He stands there, waiting to feel like himself again. Then he recalls what he saw. *Eric dropped the gun.* Could it have gone off? Or was it someone else's gun that fired?

The sound of footsteps brings him out of it. Glancing up, he sees her. Leah.

Surrounded by the muddy brown color of winter landscape, she stands out like a peek into summer. She wears a dusty blue sweater and light faded jeans.

No matter how messed up his mind, he still notices how pretty she is. Her hair is down. It sways ever so gently when she walks.

Then he notices something else. Fear. Her eyes are round with it. She's pale.

He rushes to her, resisting the urge to pull her against him. "What happened?"

She shakes her head as if it's nothing, but her eyes scream it's something.

"Are you okay?" Lady jumps at her legs, showing her concern as well.

"Yeah. I just . . . freaked a little."

"About what? What did Cassie tell you?"

"Nothing. I didn't . . . She wasn't at home. I spoke to her mother."

"Then why the scared face?"

She bites into her lip before answering. "I was nervous, and when I was leaving a cop car pulled into the driveway. For a minute I thought she'd called them on me."

"Wait." He takes her hand and leads her back to the bench, nudging her to sit down. He drops beside her. Lady scrambles to climb into Leah's lap.

Leah allows the dog up and runs her hand down its back, but she still looks scared.

"Relax and then tell me. Tell me everything."

He watches her take in a deep breath, hold it, then release. She does it again, and it almost seems as if she's counting and doing some yoga breathing technique.

Lady, appearing worried, sits up in her lap and licks her face. Leah looks at his puppy and then at him. "I'm okay."

He realizes then that he's still holding Leah's hand. Her palm feels soft in his. But damp. Whatever scared her did a number on her. He feels bad that he asked her to do it.

"I'm sorry," he says.

"For what?" She looks at him, her eyes are still large, so blue, but no longer so frightened. But she's still pale.

Guilt takes a lap around his chest. "Maybe this is a bad idea."

"What?"

"You talking to Cassie. I should do it."

Her brow tightens. "But she won't talk to you."

"I know, but I . . . I don't like seeing you like this."

She sighs, slumps her shoulders, then shakes her head. "Nothing bad happened. I just freaked out. It was silly of me."

"I'm sure it wasn't." He squeezes her hand. "Tell me everything that happened. Start at the beginning."

"I got to her place and . . . I felt strange again. Sad, like we talked about. As if Eric was feeling it."

He remembers his own Eric moment, the gunshot. "And then . . . ?"

"I notice someone looking at me from the house. I get out of my car. When I get to the door, I'm suddenly scared shitless. Ms. Chambers opens it. I ask if Cassie's home. She says she's at a friend's house."

"Here?" he asks. "She's at a friend's house here?"

"She didn't say 'here,' but it seemed implied." Leah looks at their joined hands as if it's a surprise.

Lady barks. Leah pauses, but she doesn't pull her hand away. For some reason he thinks it means something. Something good.

"Then Ms. Chambers asked me who I was," Leah continues. "I know I stumbled, but I finally said we went to the same school." A whisk of her hair flows over her face. She brushes it off with her free hand. Lady does her prenap wiggles, then settles in Leah's lap.

"She asked me if I had Cassie's cell number. All suspicious like. I lied and said I did. Then I heard a car pull up in the driveway. Ms. Chambers just stared at me, then blurted out, 'You should go.' When I turned around, I saw the cop car in her driveway. I got even more frightened. I went to my car but didn't start it up, because I thought she called the police on me. But he didn't get out. So after a few minutes, I left."

Matt sits there, taking it all in. "Why would she call the police?"

"I don't have a freaking clue."

Lady does another adjustment and almost falls off Leah's lap. Leah catches her but lets go of Matt's hand.

He closes his palm, missing her touch.

"I guess the police could have been there for a different reason." She exhales. "Shit! Now that I think about it, I'm sure I overreacted. There's no way the cop could have gotten there that fast." She stares out at the woods. "The cop couldn't have been there for me."

She lets out an apologetic sigh. "See, I was being silly."

"No." Matt leans back in the bench. "You were feeling Eric's emotions again."

She nods as if unsure. "I could have just imagined it."

He stares at her and sees disbelief. He doesn't like it. He knows she's just trying to be logical. Something he can't seem to be right now. Not when someone killed his brother.

He inhales and tries holding his breath a second the way Leah did, hoping to regroup his thoughts. "Either way, I still want to know why a cop is showing up there."

"Maybe the investigation isn't over." She shifts. "That detective you mentioned, maybe he's still looking into it."

Matt nods. "He's a detective. I don't think he drives a police car."

"He could have sent another cop to ask questions."

"I don't know." But he plans to find out. Which means he has to see Detective Henderson again, even if it means he'll tell his mom again.

Lady lifts her head and barks as if she hears something, and Leah sits her down on the ground.

Rubbing her right palm up and down her leg as if nervous, Leah says, "I had another dream last night."

"What happened?" he asks.

"About . . . the same thing." Her voice grows tenser, tighter. "I wrote it all down, but I forgot to bring the notebook." She bites on her bottom lip again.

Her lip is wet and . . . it makes him want to kiss her. Realizing he's staring, he glances away.

"Did you have a dream?" she asks.

"No, but . . ." He faces her. "I had kind of the feeling-thing before you got here. Of him running." Yeah, he's kind of lying, but he doesn't want to tell her about seeing the gun drop and possibly firing. She's already doubting. And right now her believing in him, just being here, is helping him hold his shit together. He doesn't want to lose that.

"Make sure you write it down," she says.

"I will." He pauses. "Do you want to call Cassie or . . . if it makes you nervous, I'll do it."

"No. I'll do it. I'll call her tonight."

"Okay." He remembers the pale, scared expression she wore when she walked up. "But only if you aren't freaked about it."

"I'm not," she says. "I want to help . . . you."

That pause with the added word yanks at his emotions. He feels less alone than he has since that first night he woke up to find Eric's bed empty. "You are helping." *More than you know.*

"Do you have her number? I'll put it in my contacts."

They lift up to pull out their phones from their back pockets at the same time. When they resettle on the bench they're closer. Her leg presses against him. It takes longer than it should for him to find Cassie's number in his contact list.

Right after she types it in, her phone beeps with a text. He's not trying to see it, but he does. Trent's name flashes across her screen. His mind flashes to the image of her wearing the guy's coat.

Leah swipes the screen. Lady's tugging on the leash.

"You think we should walk her?" Leah asks.

"Yeah." He's still seeing the damn coat.

Should he ask if she's going out with him? Does he want to

know? Her phone rings then, and she turns it off and places it facedown on the bench. Trent again?

"Let's walk Lady. Then it's my turn to buy lunch. And it doesn't have to be Indian food."

Her smile pulls one out of him. "Sounds good."

They stand up, and Lady bolts, tearing the leash from Matt's hands. Leah runs and grabs it.

"Good catch," he says, a few feet behind her.

"Wait." She swings around, running right into his arms. He catches her by the shoulders.

"I . . . I forgot my phone," she says weakly.

Just like that, he's back. Back in her house. Back to the second before he got the best kiss of his life.

And like before, she's against him. Her chest moves to take in air. She's close.

He likes close.

He can smell her hair, her skin, her breath. He can feel her breasts against his chest. Dare he take a chance?

Eric would call him a coward if he didn't.

"Oh," he says. "I . . . I thought you were going to kiss me."

15

For a second I think I'm imagining the words. Because the same ones are fluttering like big butterflies through my mind. But I don't waste time.

I tilt my chin up. "Do you want me to kiss you?"

He's wearing that crooked smile. "If you're Leah, I've been wanting you to kiss me since sixth grade."

I lift one brow. "I said seventh." His hands melt around my waist.

"I know," he says matter-of-factly. "I've wanted to kiss you longer than you have me."

I laugh then fall right back into the part, because this isn't finished. And that's the best part.

"Is your heart strong enough?" I ask.

He tilts his head down. "Are you that good of a kisser?" His eyes are so beautiful, his mouth so close, and my dreams are a breath away from coming true.

The fact that he remembers verbatim what was said on that day eight months ago makes me feel light, airy. I'm happy to be me. And I haven't been happy to be me in a hell of a long time.

I'm a romance heroine in my own book.

I'm New Leah.

I'm not dying.

I'm so damn alive and I feel it.

I feel everything—his hands against my waist, his muscled chest against my breasts.

It's still not enough. I need what comes next. He hesitates, as if waiting on me.

Not a problem. I'm going for what I want.

I lift up on my tiptoes and press my lips to his.

His tongue slips between my lips.

He tastes like strawberry jam, and a hint of mint. He feels strong. He feels . . . I feel . . .

His hold on my waist tightens ever so slightly. The kiss is even better than the one before. We're not in my hallway where Mom is going to see. We're not in earshot of my dad announcing he's home.

I feel myself easing closer. And we kiss and kiss until even this closeness doesn't seem like enough.

Which is the point when I know we need to stop.

I pull back. I'm breathing hard. So is he.

His lips widen in the softest, sweetest, sexiest smile I've ever witnessed. And I'm mush. I have to lean against him to keep my knees from buckling.

"Hello," he says.

"Hello," I answer.

Lady chimes in with a bark.

His chin dips as if to kiss me again, but my phone rings from the bench. His smile fades. "Should you answer that?"

"I'll check," I say.

I move to get the phone. The second his hands slip from my waist, I miss them. "It's Brandy. I'll call her later." I pocket the phone.

With him no longer close, I feel the chilly breeze. I shiver and try to shrink in my sweater to keep me warm.

"Here," he says, and before I realize what's he's doing, he's fitting his coat on my shoulders.

It's warm and it smells like him. It feels like a hug. "Thanks."

He stares at me. "No, thank you."

"Now you're going to get cold," I say.

"Not after that kiss."

I laugh. Lady tugs on her leash and we start walking.

She stops and sniffs every dead leaf and rock. I want to reach for his hand, but I think I used up my daily quota of courage when I kissed him.

Not that I'm sorry. Never. "Where do you want to go for lunch?"

"I don't care," he says. "Well, as long as it's curry-free."

I remember reading the food stories of other transplant patients. Brandy's right. It's not that weird that two people would like Indian food, and the feelings I get could just be nerves.

The dreams, however? Running dreams might be common.

But running-with-a-gun dreams? How can I explain them? I can't.

But right now I don't want to explain. I just want to enjoy being with Matt. For the next hour, I don't even want to think about Eric; I just want it to be about us.

Two normal teens doing normal stuff.

The doorbell rings. It's Brandy. She shows up at my house an hour after I'm home. I called her during lunch and we've been playing phone tag. I finally text her and beg her to come over for closet duty.

She texts back, *Whaaaaat?*

But like the friend she is, she shows up. She might not believe me about the dreams, but she'll do closet duty for me. That's the kind of friend she is.

I meet her at the door, not wanting Mom to say anything about me helping her.

"Hi, Brandy." Mom walks out of the kitchen. "How did—"

"Gotta get busy." I drag Brandy to my room.

When I shut the door, she gives me one of her signature what-the-eff looks.

"I lied to my mom, okay."

"So you've used up your lie budget for the day? Hmm . . . What can I ask you?"

"Stop," I say.

"What did you lie about?"

"Mom wanted me to go shopping today, but I had plans with Matt, so I told her I couldn't because I was helping you organize your closet."

"Why didn't you tell her you were meeting Matt? You said they like him."

I frown. "I don't want . . . They act like he's my boyfriend and I'm not sure he is. And if Mom knew I have Eric's heart, I think she'd freak out."

"Sorta like you are?" Brandy asks. It sounds like a joke, but the comment stings.

I choose to ignore it.

She flops down on the one clear spot on my bed and looks at the clothes stacked around her that I've already taken out. "So how does that translate to me helping you clean out your closet?"

"Mom thought it would be a good idea. She's been bugging me to do it."

Brandy's green eyes spark with humor. "Why do I think I'm getting the raw end of this deal?"

"You don't have to help. Just talk to me." I reach into the closet for old shoes.

"Pfff, I'm helping and you owe me." She pops up, picks up a hanger with a navy blouse. "And while we work, tell me about today?"

She gives me the evil eye. "And remember you've used your lie allocation for the day."

I drop an old but good pair of tennis shoes in the to-donate box. Because Brandy thinks Matt and I are crazy, I won't share our whole conversation. But I can share the best part.

"He kissed me again. Well, I kind of kissed him."

Brandy lets out a happy yelp. "What? Are you saying that Shy Leah, who wouldn't hold Trent's hand in front of anyone, has hauled off and kissed Matt Kenner?"

"Shh!" I say, not wanting Mom to hear.

"Don't shh me. Details! Now!"

I laugh and then . . . "I did let Trent hold my hand."

"After you'd been dating for six weeks. But forget Trent. Which obviously you have because he texted me complaining you haven't answered his calls. But that's old news. About the kiss . . ."

"He's texting you?" I feel a leak in my happy balloon. "Is he really upset?"

"He's a big boy. Don't worry about him."

"I don't like hurting him." I sigh.

"Yeah, yeah. Enough already. I want kiss details."

I push Trent from my mind, which isn't hard when I remember Matt and the kiss. I tell her how it went down and how sweet and how hot and how perfect it was. She eats it up. I answer kiss questions, while we make clothes piles. Clothes I'll donate, clothes not good enough to donate, and clothes I want to try on before donating.

"Did he say anything about the chick he was with at the fireworks?" Brandy asks.

Well, damn! A little more joy seeps out of my happy balloon.

"We didn't talk about her."

"Did he ask you about Trent? I mean, he saw you with him. He probably thinks you're with him."

"No. We never said anything about either of them."

"Do you think he's dating her?"

"I don't get that impression." I drop onto the bed, not caring that I'm on a stack of clothes. "Are you saying someone like Matt wouldn't be interested in a blatant book geek?"

"Hell no!" Brandy snaps. "He's lucky if he gets you. I just don't want to think he's using you or anything."

"He's not," I say with confidence.

"Good. I mean, he has to treat you good. You've got his brother's heart. To treat you bad is like treating Eric bad."

I look at her. For some uncanny reason, her remark opens up a whole new portal for my insecurities. "Do you think that's why he's with me? Because I have Eric's heart?"

Sure, the first time we kissed was before Eric was even dead, but what if some of the connection we feel now was because of the transplant. Matt might be drawn to me because I have . . . because I'm the last part of Eric he has left.

"No!" Brandy says. "I was . . . just making a lame comment. He likes you because you're smoking hot. And cool as shit."

"Right," I say, but my self-doubt starts feasting on what confidence I have.

I push those thoughts aside, because I know it's a slippery slope that I could find myself on, and instead I focus on the job at hand. Closet duty.

In an hour we have all the clothes in proper stacks. We talk about books. A safe subject. Or it is until she mentions the book club.

"How could you let Sandy and LeAnn change the book club rule? You should have seen her face when I said I was reading romance."

Brandy chuckles. "Did you tell her you got me reading them too?"

"No, I wasn't going to rat on you. What happened to the club?"

Brandy starts folding the giveaway clothes and putting them into a box. "I've missed a lot of the meetings, hanging out with Brian. But you know how LeAnn is."

"Yeah, I do. They'll run the club into the ground. How many members do we have?"

Brandy makes her oh-shit face. "Like seven, and they don't always come."

"I had the membership up to twenty."

"And when you come back, you can build it back up."

"Or maybe I'll let it go," I say.

"Please, it's your baby. You created it."

"Old Leah created it," I say.

Brandy stares at me. "So who's the New Leah?"

"I don't know," I say out loud for the first time. I glance at her. "Haven't you noticed I've changed?"

"Yeah. You're spunkier. But I think we've all changed. We're supposed to, right?"

"I guess."

She picks up the novel on my bedside table. "Have you finished this one?"

I nod.

"Do you mind if I take it?"

"No." I remember telling Matt I'd give his mom some romance novels. I look at the pile of books to donate and then to my "maybe" clothes. I yank my sweater off to start trying stuff on.

Brandy gasps and swings to face the wall.

"I'm sorry," she says, still looking the other way. "I didn't . . . I wasn't . . ."

I stare at the angry scar on my chest that was necessary to save my life. I remember Dr. Hughes and wonder how long it will be before mine fades like hers. Or will mine ever fade?

"It's okay." I grab a blouse on the maybe pile and slip it over my head to hide what now feels like a mark of shame.

She turns back around. Empathy rounds her green eyes. "It's . . . not that bad. I just . . ." She runs over and hugs me. "It kills me to think they actually cut you open. I can't imagine how much that hurt."

"It's okay." I repeat. And it is. I'm not going to be mad at my best friend because I have an ugly scar. Brandy's gaze lowers to my chest and steps back really fast.

I look down. The blouse fits too tight and low. My scar peeps out from above the neckline. What should look sexy is *so* not.

I put my hand over it. "Guess this blouse is a no."

"It looks good, but your girls are restricted," Brandy says, avoiding the scar topic. "Didn't I tell you your boobs got bigger?" Her grin says she's worried she hurt me. "Maybe they gave you a boob transplant with the heart."

"Maybe." I force a laugh and hope that lets her off the hook.

My own feelings are left hanging. Brandy's reaction reminds me that while I want to be normal, I'm not. More than anything, I want to be normal for Matt.

And if my best friend can't stand to see my scar, how would Matt feel about it? As much as I want to think it's too soon to consider that, I'm not naive. The feeling when Matt kisses me or just looks at me isn't a slow and easy attraction. It's fast and furious. And fabulous.

Yet even fabulous could fizzle out real fast. When school starts Matt might see things differently.

After the park, Matt takes Lady home and drives to talk to Detective Henderson. The station always smells like a locker room. Considering this is the homicide division, he supposes it's seen a lot of sweat. The gray walls, the color of a dreary day, set the mood. Two people looking claustrophobic stir in the hardback chairs in the lobby.

He moves to the front desk. The clerk, Mrs. Johnson, asks his name and then informs him Henderson isn't here. When Matt asks to speak to another detective, Mrs. Johnson—frowning—claims no one is here who can help with the case.

He knows a brush-off when he's been brushed. Amazingly, he holds his shit together. "I'll be back tomorrow."

From there he goes to the roadside park where they found Eric.

Turning off his car, his chest goes straight to hurting. He stares at the white cross and remembers the flowers and stuffed animals that had been left before. Now they're gone. People are forgetting Eric.

He swallows the golf-ball-size knot lodged in his throat. It rolls down and becomes another lump of pain in his chest.

Recalling the crazy vision he had earlier, he gets out of his car. Cold, he zips his coat. The image of Leah wearing it fills his mind and eases his hurt.

He'd really wanted to ask if she and Trent were a couple again, but he never found the nerve. He walks past the picnic table and into the woods.

Fear stirs his gut, and he's sure it's Eric's fear.

"What happened here?" He walks the path. It feels so damn familiar—not because he's been here almost fifty times since Eric died, but because he's seen it in the dreams. He inhales cold air: there's nothing here but a trail that leads nowhere.

Nowhere but to more pain.

"Tell me, Eric! What happened?" His voice rises. The cold air seems to quake. Or is that him?

After five minutes of fighting tears and walking in a haze of hurt, he realizes this is futile. Perhaps if Leah comes she might see something different. He makes a mental note to ask her.

When he gets in his car, his phone on the passenger seat flashes a new message. He swipes it, hoping it's Leah. It isn't.

It's Ted asking if he's okay. Questioning why he cut out early last night and saying they are throwing hoops this afternoon. Truthfully, every time he's been with the guys since Eric died, he's left early. He knows why.

They're always shooting the shit, having fun. It feels wrong for him to have fun. It occurs to him, though, that having fun with Leah didn't feel wrong. It felt so right. Probably because she understands.

"We need friends," he hears his mom say.

He goes to text Ted to say he'll be over, but the text bounces back. He remembers that right along this road is a dead zone.

He looks up and wonders if that's why Eric never finished his text that night. What was it he had typed? *I need . . .*

What had Eric needed?

Matt stops himself from going there, starts the car, and forces himself to do the right thing.

When he gets to Ted's, they are already playing basketball in the backyard. He joins in. They go at it hard. He works up a sweat, and for about an hour, he forgets.

16

Later that afternoon, I help Dad load the dishwasher. Chore done, I say I have a book waiting on me and start to my room. I do have a book waiting, but first I have two things to do, well three.

1. Check my blood pressure. I've felt fine all day. A little shaky when I was at Cassie's and lot shaky when I kissed Matt. Normal stuff I'm sure. However, the fact it was high this morning has tap-danced on my mind.

2. Call Cassie. And I need to check my blood pressure before I call because I know that'll make my blood pressure soar.

3. Call Matt. Or was he supposed to call me? I think we just said we'd talk. Either way, I'm looking forward to it. And I'm trying to forget about the scar. Taking the cross-that-bridge-when-I-come-to-it approach. If we come to it. A couple of hot kisses doesn't mean it's turning into something real. Something that would lead to clothes falling off.

In my room, I plop facedown on the right side of my bed, the side not covered in "maybe" clothes that I need to try on. Yeah, I decided trying on clothes in front of Brandy wasn't a good idea. I don't blame her. I don't. But her reaction still stings.

I roll over on my back and stare at the ceiling fan and do breathing exercises. Only when I feel my muscles go lax do I fit the blood pressure cuff on my arm. The machine hums, tightens, and releases. Finally beeps. I'm relieved when the numbers are good. It has been weighing on me more than I realized. I guess I'm not completely confident that I'm out of hot water. As I write the number down, I notice it's higher than yesterday's, but Dr. Hughes said it would fluctuate.

I start thinking about to-do item number 2. But I need the right words.

Hi, Cassie. Remember me, the blatant book geek? The sick girl? I was wondering what you know about Eric's death?

So not good. I rub my palm on the pink bed covers.

Hi, Cassie. Can you explain why you told the police you didn't see Eric the night he was killed, when he told his twin brother—who by the way I have the hots for—that he was going to your house?

Not good either. I sit up and rub my itchy palms over my knees.

Hey, Cassie. Matt is having a real hard time believing Eric killed himself. Do you, by any chance, know why anyone would want to hurt him?

Not great, not bad. Not how Matt would have worded it, but we differ in opinion on Cassie's possible involvement.

I sit up, fluff my pillow so I'm comfortable, and open my contacts list. I find her name, stare: all I have to do is swipe it.

Just swipe it.

Just do it.

Do it already!

My heart *thut thut thuts* in my chest. I swipe the dang thing.

The phone rings. Rings. Then rings again. Every ring ratchets up my anxiety.

Breath locked in my lungs, I wait for her voice. I hear a click.

Shit! I forgot what I was going to say? I scrub my hands harder on my knees.

A voice starts, but it's a message. I let go of a sigh. "Sorry, the person's mailbox you are trying to reach is full. Goodbye."

Click.

I sit there, my pulse swishing in my ears, phone pressed against my cheek. Then I feel it. Relief. It's over. I tried. I called. Now I get to call Matt.

But I've got nothing to give him.

I remember the look in his eyes that he's almost always wearing.

Grief.

I know that five-letter word well. It took up residence in my heart when I lost my grandma three years ago. For months, I refused to think about her being dead. I pretended she'd gone back to Florida to winter. That soon she'd show up on my doorstep, all warm, smelling like cookies and hot chocolate, and she'd move back into the fourth bedroom.

She never did.

Eventually, I stopped lying to myself. I didn't think about her that much, or at least when I did think about her, it didn't hurt as much. Then when I got sick, I thought about her a lot. It didn't hurt then. It brought me comfort.

I had this idealistic vision of what heaven would be like. A huge library of books. And Grandma. We'd sit at a table, sunlight streaming in, drinking hot chocolate or sweet peach tea. We'd spend all day reading and working the crossword puzzle together. Grandma loved books and words as much as I do.

It was when I found a box of all her old books that I started reading romance. Who knew my grandma enjoyed sexy books?

My mind flips from missing Grandma to Matt. How much harder would it have been if I thought someone took Grandma's life instead of her eighty-eight-year-old heart just giving up? Or even if she'd taken that life herself? A lot harder.

Figuring out what happened to his brother won't take Matt's grief away. But it'll offer that elusive thing—closure.

I found it with Grandma when I came across a stack of her letters she'd written me the year before she died. There was this unwritten message in all of them: *Enjoy life.*

In one letter, I found one of her amazing quotes, which I clung to when dying. One that will help me discover New Leah. *Don't do anything you know you'll regret. But do enough to know exactly what you'll regret and learn to regret less.* For a grandma, she was cool.

The thing I know I'd regret now is walking away from Matt before giving it a chance. Besides, I want to help him. If that's all there is, then so be it.

I call Cassie again.

The same message plays.

At least now when she sees the missed call, she won't think it was a misdialed number.

And she'll . . . Holy shit! She'll call me back. Cassie Chambers is gonna call me. Which means I need to be prepared.

I bite down on my lip. Why hadn't I thought about that? Probably from burying my effing head in the sand. That worked when I was dying too.

Yup, I'm glad I took my blood pressure earlier.

After a deep breath, I start to dial Matt, but my phone rings. I yelp and throw it in the haphazard pile of maybe clothes.

Which isn't smart, because if it's Cassie, I need to answer it. I scramble up on my knees—not that easy to do on a memory foam mattress. The phone's still ringing, but it's buried in a mountain of scar-showing shirts.

Shit. Shit. Shit.

I start throwing clothes willy-nilly. Left. Right. Up. Down. I finally find it. I snatch it up, without even checking who's calling. I swipe it. I spit out, "Hello."

"Leah?" The voice is male. The voice is familiar, and makes me totally regret answering the phone. My knees sink into the memory foam; my mood sinks with it.

"Leah? It's me, Trent."

Matt helps his mom in the backyard. Then they eat leftover chili and talk about what plants to buy. Thankfully, she doesn't mention anything else about Detective Henderson or about grief counseling.

After dinner, he hits the shower before he calls Leah. Or is Leah going to call him? He can't remember. A lot of what they discussed during lunch is lost to him because he was busy just watching her. The way she moved her hands when she talked. The way her eyes were so expressive. The way her smile crinkled her nose.

He's under the water, hair sudsed up, when he hears his phone. Sure it's Leah, he bolts out of the shower, reaches for a towel on the rack, but doesn't find one. He bolts naked across the hall into his bedroom, his slippery, soapy feet sliding across his bedroom floor. He almost busts his ass, but he saves it and dives across his bed for the phone on his pillow.

"Hello," he answers, winded.

"Matt?"

A smile pulls at his lips when he hears Leah's voice. It's almost musical. Not too high, but nice. Really nice.

"Yeah." He rolls over, places a hand on his chest, and remembers their kiss.

"For a second I thought you weren't going to answer," she says.

He's lost in thoughts and blurts out an apology. "Sorry, I was in the shower."

"Oh. Do you need to go?"

"No." He passes a hand over his face. His hand comes back full of suds. *Why would I need to go?*

"You could call me back." She chuckles. "If you need to get dressed."

What? "How do you know . . . ?"

She chuckles. "You said you were in the shower?"

Had he? "Shit!" he says without meaning to. Embarrassment swirls in his gut. Then her flirty laughter fills his ear.

He chuckles. "I'll call you right back." He hangs up and the awkwardness of talking about being naked morphs into something different. Different because it's warm and sweet and welcome. He's a little turned on. Which is silly and juvenile, but he likes it.

Slipping on some pajama bottoms, finding a slightly used towel on his dresser, he runs it through his hair, dives back on the bed, and hits redial.

"You're a fast dresser." Humor sounds in her tone.

"And you're not?" He adjusts his pillow.

"Not that fast."

"Yeah, I guess girls make getting dressed an art. Guys just put on clothes." He cradles the phone to his ear.

"Guys are lucky," she says.

"Yeah, because we like the art," he teases. Her laugh softens, and he imagines her smile. "Did you get your closet cleaned out?"

"Mostly."

Matt knows the real reason for this call is to talk about her conversation with Cassie, but is it wrong to just enjoy talking to her for a few minutes? "Are you ready for school?"

"No." The word sounds loaded.

"Why not?"

"Everything," she says.

"Like?"

"Schoolwork. I'm not sure I'm caught up enough. The

people. I'm not sure how they'll take being around me. And then—"

"What do you mean about how people will take—?"

"They know I almost died."

"Yeah, but . . . you didn't die. And you're fine now. So I don't get it."

She goes instantly quiet. Had he said something wrong?

She finally speaks. "It'll freak them out."

"Why?"

"It just does." Sadness brushes her tone and whispers across his heart.

"I wouldn't worry what people think. And schoolwork? I'll help. We could meet a couple times a week." He holds his breath, hoping.

"That'd be nice." She sounds like she means it too.

"What else?" he asks.

"What else what?" she asks.

"What else bothers you about going back to school?" He wants . . . no, he needs to help.

She hesitates. "I don't know. Figuring out who I am now."

"You don't know who you are?"

"Yeah." Pause. "Not really. People change."

He tries to wrap his head around that. "You think you've changed?"

"Yeah."

"I don't notice that much change."

Silence fills the line. Just when he's about to say her name, she answers, "You didn't really know me before."

That sounds almost like an accusation, but he can't be sure. "I'll bet I knew you better than you think."

"Really? What did you know about me?" Now it sounds like a challenge.

One he's up for. "That you have gorgeous eyes. Light blue, with dark blue rings around them. And your lips are—"

"Not how I look. Everyone knows that."

"Okay . . . You liked to read. You'd always had a book with you. You'd get into class and read until the teacher took over. You didn't want to stop reading, but you always did because you're a rule follower. You started the book club. You're smart. You've always taken your classwork seriously and always turned in your homework. You're thorough. You took your time doing tests. You'd finish then go over them again. You were quiet. You hung out with a small group of friends, also readers. One of which is Brandy, who lives across from Austin Walker. And in tenth grade, you had PE seventh period."

When he stops talking, the line's quiet. Sounds dead.

"Leah?"

"Yeah," she mutters, sounding lost. "Here's the thing. I still like to read, but I don't like all the same books. I'll probably join the book club, but I don't want to run it anymore. I'm not smart about everything. I want to graduate, but I'm not worried about grades. I used to freak if I got a B. Now, I think Bs and Cs are good. Brandy is my best friend and that's probably never changing, but my other friends . . . I'm not sure we connect anymore."

He almost asks if Trent is in that "others" category. He sure as hell hopes so.

Lady prances into his room. Matt helps her up on his bed before she starts barking.

"And," Leah continues, "I'm not quiet anymore. I say 'shit' way too much. Old Leah never said 'shit.' Old Leah didn't have opinions. New Leah has a hard time keeping them to herself. I find myself biting my lip trying not to say things. Or I bite it because I'm nervous over what I said."

He recalls her biting her lips—recalls wishing she wouldn't. Her mouth looks too soft to bite.

"I've noticed you're not as quiet, but speaking your mind can't be a bad thing. And 'shit' isn't the worst thing you can say."

"I know. It's just . . . I'm different. And everyone expects me to be the old me, and it feels like trying to wear someone else's shoes."

"Then don't wear them. Just be you. Wear your Donald Duck slippers." A vision of her wearing them fills his head. It makes him smile. "Just be you."

She chuckles, but it's short-lived. "First I have to figure me out." The silence returns. "How did you know when I had PE?"

Crap, he should have kept that one to himself. Or maybe not. "I uh . . . noticed you looked good in the gym shorts and tank top. So once or twice a week, I'd find a reason to leave class and walk through the gym."

She laughs. "You were checking me out? Seriously?"

Yeah, but so was Trent and he got you before I made my move. "Guilty."

Then something suddenly occurs to him. "Do you think you've changed because . . . you've got Eric's heart?"

She hesitates. "Maybe. But not completely. Being sick changes you."

He was sure it did too. As did losing people you loved.

"I called Cassie," Leah says abruptly. "She didn't answer, and I got a message that her voicemail is full." She pauses. "I waited a few minutes and called again. I'm hoping she'll see my two missed calls and try me back."

He hears something in her voice. He recalls the fear in her eyes earlier. "Are you okay with that?"

"Yeah."

"Leah, if you don't want to do this—"

"I'm fine."

His gut says he shouldn't be dragging her into this, but she's all he's got.

He hesitates. "What if we both go to her house tomorrow?"

"I can't. I have . . . I'm going clothes shopping with my mom."

The thought of not seeing her made tomorrow look bleak. "All day?"

"Yeah."

"How about tomorrow night? We could . . ." He considers asking her out. A real date. "Maybe—"

"Can't. We're leaving for the weekend. Dad's friend has a place in Fredericksburg."

Shit! If she didn't sound so bummed, he'd suspect she was brushing him off. "All weekend?"

"Until Sunday."

"That sucks. Lady will miss you," he says in lieu of saying he will.

"I'll miss Lady too."

Did she mean . . . ? "Can I call you?"

"I was hoping you would. And I'll call you too." She goes quiet. "If that's okay."

"Of course." It's right there on his tongue. To tell her how much he enjoyed kissing her. To tell her he wants to do it again. To ask about Trent. But there's a loud beeping sound on the phone.

"What's that?" he asks.

"My phone alarm reminding me to . . ."

"What?" he asks.

"I'm supposed to watch a nine o'clock show with my mom. Better go."

"Okay." There's something off with her tone again. Her quick disconnect punctuates the feeling.

Effing great. Now he's back to thinking she might be brushing him off. Why are girls so hard to read?

We're shopping. The store's filled with new winter colors and styles. I haven't been shopping in over a year. A Natasha Bed-ingfield song pipes through the sound system. Mom's already told me that there're no cash limits. She's more excited about me going back to school than I am.

I'm scared. And it occurs to me that I don't look forward to facing Trent. When he called, he reminded me that I said we'd be friends. He told me he still wants to be more and hopes I'll change my mind.

I changed the subject to books. We only talked five minutes. An awkward five minutes.

I pull out a blue shirt, see it, and rehang that sucker.

As much as I used to love shopping, I'm not into it today. Or is it that my options are so limited that shopping isn't fun? The clothes are beautiful, but high necklines aren't in. Other than turtlenecks and long-sleeve Ts. Boring. Boring. Boring.

When you have a huge-ass scar running down the center of your chest, putting on clothes feels more about hiding than try-ing to look good.

"Love this," Mom holds up a pink V-neck blouse.

She's forgotten. "I like this one better." I nod at the bur-gundy T in my basket, thinking she'll remember and we can pretend she didn't forget.

Mom moves to the next rack. "You have to try this on!" She holds up another top. The color is right. Blue looks good on me. The scooped neckline, however, is a big honking no-way-not-happening. But she's so excited I take it to make her happy. Not that I'm trying it on. *Hurry up and remember, Mom.*

"I think I'll grab a pair of those jeans and hit the dressing room." I point to the items in my basket.

"You've only got four tops."

Four boring tops. "It's a good start."

"Okay. You go. I'll grab you a few more."

I start to tell her no but can't. Instead, I snag a pair of jeans and head to the dressing room. I pull off my shirt to try on boring shirt number 1. I catch my image in the full-length mirror.

I stare at the scars. I've been avoiding looking at myself. I know exactly where to dress in my bedroom so that I can't see my reflection in the dresser mirror.

But there's no avoiding it now.

There's the puckered scar where my artificial heart was connected right under my left rib. The second small one where I had a drain pipe when I got the new heart. And then the biggie. Where they cut and cranked open my chest bone.

It's still bright red, almost a half an inch thick, and it starts a few inches below my neck and goes down a good three inches past the center of my chest. I'm not so vain I wish I didn't have it. I'm alive because of it. But I wish it would fade.

I wish I didn't still hear Brandy's gasp. I'm still not mad at her, but I'm more self-conscious than ever.

I run my finger down the scar. It's still numb in places. I wonder if the feeling will come back. Placing my hand on my chest, I feel the slight *thump-thump*.

I wonder if Eric's heart is the same size as my original one. I wonder what they did with my heart. Throw it away? Cut it up to study it?

Is that what happened to the Old Leah? Did I lose part of her when they removed it all those months ago?

Do I miss it?

I wonder if one day Eric's heart will feel like mine. Will I ever stop feeling as if I stole someone else's life? That I benefited from something terrible?

Realizing all the wishing and wondering is ruining my mood, I stop it. I slip on the new shirt. It's boring but fits nicely. I turn to the side, and for the first time I see what Brandy says.

Yeah. My boobs *are* bigger.

I put my hands on my sides. I'm curvier. I remember Matt's hands on my waist. I remember how it felt to have my bigger breasts pressed against him. His lips on mine. I get flutters in my stomach. The good kind that tickles and teases.

Then another thought crowds out the flutters.

I wonder if Matt will gasp if he sees my scar.

It's a stupid thought. Once we're back in school, he may never want to kiss me again. Maybe he doesn't even really like me. Or will he pretend he does so that I'll keep helping him look into what happened to Eric?

I tell myself to stop it again.

Taking off my jeans, I slip the new jeans on. They fit. They look good.

"Leah?" I hear my mom.

"In here." I unlock my door.

She pushes it open and sees me in the new shirt and jeans. "Hmm," she says. "I don't know, it's a little . . ."

"Boring." I try to make light of it.

"No, just plain."

As if "plain" and "boring" aren't synonyms. What can I say? Mom's always been more into numbers than words.

"I found these." She dumps an armload of shirts and sweaters on me.

Four of the six shirts have pink in them. I'll bet none of them are high-necked.

"You try them on?" I suggest.

"Today's all about you. I want to see them on you," she says in her excited voice and shuts the door.

I hang them on the hook and pull out the blue one. I hadn't wanted to tell her, because I know she's going to feel bad, but . . .

it's that or show her. I don't want to show her. I don't want to see it. To see the scar peering out behind a cute article of clothing is worse than seeing me naked.

"They won't work, Mom."

"Why? They're cute."

I touch my chest beneath the burgundy long-sleeve T. "The scar."

Her eyes widen, and tears fill her eyes. "Oh, baby. I'm sorry. I . . . forgot."

She looks as if she's just insulted me. Kind of the way Brandy looked. I hug her. "It's okay."

She squeezes me, then lets go. "I love that scar. It saved your life. You are here because of that scar. Because of it, one day I'm going be in a dressing room watching you try on wedding dresses." Tears slip down her face.

"I know," I say. "But I don't want—"

"I get it," she says. "Wait, I have an idea." She storms out and I'm clueless to what's she's up to.

I try on the next boring T. I've barely got it on when Mom storms in.

"Camisoles." She hands me three hangers. "Try one on with that blue sweater. Just a couple of months ago, I saw a show on how to wear sexy camisoles with everyday clothes." She points to my phone. "Google it if you don't believe me," she says. "I'm going to look for some more tops to pair with them." She rushes out. A woman on a mission.

I stare at the door and realize it's the same mission she's been on for almost two years. Keep Leah alive and happy.

She needs to focus on herself now. She hasn't mentioned going back to work. I should nudge her. She used to love her job working for a big accounting firm. Her friends still work there.

I look back at the lacy camisoles. I slip one on and pull the blue sweater over top of it. It doesn't look bad. Maybe Mom is on to something.

It's not boring. The sweater's neck is loose and sort of falls off the shoulder just a little. Before I wouldn't have bought it because it would show my bra strap, but with the camisole it's different. It's kind of sexy. I feel sexy. I think of Matt seeing me in it and grin.

I'm still busy admiring it when my phone rings. Brandy's supposed to call to see how shopping is going. I start looking for the jeans with my phone in the back pocket. I answer it without checking, and that very instant I remember.

I remember who else has my number.

"Hello?" The slight tremble in my voice echoes in my stomach.

"Who is this?" the caller asks. I don't recognize the voice, but I know it's her.

My mind starts whirling. Questions. Questions. What were they?

"Cassie?" I force myself to speak. Undefined emotion floods my chest. Not fear. Not just nerves.

"Who are you?" The tone is unsure, insecure. Not how I expected the beautiful, bold head cheerleader Cassie Chambers to sound. But then the image of her at the roadside park where Eric was shot floods my mind. She didn't look so bold then either.

Then it hits. Sadness. I feel sadness. For Cassie. So. Much. Sadness.

"This is Leah. Leah McKenzie. From school. You probably don't remember me." I hear footsteps outside the dressing room. *Don't be Mom. Please don't be Mom.*

I hear another dressing room door open. Not Mom.

"I remember you," Cassie says. "Why are you calling me? Are you the one who came to my house?"

I swallow oxygen. My tongue feels thick. I want to cry. I don't know why, but I do. "Yeah. I . . . I've been talking to Matt Kenner and he has questions and wanted me to—"

"Stop. I'm hurting enough already. Tell Matt to leave me alone!"

"But Cassie, as bad as you're feeling, Matt feels worse. Eric was his brother, his twin. He's just trying to understand how . . . this happened. You could help him. Please."

"I can't. I can't." I hear her shaky breaths. Crying. The heaviness in my chest swells past the legal limits, pressing against my rib cage. Too tight. I want to cry with her.

For her.

For Eric.

"Why can't you?" The words strangle through my constricted throat.

"You don't understand."

"What do I not understand? Tell me. I'll tell Matt."

The last thing I hear is her sobs. Then she's gone.

The heaviness in my chest makes my knees weak. I feel dizzy. I plop down on the dressing room bench.

The feeling fades. Replaced with another. I failed. I got nothing that'll help Matt.

Then I rehear Cassie's words. *I can't. You don't understand.* Was it just me, or did Cassie make it sound as if . . . she knew something but couldn't tell?

Is Matt right? Does Cassie know something?

Good to his word, Matt returns to see the detective the next day. He stands at the front desk and faces Mrs. Johnson. The heavyset African American woman, who looks like someone's grandmother, stares at the computer oblivious to his presence. "I'm here to see Detective Henderson."

She looks up. "Your name?" She asks that every time. He'd

bet his football jacket she knows his name. Just like he knows hers. She probably knows why he's here.

The pity in her eyes guarantees it.

He hates pity. He needs answers. Not pity.

"Matt Kenner?" He's not sure what he's going to do if they give him another brush-off.

How much of an ass can he get away with being in a police station?

Not that it'd be his fault. But it would be his problem. A problem he'd take on for Eric, but one he didn't want upsetting his mom.

He takes a deep breath, then releases it. To center himself, to think more clearly.

It's a trick he picked up from Leah. The moment she tiptoes into his mind, he starts missing her. He can't remember ever having it this bad for a girl.

He relaxes his stance. Mrs. Johnson picks up the phone and pushes in some numbers.

"Yes, Matt Kenner's here." She refuses to look at him. He watches the frown pass over her face.

That isn't good.

"Okay. Yeah." She hangs up and lifts her dark brown eyes. "I'm sorry, but he's going into a meeting."

"I'll wait." His tone's hard. His stomach knots, reminding him that he skipped breakfast.

She frowns. "It could be—"

"I'm not leaving." His jaw tightens. Hell, since he can't see Leah, he can stand here all damn day. What are they gonna do, arrest him for standing? Maybe loitering? Would they?

A door from the back swings open.

It's Detective Henderson. An unhappy-looking Detective Henderson. He glances at Mrs. Johnson. "I got this." His focus shifts to Matt. "Come on."

Matt follows, aware how tall and broad-shouldered the man

is. The detective passes his office, where they usually talk, and walks into what looks like an interview room. There are even cameras in the corner of the ceilings. And a big mirror that Matt suspects is a window.

The detective pulls out a chair from the big table and drops down. Matt chooses the chair across from him so they face each other. He meets the man's stern gray gaze. Matt almost tosses out a smartass remark, but remembers the old you-get-more-flies-with-honey theory.

"Thank you. For seeing me. I wanted to ask—"

The man holds up his hand. "Me first."

"As long as I get my turn." Matt settles back.

The man scrubs a hand over his face. "I hate seeing you."

Matt's spine tenses. "Because I remind you of what a shitty job you've done on my brother's case?"

The detective shakes his head. "I hate seeing you because you make me remember my younger brother. He died at eighteen. I had almost forgotten how much that hurt until you started darkening my doorstep."

Matt's surprised. "How did he die?"

"He got a batch of bad cocaine." He exhales. "Like you, I wanted to blame everyone else. The drug dealers, the friend who drove him to get the shit. The girlfriend who got him hooked. My parents for not intervening. Even myself. But I could never bring myself to blame my brother."

"Eric didn't—"

"I'm not done!" He holds out a hand. "I've been there, kid. I road that damn bull seven seconds, got thrown, and it nearly killed me. I wish I could help you. I wish I could say I believed you. But I've never seen such an open-and-closed case."

"You don't know—"

"Goddamn it, I wish I was wrong! Every fucking time you've walked through that door, I've opened the damn file and looked for something. It's not there. I don't know what to tell you to do to stop the hurting. Time's the only thing."

Emotion sinks into Matt's chest, stretching his ribs, crowding his heart. Tears threaten to fill his eyes. He swallows the knot in his throat. "You didn't know Eric. He—"

"I can't help you, Matt. I'd give my left nut if I could."

Matt fights the sense of hopelessness. Then he remembers the reason he's here. "Did you send a cop to talk to the Chambers?"

The detective shakes his head.

"A cop car pulled up there. I thought—"

"Don't be bothering the Chambers. If there's another complaint, I'll have to get a restraining order. I don't want to do that. Got me?"

"Who complained?" Matt asks. "Cassie?"

"It doesn't matter."

"I just think . . ."

Detective Henderson stands up. "Try not to think. Find something to occupy your time. Get a girlfriend."

Matt thinks about Leah. He almost wants to tell the detective about the dreams, about her dreams and having Eric's heart. His gut says it's useless. The detective would really think Matt has lost it. How can he make the detective believe him?

Coming up empty, he stands up, turns to go. Then turns back around and looks the detective dead in his eyes. "Was your brother trying to kill himself?"

"No, he was an addict."

"Maybe that's why he wanted to kill himself."

The detective shakes his head. "He just didn't know the cocaine was bad."

"But he knew it was dangerous. He was probably looking for a way out."

"It wasn't—" The detective's eyes widen as if he realizes what Matt's doing.

Matt's spine stiffens. "How do you know?" he pauses. "You just know, don't you? Because he was your brother. Like Eric was mine. We were identical twins. I could almost read his mind. Eric didn't do this to himself."

Detective Henderson rakes his palm over his face.

Matt continues. "I've heard of cases that were ruled a suicide then later proven differently. I know it's possible. And I'm not going to stop looking for proof. I understand that you aren't investigating. I don't like it, but I understand. But can I come to you when I find something? Will you see me? Listen to me?"

The man closes his eyes, then opens them. "I'll see you, but it has to be proof. Solid evidence. You understand what that means?"

Matt nods. "Thank you." He decides to leave on that.

"Kid?"

Matt turns around.

"I'm serious about staying away from the Chambers. The cop car you saw . . . It's not what you think."

"Then what is it?" Matt asks.

"It's Officer Yates's car. He's engaged to Ms. Chambers. Cassie isn't even there. She's living with her father in California. Yates says Cassie's mom blames you for Cassie leaving. The reason I called your mom was because Yates saw you hanging around and came to me. So don't go looking for trouble. Stay away."

"You're wrong." Matt words are as stiff as his backbone right now. "Cassie's back. And while you still don't believe me, she lied to you. Eric went to her house that night he was killed."

The detective frowns. He's already heard this, but Matt doesn't care. He'll keep telling the truth until someone listens.

"Eric told me he was going there. He had no reason to lie. I was going to order some takeout that night. He said not to include him because he and Cassie were going out."

"And she says he never showed up."

"And you believe her?"

"Her mother confirmed it."

"Then she's lying too."

The detective stares at him like a stray dog he wants to take home but can't. Matt leaves feeling worse than when he came.

18

The familiar *tap-tap* sounds against the office door and Dr. Hughes walks in.

I pocket my phone and look up. I've been mentally sitting on the edge of my seat, wanting to call Matt since Cassie called. I left Mom at lunch and went to the bathroom to call. Then I didn't.

I'm not sure what to say to him. I'm not sure if I think Cassie was hiding something. I'm not sure . . . not sure Matt and I have a chance of being anything. I'm scared that the kiss might be the last one I'll get from him. Scared to . . . hope.

For so long I didn't allow myself to hope. Hope wasn't for someone with a dying or dead heart. At least not one with AB blood.

Now I'm afraid of . . . hope. How sad is that?

"No Dumbo or Mickey?" Dr. Hughes's smile is contagious. In my state of mind, I'm surprised she pulls one out of me.

"They were sleeping in when I left." I tug the paper gown together.

She pulls a chair beside the exam bed and sits down. She's unlike any doctor I've met. She always seems genuinely happy to see me. She's never in a hurry. She doesn't just talk about my health. She talks about my life.

Probably because she saved it.

"How are you?" she asks.

"Fine, I think."

Her smile loses its sparkle. "What's going on?"

Dr. Hughes, a cardiologist who specializes in children, is a member of the transplant team. She requests to see her patients without their parents for the first half of the visit. Just in case they have concerns or questions they don't want the parents to know. I've never really had questions I couldn't ask in front of my mom.

Until now.

If I can find the courage to ask them.

"Spill." She lifts a brow.

I swallow. "Yesterday I woke up and remembered one of the dreams and then when I took my blood pressure it was high."

"How high?" she asks.

"One sixty over a hundred."

She gets that look I've seen on her face so many times. Like the time I came in and couldn't catch my breath. Or the time after I got my artificial heart and returned with a fever. "That's high. Was the dream upsetting?" She stands and pulls the blood pressure cuff from her white lab-coat pocket.

"Yeah."

"Did you retake it?" She fits the cuff on my arm.

"It was lower, but still high. Then when I took it that night, it was normal. Well, five points from my regular pressure. And it was normal this morning."

She's quiet as she checks my blood pressure. "It's fine now. Your bloodwork's fine too. It was probably from the dream."

"That's what I thought." I smile.

"I'm surprised your mother didn't call me."

I shrug with guilt. "I didn't tell her. I . . . You know how she is. She'd freak."

She cuts me a serious look, reminding me of how Mom looks at me sometimes. "Better to freak than to ignore things."

"If it'd been high later, I'd have told her."

"No other symptoms? Heart palpitations? Breathing issues? Swelling?" She reaches down and touches my ankles. "Tightness in the chest?"

I've had plenty of that but only . . . "None that aren't tied to the dreams."

She sits back down. "Are the dreams the same as before? Running? Then the headaches?"

I nod. Part of me wants to tell her everything, but . . .

"How often do you have them? Are they keeping you up?"

"Two or three times a week, but I usually go back to sleep."

She leans back. "I could give you something to help you sleep, but—"

"No. Sleeping pills make me groggy." Then I might not remember my dreams.

She presses a finger to her chin. "Maybe we should do another biopsy."

"No. You said I wouldn't need another one for nine months. Like you said, it's the dreams."

They've gone in once and snagged a few pieces of Eric's heart to make sure it's not in rejection mode. It requires a hospital stay. The last thing I want is to go back there.

She considers it. "Okay, but if your blood pressure goes up again, you call me."

"I promise."

"Are you ready for school?"

I nod.

"Excited?"

"And scared."

"Why?"

I decide to confess a bit more. "I went to a party on New Year's and hung out with my old friends."

"And?" she asks.

"And I felt different. Like I didn't fit anymore."

"What you've been through is life altering. You don't go through something like this without growing up. And when we grow up, we're different."

"I don't know if it's growing up. I'm just . . . different. People I used to know and accept now annoy me. For so long, I've wanted to get back to being me. Now I feel like I'm trying to live someone else's life."

"Then don't. Live the life you want. Be who you are now."

"I still haven't figured her out," I say.

"You will." Confidence hangs on her words.

I remember my other question. I open my paper gown. "How long until it fades?"

"It was around nine months when mine became less angry looking. Some take a year. You're using the cream, right?"

I nod.

She studies me, and I swear she's reading my mind. "What about the boy who you used to date? Have you seen him?"

Yup, a mind reader. The fact that she knows I'm thinking about getting naked with someone has me squirming inside and out. "How did you remember that? We talked about him a year ago. Do you remember everything your patients tell you?"

She smiles. "Just the good parts. Have you seen this guy?"

"He was at the party."

"And?" she asks.

"He's one of the things I don't think I fit with anymore." Before I even think about it, I add, "but there's another guy." I don't know why I throw that out there, except I don't like sounding pathetic. Or maybe I'm excited?

She smiles.

I don't.

"I'm not really sure we fit either."

"Why not?"

"Because school starts Monday and we're not . . . in the same league."

When she looks confused, I add, "He's a quarterback and I'm . . ."

"Totally awesome," she says.

"You say that just because I'm your patient."

"Please. I have lots of not-awesome patients." Honesty rings in her voice. "You do realize that after high school that whole clique stuff goes away."

"But I'm not out yet."

"Have you two dated? This new guy, I mean?"

"No. We walked his dog and had lunch . . . twice. But that doesn't—"

"Is he hot?"

"You a cougar?" I grin.

She laughs. "Depends how hot."

"Yeah. He's hot."

She pulls out her stethoscope. "How do you feel about birth control?"

I choke on air. "I . . . We've only kissed . . . twice." But I clearly recall the "more" feeling when kissing him.

She rubs the end of the scope on her sleeve to warm it. "Is he a good kisser?"

"Yes, but . . ."

She lifts one eyebrow. "Good kisses lead places."

My face warms. "But my parents wouldn't . . . If Mom knew I kissed him, she'd flip because of the germs."

"As long as he's not sick, I'm not going to tell you not to kiss. Not that you should kiss just anyone. Only the really hot ones." She pauses. "As for the birth control . . . Let me handle that. The thing you need to remember is that, while sex is on the table, pregnancy isn't."

"I know." I remember the little boy watching fireworks. "About the pregnancy." Not so much about the sex. Besides, the scar just might be all the birth control I need.

She listens to my heart. I wonder if it's too fast from thinking about sex. And Matt. I do the routine of breathing deep, holding it, breathing normal.

She pulls back. "You sound good."

I nod.

"Have you and your parents talked about college yet?"

I sort of sink into myself. It's not that I haven't thought about college, but when the thought hits, my mental brakes screech to a halt.

I realize she's waiting for an answer. "I had plans before I got sick. Dad and Mom both went to University of Houston. I was going to follow in their footsteps."

"Let me guess. You're going for an English degree?"

She's got me figured out. Maybe even better than I do. "That or journalism was a consideration."

"Was?"

"I . . ." I don't know what to say, but then it falls out of me. "I lived one day at a time for so long. I've moved up to a week at a time. I haven't gotten to months, much less years yet."

"That's a great way to put it." She sets her warm hand on my shoulder. "My job is to make sure you get years. Your job is to plan them."

Emotion crowds my throat. I don't even know why. I don't think I'm dying anymore. Do I? Maybe I just can't let go of what it felt like to . . . watch your dreams shrivel up and die, because you don't have time. Because some freaking virus that you've never heard of stole your life. To suddenly find yourself where those dreams didn't even matter anymore. To be at a place where your biggest goal was getting up enough strength to walk to the bathroom, because using a bed pan was humiliating.

"I'll try, but I don't think my parents are ready to talk about college either."

Dr. Hughes sits back. "I think going to a local college for a year is wise. But after that, the sky's the limit."

She squeezes my hand. "You've got a future, Leah. Plan for it. Figure out who you are and what you want. Then go do it. Do it large. It's people like you who make a big splash. Don't be afraid to take a chance. Win or lose. That's what life is, a bunch of chances."

"You sound like my grandma."

"As long as I don't look like her," Dr. Hughes says.

I smile. Emotion stirs in my chest. My emotion. Mine. I can feel the difference from this and what I felt when talking to Cassie.

"Any other questions or concerns?" she asks.

I hesitate. I swallow. Dare I ask her? My own best friend doesn't believe me. *Take a chance.* "Sometimes I feel . . . Have any of your other patients felt as if . . . ." I put my hand on my chest and start over. "I have someone else's heart and I think this heart feels things and I'm not feeling."

Dr. Hughes uncrosses her legs and her shoulders tighten, making her appear taller. I wish I could suck the words back in. Instead of looking at her face, I stare at her name embroidered on her white coat.

"Have you been reading the Internet?" she asks.

I look up. "Only after I started feeling like this."

"What exactly are you feeling?"

"Just emotions."

She studies me. "The dreams part of this?"

I nod.

She crosses her arms. "What do you think the dreams mean?"

That someone killed Eric. I hold back. "I'm not sure." It's a lie. How many does that make today?

"Leah, medically, there's no proof that the stories you read are true. The claims are based on the fact that all cells have memory and that hasn't been proven. Experts believe it's nothing more than anecdotal evidence."

I hear what she's saying, and I think I hear what she's not saying. "So what do you believe?"

Dr. Hughes exhales. "I just told you."

"No, you said 'medically' and that experts believe. I want to know what you believe and if other patients experienced this."

She sighs. "You're going to put me on the spot, aren't you?"

"Sorry."

"Okay. Yes, I've had patients tell me things like this."

"How many?"

"Less than ten, and I've worked on over a hundred transplant cases."

"And you still don't believe it?"

"In most cases, the patients were highly susceptible to believing anything. The stories were vague and lacked substance. Like a patient who suddenly developed a sweet tooth, so the donor must have loved candy. They don't realize the prednisone they're taking increases appetite."

I wonder if that could explain the Indian food. Probably. I wonder if I'm one she considers highly susceptible.

"And the other cases?"

She frowns. "A few have been more convincing." She hesitates. "I'm not saying I believed it. I'm saying my patients believed it and their stories held more merit."

"So you think it's possible?" I ask.

"I didn't . . . What I think is that I offer hope to people who didn't have any. I offer life. And the last thing I want is these unproven cases to cause even one person to be afraid to take the chance modern medicine offers them."

"It wouldn't have stopped me, even if someone told me this," I say.

"Not everyone is as brave as you are."

I laugh. "I think you have me mixed up with someone else."

"No," she says. "Would you like to talk to someone about the dreams? A psychiatrist?"

"No." I answer quickly.

"You sure?"

"Positive."

At least I know I'm not the only heart patient who has experienced this. Dr. Hughes may not completely believe it, but I see the glimmer of uncertainty in her eyes.

Then I hear her words of wisdom: *Don't be afraid to take a chance. Win or lose. That's what life is, a bunch of chances.* Am I really going to take a chance on Matt?

Mom's quiet on the drive home. Too quiet. I'm guessing it's the talk Dr. Hughes had with her when she sent me out to the waiting room. The birth control talk. A couple of times, I see Mom look at me as if to say something. Then she turns back and faces the road.

I'm normally all for speaking your mind—especially lately— but right now I'm glad she's holding back. I'm not ready to have this talk.

She pulls up in our drive. "We're running late," she says. "Your dad wanted us to be ready to go when he gets home. So grab your stuff. We have less than an hour."

"Okay." I'm mostly packed, but that gives me time to call Matt. I have to tell him about Cassie calling me.

We get out and walk into the house.

I start toward my room and Mom says, "Leah? Uh, can we talk a minute?"

I swallow. "I thought we had to hurry."

"Just a minute."

Shit. Shit. Shit.

19

I follow her into the kitchen. "Let's get some hot chocolate."

Oh, damn. Whenever Mom brings hot chocolate into a conversation, she means business.

My pulse races. I don't know why. We've had the sex talk. But then we haven't had the get-you-on-birth-control talk.

I drop into a chair. Mom puts two cups of hot water in the microwave and busies herself gathering spoons, hot chocolate, and marshmallows. She's rubbing her palms on the sides of her jeans. I'm not the only one who's nervous.

She sets everything down in front of me, but stares at the microwave, waiting for the ding. The only noise in the room is the electric hum of the appliances. The beep breaks the silence, and she delivers the hot water and sits down.

We add the chocolate powder to our cups. I even pour a handful of marshmallows from my bag. They bob up and down, then start to melt. I wish I could melt away.

"Dr. Hughes suggested I take you to a gynecologist and get you on birth control."

I knew what this was going to be about, but I panic hearing

it. I snag my spoon and run laps around my cup, watching the last of the marshmallows dissolve into sweet white foam.

I need to say something. I have choices. I can probably nip this conversation in the bud by telling the truth. Tell her I'm not having sex. That I wasn't the one to mention birth control. But if I do that, she'll decide it isn't necessary. Then when I start thinking about having sex, I'm going to have to bring this up again. And then she'll know I'm planning to have sex. I so don't want my mom to know when I'm planning to have sex.

"Yeah." My tongue feels too big for my mouth. My mouth is too dry. I take a sip of hot chocolate. It burns my tongue and I can't taste it. The marshmallow foam coats my upper lip.

"Are you and Matt, uh, that serious?"

I open my mouth to explain. Nothing comes out.

"Two days ago you said he wasn't your boyfriend."

"Yeah." I'm not sure what I said "yeah" to. By the look on her face, Mom isn't either. "I like him," I spit out.

"So he's your boyfriend?" She looks confused.

"I don't know. When we start school . . . He'll have his friends."

"What do his friends have to do with it?"

"He's quarterback and they normally date cheerleaders. I don't know if he'll still notice me then."

She nods like she understands. "I see." Her brows tighten. "I don't think you realize how beautiful you are, but that's not what I'm talking about."

"I'm not having sex with him," I blurt out. *Don't leave it there. Don't leave it there.* "But . . ." Damn, damn, damn. I can't do it.

"But what?" she asks.

"But I'm almost eighteen and . . ." I can't say more, and not because it's about sex but because . . . it's months away. I'm barely thinking a week at a time.

I take a deep, shaky breath. *Don't be afraid to take a chance.*

Win or lose. That's what life is, a bunch of chances. "Maybe it's not a bad idea," I finally finish.

Mom's pupils dilate. I don't know if it's disappointment or shock. Part of me feels she's about to ground me.

"I'll . . . make you an appointment. I just don't want . . . Being on birth control doesn't mean you should do something before you're ready."

"I won't." I'm shocked it was this easy.

She nods. I glance at the door. "I should go and start . . ." I don't want to lie, so I let her assume I mean packing, but I really want to talk to Matt.

And announcing I need to speak to Matt feels like a bad idea. She might think I'm going to tell him about the birth control. I'm so not going to tell him about birth control. But right then I realize I like thinking I'm moving in that direction. I kind of like this elusive thing called a future. I'd really like Matt to be in it.

"Go," she says.

I stand, but before I even turn she's up and has me in a big bear hug. "My little girl is growing up and I'm not sure I'm ready." She pulls back. Tears are in her eyes. "I still want to comb your hair and put it up in pigtails."

I smile. "And dress me in pink."

She nods and then says, "What's wrong with pink?"

It's now or never. "Pink isn't my best color."

She looks surprised. "But I thought you . . . What about your room?"

"It's great." I say quickly. Too quickly.

She hears my lie. "You wouldn't have chosen pink?"

"No, but—"

"Well, shit!" she says.

I gasp dramatically. "Just because I curse, doesn't mean you can."

We laugh together. "We'll do something about your room. You can pick it out this time."

I know she paid a fortune for all the pink. "Maybe next . . ." The word years catches on my tonsils. "Later."

She brushes my hair off my cheek. Her eyes sparkle with mama emotion. "As much as I hate to see you grow up, less than a year ago my worst fear was that you wouldn't. Just promise me you'll make wise choices."

Choices and chances, I think. That's what having a future is all about. "I promise." And I mean it. This is my second or perhaps my third chance at life. I don't want to screw it up. I know not every choice I make is going to pan out. But I won't know until I try. And not trying isn't living.

I give her another hug. The choice made, I hurry to go take a chance on Matt.

Matt's resting on his bed with Lady sleeping at his side, as he stares at his phone. He'd tried to call Leah three times and chickened out. Eric would be so damn disappointed in him.

Matt tells himself he doesn't want to interrupt Leah's shopping spree.

The truth is he's afraid she won't answer. He's afraid she really was brushing him off yesterday. But damn it! He needs to talk to her.

He needs to tell her to stay away from Cassie. Something tells him that Detective Henderson wasn't bullshitting him about Ms. Chambers having her fiancé get involved. And the last thing he wants is to get Leah in any trouble.

Man up! He can hear his brother say.

Angry at himself for being a wimp, he dials her number and presses it to his ear.

"Hi." She answers before he hears it ring. Her voice, her one word, sends a wiggle of happiness to his chest. "I was calling you."

"Really?" he asks.

"I was dialing when it rang."

So it wasn't a brush-off. He smiles.

"Did you take Lady for a walk?" she asks.

"Yeah. We missed you."

"I miss you two too." She sounds a little shy.

He sits up, careful not to wake Lady. "How did everything go today?"

She pauses. "How did what go?"

"Shopping?"

"Oh, great. I got some clothes."

"Good." He hesitates. "I went to see Detective Henderson." His chest locks out some of the happiness talking to her brings.

"Did you ask him about the police car?"

"Yeah. He said they're not looking into the case anymore. That police car belongs to Ms. Chambers's fiancé. Henderson said Cassie's mom blames me for Cassie leaving and her fiancé is stepping in on her behalf. So I don't think you should go there anymore."

"Cassie called me," Leah says.

His gut tightens. He sits up. Lady whimpers. "What did she say?"

"It was weird. She said to tell you to leave her alone and that she was hurting. I told her you just wanted some answers. She started crying and said that I didn't understand."

"Understand what?"

"I don't know. I may be making more out of this, but it almost sounded as if there was a reason she couldn't talk. Something besides you reminding her of Eric."

Validated, his muscles tighten. "I told you she knows something."

"I know. I just . . . I still don't believe she did it. She didn't sound guilty. She sounded hurt. Maybe scared."

"Of who? And why would she be scared if she didn't do anything wrong? Why did she lie, unless she had something to do with it? And why did her mother lie and say Eric wasn't there that night?"

"Maybe they aren't lying," Leah says slowly as if choosing her words cautiously. "Maybe he didn't get there. What if we're looking at this wrong? What if what happened to Eric didn't have anything to do with Cassie?"

"But everything points to Cassie. She wouldn't talk to me at the funeral. Then she left to live with her dad. And then there's whatever was wrong with her that made Eric go back to her to start with."

"Did you two have all the same friends?"

"Mostly," he says. "There's a few that go to another school that he was closer to."

"Have you asked them if they knew something was up?"

"Eric and I were close. We didn't keep secrets from each other."

"I don't mean this the wrong way, but he did keep something from you," she says. "He took your father's gun, so something was up."

Matt closes his eyes. She's right. There was even a part of him that knew something was up with Eric, and he'd pushed for his brother to tell him. But Matt hadn't pushed hard enough. If he had, his brother would still be here.

If only . . . If only . . .

"I'm sorry, I didn't mean—"

"No. You're right. I'll talk with his friends." Except he hated the way they looked at him, with all kinds of pity. He suspected they believed Eric did this to himself. That just proved they didn't know Eric that well.

He closes his fist. "But, damn it, Cassie needs to talk too."

"Didn't you say she was going to finish the year of school here?"

"That's what I heard."

"Then wait until Monday. We can talk to her there."

He shuts his eyes and tries to push back the grief and guilt he feels. "I should try talking to Marissa again. Maybe Cassie's talked to her since she's been back."

"Do you want me to call Marissa?" Leah asks.

Her offer comes out so sincere and it means a lot, but he can't forget how scared she looked yesterday after coming from Cassie's house.

"No, I'll do it."

"I want to help, Matt. I think Eric wants me to help."

"I know, but I don't want any of this to come back on you. And Marissa's not avoiding me." Probably because she liked him, but he's made it clear the feeling isn't mutual.

Leah gets quiet. "Okay. But I'm offering."

"I know. Thanks. For everything. Not just this. Having someone to talk to means a lot."

"I like talking to you too. Sorry I couldn't meet you today or this weekend."

"Me too." It feels like the end of the conversation and he's not ready. "What are you doing fun this weekend?"

"Maybe a museum, or more shopping. Fredericksburg has a cute downtown area with unique stores. I'll mostly be reading. I actually prefer that to shopping."

"How many books do you read in a month?"

"It depends on how good the books are," she says. "In the last year, I've read seventy-eight."

"Wow! You do love to read."

"Yeah, but I was sick so I couldn't . . . I just read."

He hears something in her voice. "I wasn't making fun of you. I think it's great."

"Thanks," she says. "My bucket . . . my goal is to get to a hundred."

"Then what?" he asks.

She chuckles. "Read a hundred more."

"You make me feel like a slacker. I'm going to have to find a book to read."

"You aren't a slacker, but you should read. Reading is a vacation for the mind. Well, if the book is good, it is."

"Do you want to write?" he asks.

She gets quiet. "I did. I actually started a project before . . . I got sick. But it was too hard to be creative. So I just read."

"You should try again."

"I probably will."

"What are you taking in college?" he asks.

There's another lull as if she's thinking. Then he hears someone call her name.

"That's my mom. I should go. My dad's home."

"Call me if you get bored of reading. As a matter of fact, don't take the good books with you, so you'll get bored and call me."

She laughs. "I will. Call you. Not bring boring books. I don't read boring books."

She hangs up. He drops his phone on his chest. Then he realizes he's smiling. Just talking on the phone with her makes him feel . . . lighter. Free. As if he's not trapped in the dark place he usually stays.

But, damn, he really wishes she weren't leaving for the weekend.

Lady moves to the edge of the bed and whines. She's still too frightened to jump off.

He takes Lady out. When she's done her business, they come

back in. He checks to see if his mom's home. She isn't. He re-calls her mentioning going out for an early dinner with friends before going to grief counseling.

He thinks about calling Marissa. But it's Friday evening. She's probably out. The same with John and Cory, the guys Eric hung out with who go to Southside High.

The thought of calling Ted and seeing what he's doing crosses Matt's mind. But he's not sure he's in the mood for that. He wants Leah. He wants the lightness she makes him feel.

He pushes his fingers through his hair.

He starts back to his room. He stops at Eric's closed bed-room door. The room has become like his dad's study. Nobody goes in there. It hurts too much.

Before Eric died, they'd read some articles on coping with grief, hoping to help their mom and maybe even themselves. One of the articles suggested clearing out the departed's things. It was okay to hold on to keepsakes, but clearing out a closet or a room was part of the healing. Part of letting go.

Matt reaches for Eric's doorknob, but he can't even turn it, much less walk in.

He's not ready.

He should probably clear out his dad's study first. But he's not ready to do that either.

He starts back to his own room to just sit there, to think, to hurt. He doesn't want to hurt. He's tired of hurting.

Reading is like a vacation for the mind. He hears Leah's words.

He needs a vacation.

He walks past his room to what his mom calls her library. Two of the walls are floor-to-ceiling bookshelves. There's a shelf of books Mom bought for him and Eric.

Matt runs his fingers over the spines. He's read them all. Moving to the next shelf, he sees his mom's romance novels. He sees an author's name he thinks he remembers Leah saying she read. He pulls it out.

He reads the blurb on the back. Definitely a chick book. But he's curious. So he takes the book and goes back to his room.

At first he has to force himself to keep reading, but then he gets caught up in it. He laughs at the character's antics; he can't turn the pages fast enough when the suspense element is brought in; and then uh . . . it gets . . . hot.

He cannot believe his mom and Leah read this. He puts the book down, swearing it's too much. He's a guy. Guys don't read this stuff. They don't . . .

Shit!

He picks the book back up.

It's three hours later when the sound of his empty stomach grumbling makes him close the book. He's almost finished with it.

Reading is like a vacation for the mind.

She's right. He feels refreshed. Hungrier than a bear, but good.

He's raiding the kitchen, eating chips and drinking milk, while the pizza cooks, all the while thinking about the book. Thinking about Leah reading the book, especially the sexy parts.

He wonders if he'll ever get the nerve to tell her he read it? Probably not. Then again, if . . . if this goes where he wants it to go, yeah, maybe.

He likes that maybe.

The memory of his and Leah's kiss fills his head. That brings on thoughts of other scenes in the book. The bedroom scenes.

Damn, he wants that. With Leah. The teasing. The laughing. The touching. The getting naked. He really wants all that.

Five minutes later, he's trying to stop wanting it when he hears his mom's car. He starts toward the front door when the oven dings announcing the pizza's done. He's pulling it out, when he hears her walk in. He's setting the pizza on the stovetop, when he hears her crying.

Vacation's over.

Reality hits.

Pain hits.

Guilt hits. Guilt for being excited about living when two people he loved are dead.

20

Matt turns around. His mom walks in. Her eyes are red; her makeup's smeared down her cheeks.

"You okay?" He walks over.

"I'm so sorry, Matt. I feel so guilty. It's my fault. If I hadn't been—"

"No." He steps closer and folds his mom in his arms. "I don't think Eric did this to himself, but even if he did, it's not your fault any more than it's . . . mine." The moment he says it, he feels something release in his chest. It's not his mom's fault. It's not his fault. It's true. "We were all hurting, Mom."

"But it was my job to take care of you two."

"It's not your fault. Listen to me. It's. Not. Your. Fault."

When she pulls away, he says, "Maybe grief counseling isn't what you need."

"No. I think it's good. They said I need to cry, until I don't need to." She looks up and puts her hand on his chest. "Have you cried?"

He nods and, without meaning to, proves it. Tears fill his eyes.

They sit in the kitchen crying, then talking, then crying, then talking. And hurting. Only this time the hurting feels different. It's almost cathartic. Or maybe it's just that this is the first time he and his mom really shared the grief. He doesn't know. He doesn't even care. He feels a little better.

His mom finally gets up and slices the pizza and sets it on the table. She's about to sit down when she suddenly folds her arms around herself and lets out another sad sound.

Moving to the counter, she opens a drawer and pulls out the M&Ms bag. She empties the bag of colorful chocolate candy on the pizza.

They both laugh again, then cry again, then force themselves to eat pizza, Eric-style.

My shoes feel weighted, a thousand butterflies are calling my stomach home, and my lungs are filled with liquid fear. Do I really hate this place that much, I ask myself as I walk toward the doors of Walnut High Monday morning.

I'm thirty minutes early. I have to pick up my class schedule and books from the office, find my locker, take my pills to the nurse's office, and try to remember how to play the game.

The high school game. The one where you have to know how to fit in, know whom to ignore and whom to smile at, know how to get through the day without wishing you were someone else.

It's not as if I had a really low self-esteem before. But I knew my place, my people, and my plan. Now, I don't know shit.

Why did I want to come back here?

I'm wearing the royal-blue sweater with the tan lacy camisole under it and the new jeans. I paired it with my new black ankle boots.

I spent a good thirty minutes fixing my hair and makeup. I

even gave my nails a coat of clear polish. Before I left home, I'd stood in front of the mirror and felt pretty damn confident about how I looked. Pretty sure Matt would appreciate . . . what did he call it? The art of getting dressed.

But right now all that confidence is gone. Yesterday's news. Dead. History. I'm nothing but a tight ball of nerves that's about to start unraveling.

I tell myself it's silly, but nothing feels silly. Leah McKenzie is going back to school. And I'm not sure who she is anymore.

I open the heavy front doors. The smell hits me. I can't define the scent but I know it. I haven't smelled it in over a year and a half. It's school. It's over a thousand kids in one building with their hormones, anger, dreams, egos, and identity crises. It's the slight smell of the lunchroom's hideous tuna casserole. It's people. Lots and lots of people. I haven't been around a lot of people in a long time.

Several students shuffle around in the halls. I recognize some of them, and know a few of their names because I've had classes with them. But if the way they're staring is any indication, they don't know me. Their eyes stay glued to me as if I'm a stranger in their world.

I feel like a stranger. Like I don't belong. Like I'm supposed to be dead.

Then a crazy thought hits. They all knew Eric. They all loved Eric. What they don't know is I have his heart. That I'm alive because he's dead.

Thank God they don't know.

A couple of times, I look down and just stare at my black boots moving, but I don't want to appear weak or like a dweeb. So I lift my chin, exist in their stares, meet their gazes, keep walking. *Thank God they don't know.*

I feel their gazes crowding me. Eric was their hero. I'm not sure I'm worthy to have a hero's heart. I want to run, run away. *Please God, don't ever let them find out.*

I turn the corner and spot the office. I breathe easier. I lift the backpack higher on my shoulder and open the door.

I hate carrying the backpack. It reminds me of the one I had to carry for almost six months.

There are two people talking to the office staff behind the desk. Another five or six students stand around as if waiting for something. Several have their backs to me, and I don't have a clue who they are. I stand still and wait for my turn.

Then I recognize one of the ladies behind the desk: Ms. Clarkson. She was always nice. She liked to read and thought it was cool when I started a book club. She even helped us raise money so the students who couldn't afford to buy the book still got one. She was also the one I spoke to about the classes I wanted when I called a couple of weeks ago.

She glances up and our eyes meet. I don't think she recognizes me. Have I changed that much? Then she smiles and does a tiny wiggle-like happy dance.

"I'm so glad you're back," she says loud enough for the whole room to hear.

Everyone looks at me. I force myself to smile but wonder why she couldn't have waited to tell me that personally.

One of the girls looks at me really hard then gasps. I recognize her too. Lisa Porter. The bully who tried to make my life miserable for so many years. The girl who nearly pushed me out of the locker room while I was changing so everyone would get a sneak peek of my boobs.

I'm glad I'm done with PE. If she tried that trick now and exposed my scars, I . . . I don't know what I'd do. But it wouldn't be nothing.

She moves closer. "I thought you were dead."

I'm stunned at her rudeness. Old Leah would just look away, ignore her because she's an idiot. But I sense that my silence gave her some of my power. I don't have enough power to share.

Then I feel it. My backbone. I lean in and toss out the only thing I can come up with, "Are you sure I'm not?" I manage to make my voice sound spooky.

I didn't speak nearly as loudly as she did, but people must have heard because they chuckle. Lisa blinks, frowns, and mutters something under her breath and walks out. She probably called me a book dork. That had been her nickname for me since I started the book club. I pull my phone out and pretend to be enthralled. Pretend I don't feel the others staring at me.

"Leah?" I look up. "Come on back?" Ms. Clarkson pushes open the half door for me to walk through.

I sit down with my new counselor, Ms. Milina, to get my schedule, my locker info. She also wants an update on my health. I pretend I don't hate talking about it—pretend I don't see the pity in her eyes. But I stop pretending so hard when she tells me they've reserved a scooter for me to get from class to class. I nix that idea really fast. She backs down graciously. Then I go straight to the nurse to drop off my pills. Mom's already faxed the info.

In and out. One less thing to do.

As I walk to find locker 169, there're students everywhere. I ignore the looks. A couple of times I hear my name and the words "heart transplant." It makes me feel like a freak.

Classes should start in fifteen minutes. I keep a lookout for Brandy or Matt. The only two people I want to see.

I'd spoken to both of them three times over the weekend. Both offered to meet somewhere, but I didn't have a clue where I needed to be, so I suggested we just find each other. Now I wish I hadn't.

Then again, I need to do this on my own. I can't depend on others to just walk down a hall. I may not completely know who

I am, but I've never been overly needy. Hey, I've had my chest cracked open twice. I'm no coward.

I find my locker and stand in front of it, like it's my friend. I finally take the time to check out my schedule, then stuff what I don't need for the first two classes into my locker. The hall noise is loud, people talking, lockers being opened and banged close.

The chorus of noises plays around me like a symphony. I look around and again I wonder why I wanted to come back.

I shut my locker when I hear a familiar voice. "Hey, you."

Finally, I think, and turn around to find a someone I wanted to find.

I visit with Brandy for about three minutes. We share our schedules, and I draw strength from knowing I'm not completely alone.

When she walks away, I take a deep breath and head for science. I'm almost there when I see Matt. My heart does a double cartwheel and I smile. I start toward him. His name's on my lips; then I see he's not alone. He's with a blonde. A beautiful blonde. They're talking, no, whispering, leaning against a wall.

Considering how close they are, it's a private conversation. Emotion shrinks my chest.

I recognize the girl. Don't know her name, but I know she's a cheerleader. Then I recognize more than her face. Much more. I also recognize the emotion taking up residence in my heart. Jealousy.

In a blink, it occurs to me that the blonde is probably Marissa. The conversation they are having might be all about Cassie and not about hooking up.

I give myself a good swift mental kick in the ass and hotfoot it to class. But, damn it, even rationalizing that it's Marissa, the jealousy yanks at my heartstrings. For good reason, of course.

The girl is gorgeous. She is totally in Matt Kenner's league. And she is wearing the same sweater that I am, except in red, but she doesn't have a camisole.

She doesn't have scars.

Matt walks the halls looking for Leah. He doesn't find her. But he finds Marissa. He called her three times over the weekend. He wants answers, so he pulls her to the side of the hall for a chat.

"Okay, one more time. I don't know anything," Marissa says. "Hell, I didn't even know Cassie was back. She's dropped me. It's like we were never friends."

"Why? Why would she do that?" Matt asks.

"Because she loved Eric and he died." She frowns. "Well, it can't just be that. She started pulling away a couple of months before. But I blamed it on her and Eric breaking up."

Matt takes in her every word. "But the breakup wasn't Eric's idea. Why did she break up with him?"

"Don't know," she says. "She told me she needed space. But she never told me why. That's when she started acting . . . different. I thought it was that guy?"

"What guy?" Matt asks.

"James or Jake, starts with J. He drove a motorcycle, had tattoos, older, like twenty-one. Dark hair and a bad-boy look. He had a thing for Cassie. His family moved next door to her."

"When was this happening?"

"Before she and Eric broke up. I'm not saying she cheated on him. I don't know if they went out. All I know is before Eric and her broke up, that guy was showing up."

"Why didn't you tell Eric?" Matt's frustration feels like thunder in his chest.

"Because I'm Cassie's friend. Or was. And it seemed harmless. Yes, it made Cassie happy that an older guy was hitting on her, but she said she loved Eric. Later, when she told him about needing space, I thought it was that guy."

Matt grits his teeth so tight he feels they might crack. "When Detective Henderson talked to you, did you tell him this?"

"No, that was like five months before Eric killed . . ." She stumbles then rephrases. "Before he died."

Matt's frustration thunders louder. They knew Eric. How could they believe he'd kill himself?

"Can't you see that this guy was probably pissed when Cassie went back to Eric? He had a motive to kill Eric!"

Marissa blinks. "How would he have gotten your dad's gun?"

"Maybe Eric got the gun because he was afraid of this guy. Then maybe the guy got the gun and used it on Eric."

Pity fills her eyes. "That's a lot of maybes."

He swallows. "Is Cassie here today?"

"I haven't seen her."

The tardy bell rings. Damn it, he needs to get to class, and he hasn't even found Leah yet. "Will you call me if you remember anything else? And stop avoiding my calls?"

She sighs. "Take me out Friday. We can talk then."

Hell no! "I can't . . . It's not like that between us."

"It could be. We had a good time when we went out, didn't we?"

No. "Yeah. But I just need your help figuring things out. Please."

"Fine," she says in a tone that sounds like she thinks it's really less than fine, and takes off.

Fighting oncoming hall traffic—fighting the frustration simmering in his gut—he hurries to his first period. Suddenly really needing to see Leah, he claims a corner in the hall to text her. *Didn't find you. Where are you?*

She doesn't answer. Walking into his class, his gaze searches for a dark-haired girl that makes him feel whole, that pushes the darkness he feels farther back inside him.

She's not there. Voices bounce around the room. Mr. Muller, a teacher he had last year, is straightening his desk.

Matt suddenly doesn't just want to see Leah, he needs to. He needs the calm Leah offers him.

He almost shoots out of class but spots Brandy, Leah's friend.

There's an empty seat next to her. He claims it and leans in. "Have you seen Leah?"

Her eyes widen as if surprised he spoke to her. "Briefly."

"Do you know her schedule?"

"I glanced at it. She has science first period, and we have English together fourth period. Mr. Applegate's class."

He pulls his schedule from his pocket and unfolds it. Since he hadn't kept up with his AP classes, they'd rearranged his schedule. "Who's her first-period teacher?"

"Whitney." Brandy glances at his schedule. "You have the same schedule as me, except English."

"Are you in any of her other classes?"

"Just English."

"Shit." He wads the schedule in his hand.

"Can I say something?" Her tone is cautious.

"Yeah."

"Don't hurt Leah. She's been through enough."

His shoulders harden defensively. "I don't plan on it."

She leans closer. "Don't forget that if you break her heart, you're breaking Eric's."

Air hiccups in his chest. *Leah told Brandy?* He knows girls talk. He's not upset, just surprised.

"Okay." Mr. Muller's voice echoes above the chatter.

Matt pops up and heads for the door.

"Matt?" Mr. Muller calls out.

Matt turns but keeps walking backward. "I remembered I'm supposed to check in with the office about something."

"Can't it wait?"

"No, sir." Shooting around, he darts out.

21

I'm halfway through science, taking notes, when a girl walks in. She moves over to Ms. Whitney and whispers some important message worthy of class disruption.

Ms. Whitney looks up. I swear she zeroes in on me.

It can't be about me. I'm just feeling paranoid. About school. About Matt. About my scar. But I got a text from Matt. Unfortunately, I was already in class and didn't want to risk having my phone taken away. But as soon as class is over . . .

The girl walks out. Ms. Whitney starts down the aisle.

My aisle.

Could it be about my pills? I check the clock on the wall. It's not even eight. I take them at nine.

Ms. Whitney stops beside me. "You're needed in the office."

"Why?" I ask, then wish I hadn't, because everyone's listening.

"I'm not sure. Probably nothing."

You don't get called into the office for nothing. I walk out with my books, my pen, and a backpack full of fear. I'm shaking. I've never been called to the office before. Book dorks and blatant book geeks are good kids.

I walk the green mile to the office. Ms. Clarkson smiles at me.

I ease up to the counter. "Is something wrong?"

"No. Ms. Milina, your counselor, wants to speak to you again."

Crap. I hope this isn't about the scooter.

Her door's open. I still stop outside of it.

"Come in." Her voice flows out.

I ease in. Should I close the door? Then not wanting anyone to eavesdrop, I shut it. "What's wrong?"

"Nothing." She motions to the chair. "Do you know Matt Kenner?"

Air catches in my throat. I plop into the chair.

She leans in. "I hear you two have a . . . special connection."

My knot of nerves starts to unravel in my stomach. She knows? Shit shit shit!

But—I breathe in, I breathe out—how could she know?

She's staring at me. I manage to nod.

"Matt stopped by earlier. He mentioned that . . ." She's speaking slowly. I wish I could yank the words out. But then maybe I'm not ready to hear them. I'm not ready for the world to know. They'll blame me . . .

Because deep down, where I don't like to go emotionally, I blame myself. Not for his death, but for benefiting from it. Part of me wonders how Matt doesn't blame me.

"Matt made a request. I wanted to confirm it was okay with you."

I shift in my seat. The chair scrapes across the wood floor. "A request?"

"He said he's been helping you study."

"Yes. He is." The tension holding my spine hostage releases.

"He requested to be moved into your classes."

He did? *Oh shit! Good shit.* I probably shouldn't smile, at least not this big, but I can't stop myself. Matt Kenner wants to be in my class.

"I wanted to check with you first."

"It would be so helpful if that's possible."

"I can only get him into your math and science classes."

"Those are the subjects I'll need the most help with," I tell her.

She leans back. Her chair squeaks. "The schedule will start tomorrow." She pauses. "I normally don't grant this kind of a request, but Matt made it clear that you two have had a rough year and because of it you've bonded."

My smile goes bigger. *Matt thinks we bonded. Bonded.*

The moment I'm out of the office, I grab my phone to text Matt. I don't know what to say. I hesitate, then write. "Science and math with you. Awesome."

I get a text right back. *I agree. When do you have lunch?*

I text back *11:40.*

Me too. Meet me by C entrance. I've learned something about Eric.

I text back *OK* and float back to my class, happier than I probably have a right to be.

I don't find Matt during the next bell, but there's no time to look since we only have six minutes between classes. The bubble of happiness follows me as I move into history and go straight to Mr. Perez's desk. I stand close enough to not be heard by the students piling into the classroom. He's staring at his phone.

Feeling awkward, I clear my throat so he'll notice me. He looks up. His frown's chiseled so firmly in his face, I step back.

"I want to let you know I'll be going to the nurse's office to take medicine at nine."

"No. You can take them after class. Now be seated so we can start." His words blast out, and I feel everyone's stares stick to me like gum on the bottom of a desk. My happy bubble pops.

I'm stunned. I don't move. I assumed the teachers would've been notified. "I'm sorry, but I have to take them at nine."

"What's your name?" His voice booms out, gathering more stares. I'm in the limelight, and I want to fade to nothing.

"Leah McKenzie." My name scrapes out of my tight throat. I've never felt more uncomfortable in my own skin.

"Well, Miss McKenzie," says with disdain. "I'm positive taking a pill twenty minutes late isn't going to kill you. Now be seated."

But it can. Just ask the transplant team. "Sir, I—"

His thick, hairy brows knit together. "Sit down!" He yanks papers from a briefcase and addresses the class: "The first day back, and I already know who's going to be trouble."

My face goes hot. I'm shifting from embarrassment to anger. This, being here with Eric's heart, is all so damn hard. I don't need this. I don't need a rude, obnoxious asswipe throwing verbal darts at me. My sinuses sting, but I'll die before I cry.

When he realizes I haven't moved, he scowls up again. Anger fattens his face. I don't think it's even aimed at me. He's just one of those angry souls, and I happen to be his target. I'm tired of being someone's target.

"Are you hard of hearing? Sit down!" he orders.

Several rude responses tickle my tongue, but I can't push them out. I don't move either.

"Seriously?" He slaps a hand on his desk. "You really want me to send you to the office on the first day back to school."

Old Leah wouldn't stand here. Old Leah would've already been in her seat. I'm not Old Leah. I tilt my chin up.

"Yes, sir. Please send me to the office." My words are polite. The sharp edge of my tone isn't.

"Go." He orders me like a dog.

I'm not out of the room before I hear someone say, "Perez, you know she has a dead heart, don't you?"

Another student counters, "It's not dead. It came from a dead person."

"She's practically a zombie," another says.

I bolt out. My chest hurts. The damn knot in my throat doubles.

I don't go to the office. I go to the front exit. I don't want to be here. I shove the door open. Cold winter wind washes over me. It feels good. I'm hot. I'm angry. I'm so pissed that this is my life.

That some effing virus took everything away from me.

What did I do to deserve this?

I stand right outside the door. The wind scatters my dark hair on my face.

Staring at the parking lot, I see my car. It's calling me. Tempting me.

I could go home. My keys are in my pocket. But if I leave, I won't come back.

I have to come back. I have to. I have two classes with Matt.

I grip my fists. I'm not leaving, but I'm not ready to face anyone. I move away from the door, slink behind some bushes, and lean against the rough redbrick building. It's where I used to wait on Mom after school. A hidden place I could read and go unnoticed. It hits me then. That's what Old Leah always did. Old Leah really didn't like school any more than New Leah. I've spent all of my school life staying out of everyone's way.

I stand there, angry that I don't feel like I'm enough. I breathe in. I breathe out. In, one-two-three. Out one-two-three. Time ticks past. One minute, two, three.

Ten.

I'm almost calm enough to go to the office when a white car pulls up.

I shift to the right so I can't be seen, hoping Mr. Perez hasn't called the office and announced I'm MIA.

A girl gets out of the car. My chest instantly grows heavy. At first I don't recognize her. Then I do. "Cassie."

She looks bad. Her mascara's smeared. Her face is red. Her hair's a mess.

What's wrong with her?

I flatten myself against the brick wall. My heart swells with emotion. Some of it's mine. Most of it's not.

I hear a slight buzz and see the passenger-side window lower.

"Cassie! I love you," the woman in the car says. I can't see her, but I recognize her mom's voice, from the time I visited her house. "Go to the bathroom and clean your face, okay?"

"Go to hell!" Cassie storms back to the vehicle. She hits the passenger door. "I can't believe you're making me do this. Do you love him more than me?"

Love who *more?* I remember Matt telling me Ms. Chambers is engaged.

"You have to go to school!" she snaps. "Go. I called and they're expecting you."

The window goes up. The car drives off.

Cassie stands there looking defeated, alone, in pain. I want to step out and offer her comfort, but something tells me she wouldn't want it. I wouldn't want someone seeing me after a meltdown.

I hear a sad sound leak from Cassie's lips; then she darts to the school doors. But she doesn't go in. She stands there, as if debating something.

Then, almost as if she feels me looking at her, she glances around. After a moment, she hitches her purse on her shoulder and walks away.

Away from the door.

Away from the school.

Away from what her mother told her to do.

I watch her cross the street before I walk back inside.

Funny how when you see someone else hurting, you stop

feeling sorry for yourself. Or maybe it's my heart, Eric's heart. He cares more about Cassie than me.

But as I get closer to the office, I return to my own problem. I'm being sent to the principal's office.

I've done nothing wrong. But it doesn't matter. Life is one big effing virus.

When I step into the office, Ms. Clarkson sighs. "We were so worried."

Principal Burns rushes out from the back. "Have we found her?"

I know "her" is me. I'm in all kinds of trouble now.

"She just walked in," Ms. Clarkson says.

Relief flashes across his chubby face. I remember the catch-phrase all the kids used to say. *Get in trouble at school, and you'll feel the Burn.*

"Come on back." His tone is direct, maybe even angry.

My palms go suddenly slick. I follow him.

I already feel the Burn.

22

Burns settles behind a big dark wooden desk that looks intimidating. His office is decorated in browns and blacks.

I settle in one of the leather chairs across from his desk and take in a deep breath. I swear I smell fear. Maybe my own, or maybe all of the students' before me.

Our gazes meet. My heart thumps.

"I want to apologize," Mr. Burns says.

Did I misunderstand? "Huh?"

He repeats himself and settles back in the chair. A pudgy guy in a not-so-pudgy chair.

"We sent the e-mail to your teachers about your condition."

My condition?

"Somehow Mr. Perez wasn't on that list. Ms. Clarkson explained it to him. This won't happen again."

Maybe I'm not going to feel the Burn.

"However, if anything like this happens again, you should explain it to the teacher instead of showing a temper."

A temper? It's a slap on the wrist. Not even a hard one, but it stings.

My phone alarm goes off. It's 8:55. His brow pinches.

"Time for my pills," I say.

"Of course. Go." He smiles as if everything's fine.

But I'm still stinging. I get to the door. I pause.

Keep going. Keep going. I tell myself . . . I wasn't punished. I should let it go. Old Leah would let it go.

I'm not her anymore.

I turn around. He's focused on his computer.

"Mr. Burns."

He glances up.

"I tried to tell Mr. Perez. Every time I opened my mouth, he interrupted me and ordered me to sit down. Then he announced loud enough for everyone to hear that he could already tell who the troublemakers were going to be."

Mr. Burns open his mouth to speak, but I continues. "Mr. Perez was rude. I didn't deserve that. Not because of my condition. Every student here deserves respect. It's him you need to have a talk with. It's him who showed his temper and his ass."

I walk out. *Did I just say "ass" to the principal?*

My chin remains high. I'm fretting and smiling on the inside. I'm proud of myself. I kind of like New Leah's approach.

I glance down at my chest. My boobs might be bigger, but that's not the only thing that grew. Somehow I managed to grow me a pair of balls.

I don't see Matt until I'm heading into English. I'm running late because my locker is on the other side of the school. Our eyes meet. There are five students between us. He barrels through them, catches my hand, and pulls me out of the hall traffic.

"Hey." His smile is wowing. His hand is warm. His touch welcomed.

His gaze whispers up and down me. Not indecently, just an appreciative glance. "You look good."

"Thanks." I try not to think about the blonde wearing the same sweater. His thumb moves in slow circles across the top of my hand.

"I can't believe you got Ms. Milina to change your classes," I say.

His smile reaches his eyes. "It means we're really going to have to study together."

"Shit," I say, joking.

The bell rings. I want to ignore it. I want to be with him—forget school. But New Leah still follows rules.

"I should go. But I'll see you during lunch."

"Yeah. He still hasn't let go of my hand. He looks around, leans in, and presses his lips to mine. It's brief, but beautiful.

He hurries off. I don't. My knees are jelly. It's a first. The first kiss I've ever gotten at school. It feels special. Forbidden.

It makes all the bad parts of today feel smaller. Tolerable.

I remember the bell has rung and force myself to move.

I walk into room 12. Thankfully, two other students move with me, so I don't feel late. Brandy waves to an empty seat beside her. Trent is on the other side of the room.

I saw him once in the hall, but I didn't think he saw me, so I ducked behind a group of girls and moved past him.

Now he sees me. He's checking me out and looking sad. I don't like being the reason someone has sad eyes. But I don't dislike it enough to go back to him.

Sandy and LeAnn wave.

Carlos lets go of a whistle. "Looking good, Leah."

I smile. He's such a flirt. Always has been. But he never means anything by it. I claim the desk beside Brandy.

She leans in. "How's everything?"

I think of the kiss. "Great." I almost texted her about the whole Perez issue, then decided to explain it later. Now I'm in too good of a mood to spoil it.

She leans closer. "Does a certain dark-haired hunk have anything to do with that?"

"Maybe." A smile bubbles out of me.

She grins. "Matt said he changed his schedule to be in your classes. He's so into you."

I love hearing that, but I'm shocked. "You've seen him?"

"I have four . . . I had four classes with him before he changed them. He sat beside me. You should have seen the looks on the snooty girls' faces."

I like that Matt's being nice to my best friend. I realize I should do the same with his friends. Problem is, I don't know them well enough to be nice to them.

"Oh. Mr. Applegate agreed that the book club can meet in here during lunch. So we'll grab food and eat in here."

I shake my head. "I can't. I'm meeting Matt for lunch."

Brandy makes a face. "Hmm . . . a hot guy or the book club? Good choice."

"Thanks."

"But I should warn you. If you're not here, you won't get a say on the next six books we read."

"I'll pick something later." I've gotten good at speaking up.

"No. It's a rule. People who don't show for the first meeting don't get to vote."

"Who set those rules?" I'm again questioning if I want to be in the book club.

"Sandy and LeAnn." Brandy's voice lowers.

"Well, since I don't know the rules, I'll speak up anyway."

She looks at me weird.

"What?" I ask.

"You're different."

I know I am, but I'm curious how she sees me. "How?"

"You used to be quieter, and you always went with the flow. Maybe too much. Now you don't take any crap. I like it."

"Or maybe I grew a pair of balls."

We laugh. And it's not quiet.

"Okay, class." Mr. Applegate stands from his desk. "I see two new students. So let me start by introducing myself. I'm your English teacher, and I'm a book lover." I know I like him.

Forty minutes later, class is dismissed for lunch. I finish putting my books in my backpack, and when I look up I'm surrounded by the book club. Trent included. I'm reminded of how I felt at Brandy's New Year's party. I don't fit.

Sandy speaks up. "Why don't we grab a piece of pizza and hurry back so we can get busy."

I start to answer, but Brandy does it for me. "Leah can't make it today."

"Why?" LeAnn asks.

Brandy always had a way of speaking up for me, and I love her for it, but it suddenly feels wrong. "I'm meeting someone for lunch." I pick up my backpack.

"Who?" Trent asks.

I swallow.

Before I answer, Sandy speaks up. "Don't tell me. It's Matt Kenner?"

I nod.

"Book club comes before boyfriends," LeAnn says.

I almost say he's not my boyfriend. But he kissed me in the hall. Maybe he is my boyfriend. LeAnn's looking at me as if waiting for an answer. But it wasn't a question. I nod goodbye at Brandy and walk off. Right before I'm out, I hear LeAnn say, "She's different."

Matt's where he said he'd be. "Hey." He offers me a shy smile and studies me. I almost think he's worried the kiss upset me.

I smile.

"Let's grab something quick so we can talk," I say. The lunchroom noise is booming. The smell of tuna casserole is thick.

"Yeah." He walks to the pizza counter. "This okay?" He makes a face. "Or do you like tuna casserole?"

Pizza's great, even though I suspect the book club will arrive shortly. But I can't avoid them forever.

We stop in the line. He moves closer. His arm is against mine. Then he ducks his head close to my ear. "How's your first day so far?"

Besides having a little run-in with the school bully, and being sent to the office? "Pretty good." I'm still high from his kiss.

"So you don't feel as if you're wearing someone else's shoes?" He glances down at my boots.

The fact that he remembered what I said means he was really listening. I like that.

"A little, but I'm getting used to them." I put one heel up and turn my ankle.

He glances down. "I hate to say this, but I like the Donald Ducks better."

I grin. "But you haven't seen the Dumbos yet."

He laughs. This close, I hear the different tones in his laugh. Low then high. I love the sound. And every time he laughs, it sounds less rusty.

"How's your day?" I ask.

"It started off bad. But it got better about forty-five minutes ago."

I realize he's talking about the kiss in the hall. I grin. "Funny, that's when my day started uphill too."

The line moves up.

I hear familiar voices and glance around. It's the book club.

Brandy mouths the words "good luck."

Matt starts talking about the classes we'll have together and asks if I met the teachers.

"I haven't had math yet. Ms. Whitney, our science teacher, is okay. But I have Mr. Perez for history. He's an asswipe." My gut tightens.

"Last year he taught eleventh-grade history. Eric had him. He said the same thing."

We get our pizza and drinks and pay. The back of my neck tingles, and I turn around. LeAnn, Sandy, and Trent are staring. Matt and I move away from the counter.

Matt stops and looks around. "I see a couple seats in the back."

We start that way, and I hear someone call out, "Matt, I saved you a seat."

I turn and see it's the table closest to the one big window. The popular kids' table. Where the cheerleaders and jocks sit. The whole school knows it's their table. No one else even tries to sit there. I spot the girl Trent was talking to, the one I think is Marissa. I notice there's more than one seat free. I'd told myself I needed to be nice to his friends, but to sit with them . . . ? Now? Am I ready?

I wait to see what Matt will do, worrying he's going to say he'll catch up with me later.

"Thanks. Next time," Matt calls back.

I let go of the breath I'm holding. I'm ashamed I expected him to drop me in the grease. Then my emotions start zipping everywhere. I don't know if I'm thrilled he wants to be alone with me or bothered that he doesn't want me to sit with his friends.

What is it about school that drains a girl's self-confidence?

We set our trays on the table, away from the others, and settle in. He's sitting so close I feel his leg pressed against mine. It sends all kind of sweet tingles through my body.

He opens his milk. I unscrew the lid off my water bottle and take a sip. People are staring. Probably wondering why a popular boy is sitting with a blatant book geek.

Matt reaches for his pizza. "Can you go with me to walk Lady after school?"

"Yeah. But Mom's going to want to interrogate me about my first day back to school before I leave."

"So how about four?" He takes a bite.

"That's good."

He looks at my untouched pizza. "You'd better eat. Time passes fast."

I pick up my cheese pizza and take a bite. "Hmm," I say, talking around the flavorless food. "I forgot how good school pizza was." I'm being sarcastic. He must get it because he laughs.

"You could have gotten tuna casserole," he says.

I roll my eyes. "Kill me now."

He brushes a finger across my lips.

I reach for the napkin thinking I had sauce on my mouth.

"You're fine." He grins, almost appearing embarrassed, but then he presses the finger he'd had to my lips to his. Something about it is . . . sexy.

I feel the good flutters in my stomach again. I swear, if he tries to kiss me right now, even in front of over two hundred peers, I'd let him.

We stare at each other for several seconds.

He looks down at his pizza. "Can I ask you something?"

He sounds nervous. "Yeah." I take another bite of pizza.

"What's the deal with you and Trent?"

23

I'm caught off guard by the Trent question. "Uh, there's no deal."

He remains silent as if waiting for me finish. Feeling pressure, I push more words out.

"We dated . . . before."

"Before . . . ?"

"We broke up when I got sick."

"What an ass!"

I realize what he assumes. "I broke up with him. Not the other way around."

"Why?"

I shrug. "It didn't seem fair."

"Okay." He pauses. "It still seems he'd have wanted to be there for you."

There was my feeling-sorry-for-myself stage when I went down that lane. When even though I pushed Trent away, it hurt that he didn't push back. But it didn't hurt that much. Truth is, I was hurt more when Matt didn't call.

It's different. I know it is. He'd lost his father and we weren't going out, and I was . . . sick, but . . . I'm scared. Scared he'll realize that even with Eric's heart, I'll never be a hundred percent. And if he walked away once . . .

Damn that stings.

"And now?" Matt asks. "You're not sick anymore."

I kind of am, but you couldn't pay me to say that.

Matt stares at me right in the eyes. "Are you going back with him?"

"No. I . . . don't feel the same way."

"But he does, right?" His words come with a frown.

When I don't answer immediately, Matt continues. "I know, because if looks could kill, I'd be worm bait."

"I'm sorry," I say. "I told him I just wanted to be friends."

"Good." Something like relief softens his eyes. "I don't want to be falling for someone else's girl."

He's falling for me. That giddy feeling returns. I see the opportunity and I go for it. "What about you?"

"Me?"

"Am I falling . . ."

"No. I . . . I haven't dated since . . ." He pushes his pizza around on his plate. "I stopped dating when Dad died. I only went out twice afterward. Eric set me up. I didn't want to go, but Eric could be pushy."

Matt downs a couple more bites of his pizza, then reaches for his milk and takes a big drink. He gets quiet for a few seconds. "Maybe this weekend I can take you out for good pizza? If you're going to be in town."

He's asking me out. He's really asking me out. "I'm not. I mean, I am." He looks confused and so do I. "I'm trying to say . . . I'd like to go out for pizza." My giddiness is at an all-time high.

A burst of laughter rings out. We both look up. It's coming from the popular table.

I see who I think is Marissa standing up, holding out napkins as if something got spilled down the neck of her red sweater. She's dipping the napkin down the front. The front without a camisole.

I try to ignore them and lean a little closer to Matt. "What did you learn about Eric?"

Matt looks at me. "I spoke with Marissa this morning. She said that Cassie had an older guy hitting on her when she was still dating Eric. She said at first she thought that was why she broke up with Eric."

"Did she tell you his name?"

"She said it started with a J. But she said that he and his parents moved in next door to Cassie and he rides a motorcycle and has a tattoo."

I digest what he's saying. "You think he could be the one who shot Eric?"

"Isn't jealousy one of the main motives for murder?"

"Yeah." Chills dance down my spine. I'm reminded this could be dangerous. "Did Marissa say whether Cassie is still seeing him?"

He shakes his head. "She doesn't know. Cassie dropped out of her life."

"That's weird." I watch him eat the last of his pizza.

"Really weird." He exhales. "Now I don't know if I should go to Detective Henderson with what I know or if he'll just say it doesn't matter."

Surely he didn't plan to approach this guy alone. "Didn't you tell me he said you could come to him if you found something?"

"He said solid evidence."

"This is solid."

He nods. "I think I'll check and see if the guy still lives there first. If I send the detective there and the guy doesn't even live there now, he'll think I'm crazy. And he'll never listen to me again."

I touch his arm. "You aren't crazy. But how are you going to check? Didn't the detective tell you to stay away from the Chambers?"

"I'm not going to the Chambers. I'm going next door."

I shake my head. "I don't like that idea. If this guy did this, he's going to recognize you." Suddenly I'm less afraid for me and more for him. "I should do it. He won't know me. I could pretend to sell magazines or something and—"

"Right?" He smirks. "I'm going to let you go talk to a guy who may have killed my brother."

I lift my brow. "Then just tell the detective."

Determination tightens his eyes. "I don't have to talk to this guy. Just make sure he still lives there. Just sit in the car and see if he shows up or see if there's a motorcycle there."

I shake my head. "I still don't like it."

He tucks a strand of my hair behind my ear. I swear I can feel his finger print sliding across my cheek. "I promise to be safe. But the fact you care makes me feel good." He smiles.

I frown.

Keep frowning even when his touch makes my skin feel electric and his smile makes me melt inside. I. Do. Not. Like. This.

Then I remember what I needed to tell him. "I saw Cassie this morning."

"She's here? I've been looking for her and haven't seen her."

I tell him about the car pulling up and about what Cassie said to her mom. Though I skip telling him the reason I was outside. Any mention of pills makes me sound . . . sick.

"She was upset," I say. "She didn't even go into the school."

He shakes his head. *Do you love him more than me?* " Matt repeats what I told him Cassie said to her mom. "She has to be talking about the fiancé."

"That's what I thought." I sigh. "She looked like a victim, Matt, not like a villain."

His brown eyes darken. "Victim or not, if she knows some-thing and isn't saying anything, then she's guilty." He sounds angry. Not at me, but at Cassie. And whoever killed his brother. I don't blame him for feeling it, but I've been told over and over again, anger isn't good for your heart.

A couple of kids come and sit down at the table. I can tell from his expression that we're changing the subject.

He picks up my pizza and holds it to my mouth. I chuckle. I take a tiny bite, then push it away. "I'm done."

He finishes it off. Call me silly, but I like seeing him eat my food. It's . . . as if we're somehow closer because of it. My par-ents do it. Mom will eat all her fries and sneak Dad's. He always teases her. She kisses the complaint out of him.

I'm tempted to complain, hoping Matt will kiss me.

Sitting there in the lunchroom filled with clinking forks, chatter, and unidentifiable lunch smells, we talk about Lady, about working out a study schedule, about small things.

I like talking about small things. It makes me feel as if he's falling for me because of me.

Not because I'm helping him out.

Not because I believe him.

Not because I have Eric's heart.

"So?" my mom tosses the one-word question out the second my feet cross the threshold. She pulls me into the kitchen.

I should have already figured out what to say. But on the way home all I thought about was Matt.

I look at Mom. Would she freak if I told her Matt kissed me in the hall? I think she's still on her germ-phobia mode. Should I inform her what an asswipe my history teacher was? Tell her if it wasn't for Matt, I'd be begging to go back to home-schooling.

Decisions. Decisions. I drop my backpack on the table.

"Well?" she asks.

"It was bad and good." I reach for a peanut butter cookie. It's so warm it breaks apart in my hand.

"Thank you," I say. I'll bet I'm the only senior who has homemade cookies today. I lucked out on parents. Too bad they can't say the same thing. They deserved a healthy kid. Grand-kids. *Sorry, Mom.*

"So spill." Mom pours me milk. "Did you attend the book club?"

"No. They held the meeting at lunch. And Matt has the same lunch as I do and I wanted to visit with him."

Her eyes widen. "Boys over book club?" she asks, remind-ing me of what LeAnn said. "What have you done to my daughter?"

I almost tell her I don't have an effing clue where she is. I'd be freaking if I wasn't so excited about seeing Matt. "LeAnn and Sandy have taken over the book club. It feels different."

"Give it some time." She sighs with mama sympathy. "Did you get everything solved with your history teacher?"

I choke, grab the milk, and swallow. "How . . . ?"

"Mr. Burns called me. He wasn't happy with the teacher. He assured me that it wouldn't happen again. He also said if you felt the need to move out of his class, he could arrange that.

My first thought is hallelujah. My second: it might mess up Matt and I being in the same class. Third: I didn't like the prin-cipal calling my mom.

"No, I'm fine," I push out.

"Tell me about the other good stuff," she says.

"I really like Matt." I smile. "I like my English teacher."

"Good." She rests a warm hand on my arm. "I missed you today."

Crap. Now I'm going to feel bad about leaving. I grab an-other cookie and it hits me then. When I got sick, my world got so small, but so did my mother's. I can't remember when she's gone to lunch with a friend. Or gone for a pedicure. How unfair is that?

"I've been thinking," I say. "You need to go back to work."

She lifts a brow. "That's odd. My old boss called today asking me to come back part-time."

"Say yes, Mom." I remember thinking I needed to cut the apron strings, and I realize that so does my mom. She's got to learn to live again too.

"I'm considering it."

"Mom. You quit a job to take care of me. And I'm fine now. Get back to your life." Guilt makes my words heavy.

Tears fill her eyes, and it's contagious. My own grow wet.

She blinks. "You and your dad are my life."

"Your other life then." The one you loved before I stole it from you. I see the clock on the wall. I hug her. She smells like cookies and love. But I still want to be with Matt. "Matt will be here soon. We're walking Lady and I want to change clothes."

"Are you not too tired?"

Am I tired? A little, but . . . "I'm fine." I stand up.

"At least take your blood pressure."

I start to argue. I'm only required to do it morning and night. And that only for another week. But to make her happy, I nod.

Then I remember, "Oh, Matt asked me out for the weekend. Since Dad's met him, I'm assuming it'll be okay."

She doesn't look thrilled. "Your doctor's appointment is on Friday."

"No. I shouldn't have to see Dr. Hughes for another month."

"Not Dr. Hughes. The gynecologist."

"Oh." My face heats up because I know Mom's thinking about Matt and I having sex.

I hotfoot it to my bedroom, dragging my embarrassment with me. Not that I haven't thought about us having sex. Well,

I start to think about it, but when the thought leads to me taking my clothes off, all I can think about is Brandy gasping.

And Matt not being able to look at me.

After school, Matt had walked Leah to her car. He'd hoped to steal another kiss, but people were everywhere and the moment wasn't right.

So he squeezed her hand and told her he'd see her at four.

As soon as she drove off, he texted his mom saying he was going to hang at school and would be home a little before four to take Lady for a walk.

It wasn't a complete lie. He's hanging. Just not at school.

He remembers Leah telling him he shouldn't come here. But he's not doing anything stupid. And he's not going to be here that long. All day he keeps seeing Leah's face when he kissed her in the hall. She looked surprised and so damn sexy.

He's parked across the street, where he can have a good view of both houses flanking the Chambers's house.

There's no motorcycle out front. As a matter of fact, there's nothing happening at any of the houses, not even Cassie's.

Finally, a jeep pulls into the driveway of the house to the right. Matt scrunches down in the seat, hoping a guy with dark hair and tattoos gets out.

But a woman, blond, steps out. And from the backseat emerge two blond girls.

He looks at the house on the other side of Cassie's. Just because this family doesn't match the guy's description doesn't mean he doesn't live there. But Matt notices the woman looks too young to have an older kid.

He's there for another thirty minutes. No one shows up. No motorcycle, no dark-haired guy with tattoos. Unexpectedly, Matt's chest grips. His frustration rises.

"Eric?" He says the name as if he half expects him to answer.

His skin tightens, as if someone's watching him.

Slinking in the seat, he peers at the houses to see if anyone is staring out. He doesn't see anything.

He wonders if Cassie is home. It's tempting to knock on her door.

The more he thinks about this tattooed guy, the more he feels he's on to something. Eric and Cassie hadn't been back together long when Eric died. This guy probably saw Eric picking Cassie up, got pissed, and . . . murdered him.

The hair on the back of his neck tickles as if someone is breathing down it. Looking over his shoulder, expecting . . . Hell, he doesn't know what he expects. Then he sees her.

She's walking down the street. He inhales. She gets to her yard. He gets out of the car.

"Cassie?"

She turns, shakes her head no, and starts to the front door.

He rushes over as she's trying to unlock the door. "Just talk to me."

"Leave!" she yells at him.

"Please . . ."

"Leave!" She bolts in and slams the door.

Frustrated, he clenches his jaw and swings around. Air catches in his lungs when he sees the cop car in Cassie's driveway with a cop inside. Officer Yates. Breath held, Matt goes to his car, gets in, and focuses on the rearview mirror. Is he going to be arrested? He supposes they could nail him for harassment, maybe even stalking. Which was frustrating because he was just trying to talk to someone.

Matt sinks into the seat. Still staring in the mirror. The officer gets out of his car. The sound of blood gushing in Matt's ears is so loud he can't think. He can't breathe.

When he looks in the side mirrors, the police officer has stopped but is pulling out his phone. And he's staring at Matt's car.

Matt's hands shake, but he finally realizes no one has said he can't leave. Matt starts his car and drives off.

But he can't help wondering if the officer was going to call Detective Henderson.

Eric, what the hell do you want me to do?

24

I no sooner get into my pink bedroom than Brandy calls. I tell her what Lisa said to me about thinking I was dead and what I said back. Brandy laughs her ass off.

I tell her about Mr. Perez. About getting sent to the office and what I told Mr. Burns before I walked out.

"Okay, it's official," she says. "You definitely grew a pair of balls."

I tell her about Matt kissing me in the hallway.

She squeals and says, "Next thing I know you'll be going to third base in the art-supplies closet."

"The art supply closet?" I've never taken art. But Brandy has. "Is that where you and Brian go?"

She doesn't answer but doesn't deny it.

I ask about how things went in book club. I listen but still manage to think about Matt and find myself wishing I took art.

Eventually, she tells me about her day. Her conversation moves into how she and Brian are making plans to spend the whole weekend together when her parents are going away. I hear the excitement in her voice. I wonder what it would feel like to sleep with Matt. Not have sex—I've already wondered about that—just sleep next to him, to use his shoulder as my pillow. To feel myself wrapped in his arms.

Brandy doesn't ask about my dreams or any of the Eric stuff. Which probably means she still doesn't believe me. It stings, but I love her anyway.

How could I not? She could've dropped me in the grease and found a new best friend who wasn't dying.

I look at my pink clock. "Shit. I gotta go. Matt's supposed to be here."

I take my blood pressure. It's ten points high, but I was in a rush and thinking about Matt. I run into my bathroom, put on powder, blush, and lip gloss. I look at my messy hair, moan, and put it up. Ponytail in place, I dig through my closet for my new long-sleeved burgundy shirt and matching hoodie. I remember I'd worn it over the weekend.

I tear off to the laundry room to see if Mom washed it. It's in the dryer. Still warm.

I ditch the blue sweater. Yank the static-electrified T and hoodie from the dryer, and put them on.

I'm still dressing when the doorbell rings. I fit my arm in the hoodie, grab my purse, and run out.

Mom, phone to her ear, comes to the kitchen opening. She offers me a wave and returns to the kitchen and her conversation.

I open the door.

Matt's there. He wears the same thing he wore to school, but he gives me a quick once-over.

Approval lights up his eyes. I like approval.

"Where's Lady?"

"In the car. I didn't know if I had to come in, and I'm not in the mood to pick up shit in your house again."

I laugh. We head out. I feel him staring, but when I glance at him, he looks away.

When we get in the car, I drop my purse to the floorboard. Lady tries to get in the front seat. Matt tells her no.

"Uh . . ." Matt's looking at me strangely again. Almost smiling. Almost not.

"What?" I ask.

"You have . . . something stuck to the back of your jacket."

"What?" I look over my right shoulder.

"Here." He reaches behind my left shoulder and pulls off a wispy piece of material.

It takes me one second to recognize my new lacy wine-colored panties. The static must've gotten them caught on my hoodie.

Time freezes. I have options. I can be humiliated or I can make light of it.

I go with the latter. Before I know what I'm saying, the words slip out. "I was looking for those."

A deep belly laugh escapes his lips. His eyes light up in a sexy I-just-saw-your-panties kind of way.

I reach for them. "This isn't finders keepers?" His tone's packed with tease.

"No. And why would you want to keep my mom's underwear?"

He looks mortified, drops the garment in my lap, and this time I'm the one laughing.

I stuff them in my purse.

When I look back, Matt's leaning over the console. He kisses me. It's soft. It's hard. It's powerful. It's tender.

I melt. I want this. I want more than this.

"Wow," I manage to say when he pulls back.

He brushes a finger over my lips. "I guess your mom's underwear really does it for me."

We both crack up laughing.

"They aren't hers," I say.

"I know." He taps my lips with his index finger, playfully.

He's still close. His eyes are wide, filled with heat. They're brown but have green and gold flecks that I want to study. What really catches my attention is what I don't see. No pity. No pain. No grief.

I want to take credit for the last two—to believe I'm helping him. I know he's never going to stop missing Eric or his dad. I haven't really stopped missing Grandma, but there's missing and then there's missing—the kind that eats at your soul.

He drives to the park. We walk down the trail and talk about school. Matt alternately has his arm around my waist, or he's holding my hand.

We end up back at our bench. Funny how we've only been here twice, but it feels like it's ours. Our place. As if it knows us. As if the trees, the ground, and the wooden bench preserve our memory. The story of us lives here.

He ties Lady to the arm of the bench. She drops to the ground in a drowsy puppy pose. Her sweet yellow face rests on her paws, and her sad, sleepy eyes glance up at me.

Matt puts his arm around me as if to keep me warm. It's not as cold as it was earlier. I think it's just an excuse to be close. But I'll take any excuse he comes up with.

I lean my head on his shoulder.

We stay like that for several moments. Birds flutter above, some little creature scurries below. The lightest breeze whispers through the trees. And inside me is another echo. An echo of happiness. I'm happy. New Leah is happy.

I want to remember this. Always.

I sit up. "You mind if I take some pictures?"

"No," he says. I take a few shots of the two of us, and Matt and Lady. "Send them to me."

I do. After a second, we're back to snuggling.

"I had classes with Brandy today," he says.

I don't look at him, just answer. "She told me."

"She gave me a talking-to about treating you right."

"Sorry. She's a good friend. A little protective."

"What surprised me was she knew about you having Eric's heart."

I sit up. I look at his eyes and it's back. The pain. "Yeah. I was . . . freaked, and needed someone to talk to. I hope you don't mind."

"No, I was just surprised." He hesitates. "Did you tell her about the dreams?"

"Yeah."

"What did she say?"

I debate skirting around the truth. I don't want Matt upset with Brandy. But I'm already skirting around so much with Matt. "She thinks we're dealing with a lot of crap and are confused."

"So she doesn't believe you." His tone sounds apologetic.

"It *is* kind of hard to believe."

He exhales. "Sometimes I want to tell Mom or even Detective Henderson, but it's like saying I'm seeing ghosts. But it's him, Leah. Just today I felt . . . him. It's like recognizing a part of myself."

"I believe you."

We sit there in silence, until he glances at me. "Have you told your parents?"

"They know I've had dreams, but they don't know anything else." I remember something that might make him feel better. "I've read stories about identical twins having that connection. And there's a lot of transplant patients who experience this. So it's not just us."

He nods and in few second asks, "Have you told your parents that you got Eric's heart?"

"No. I'm . . . afraid they'll make a big deal out of it."

"What kind of big deal?" he asks.

"That . . . they might think we like each other for that reason." I wait and hope he'll assure me that it's not so. He doesn't say anything.

He glances around. "I think the tattooed guy lives in the house to the left of Cassie's."

"You went there?"

He looks guilty. "After you left school. I didn't see him, but a young blond woman with two girls pulled up to the other house. Then Cassie showed up." He frowns as another cool breeze brushes past. "A cop pulled up. I left, but he stared at me as I drove off."

"Matt, you can't do this. Seriously, you could get in trouble. And not because of the cop. If this tattooed guy sees you and thinks you know something, he could . . . kill you."

I stand up, staring down at him still sitting on the bench. He gets up.

I bury my hands in my pockets. "Promise me you aren't going back there." The wind picks up again.

He wraps his arms around my waist. He half smiles. "Has anyone told you that you have the cutest nose in the world? It's perfect. A little turned up, and small, and . . ."

"Are you really using my nose to change the subject?"

"Maybe, but it's the truth. Your nose is perfect."

I lift one hand from my pocket and press it against his chest. "Promise me you won't go back."

"Your lips are almost as perfect as your nose." He tilts his head down as if to kiss me.

I put my hand up and his mouth lands there. "Promise me." His lips feel moist on the back of my fingers.

He makes a low growling sound. "I can't promise. I have to find out who did this to my brother. If that means getting in trouble or putting myself in a little danger, so be it."

I hate hearing that. Hate it. I step back, away from his warmth. "Go to the detective and—"

"I will. When I have proof."

We stand there and stare at each other. I can see the pain in his eyes. I understand it, but doesn't he realize what could happen? He could die. He inches in.

Tilting his head down, his breath is on my temple. "Please understand. I have to do this. Don't be mad."

"I'm not mad. I'm scared." He puts a hand on each side of my face. His touch is warm and so welcome.

"I'll be careful." He lips touch mine. He brushes a soft kiss on the side of my mouth. Testing. Tasting. Tempting.

I know what this is. Pure distraction.

And I'm falling for it, hook, line, and sinker.

His tongue eases inside my mouth. I tilt my head and take it deeper and we stand there, the cold breeze around us, the echoes of small animals, but the only thing I care about is his kiss and his hands holding my waist.

Before I realize it, his hands shift just under the hoodie, under my tee. His hands are on my bare skin. Fitting to the curve of my waist. He moves up an inch. Down and inch. I want more inches. I want his touch everywhere.

Sweet vibrations whisper over my body. The muscles in my lower abdomen tighten almost painfully. My breasts, pressed against his chest, feel heavy and sensitive.

I feel electric.

I feel a weird kind of empty and I want him to fill it.

I feel as if I'm floating. I'm moving through the air on something light—something mystical.

Then I want to touch him. I reach under his jacket. I move up and under his shirt. I'm touching his lower back. His kiss becomes more intense. I let my fingers move up and to the side, exploring how he feels against my palms. But I still want more.

The need to touch more, more skin, more Matt. I glide my hands up his back. His skin is soft, but beneath it is muscle. He's firm. He's hard. I'm lost.

I rock against him ever so slightly, wanting to be closer. That's when I feel that he's hard in other places. It's like a wake-up call. But I'm not sure I'm ready to be woken up.

Still, I pull back. My lips slowly part from his. When I open my eyes, his are wide, bright, filled with heat. His lips are wet from our kiss. I know mine are the same. I hear him breathing, or is that me? His taste lingers on my tongue.

I'm almost embarrassed, but not. Despite being the one to end it, I feel bold. Bolder than Old Leah ever felt. I realize I don't care if the reason I feel this is because I have Eric's heart. I feel it. I'm owning it.

"Sorry," he says as if he knows I noticed his below-the-belt problem. As if he knows that it's the reason I pulled back. His cheeks are pink, and I don't think it's from the cold. The last thing I want is for him to feel bad.

I force a smile. "I'm not sorry. Not even a little bit."

He grins. It reaches his eyes. "Then I'm not either."

Lady barks at some small noise in the woods. "We should go," he says.

I nod. He puts the sweetest kiss on my cheek. Pulling back, he touches my nose. "Your nose really is perfect."

He grabs Lady's leash, and we start to the car, his hand in mine. I love the feel of it. We walk in silence. I'm busy storing the memory for safekeeping so I can go back to it. So I can relive it.

I hear his words again. *Your nose really is perfect.*

My giddiness fades because I realize not all of me is perfect. I remember the scars.

Matt squeezes my hand. "I've been meaning to ask you. Do you have college plans?"

Air hiccups in my throat. Plans require a future, and until recently I didn't have one. And now . . . ?

I realize he's waiting for an answer.

"No big plans," I say, and bam: I realize what this might mean. Matt has plans. Matt's going to leave. Leave town. Leave me. I'm already missing him.

"So no plans?" he asks.

"I'll . . . probably do my basics in a junior college here." Just saying that gives my pulse a zing because that's . . . nine months away. I look at him and think of his leaving, and for the first time nine months doesn't seem long at all. I notice he's smiling. "What?"

"Me too. I'm going to college here for at least a year."

Relief flutters through my chest.

He squeezes my hand. "I don't think it's a good idea to leave Mom just yet. I can do a lot of what I need for a business degree here."

"Business? That's what you're taking?"

"Yeah. I considered law, but . . ." He pauses. "I know what I want to do. I'm just not sure if it's feasible."

"What?" I ask, wanting to know everything. What makes him happy. What makes him sad. Everything about him. Every tiny nuance.

"Don't laugh." He rears back on his heels.

"I won't. Promise."

"I'd love to open up my own garage. Maintenance. Redo engines. Restore old cars."

I recall a piece of the past I'd filed away. "You were in auto tech in tenth grade. You used to come into class with grease on your hands."

"Yeah, I took it in eleventh too. I didn't get my shit together soon enough to make it in this year."

"How did you get into working on cars?"

"My granddad was a mechanic, had his own shop. As a kid, I loved going there. Even after my grandfather died, Dad always made Eric and I help him work on cars. I think my grandfather made my dad help him. It was like a tradition. I loved it. Even when I was eight, I could stay under a car all day. I worked part-time for a garage for a while." He pauses. "Before Dad died, he bought this Mustang for us to restore."

Matt swallows. "Eric and I decided to do it together."

My chest tightens, and I press my palm closer to his. "You should still do it. Do it for them."

He nods but doesn't answer. Then he looks at me. "You used to want to write? Are you going for an English degree?"

"I think." And for one second I let myself go there. To the future. To the faraway future. Not just to graduating high school, but college. Then I feel myself pulling back, afraid to plan. Afraid to hope.

"I'm not sure," I mutter.

"You can start with the basics."

"Yeah." My chest feels like it has marbles in it. Round knots of fear, crowding out my newfound joy. Why am I scared to plan the future? Do I know something I don't want to know?

25

Wednesday afternoon, after spending an hour parked in front of Cassie's house, Matt walks into the Whataburger. The air is thick with the fast-food scents. John and Cory, Eric's friends from Southside High, finally called and agreed to meet. They're late, so Matt moves to the counter to order a Coke and fries.

When he looks up at the shake menu, grief knees him in the balls. Hard.

Crazy how the simplest things bring it on.

At least twice a week, he and Eric came here. His brother always ordered a vanilla shake and fries. He used the shake like ketchup. Or the fries like a spoon.

But, damn, Matt misses him, misses those ordinary moments of togetherness—of being a twin. Most people don't know what that means, and maybe it means different things to different twins, but for Matt being a twin felt like . . . like the opposite of how lonely feels. He'd taken it for granted, because he'd never known what it felt like to be just one—not until Eric died.

Sure, they had their own lives and hobbies and, in some cases, even friends, but he always felt that sense of being half of a whole.

Remembering Leah's breathing trick, he inhales, holds it, then slowly releases. The grief is still there, but the pressure lessens.

Tray in hand, he moves to a table and waits for John and Cory. Of course, he knew these guys and had spent some time with them. Eric mostly hung with them when Matt was working at the garage. His brother liked drinking beer and occasionally smoking a little weed. And these guys were into it more than their friends from Walnut High.

John's black Honda pulls up, and they walk in. Matt motions them over and tries to decide how to ask his question. He hasn't yet spoken to their mutual friends at school either. It's harder to talk to them, because he knows what side of the fence they're on. They're on the "suicide" side.

The second John's and Cory's eyes land on him, he sees it. They blink. They look at him, but he knows they see Eric. And, freaking hell, he knows how that feels. He feels that burn every morning when he looks in the mirror and Eric's looking back at him.

He remembers Leah saying that's why Cassie wouldn't talk

to him. He believes it more. Everything inside him says it's more.

"What's up?" Cory asks as they both drop into seats.

Matt suddenly isn't sure how to put it.

"Yeah, I was . . ." He stumbles. "I know Eric spent time with you the day before he got shot. I was just wondering if . . . if he said anything?"

Cory's shoulders crowd the back of his chair. "I went through everything he said, wondering if I could have said something to have stopped him. I knew he was upset, but not that bad."

Matt's gut tightens. Didn't anyone know Eric like he did? Matt hesitates to correct them. He just needs information, but then not correcting them feels disloyal to Eric. To his memory. To his brother's pride.

"Eric didn't do this. He wouldn't—"

John leans in. "Wasn't it your dad's gun?"

That's the argument everyone throws out. But it's not proof. Just because he got the gun doesn't mean he used it to kill himself.

"I think he took the gun but someone used it on him. If you'd tell me anything he said, or what he was upset about? Maybe I can figure it out."

They look at each other. Cory speaks up. "It was his girl. She had him in knots."

That's old news. Matt needs more. "And?" Matt focuses on John.

"We tried to fix him up, get him laid. Figured he'd move on. He wouldn't hear of it."

Matt turns the soda in his hands. "Did he say why they broke up?"

Cory shakes his head. Matt can't let it go. "Anything?"

John shrugs. "He said . . . something that sounded like she was cheating on him."

Matt's backbone ratchets up. "What did he say? Did he say who?"

"No." John shifts. "I can't remember his exact words, but something like he couldn't handle thinking about him with her. I told him to forget the bitch. He flipped. I've never seen him get pissed like that. He said she wasn't a bitch."

So it was true! Cassie was seeing the neighbor? That asswipe killed his brother. Anger burns Matt's gut.

"Eric wasn't himself," Cory says. "That's why it made sense he did it."

"He didn't. Damn it, guys. Didn't you know Eric? Don't you see, the guy Cassie was seeing killed Eric."

Cory leans in. "But I thought . . . Didn't the cops investigate?"

"Eric didn't do it!" Matt snaps. But he can't help wondering why Eric hadn't told him about this. Why the fuck hadn't Eric confided in him?

"Matt?"

Thursday afternoon around six, Matt hears his mom call his name and he flinches. He hadn't heard her car pull up.

He considers sneaking back into the house. But she probably already saw the light on.

Coming out here was a bad idea. But after talking to Leah, he'd been thinking about the Mustang, about restoring it. Not that it's happening soon. Right now he plans to put all his energy into getting enough proof to take to Detective Henderson. While his chat with Cory and John helped, he still needs more. The next time he walks into Detective Henderson's office, he wants to leave smiling.

He inhales. The smell is so familiar: Old tools. Old oil. It's a smell he always associated with his dad. When he wasn't deployed, he spent his time in here.

"Matt," his mom calls again.

"In here," he answers.

"What are you doing?" Tension thickens her voice.

She stops at the door, as if walking in would be too painful. Like his dad's office, they've stayed out of the garage.

He takes a step to go in, but she bolts out, almost as if doing it would prove something. Crossing her arms, she hugs herself, and stares at his dad's and Eric's cars—parked and forgotten.

"I was thinking," he says. "About the Mustang."

She looks up; there's a teary sheen to her green eyes. "I remember the day you guys brought it home on that rented trailer. It was like Christmas for all three of you. You were so excited."

Her breath shakes. "I remember thinking what a great father your dad was. He loved doing things with you two."

Matt's chest tightens. He breathes, Leah-style. "He was a great father."

Matt stares at his mom and wonders if it's too soon to tell her his plans. "I was thinking about restoring it."

She catches her breath. "That would be great."

He rubs his hands together. "It would be expensive, but since I'm going to college the first year here instead of Texas A&M, I thought I'd pull a little money from that. And I dropped by Jim's Garage, and they said I could work weekends." It wasn't that they didn't have money. Both sets of his grandparents had left sizable inheritances, and with his dad's life insurance, they weren't hurting, but he didn't want to run through that.

"What? You aren't going to Texas A&M? Son, that's been the plan all your life. Your grandparents put money in your college account for that."

"I'm going. Just not the first year."

"No. You're doing this for me. And—"

"Wrong," he says. Earlier it had been for her, but now . . .

"It's not just you, Mom. It's me. I need to heal too." And he feels closer to doing that. Closer to finding the truth about what happened to Eric.

She hugs him. "Are you sure it's not about me?"

"Positive," he says.

They stand in the garage neither have entered in a long time. He knows this is a step. A step toward letting go. And it's because of Leah. She's so damn good for him.

The silence in the garage is comfortable. Then his mom speaks up. "Do you want your dad's and Eric's cars?"

He looks at Dad's Lexus SUV and Eric's Subaru. He feels an attachment to them because they belonged to them, but he remembers the article he'd read about cleaning out the departed's things.

"No," he forces himself to say, even when his heart says yes.

"Then maybe we should sell them and use that money to restore the Mustang. I think your dad and Eric would approve, don't you?" She presses a hand over her trembling lips.

Matt nods and swallows his own emotion. *Why did healing, letting go, have to hurt so much?*

"Speaking of money," his mom says. "I'm going back to work."

He looks at her. She used to love her job as a real estate agent. "Are you ready?"

"Some days I feel more ready than others. But I think it's time I push myself."

"Yeah." He's proud of her. "I'll put an ad on Craigslist for the cars."

She nods. "Come help me. I've got groceries in the car."

They walk outside. "Speaking of school . . . How are you doing? I don't want you to let your grades drop again." His mom had a fit last semester when he'd had two Cs on his report card.

Grabbing a few bags of groceries from her trunk, he looks at her. "I'm not. Actually studying with L . . . ori is helping."

"When am I going to meet this Lori?" she asks.

He swallows. "Soon maybe." He wonders what Leah would say if he told her he's lied to his mom about her name. But, damn it, his mom is doing so well. He doesn't want to risk her figuring out that Leah has Eric's heart. It might drag her back into depression.

His mom moves beside him and grabs a couple of bags herself. "Why is Ted's car here and your car isn't?"

Because I'm using Ted's car to spy on Cassie's neighbor's house. Since Ms. Chambers's cop boyfriend had seen him last, he'd been swapping cars with Ted for a few hours every day. Only today, Ted had somewhere to go, and they wouldn't swap back until later tonight.

But he can't tell his mom that. "Ted's car was making a weird noise, and he wanted me to drive it and see if I could identify the problem."

"That's nice of you," his mom says.

"Yeah." He hates lying. But his mom would flip if she knew. Leah would too. Hence the reason he hasn't told her.

Not that anything has happened. So far, he's got nothing. He hasn't spotted a motorcycle or a tattooed guy. He hasn't seen Cassie or her future cop stepdad again. But he still feels things when he's there. He feels Eric. He feels unhappiness. Lately, the dreams are driving him crazy. He keeps having the one where Eric drops the gun, followed by the sound of a gunshot. Each time, he wakes up with the throbbing pain in his temple.

He refuses to believe Eric killed himself. Or that it was an accident. And he's not stopping until he proves it.

"So what's going on?" Brandy asks as I drag her to my bedroom. I don't answer and won't until we're in my room, doors shut, alone. "Come on, spill." She drops on my bed and gets comfortable.

It's Thursday afternoon, and after "the talk" with my mom a little earlier, I needed a sounding board. So I called Brandy.

"Is this about Matt? I noticed you didn't say you went walking with him yesterday or today."

I shake my head. "No, it's not . . . He had something he had to do." I stare at Brandy and debate where to begin. "I'm going to start taking birth control pills."

Brandy's mouth drops open and closes, making her look like a fish out of water. "What?"

I give her the lowdown about Dr. Hughes wanting me on the pill. I don't tell her I can't ever have kids. I'm not ready to share that.

"But the pill isn't the problem," I say.

"Oookay," she says, stretching out the O. "What's the problem?"

"I'm going to the doctor tomorrow. This afternoon, mom told me what the doctor will do."

"What will he do?" She looks confused.

"She," I correct quickly and drop down and start strangling a pillow. "Thank God it's a she, but it's still terrifying?"

"What's terrifying?" she asks.

"A pap smear! I've heard of them before but never thought about them." I clutch the pillow tighter. "They used to do them to all teen girls, but stopped because it was so traumatic, but because I'm on the immune suppressant drugs, I have to do it. I mean . . . They are going to spread my legs open and stick something inside me and—"

"Kind of sounds like sex." Brandy belts out with laughter.

I hit her with my pillow. "I'm serious." She keeps laughing. I hit her again.

She finally sobers.

"Have you had one?" I ask.

"No. But women everywhere have them. I don't think they hurt too bad."

"It's not just the pain," I say. "It's that this doctor is going to see parts of me that I've never seen."

Brandy falls back over, laughing again.

It's suddenly contagious, and we laugh a long time. Then I say, "I'm scared."

She wipes the smile off her face. "Someone cut open your chest, not once, but twice. I'm sure this will be a piece of cake."

"I don't know. Mom says they use a metal thing to kind of crank you open. That sounds painful."

"I'm sure it's not fun, but . . . I'd do it to go on the pill. About six months ago, Brian's condom burst. I was terrified I was pregnant. I even took a pregnancy test. I didn't let him touch me again for a month."

"You didn't tell me this," I say.

"You'd just gotten the heart and it didn't feel right whining to you."

"You can always whine to me," I say. "That's what best friends are for." But I haven't been a very good one.

"I know." She grabs a pink pillow and stuffs it behind her.

"You don't think your parents suspect you are having sex?" I ask.

"Are you kidding? They live in an alternate universe. They still give me stuffed animals for my birthdays." She suddenly sits up. "Wait. You're going to the doctor tomorrow?" She frowns. "We're meeting after school for book club again."

"Sorry."

She gives me the evil eye. "I don't think you're that sorry."

"Please! Like I'd rather have a pap smear."

She giggles. "But seriously, are you joining the book club or not?"

"I'm not sure I belong. And Trent will be there, and things are weird with us. Today he walked by my car just as Matt kissed me goodbye. He looked devastated."

"Don't worry about him. He'll move on."

"Right. It's been almost two years since I broke up with him."

"Yeah, but . . ." Brandy scrunches up her shoulders as if guilty. "I never told you, but two weeks after you two broke up, he was dating Tammy Wilcox. Word is she slept with him. They broke up, but he's dated at least five girls since you."

I'm sitting there, trying to digest something that feels indigestible. "Seriously?"

"Yeah."

"I thought . . . why didn't you tell me?"

"You kind of had other things to worry about."

I toss a pillow at her, glad to finally be free of feeling sorry for Trent. "No more secrets. Seriously."

"Okay." She pauses. "So you really think you and Matt are going to have sex?"

I remember our kisses. The way his bare skin felt under my hands. I know where it'll take me, and I want to go. I just haven't figured out how I'm going to hide my scar. I'm afraid if he sees it, he won't want to have sex. That'll kill me. Just kill me.

"Yeah." I finally answer.

"This weekend?" she asks.

"No," I choke on the word. "This is our first date."

"You've been with him all week. And I see the way you two look at each other."

"Yeah, but all we've done so far is kiss."

"So you jump ahead." She hugs the pillow tighter.

"I don't think so."

Brandy pauses. "Are y'all still having dreams?" Her tone is different, walking-on-eggshells careful.

I consider lying. But she's my best friend. "Yeah."

Thankfully, Mom calls us to dinner. We drop the dream talk and go eat. But as I move into the kitchen, I remember the whole pap-smear conversation and lose my appetite.

26

After second period on Friday, and during our fifteen-minute break, Matt texts me and tells me he'll meet me at my locker. I'm changing out my books in my backpack when my locker neighbor, Devon, walks up. We've spoken a couple of times between classes.

He's nice. Maybe too nice. Sometimes I wonder if he's hitting on me.

I'm flattered, but soooo not interested.

"Ready for the weekend?" Devon asks.

"Yeah," I answer in a polite, uninterested way.

The hallway is noisy, so he takes a polite, interested step closer. "I was wondering if you might like to hang out this weekend."

I take a polite, uninterested step back.

It takes me a minute to find my words. "Sorry but—"

I'm suddenly grabbed and gently swung around. Almost before I see Matt, his lips are on mine.

This isn't anything like the other hall kiss. It's deep, it's with tongue, and it's . . . wonderful. I forget we're being watched by probably hundreds of students. All I can think about is his chest on mine, his hand behind my neck, angling my head so the kiss moves deeper.

I hear loud whistles, and I'm guessing they're directed at us. I still don't stop. Old Leah would be humiliated. New Leah is in hog heaven.

Matt pulls back and meets Devon's gaze. He doesn't look angry; he's even grinning. "Hi, Devon."

Devon laughs and looks at me. "I'm going to take that to mean you already got plans."

"Yeah." Now Old Leah creeps in a little, and I'm embarrassed. But not too much.

Devon walks off and Matt looks at me. "I hope you didn't mind."

"No. I was telling him—"

"But seeing it is better than hearing it."

"Are you two finished?" A teasing voice pipes up.

I look up. It's Ted, Matt's friend, whom I have yet to be introduced to.

"Yeah." Pride etches into Matt's smile.

Ted grins. "You're Leah, right? The reason I haven't seen much of Matt here."

"Yeah. Sorry," I say, but I'm not.

"It's okay." Ted looks at Matt and holds out a hoodie and a book. "You left these in my car. And thanks for the gas, but you didn't have to do that."

"Yeah," Matt takes the items and looks . . . somehow guilty. Then he glances at me.

Ted leaves, and I'm still trying to figure out the guilty look when Matt blurts out in low voice, "I used his car to see if I could spot the motorcycle guy on Cassie's street. I know you don't like it, but I'm being careful. Wearing a hoodie."

Frustration fueled by fear rises inside me. "It's still dangerous."

He pulls me close and leans his forehead on mine. "I'm a big boy."

Yeah, one I care about. I swallow my frustration because now isn't the time. The bell rings.

"See you at lunch," he says, still studying me.

"I have a . . . dentist appointment. I'm leaving right before lunch." The lie turns my tongue bitter. But I tell myself it's practically the same thing. Someone's gonna stick something somewhere I don't want them to.

"You got a cavity?" He touches my cheek.

"Just a checkup." I almost blush realizing what's going to be checked.

"Were still on for tonight, right?"

"Yeah." I even asked Mom if I'd be too sore to go out. She assured me I wouldn't.

"Six, okay?" he asks. "We can eat some pizza and then go to the movies at seven thirty."

"That's good."

He brushes a finger over my lips. "I'll be thinking about it all day."

I put my hand on his chest. "Promise you're not going to watch Cassie's house this afternoon."

He frowns but answers. "I'm not. I've got a hot date tonight."

Walking away, I watch him. Even with my nerves on edge, I'm looking forward to that hot date.

At lunch, Matt grabs milk and a muffin and goes in search of Marissa. She's where she always is, with the other cheerleaders and his friends.

There's a spot open beside her. He drops down. She frowns.

"You lose your girl?" Ted asks in a teasing tone.

"She had to leave early," Matt says.

234 C. C. HUNTER

He waits a minute, then leans close to Marissa. "Can we talk?"

"I'm eating," she says.

He makes small talk with the guys, waiting for her to finish lunch. He leans in again. "Now?"

Frowning, she jumps up. They aren't out of the lunchroom, when she snaps, "What's wrong, you lonely without your book dork?"

Matt frowns. "Don't be like that."

"Like what?" She continues out of the lunchroom and stops right outside the double doors. "You mean upset that you lied to me?"

"When did I lie?"

"Seven months ago when you told me you weren't in the right place to start dating. I've been waiting, and now you're steaming up the halls with her."

"I never told you to wait."

"You didn't tell me not to."

No, but he thought he'd sent out enough signals that she'd know he wasn't into her. The only reason he dated her was because of Eric.

"Can't we just be friends?" he asks.

"Friends don't just talk to you when they need something. Which brings me to my next question. What do you need?"

He feels guilty. "I'm sorry, but you know Cassie better than anyone."

"I knew her. After I spoke to you on Monday, I called her. She didn't answer. Her phone's full of messages. I called her again later. She didn't call me back. She's gone psycho."

"Yeah, but I want you to call her home phone. Try to reach her that way and—"

"Why don't you just call her yourself?"

"Because I was told not to."

"By who?"

"Cassie. The police. And Cassie again."

Her eyes round. "What are you doing, Matt?"

"I'm trying to find out what happened to Eric."

She rolls her eyes. "When are you going to accept what happened?"

"Eric didn't kill himself." He tries not to sound angry. But it hurts.

Marissa groans. "Okay, I'll call her. But after this, leave me out of it, okay?"

He nods, and he's so thankful he has Leah.

Marissa moves to a less-crowded corner and dials. Matt follows.

"Hi, Mrs. Chambers. It's Marissa." She pauses, Matt leans closer to see if he can hear Cassie's mom. "Fine, thanks." Marissa frowns at him. "And you?"

"Good." Marissa pulls the phone from her ear and hits speakerphone. "I can't seem to reach Cassie," Marissa continues. "I thought something might be wrong with her phone."

"She's probably not answering it because she's in school." Ms. Chambers says. "Are you skipping school, young lady?"

Marissa looks at Matt and answers, "Uh . . . No ma'am. It's lunchtime."

Ms. Chambers continues. "I asked Cassie why you haven't come by. She said you two only have one class together. You should come over. Cassie's still dealing with things. She could use a friend."

Matt sees guilt flash in Marissa's eyes. "Yeah, I'll talk to her."

"Good," Ms. Chambers says.

Marissa hangs up. "Did you get what I got from that conversation?"

Matt nods. "She's living here, and her mom thinks she's attending school. But she's nowhere to be found."

Marissa looks concerned. "Do you think she's gotten into drugs or something?"

"I don't know," Matt says. But he intends to find out.

Sitting in a paper gown, I can't stop fidgeting. Dr. Stein finally comes in. She's young and nice. Even tells me how scared she was at her first gynecological checkup. Then she goes through a quick questionnaire.

Tobacco? No.

Alcohol? No.

Sex? No.

She explains everything she's going to do.

When she goes to pull my paper gown open to examine my breasts, I warn her about my scars. I didn't want to hear her gasp. One gasp memory is enough.

She smiles and says she knows. As she checks my breasts, she gives me tips on how to examine them. Really? I already need to do that?

As she moves below, she keeps talking, which I find awkward. And the stirrups don't help. It isn't painful, but it isn't pleasant. I have my eyes closed so tight, my jaws ache.

Mid pap smear, she informs me that my hymen is already broken. My eyes shoot open. I lift my head up, look right at her between my knees, and swear to everything holy that I haven't had sex. She explains it sometimes happens with girls who wear tampons.

I don't think I breathe again until she leaves the room.

When I'm getting dressed, I look down at my scar and run my finger over it. It's fading. It isn't as light as Dr. Hughes's yet, but it's lighter.

When I walk out front, Mom's paying.

Heading to the car, she asks, "So you survived?"

"It wasn't as bad as I thought."

"Told you." Mom drapes her arm around my shoulder. "Did you like Dr. Stein?"

"Yeah," I say. "She said she called in a prescription to the same pharmacy you use."

Driving out of the parking lot, she asks, "Why don't we pick up your pills, then grab something to eat. You barely touched your lunch."

"Sorry. I was nervous. As a matter of fact, I'm still not hungry."

"How long have you not had an appetite?" Mom asks in her my-daughter's-dying tone, which stirs up painful memories that I push back.

"Since I've been thinking about someone cranking open my vayjayjay. Stop worrying."

Mom laughs and pulls into the drugstore. While she takes the doctor's order back to the pharmacy, I walk around. Yeah, I figure I'll just let the pharmacist think the pills are for Mom.

I end up in front of the store's small book selection. I don't need one. I had six delivered to my Kindle last night, but I prefer a real book. Running my fingers along the spines, I find one that looks interesting. The blurb on the back makes it sound light, and I just know it needs a home.

And after a pap smear, I could use some humor.

I'm paying when Mom walks up.

We are halfway home when Mom drops the bag in my lap. "Here. There are directions, but if you have questions, just ask."

"Thanks." I pull out the bag's contents. I pick up the first box, read it, squeal, and then throw it in the backseat.

Mom giggles.

I don't.

I look at her. "Why . . . why did you buy me condoms?"

"Because . . . if you decide to have sex, you need to protect yourself from more than just pregnancy. And . . . the pill won't protect you for at least a month."

I gasp. "You think I'm having sex tonight?" First Brandy and now my mom?

"No," Mom says. "I just want you to be prepared when it happens."

I sit there shaking my head in disbelief.

"I know sex is difficult to talk about, but if you need to talk . . ."

"We had that talk, remember?"

She nods. "You know your grandma was a little too forward thinking with me."

I look at her, unsure what Grandma has to do with the sex talk.

"She took me shopping for condoms on my sixteenth birthday. I thought I'd die." Mom focuses on the road. "Turned out, I was glad she did because I . . . had them when the time came. The condom the boy had in his wallet was one he'd carried around before puberty. There was no way I was letting him use that thing."

I put my hands on my ears and start humming the birthday song like I'm brushing my teeth. When she stops talking, I look at her. "I do not want to hear about you having sex."

She laughs. We keep driving.

Curiosity hits. "That boy? Was it Dad?"

Her expression answers the question before she does. "No."

"How old were you?" I ask. So I guess I do want to know.

"Too young," she says.

"How old?"

"Sixteen. A week after my birthday, which is why I hesitated putting you on birth control. It felt as if my mom had given me her blessing, so I didn't wait."

We're close to our house, but I'm wishing we were closer. I'm imagining my mom having sex with someone and I can't look at her. It's all just too gross.

I stare out the passenger window as the cars pass. A feeling hits. Emotion. Not being-disgusted-by-my-mom's-sex-life emotion, this is like . . .

A motorcycle pulls beside us. I stare at the passengers.

I gasp. The girl who has her arms wrapped around the driver's waist is Cassie. That's when I know for sure that Eric can make me feel things. I want to jump out of my skin. Chills run down my arms, up my spine, and do a choreographed tap dance on the back of my neck.

Then I remember what Matt said about Cassie seeing a guy who drove a motorcycle.

A guy with . . . dark hair and tattoos. This guy has black hair, but he's wearing a leather jacket so I can't see if he has tattoos, but . . . but . . . Shit shit shit!

I'm back to feeling Eric's emotions. I'm sad. I'm mad. I'm jealous.

We come to a red light. I don't want to look at them, but I keep glancing sideways out of the corner of my eye to make sure I'm right.

I am.

That's Cassie Chambers. And there's a good chance she's on the back of a bike with a killer.

The light changes. The motorcycle turns onto South Pine Street. My panic is playing full volume. I look at my mom and almost blurt out, *follow that motorcycle!*

I don't. And I'm relieved because then Mom would ask why. And there's not one feasible explanation I can give her. Not even the truth. Especially not the truth.

My heart is *thump-thudding* in my chest. I'm doing my deep breathing to calm down, but it's not working. The light changes. Our car moves forward.

"You okay?" Mom asks.

"Just traumatized by all the sex talk." I try to smile, but I can't.

Mom chuckles again. I sink deeper in the seat and try to think. If Cassie's still hanging out with the guy who possibly killed Eric, then maybe Matt's right.

Maybe she's not so innocent.

I'm itching to call Matt. But I can't with Mom listening. I consider texting him. I grab my phone out of my back pocket. I type, *Just saw Cassie on a motorcycle.*

I stare at it, then realize what he'll do. He'll leave school and try to find them. Matt said he won't confront this guy, but I know how angry he is. I know anger makes people do stupid things.

And if this motorcycle-driving, dark-haired tattooed guy sees Matt, and if he did kill Eric, he's gonna want to shut Matt up. Maybe permanently.

Just like that . . . I know what I have to do.

27

Twenty minutes later, I park my car and play with my silver hoop earrings because I'm so nervous. I'm not parked directly across from Cassie's house. I don't even look at her house, but I hear her guard cat meowing. I ignore it. My blood's whooshing through my veins so fast I'm almost dizzy. I do the breathing exercises.

If motorcycle guy is here, he won't recognize me. There's no reason for anyone to think I'm here to confirm a guy with a motorcycle and tattoos lives here.

I get out of my car and walk to the house on the left. It's

fifty degrees outside, but I'm sweating when I get to the door.

I knock.

I hear a television.

I hear footsteps.

I hear the lock on the door turn. Fear curls my stomach, and I want to puke. I take a deep breath. In. Out.

Oh, shit. In one second, I might be face-to-face with a killer. And this isn't fiction.

The door opens. A woman stands there. She's blond and about forty. "Yes?"

"I'm . . . I'm looking for your son."

"You mean my stepson?" she asks.

I inhale. "Drives a motorcycle?"

She rolls her eyes. "Jayden's not here. He ran away about seven months ago. Just disappeared. Worried his dad sick."

Which is right about the time Eric died. I swallow and try to find my voice. But it's gone.

"I wasn't so upset, until I found out that my husband is now helping the no-good delinquent pay for an apartment."

"Apartment?" I ask.

She takes a step back and eyes me up and down.

"God, don't tell me you're pregnant?"

"No! Promise. I . . ." I need a lie and need one fast. "We went out a while back and he has my driver's license. I forgot to get it back." I'm proud of that answer. Sounds legit.

"Well, I don't know what apartment. One off Pine Street. But I can tell you this"—she slips a hand on her hip—"it'd behoove you to just get another license. Jayden's trouble. I know he has that bad-boy charm, but he's twenty-one, already spent a year in prison. Is that really who you want to hang out with?"

Chills run down my spine. *Nope. Don't wanna hang with him.* I shake my head.

She stares at me, unconvinced. "Ahh, shit. I'll take your

number and ask my husband to give it to him. But God's my witness, you're gonna end up pregnant. And don't think his dad and I are going to raise it." She turns around to a side table and grabs a pen and paper. "Your number?"

"No, I . . . I'll just go to the DMV."

"Smart girl!' She shuts the door in my face.

I hurry across the street. My hands are shaking. My knees are shaking. My freshly cranked-open vayjayjay is shaking.

But I'm smiling.

I did it.

I got something that will help Matt. Jayden's already been in prison. The detective would be a fool not to check it out.

I'm crossing the street when Cassie's guard cat nearly trips me.

"No. Get out of the street," I wave the cat off. It purrs and wraps itself around my leg.

"Go!" I shoosh him away. He purrs harder. I could just leave, but if it gets killed, it's on me.

I pick the thing up. Keeping it away from my body, I take it to Cassie's yard. I turn to go back to my car. And freeze. A cop car's pulling into the driveway.

Shit shit shit!

But since I'm not doing anything wrong, I continue to my car and start the engine. I'm putting it in drive when I see him walking to my car.

Fracking hell! I'm going to puke.

I'm not doing anything wrong, I tell myself. I don't need to be afraid.

So why am I afraid? Sure, the detective warned Matt to stay away, but I'm not Matt.

I roll my window down.

"I'm Officer Yates. Do you mind telling me what you're doing here?"

I swear my heart, Eric's heart, is beating so loud the officer could hear it. "I was looking for Jayden?"

"Jayden Soprano?"

"Yes, sir." Then I cringe, realizing I just admitted to a cop I'm looking for an ex-con.

He frowns. "Can I see your license?"

My hands are trembling and it takes me forever to pull it out of my wallet, but I finally hand it to him.

"Leah McKenzie." He reads my name aloud.

"You were here last week. I saw you."

My heart stops, drops, and rolls. "Yes, sir."

"So why are you lying about why you're here?"

"I'm not, sir." I reach deep for a convincing lie. "Last week I wanted to see her because I thought Cassie might know where Jayden was."

His dark eyes tighten. He doesn't believe me. And here I thought it was good.

"Look, someone's stalking Mrs. Chambers's daughter. Calling her at all times of the night. She's upset, can't sleep. It's hurting her. It has to stop. If you're part of that?"

"I'm not." *I only called her twice, and it wasn't late.* Shit shit shit. I came to help Matt, and I might have gotten him in more trouble.

"Don't lie to me. Jayden doesn't even live here anymore."

"I . . . know. I just found out when I spoke with his stepmom."

"You talked to her?" He almost smiles.

I nod, realizing the man probably saw me leaving Cassie's yard. "The cat followed me. I was getting it out of the road before it got . . . killed."

"If I ask Ms. Soprano right now, she's going to tell me you just spoke with her?"

"Yes, sir."

"Wait here." He looks right at me, then drops my license in his front pocket.

He takes a step, then turns, bends down, and reaches into my car. He removes my keys. I flatten myself against the seat so his arm doesn't brush across my breasts. They've already been examined today, and once is enough.

He stands up. "I'll hold on to these." He starts toward the house. With my license and my keys.

I am so caught. He's going to show the stepmother my license, and she's going to tell him I said I lost it. Is lying against the law? I didn't lie to the cop. Just . . .

I feel that one bite of lunch crawl up my throat. I consider calling Mom.

But how would I explain?

The officer knocks so hard I can hear it.

The same blond woman answers his knock. He points to my car. They exchange a short conversation. He starts back, walking slow, as if saying he doesn't value my time.

He stops at my window. "Looks like you're not lying." His dark eyes stare at me in a way that makes me nervous. Probably the official police-regulated look. Or does he get off intimidating people? "But why do I not believe you? Let me say this one more time: if you're bothering Cassie Chambers, it has to stop. She doesn't deserve this."

He hands me my license. I take it.

"Can I go?"

"Not without these." He dangles my keys from his fingers and expects me to reach for them.

I reach. But he pulls his hand back just a little, and I miss. He's a jerk.

He dangles them again. Yup, my internal jerk meter is *dinging* right now.

I get the keys, but I don't look at him. I put the car in drive, drum my fingers on the wheel, and wait for him to step back so

I don't run over his feet. Truthfully, if I didn't think he'd hunt me down and shoot me, I'd love to take out a few of his toes.

I'm hot-date ready at 5:45. I texted Matt and told him to bring his notebook. I didn't say anything else. I'd rather tell him about my afternoon calmly over pizza.

And I am calm. Now. I was shaking when I got home. But I knew how to take care of that. I found the scariest book I had on my Kindle and dove in. In the beginning of my heart failure, when I was scheduled for some scarier-than-hell, life-or-death procedures, I discovered that nothing chills me out more than murder mysteries.

When a heroine is being chased by a bad guy in a parking lot, trapped in the house of a serial killer, or hunted by a guy with a knife, my brain sends the message to my nervous system: *See, your life isn't that bad.*

And it's not. Although I know Matt's going to be pissed at what I did. Then he'll be happy. Hey, I got what he needed. More than he needed. I know his name, Jayden Soprano. I know he's still seeing Cassie. I know he lives in an apartment on Pine Street. I know he's an ex-con.

I know Matt doesn't need to be near him.

I dab on lip gloss and look into the drawer where I've hidden the box of mom-blessed condoms.

I don't need one. I don't. I don't.

But considering Mom thinks I'm possibly having sex, Brandy thinks I'm possibly having sex, and I don't know what Matt thinks, I wonder if putting one in my purse wouldn't be wise. What if we kiss again? What if this time I don't want to stop? What if his condom is one he carried since puberty?

I open the box. I've never held one. The slick foiled plastic feels liquidy inside.

Racing back to my room, like I'm stealing something, I find

the secret zipper in my purse and hide it inside. I feel naughty.
I feel brave. I feel like a nervous twit.

What if I drop my purse and it falls out? I make sure I zipped
the pocket closed.

Then remembering something else I have to worry about, I
check to make sure I have my medication. How I'll manage to
take them at nine without Matt knowing is a mystery. But if
we're in the movie, I can always go pee.

Maybe I should just tell him I take pills. Maybe he won't
care that I'm not normal, that my body could reject his brother's
heart, that I'd die and take his brother's heart with me? That's
a big freaking maybe.

Feeling out of breath, I sit on my bed. Then bam, I worry.
I shouldn't be out of breath. Is this . . . ? It's not my heart. I'm
just nervous.

The doorbell rings. I shove my notebook in my purse. I rush
out. My phone dings. I look down. It's Brandy. Her text reads,
Call me.

She's gonna have to wait.

Dad, who popped into my bedroom briefly when he got
home, is already at the door. I tell myself he likes Matt and I
don't have to worry, but then again I also bet Mom told him
why I went to the doctor today. She probably told him she
bought me condoms.

I'm not so sure Dad likes Matt anymore.

"I'll get it," I yell out.

"Nope," Dad says in his stern-daddy voice. "I got it."

Oh, damn!

Leah looks fantastic. She looks hot. She looks nervous.

Matt's with her on the nervous part. Mr. McKenzie's order
of *treat her right and with respect* was father speak for *don't you
dare even think about having sex with my daughter.*

Matt answers with a big *yes, sir,* but it's too late. He thought about having sex with her when he first saw her in her jeans and a fitted shirt. Not that he planned on them going that far tonight.

They crawl into his car. Matt smiles at her. After losing control at the park last Monday, he felt like a horn dog. He's not a horn dog. Yes, he wants to have sex with Leah. He wants to have lots of sex with Leah. He wants to lie in bed and laugh about having sex like the couple did in the romance novel.

Late at night, if he's not dealing with an Eric dream, sex with Leah is all he thinks about. But he's not going to push her. He needs to at least tag a few bases first. What was it Eric had said, "Base jumping with a girl you like will likely lead to a foul ball or a complete strikeout."

Matt almost smiles. Eric had a sports metaphor for everything. Sometimes Matt wonders how he's ever going to make it through this life without his brother.

He starts the car.

"I'm sorry," Leah says. "My dad's acting like a jerk."

"He's your dad. Protecting you is his job." Matt means it too. And saying it has him remembering where he learned the term "horn dog." He had been working with his father and Eric in the garage, door open, changing oil in their cars. The neighbor's college-age daughter was gardening in her bikini, and Eric made a comment about how he'd like to get her to *handle his tool.*

His dad gave Eric a thump on his head and said he thanked God he didn't have a girl because he'd never trust any guy with her. "We're dogs," he said. "No offense, sons, but we are. It's our basic instinct." Then he gave them a stern look and said, "Try not to be too big of horn dogs."

His dad had been pretty good at advice too.

"He doesn't have to be rude," Leah says.

"He cares about you," Matt adds.

"Yeah, but you're not the big bad wolf." Leah buckles her seat belt.

No, he isn't. But he's still a dog. To prove it, while she's buckling in, his eyes, with a mind of their own, shift to her breasts, pressing against her royal-blue shirt. It's a scooped-neck shirt, but she's wearing a white tank underneath it.

She looks up, and so does he, albeit guiltily.

"How's your mouth?" He drives off.

"What?"

"Your mouth?" He glances at her.

She stares at him as if he's talking Chinese. "You went to the dentist, right?"

"Oh. It's fine."

She's fine. And he's not the only one who thinks so. He remembers Devon hitting on her. Remembers the hot kiss Matt gave her as a back-off message to the guy. "So no cavities?"

"Nope. Did I miss anything in math?"

"We went over some problems. Maybe we can do them tomorrow or Sunday." He waits to see if she plans on seeing him only once this weekend. After seeing her at school every day, the idea of not seeing her for a whole day gives him an empty feeling. Last weekend had been torture.

"That'd be good." She says it like she means it.

She starts talking about a scary book she's reading. Matt listens but recalls Eric being attached to the hip with Cassie. Is this what Eric felt for Cassie? Matt's never experienced this before.

Not even with Jamie Anderson. She went to Southside, and they dated for six months. They'd been sleeping together for three. He'd even tossed out the L word, but when he started football practice and working at the shop, she said she got lonely and wanted to see someone from her own school. It had hurt, but not bad. And whatever that was he felt for her, it doesn't compare with this.

"Did she get away?" he asks about the book.

"And kicked his ass." She smiles.

Spotting the restaurant, he pulls in and parks, then turns to her. "You hungry?"

"Starving. I barely ate lunch. Did you bring your notebook?"

"Yeah, but . . ." He leans over and kisses her. Her mouth is so soft. He doesn't want it to end. But he knows he can't take it too far. When he pulls back, he says, "I don't want the whole night to be about . . . that. Yes, we need to talk and there's something I need to tell you, but I want tonight to be about us too."

"Good." Her smile flashes in her eyes and lands right in his heart. "I like us."

"Me too." He kisses her again. When the kiss ends, he keeps his forehead against hers. "You smell like strawberries and vanilla."

"My shampoo." She buries her nose in his neck. "You smell spicy." She lifts her head up slightly. Their eyes meet again. "We should probably go eat and stop sniffing on each other." She laughs.

It's the sweetest damn sound. She still doesn't pull away.

Neither does he. Their eyes remain locked. He feels it. Want. Desire. He knows she feels it too.

She finally pulls back, but she puts her palm on his chest. He can feel her hand through his shirt. It's right over his heart. He loves it when she touches him. Too much. That's what caused the problem in the park. When her hands moved under his shirt . . .

She bites down on her lip like she does when she's nervous.

"What?" he asks.

"I learned something too."

"About Eric?" He's shocked.

She nods.

"What?"

"Let's talk while we wait on the pizza?"

He grabs his notebook and moves beside her. Something about her tone tells him she doesn't think he's going to like this. And there's only thing she could have done that'd upset him. Gone to Cassie's house.

28

Matt slips his hand in mine.

I sneak a peek at him. He's wearing his football jacket, and beneath it, clinging to his abs, is a dusty-green T-shirt. The jeans he has on look worn and soft and mold to his shape. A shape I'm getting fonder of each time I see it.

"What did you learn?" he asks.

"Let's get seated." Is he going to be mad?

The tangy scent of pizza sauce and yeasty crust welcomes us inside. A red-haired hostess seats us in a booth in the back.

Matt settles across from me. "You went there, didn't you? You went to Cassie's house." His brows pinch together. Concern turns his brown eyes a shade darker.

I try finding words in my defense. I come up empty, but then . . . "You have a cute nose."

He frowns.

I lift my chin defiantly. "That's what you told me when—"

"I know," he says. "But—"

"And you went anyway."

"I never promised I wouldn't go."

"Neither did I," I say with a touch of attitude that's new for me. But I like it. New Leah has spunk. Maybe not enough to run over a cop's toes, but maybe in time . . .

"If something happened to you, I . . ." He grounds out the words.

"Nothing happened. Almost nothing," I correct myself.

"What happened?" he growls.

"The cop, Mrs. Chambers's fiancé, Officer Yates, he sort of questioned me."

"Sort of?"

"Okay, he questioned me, but all's well that ends well."

Matt presses his palms on the table and leans in. "Do you realize the trouble you're in? The cop's going to call Detective Henderson, and he'll call your parents and . . ." He pushes an angry hand through his hair. "Your dad's not going to let you see me anymore."

"Slow down," I say. "The cop's not calling my dad. He thinks I was there about Jayden."

Matt looks confused. "About who?"

"Jayden Soprano. That's the guy who lived next door to Cassie—lived, past tense. He doesn't live there now. However, his dad and stepmom do. He moved, or ran away, right about the time Eric was killed. And listen to this: he's already been in prison."

Matt's eyes widen. "How do you know . . . ?"

I tell him everything from seeing the motorcycle to going to her house. He fills me in on what he learned from Marissa.

"Why would Cassie not want to go to school bad enough that she'd lie to her mom?" I ask.

"Because of me." Matt says. "She knows she's lying to me. She knows what happened to Eric and she's scared."

"But why turn away from her friends?"

He slumps back. "That I don't know." His gaze takes on a faraway look. "You said Yates mentioned someone calling her all the time. But it's not me. I stopped after Henderson warned me. So who could it be?"

"Someone else she's hiding from. Someone other than you."

We both sit there thinking. I pull out my notebook. "We're missing something. Lets go back to the dreams. You say you see the gun fall, then you feel pain. You don't mean that . . . that he dropped the gun and it went off, do you?"

Matt grabs his soda, gives it a couple turns, and doesn't look at me. And I see it. Doubt.

"No. I . . . I thought about that, but I had the dream again. When he fell, he fell facedown. You can't shoot yourself in the head like that. And anyway, he was shot at a closer range. I read the police reports. It doesn't support the gun falling and firing."

"What if Eric was holding it close to his head, and it just went off for some reason?"

"It didn't just go off," Matt blurts out. "It would make doing this a waste of time."

"Not really," I say carefully. "You need answers. I think Eric is trying to give them to you. To us. If it was an accident—"

He shakes his head. "Have you had dreams that make it look like that?"

"No," I say honestly.

"Then why would you think that?"

I carefully digest his question. "I don't think it, but anything's possible."

He closes his eyes. "Sorry, I didn't mean to sound . . ." He looks at me. "I wish I could believe it. Then I could lose this . . . anger. Or . . . maybe I'd still be mad at life."

I feel his pain. "I remember being angry when my grandmother died."

He nods, and after a second he says, "But it's getting better. I don't feel like I'm drowning in it anymore. It comes and goes.

I find myself thinking about other stuff." He offers me a sad smile. "Like you, for example."

"Good," I say. "I think about you too."

We can only look at each other with puppy-dog eyes for so long. We return to reading as the waitress takes our order. "You know what's strange?" I say after I read another of his passages. "We both hear shots going off, in different dreams. Did the detective say if more than one shot was fired from the gun?"

Matt leans back. "No. He said only one bullet was fired. I'm assuming the chamber was full except for one."

"Could someone else have fired? Did they look for other bullets in the area?" The moment I ask the question, I realize how much these questions must hurt Matt.

My chest aches, and I want to do something, anything, to make this right for him.

"I don't remember them saying they looked. But they found his body right outside the woods. According to both of our dreams, he was running for a while. So . . . if he was fired at, those bullets could be anywhere along that walking path. Or off of it, for that matter." He points to my book. "You wrote that he was running in the brush."

I cautiously ask my next question. "Is there any reason we can't go there? To the roadside park? Or do you . . . not want to? I understand if—"

"No," he says. "For a while I went there every day."

"I only went there once," I confess. "I didn't even get out of the car. That was the day I saw Cassie. It scared me. But I think I'd be fine if you were there."

He touches my hand. "We could do it this weekend."

Our waitress shows up with the pizza. Matt pulls away.

"Sorry, it's gotten busy." The waitress moves to put down our pizza, but her foot catches on the table and she jerks. The pizza flies right toward Matt and falls, cheese and sauce side down, on his light-green T-shirt.

"Come on in," Matt says as he pulls up to his house. "Mom's not here. It'll just take a second to change my shirt."

I follow him inside, curious to see where he lives. I'm imagining seeing all of the trophies he's earned in all the different sports he's played over the years.

Right before I step inside, I imagine the home feeling depressing since two people who lived and loved here have died. But as I walk into the living room, I make a complete circle and soak in the bright colors. Yellows, greens, and even some reds.

"Wow."

"What?" Matt asks.

"It's bold. I like it."

"Yeah. I'm kind of blind to it now. After Dad died, my aunt told my mom she needed to repaint with cheery colors so it wouldn't feel sad."

"Did it work?" I ask.

"No," he says. "She didn't start getting better until a few months ago. Thanks to my aunt again."

"What did she do?" I ask.

"She gave my mom a come-to-Jesus talk. Basically, she told her she had to get her shit together . . . for me." His tone holds echoes of sadness.

I hug him. "Your aunt was right."

"Yeah." He rests his hand on my waist. "I'm just glad she's getting better. She told me she's going back to work."

"What kind of work does she do?"

"Real estate."

I look around the house. "So where are your trophies?"

"My trophies?" He makes a funny face.

"Yeah. Every week I read in the school newsletter that you'd won another trophy."

He grins. "I remember reading the article about you starting the book club. I was actually going to join, but it conflicted with another class."

"Seriously?" I laugh.

"Yeah. Isn't it crazy that we both had crushes on each other all these years?"

"Yeah." I'm smiling again.

"Okay, come see my trophies." He takes my hand. He leads me down a hall and into a bedroom. His bedroom. I know because it smells like him. Spicy, male, and warm. One entire wall is bookshelves filled with trophies.

"Holy shit!" I start reading the inscriptions. Matt walks up behind me and wraps his arm around my middle.

"You should see Eric's. He has more than I do. Oh!" He jerks back. "I don't want to get pizza grease on you."

I continue reading. "Bowling?" I turn around. "You . . ." My words dissolve on my tongue. He's taking off his shirt. His muscles roll as he pulls it up. He's facing to the side and doesn't see me . . . seeing him.

My mouth is still open, words sit on my tongue, but I don't even remember what those words were. All I can do is stare. At Matt. At Matt shirtless. At Matt perfect.

His abs are so tight.

His chest so sculpted.

His skin so golden.

When he pulls the shirt over his head, the muscles in his biceps roll. My palms itch to feel those warm muscles move under my hands.

I'm breathless. Gawking is rude.

So I'm rude.

He even has a treasure trail of hair—which I learned about in romance novels—that starts right below his navel and dips down behind his jeans zipper and leads to his . . . treasure.

He's busy tossing his shirt into a basket. He's going to turn around any second and catch me.

I swing around and stare at the trophies.

"My mom loved to bowl. We were twelve when Mom signed us up to a league."

"Oh," I manage to say.

His footsteps ease in, and I feel his arms come back around me. His bare arms. Oh, heck, he hasn't put on a shirt yet.

His naked chest presses against my back. I swear I can smell his skin.

"Have you ever bowled?" he asks.

"Not . . . in years. My . . . grandma bowled." I'm pretty sure my words sound empty, or incoherent, because I'm fixated on him. Him practically naked.

One of his hands releases around me and he brushes my hair up. His lips press gently to the curve of my neck. Sweet tingles flow through my body.

I wish . . . I want . . . Why not? I turn around.

Boldly, I lift my hand and put it on his chest. He's so warm. I lift up on my tiptoes and my lips meet his. I don't wait for him to deepen the kiss, I go in deep, I go in with tongue, I go for it.

He pulls me close. I don't know how it happened, but we are suddenly on his bed. On our sides.

Still kissing.

I'm still touching his chest.

He pulls back and frowns. "We should . . . stop."

I don't want to stop. I don't want words. I want more of this. I almost died without knowing this. I want this now.

29

I go in for another kiss. I shift closer. My leg slips between his. I hear him moan, and his right hand moves up under my shirt to touch my back. All over my back. It sweeps around to the front, and he cups my breast. I feel his touch through the thin lacy bra.

I remember. The scars. I freeze.

He pulls back. His deep breath spills against my cheek. I force my eyes open. His eyes are wide, filled with heat, and an apology.

"I'm sorry," he says. "I didn't mean . . . I didn't bring you here for this. I swear."

"I know." I shift my legs out from between his. "I started it. I should be the one apologizing."

He brushes a few strands of hair off my cheek. "I want this so bad, but I don't want to rush you. I'm not just after that."

"I know." I must sound disappointed.

"Not that I don't want it. I do. I really do. And if you're ready . . ."

"A little later," I say. "Not too much later," I add.

"Thank God," he says, then looks embarrassed.

I chuckle.

He flinches. "I didn't mean . . ."

"It's okay. I feel the same way." That smile, the one that comes from so deep inside, shows up on his lips again.

The uncomfortable look in his eyes fades. He brushes a hand over my abdomen and fits it in the curve of my waist. He's careful not to touch my breasts this time, but he's close enough I wish he would.

"You're beautiful."

"Have you looked at yourself lately?" I say.

His brows knit together. "I wouldn't describe myself as beautiful."

I grin. "Okay, let's go with hot."

His eyes light up with playfulness. "You think I'm hot?"

I'm suddenly feeling extra bold. "Why do you think I literally threw myself at you? You took your shirt off." I give his chest a light slap.

He drops off his elbow onto his back, laughs, and turns his head to me. "You threw yourself at me?"

"Practically."

He kisses me again. It's sweet, sexy, but he stops before it becomes too seductive. "For the record, anytime you want to throw yourself at me, I'll catch you."

"Deal." I rest my head on his bare shoulder.

His hand moves over my back. Up. Down. I love the way he touches me.

"Thank you," I say with complete sincerity.

"For what?" His words brush against my temple.

I lift up and meet his eyes. "For not pushing me. You're not like other guys."

"I don't think you're like other girls either. I don't want to mess this up."

"Me either. My gaze suddenly catches on his bedside table. I blink, unsure I'm seeing what I think I'm seeing. "Is that . . . a romance novel?"

His cheeks turn pink. "I . . . Isn't that one of the authors you said you read?"

"Yes. You read it?"

"I went to find a book to read on our bookshelf and I saw it. I was curious."

"Did you read it?"

He smiles. "I'm afraid so."

"And it was good, right?"

"Yeah, I enjoyed it. It was . . . uh, very interesting in some parts."

I laugh. "Hey, I'll bet there's not more than six pages of sex scenes and there's more than three hundred pages in the book."

He chuckles. "There was nine and half. And they were very memorable pages."

"Well, you would hope so." I blurt out.

He starts laughing again and rolls on top of me, keeping most of his weight on his elbows. "When I finished reading it, all I could think was . . . I want that. The teasing, the flirting, the . . . sex. I want it with you." He kisses me.

I feel his weight, his body on mine in all the right places. I want the same things he does. But when I think about getting naked, I'm not ready.

He ends the kiss then and rolls off of me. "I think we should . . . uh, get off the bed."

We both get up. I watch him move to the closet to find a shirt. I watch as he slips it on. It's not quite as sexy as it was watching him take one off, but I'm still mesmerized.

Saturday morning, the alarm is the most unwelcome sound. I slap it off. Take my temperature, take my blood pressure. All's normal. I lay there, let the lazy feeling pull me back in. I think of Matt's kisses. I think of making love. I think about us going to college together. Of making career paths.

I doze off. So lazy. Gotta take my pills. I try to get up, but my body won't let me. I'm tired. No. More than tired. I'm debilitated.

Bam! I remember. I remember feeling this way 24/7 before I got the artificial heart. When my heart was . . . dying. When I was dying.

I force myself to sit up. Am I okay? Am I dreaming this?

I sit there, breathe in, breathe out. I do a mental medical check. The fogginess of sleep leaves me. Maybe I was just half asleep? I stand up. I sit back down. I lift my hands up in the air. Hold them up. To show myself I can. Because there was a time when I could only hold them up for five seconds.

I start counting.

One.

Two.

Three.

I get to ten. There's no effort needed. Tears are falling from my cheeks. I'm fine. Then again, I'm not fine. I'm afraid.

I'm afraid of dying. I put a hand over my mouth to keep the cry from escaping.

I don't want to go back. Haven't I already been there? Forced myself into accepting death. Now is it too much to ask that I can accept living? That I can count on it? Plan for it.

Then it hits me. I know what brought this on.

I'm afraid to believe I can think as far ahead as years. I suppose living with an expiration date on your ass can screw you up a bit.

But living in fear isn't living. I have to stop.

I sit back down. Give myself a pep talk. I'm alive.

I finally stand up. I'm tired, but not debilitating tired. It's my first week back to school, and I was out until midnight; then I stayed awake thinking about how good it felt to kiss Matt. How it felt to touch him and how his hands felt touching me.

Then I recall the dream that woke me up again. I frown when I realize I didn't write anything down. I close my eyes and see a flash. I see a gun falling, and right after I hear the explosion. I don't know how much the cops could tell if the bullet came from below, or if Eric would still have gunpowder on his hands.

Then it hits. Shit. Am I now having the same dream as Matt?

I drop back down, pick up my notebook, trying to remember, but I realize it's five past nine and Mom's probably drumming her fingers on the table impatiently.

I pop back up and head to the kitchen. Mom and Dad are at the table. Mom looks worried.

I see the words on her lips. *You're late.*

They remain unspoken but they're still loud. She needs to stop worrying. So do I.

I pull a glass from the cabinet, go to the fridge, and pour a glass of milk. Grabbing my pills, I drop into a chair beside them and take my pills.

I remember leaving Matt to run to the restroom at the theater and to take my pills, so he wouldn't see. I need to explain things to him.

Mom and Dad are staring. Something else is going on.

"What?" I say.

"Did you have a good time?" Mom asks.

Then I feel it. I feel the elephant in the room. *Oh, shit.*

This isn't just any elephant, it's a pink polka-dot one and it's wearing a purple tutu.

"I did not have sex!" I say.

"We didn't ask." Dad blushes. He bypasses pink and goes all the way to red.

Mom grins.

"Yeah, but you're thinking it. I see it on both of your faces." Neither of them denies it.

"I don't think you're ready," Dad mouths off. "You're only in high school, young lady."

My mouth opens and words spill out. Words that I didn't plan. "Well it's not like you two are virgins. If you were, I wouldn't be here. And don't think I haven't heard your creaky bed springs." I grimace and shiver at the thought. "When I do, I can't get to my iPod and headphones quick enough."

Holy mother of pearl! Did I just say that? Now I'm blushing.

Mom laughs. Dad looks horrified. I jump up, grab a breakfast bar, and shoot off to my room.

I'm barely out of the kitchen when I realize I'm smiling. Maybe it's seeing Dad embarrassed. Maybe it's just me being embarrassed. Or maybe it's because I'm honestly thinking about having sex. No, not just sex. Sex with Matt.

As awkward as that conversation was, it makes it feel . . . real. And it makes me feel normal. A normal girl doing normal things. Like fighting about having sex with your parents. I like being normal.

And normal means having a future. I need to start planning for one.

Four hours after the sex talk with my parents, the doorbell rings. I run to open it. Mom and Dad are in the breakfast room, which offers a full view of the living room and front entrance. Matt nods a quick hello to my parents. They nod back. Mom smiles. Dad gives Matt the stink eye. I'm almost worried Dad's gonna blurt out something embarrassing.

I'll die if he does.

"Where's Lady?" I ask Matt, hoping to dissolve some of the tension.

"I . . . left her at home . . . didn't want to chance her having another accident in your house." Subtly, he shifts from foot to foot. He's nervous but trying to hide it. I'm as nervous as he is.

I shoot Mom a pleading look to reign in Dad. She elbows him.

"Uh, let me grab my coat and we'll go walk," I blurt out.

Matt appears surprised. Originally we'd decided to study

first, but his quick nod tells me he's as eager to get the hell out of here as I am.

In less than one minute we're out of the house. As we move to his car, Matt doesn't even touch me. Doesn't speak.

We crawl into his car. I'm trying to figure out what to say.

He drives off, and we get a block from my house when he pulls the car to the side of the road and puts it in park. Then he leans over the console and kisses me. It's not a short kiss.

When it ends, he keeps his forehead on mine and opens his eyes. "I missed you. I barely slept last night. Every time I rolled over, I could smell you on my pillow."

I grin. "I'm not sorry for keeping you up, but I'm sorry about . . . my dad."

"He doesn't like me, does he?"

"Actually he does. He's just being overprotective. Don't let him . . . scare you off." The moment I say the words, I realize how much I mean them. I can't lose Matt. I'm not sure how he's become such an essential part of me, or of the New Leah, but he has.

"Never." The one word holds a promise. He drives off.

I'm feeling so light, so gushy warm from being with him, that I forget where we're going. When we get to the roadside park, the glow inside me fades to black.

There's a white cross at the edge of the property that someone put there in memory of Eric. It's fallen. It looks forgotten.

So are my lungs. I draw in a needed breath. We get out of the car, and I wonder exactly where they found Eric.

Matt doesn't speak—not one word. I know he's feeling this. This overwhelming spooky sadness.

We walk past the picnic table toward the path. I'm the one who suggested we come here. Is it too late to unsuggest it?

It's so weird. Like walking into a bubble of déjà vu. Or entering into an alternate world.

I know these woods. The smells. The sounds. I've listened

and memorized the way the wind blows through the trees. Even as I stand, completely still, I can feel the bottom of my feet pelting the ground. I've run these paths. The fear swelling inside me isn't new. It's not just inside me. It's here. It lives and lingers here like invisible footprints.

My footprints. But only in my dreams. When I wasn't me— when the heart thumping in my chest wasn't mine. But Eric's.

A shiver tiptoes up my spine. My lungs cling to my last breath, as if fearing it will be the last. Right then I know that's how Eric felt. He knew he was dying.

Matt starts walking, and I grab his hand.

He stops, faces me. "You okay? If you don't want to do this, we can leave."

No, I will not let fear win. "I'm fine. It's just eerie. I . . . feel like I've been here. But I haven't."

"I know." There's pain in his voice. "We can leave."

"No," I say with confidence.

He presses a soft worried-about-you kiss on my lips.

When he pulls back, I force a smile. "I'm okay." It's only a white lie.

We walk hand in hand down the path for the next ten minutes, both of us looking from side to side. Both quiet.

I tell myself I'm not alone. Matt's here.

As is Eric. I feel him. Another chill dances across my skin.

The breeze picks up. I stop when I see a dense stand of trees. The sensation that I've been here, right here, is stronger.

30

Matt studies me as if worried I'm freaking out.

Maybe I am, a little.

I sink into my jacket. The temperature is down in the forties. It's not just cold. It's a wet cold. Bone-chilling cold. It rained earlier, and the smell of damp earth is pungent.

As a winter wind brushes past, Matt's palm is reassuringly warm against mine.

I look down, brushing my foot across the dead brown leaves littering the ground. I think of the murder books where the police find bullet casings.

"Next time we should bring metal detectors," I say.

"Can we rent those?" He steps away; his palm slips out of mine. I feel the loss.

"We have some." I'm looking at the ground. "I used to go to Galveston Beach treasure hunting."

"Did you ever find any treasure?"

"A necklace." I brush my foot back and forth, stirring the wet leaves. "A locket, real gold. I keep it in my jewelry box on my dresser."

"Why don't you wear it?" He's pushing leaves away with his foot as well.

I glance up. "Because it's not mine. And . . . it feels sad."

"Sad?"

"It was empty. No pictures."

"Maybe she just hadn't put a picture in it."

"Maybe." Then I say what I really think. "I think she drowned. No one missed her. Her life was empty like the locket.

I used to think about her a lot." Especially when I was dying. I told myself I was lucky. At least I had parents who loved me.

He bumps his shoulder against mine. "See, you should be a writer. You can give her a happy ending."

I smile and wish I hadn't sounded so melodramatic. Back when I was dying, I had a real problem with that. I don't think I was depressed. It was as if thinking about other people's pain kept me from thinking about mine.

Matt continues to look at me. "Maybe we should come back later with the metal detectors?"

I pull my coat tighter. "Yeah." We start back, and he holds my hand. "Next week, do you want to go to the college for a tour?" My voice is low.

"Yeah." He looks surprised. "Why did you think of that now?"

"I don't want my life to be like the one I imagined for the girl who owned the locket. I want to live." And I want someone special in my life. Someone I'd put a picture of in a locket. I'd like it to be him.

We get out of the woods, and I see the downed cross. My mind whispers back to Eric. Matt lets go of my hand.

He walks over. Picking up the weather-worn cross, he pushes it back into the soft ground.

I fight the sting in my eyes. I refuse to cry when I know it hurts him more. But, damn it, I want to help him—to stop his pain. If I had a choice, I'd give Eric's heart back. I would.

He starts back to the car. I follow. He hits the clicker to unlock it. Instead of getting into the car, I turn and hug him.

"I'm sorry." My words are muffled by his shoulder.

We don't kiss. We stand there for the longest time. Matt leaning against his car—me leaning against him. Our arms around each other.

Our hair is tossed in the breeze. A few cars pass, just a reminder that the world is happening around us. But for me none of that world matters. It's just me and Matt.

It feels right. I could stay like this forever. It's not so cold when I'm in his arms. I'm not someone who was recently dying. I'm someone who is living.

His warmth is mine, and mine is his. Together we are stronger.

He pulls back. "Thank you."

I don't ask for what. I know he feels this. The connection. The way we are together. We're better.

"I called Detective Henderson." Matt says.

"And?"

"He wasn't in."

"We're going to solve this," I say. And I pray I'm right.

On Monday, Matt still hadn't heard back from Detective Henderson, so he calls the office again. Mrs. Johnson informs him that the detective is on vacation and won't be back until next week. Matt's frustrated—he even wonders if she isn't lying—but without another option, he resigns himself to wait. Thanks to Leah, focusing on her, he gets through the next few days.

On Wednesday they go to the park with the metal detectors and find nothing, and his frustration ignites again.

Thursday after school, feeling as if he's losing it, he drives over to Ted's house, where he knows his friends are shooting hoops. After all the hellos, they toss him the ball and expect him to join in.

He stands there, looks at them, and does what he's been meaning to do. "Did any of you see Eric that last week? Did he say anything, anything about Cassie and why they broke up?"

Their game-on expressions drop. Most of them won't look him in the eyes. He knows this makes them uncomfortable. But they were Eric's friends, too, damn it. Why can't they help? Why can't they at least talk about Eric? It's not like he didn't exist!

Matt doesn't move. He stands there staring, the basketball clutched between his hands. They finally start talking. Only to claim they don't know anything. Ted's the only one who doesn't speak up.

And because Ted was the closest to him and Eric, it hurts the most. "Did you talk to him?" Matt asks.

Ted still doesn't look at him.

"Talk to me, damn it!" Matt snaps.

Ted lifts his gaze. "You asked us already."

"I thought maybe you might have remembered something."

Ted rakes a hand through his hair. "It's hurts, man. It hurts thinking about him. And it's hurting you too. Isn't it time you . . ."

"Forget about him?" Matt yells. "It's so damn easy for all of you, isn't it? What kind of fucking friends are you?"

Matt knows it isn't fair. He knows it when he leaves.

He knows it on Friday when he finds Ted in the hall and offers a quick, "Sorry."

Matt starts to leave, and Ted speaks up. "I haven't forgotten. I think we're all just trying to move past it."

"I know," Matt says, then goes to find Leah. The one thing he knows—at least for a moment—can help him move past it.

He finds her just before she steps into class.

"Hi." She looks at him through dark lashes, her lips pursed in a bow. He wants to kiss her now. Not just a sterile, stolen kiss—but one that ends with them both out of breath.

He stops himself. They're going to study at her house after school, and with her mom now working, he can kiss her all he wants then.

"Still nothing from Detective Henderson?" she asks.

"No, but I'm leaving after first period to talk to him."

"You're skipping school?" Her oh-gawd tone tells him she's never done that.

"Not skipping," he says. "I wrote a note and faked Mom's signature that I have a dentist appointment."

She stops walking. "That's brave."

"Not really." He smiles at her innocence. "How about we skip school one day. Spend the whole day, just us, doing . . . whatever. Movies. Go to the bookstore." *Make out.*

Her eyes widen. "I've never skipped." Doubt shows in her voice.

"We're seniors. We're supposed to do that. It's a rite of passage."

They hurry to his locker to grab his notebook. Right before they walk into the classroom, she comes to a quick stop and faces him.

"Okay," she says.

He's lost. "Okay what?"

"Let's skip school. Soon."

Biting her lip like she does when she's nervous, he gets the idea he's pressuring her. "We don't have to—"

"No." She looks so serious and scared. "Old Leah wouldn't do it. But New Leah . . . It's like you said: it's a rite of passage. I don't want to find myself dying without having done it."

Her words rake over nerves, bringing pain to the surface. "Don't!"

"Don't what?" she asks, frowning.

"Act like you're dying. It's not the first time," he says. "It scares the hell out of me."

She buries her teeth back into her bottom lip. They stand in the doorway staring at each other. He suddenly realizes he's being an ass. "Sorry," he whispers.

The bell rings and students are waiting on them. Matt finally starts walking in, and Leah does the same.

The next hour, instead of paying attention to the teacher,

he's thinking about Leah. About how part of him is scared to love this much. He's lost too much.

No.

More.

Death.

The second the bell rings, and he pulls her out of class and into the lab he knows will be empty.

He pulls her against him. "I'm sorry. I just get scared sometimes."

"No. I'm sorry." She puts two fingers on his lips. "I lived one day at a time for so long, sometimes it just . . . It haunts me."

"But you're fine now. Look at you—you're completely normal."

She lifts up on her tiptoes and kisses him. The kind of kiss he'd been wanting earlier.

When Matt leaves school to go see the detective, the bright sun has burnt away the gray haze and the sky is a cobalt blue. It's still cold, but the damp gloom is gone.

He thinks about Leah, how much he depends on her, and wonders what he can do to make her happy. To make up for the all the bad shit she's had. To thank her for believing him when no one else will. Suddenly, he wants to get her a gift. Something to make her realize how much she means to him.

He's driving, plotting gift ideas, when he sees a jewelry store. He pulls in. The store is empty except for the older lady standing behind the counter.

"Can I help you?" she asks.

"Just looking." He realizes Leah doesn't really wear a lot of jewelry. Maybe this is a bad idea, but then he sees . . . a locket? Gold. Heart shaped.

"Would you like to see it?" The clerk pulls it out, opens the heart, and hands it to him. He sees the price tag.

It's more than he'd hoped, but after he sells the cars . . . He smiles at the woman. "I'll be back later."

Hungry, he hits a fast-food joint next.

He's attempting to pull out of the parking lot while unwrapping the hot biscuit when he sees . . . her. She's walking across the street. Cassie.

He almost floors his gas pedal to follow her, but realizes chasing her in his car would scare her.

Putting the car in reverse, he backs into the parking lot. There isn't a single parking spot. He sees Cassie's halfway down the block, turning a corner. Damn!

Tossing the biscuit in the passenger seat, he parks next door and hauls ass to catch up.

Unfortunately, the light changed and cars are flying past. He waits . . . Cars keep zipping past. Finally, he sees a small opportunity. He darts across the street.

When he gets to the corner where she turned, she's not there. "No!"

He takes off, looking in the business windows and praying he'll find her. Praying she'll talk to him. Praying what she has to say will offer him more ammunition to take to Henderson.

"Shit!" he mutters when she's nowhere to be found. He hears a dog barking and sees a woman walking a poodle, coming out of a small park another block down.

He runs down the street; his breath's uneven, his chest tight. He takes a second at the park's entrance and forces air into his lungs.

Trees and shrubs make up the landscape and create little alcoves. He walks down one side of the park, his frustration growing every second he can't find her.

Then he spots her. She's sitting on a park bench, staring at her phone.

Taking a deep breath, still unsure what he plans to say, he walks toward her.

31

She doesn't look up at first when he sits beside her. When she finally does, she gasps.

"Go away!" she screams.

"We need to talk." He uses the calmest voice he can muster.

Tears fill her eyes. "Do you know how hard it is to look at you?"

"Yeah, I do!" he snaps. "I see Eric every time I look in the mirror."

Her intake of air is an emotional sound. She jumps up and starts running.

"Cassie, please." He bolts after her.

He catches up and gets in front of her. "Damn it, Cassie. Just answer a few questions and I'll leave."

"I can't even look at you! It hurts." Tears sound in her hiccupy voice.

"Why?" He grounds out the one-word question. "What did you do? Why did you lie about Eric coming to your house that night?"

"I didn't lie!"

"Bullshit!"

She moves to go around him, and he blocks her again. "Talk to me! Tell—"

"Leave her alone!" The voice explodes behind him.

Matt swings around. The guy has dark hair and a tattoo peeking out of his collar.

"You son of a bitch!" Matt yells.

The guy throws a punch. His fist lands on Matt's left eye.

Bright flashes of light appear in his vision. Pain sparks in and around his eye socket, and he goes down.

"Stop, Jayden!" Cassie yells.

Confirmation that he was right about the guy's identity ignites another explosion in Matt's chest. Matt shoots up and strikes before the guy even sees him. Matt's fist slams into Jayden's mouth. He doesn't fall, but wavers on his feet.

Matt's holds both his fists up, shielding most of his face, and prepares for another swing. He notes his right fist is covered in blood. But so is Jayden's mouth. The asshole has sharp teeth.

Jayden goes for another punch. Matt dodges it.

"Stop!" Cassie jumps between them. "Both of you stop!"

"He killed Eric!" Matt seethes.

"No." She shakes her head. "He didn't."

"You went back to Eric and this guy got angry—"

"No, he's not who Eric was pissed at!"

Matt stares at Cassie. "Then who was he pissed at?"

"I'm here to see Detective Henderson!" Matt grinds out, standing in the homicide division department.

The receptionist looks up. Her eyes round. He hadn't even taken the time to look in the rearview mirror to see how bad he looks. But he knows one of his eyes is almost swollen shut.

"What happened?"

"I ran into a wall." He tries to keep from frowning, but he's hurting and he's mad.

"One minute." She jumps up and walks in the back.

Three minutes later, she walks out, and with her is Detective Henderson.

He walks up, eyeing Matt's face, and exhales. "Come on back."

Matt follows. Detective Henderson leads Matt to his office and says, "I'll be right back."

In less than a minute he returns with a bag of frozen peas and hands it to Matt.

"I'm fine," Matt says.

"Put it on your eye." His words string together like an order. Matt complies.

The detective drops in his seat. "What have you gone and done?"

"I left you a message. You didn't call me back."

"Yeah, and I was on vacation. And I mistakenly thought you'd be in school this morning. Not that I have to explain that to a kid who's nothing but a pain in my ass."

"Sorry," Matt mutters at the same time his phone rings. He pulls it out, glances at the number, doesn't recognize it, and turns the volume down. The vibration can still be heard, but he ignores it.

Matt looks back at Henderson. "I got evidence."

Detective Henderson frowns. "You've also been hanging out in front of Cassie Chambers's house too. Calling her all hours of the night. I got an earful from Officer Yates this morning."

Matt frowns. "I wasn't hanging out in front of her house. I was next door. And I haven't called her. Not once. You can check my phone." He pushes it to him.

The detective shakes his head. "Don't bullshit me."

Matt sits a little straighter. "I'm not. I went there to find Jayden Soprano."

"Who's that?"

"The asshole who murdered Eric." Matt's phone starts vibrating on the table again. He ignores it.

The detective runs a hand over his face. "I told you: I need solid evidence. I can't—"

"It's solid. Cassie and Jayden dated. That's why she broke up with Eric the first time. I'm sure he was pissed that she went back to Eric. Isn't jealousy one of the main motives for murder?"

"That doesn't—"

"He's an ex-con. He ran away from home the same time Eric was shot. Cassie's dating him now. He lives in an apartment on Pine Street. I don't know which one, but he drives a red Honda motorcycle."

Eric isn't sure what piece of information changed Henderson's mind, but the doubt fades from his eyes.

"How do you know all this?"

"Because I've been doing your job." Matt immediately realizes he shouldn't have said that. He needs the detective's help, and antagonizing him isn't the way to get it.

"I'm sorry. I'm just . . ." Matt inhales. "Marissa Leigh—she was Cassie's best friend. You talked to her. I spoke to her again and she told me about Jayden. Then Leah knocked on the Sopranos' door. The stepmom gave her this long talk about how he was already in jail once. Then I spoke to some friends of Eric's from a different school. They saw Eric the day before he died. They told me Eric said Cassie was seeing someone else."

Matt's phone starts buzzing again. Nervous it might be important, he pulls it over to see the number. He doesn't recognize it. But he remembers the Craigslist ad.

"You need to get that?" Henderson asked.

"No. It's just . . . I posted two cars for sale on Craigslist."

Henderson runs his right index finger over his chin. "How do you know Cassie is dating this guy now?"

"Leah saw her on the back of his motorcycle and . . . I just saw them together."

"Leah McKenzie?" he asks.

He realizes he never told him Leah's last name. "How do you know Leah?"

"Officer Yates." Henderson frowned.

"She wasn't there to harass Cassie. Just to get information on Jayden."

Henderson's jaw tightens. "And that shiner?" He frowns. "Tell me you walked into a wall and I'm walking out that door!"

"Jayden. He threw the first blow."

The detective groans. "You think he killed your brother, your identical twin, and you confront him. Are you stupid?"

Matt's gut tightens. "I didn't go looking for him. I saw Cassie on my way here. I followed her. Just to talk. Jayden showed up."

"Did this Jayden guy say anything? Confess to anything?"

"No, he . . . he saw Cassie arguing with me and started swinging."

"Did she say anything?"

Matt hesitates. "She said Jayden didn't do it. She claimed that Jayden wasn't the one Eric was pissed at. I asked, even begged her, to tell me who he was pissed at. But she clammed up. Wouldn't say anything. She's just protecting Jayden."

After a few more groans, Henderson has Matt write everything down.

"So you're going to reopen the case?" Matt asks, his gut crunching on hope.

"I'll look into it if you can promise me something."

"Anything you say."

Detective Henderson hesitates. "Promise me that if I don't find anything this time, you'll let this go. Deal?"

Matt nods even though it's a promise he's not sure he can keep.

"I'm going to check and see if this Jayden character really has a record. If he does, it might merit talking to him."

"Thank you," Matt says with emotion. His phone buzzes again. The detective eyes his phone. "You know about our safe exchange zone, don't you?"

"What?" Matt's lost.

"For selling your car. There's two spaces marked off and under surveillance in the station's side parking lot. Don't give any information about where you live or anything, just set up for them to meet you here. When people know they're being watched by a camera, they're less likely to try something dirty."

"Do I need to let you know if I'm coming?"

"No. Just drive up. The spaces are marked. There's a sign that lets everyone know they're under surveillance. Do it during the day."

Matt nods. "How long before I hear from you on the case?"

The detective frowns again. "As soon as I find something. I have other cases, so it's not as if I can drop everything. But you have my word I'll look into it."

Matt believes him and realizes he's smiling. He stands up and offers the man his busted hand.

The detective hesitates. "One more condition."

"What?"

"You and this Leah chick don't go anywhere near Cassie or this Jayden guy. Not them, their houses, or their neighborhood. I'm already gonna hear about this fight. Yates is pressing to get a restraining order out on your ass. And after this he might get it. He's superprotective of Cassie. And I don't blame him. The girl's had a rough time too. So, I'm serious. Got it?"

"Got it." They shake hands. Gently, because his hand's still throbbing. He's still smiling when he leaves.

I'm standing in the lunch line, still debating if I'll join the book club back in the classroom or just sit by myself. I'm not doing cartwheels about either. All I want is the day to pass so I can be with Matt. Alone.

I've had a pissy day. I pull out my phone I retrieved from Mr. I'm-an-Asshole Perez after class. He confiscated my cell because he saw me looking at it. He accused me of texting. I told him I was only checking the time to go to take my pills. I was certain his clock was ten minutes off, and it was. Not that he cared.

I asked him to look at my phone to confirm I wasn't texting, but he wouldn't, and he didn't believe me. It sucks to be a rule follower and be accused of not being one. I mean, if I'm going to be punished, shouldn't I just break the rules anyway?

Now, since phones are allowed in the lunchroom, I look at my text messages. Matt still hasn't texted me about Detective Henderson. I worry that's bad news. The cluttered lunchroom noise echoes around me, making me feel more anxious. The smell of tuna casserole fills my nose.

I hear the words "heart transplant" sound behind me. A toad-size lump is bobbing in my throat. I want to be alone, so I bolt out. I think I hear my name. Thinking Matt might have returned, I look back.

It's not Matt. It's Ted. Matt's friend. He's pushing through a crowd to get to me.

I shove my emotions back.

"Hey," he says when he gets to my side. "Can we talk?"

About what? "Uh, yeah."

I follow him to a quiet corner outside the library. He drops back against a wall, looking nervous. My heart starts that strange kind of pounding. "Is something wrong?"

"Sort of," he says.

I imagine the worst. "Is Matt okay?" Instant emotion tumbles around in my chest. It feels like it's Eric again.

"Yeah. Look, last week Matt tried to talk to me and our friends. About Eric."

I remember Matt telling me he'd spoken to them. He hadn't said how it went, but I could tell it wasn't good.

Ted starts again. "Matt refuses to believe Eric killed himself. It's been months, and he's still on this mission to prove differently. I'm worried. I was hoping when he started dating you that . . . that he'd let it go. It hasn't helped. He can't keep doing this to himself."

I try to decipher the emotions that are mine and those that might be Eric's.

I breathe in and out.

"I was hoping . . . maybe you could talk to him. Convince him to let it go."

I bite down on my lip. "Thing is, I'm not sure I believe Matt's wrong." I start to tell him about Jayden, but it's not my place.

Ted frowns. "The police proved it."

"But . . . the cops are wrong sometimes."

"Not this time!" He glares at me. "I thought you were the sensible type."

He's angry. I'm not sure how to react.

"I am sensible. Matt just wants—"

"I know." Emotion laces Ted's voice.

"What do you know?" I'm sensing he has some knowledge he's not sharing.

He shakes his head, then blurts out, "Fuck!"

"If you know something that Matt doesn't, he . . . he needs to know." Ted's eyes are damp with tears. "He'd hate me. I already hate myself. I should have done something."

My chest swells with emotion. "What happened?"

"I . . . I saw Eric that day. He was getting gas at the service station. I pulled in and asked him to go swimming. He was so mad. I asked him what was wrong and . . ." He inhales another shaky breath. "Eric said . . . He said he'd rather die than . . . than do nothing."

Ted bangs his fist on the wall. "I didn't understand what he was taking about. I asked him, but he wouldn't say."

Ted scrubs his hand over his eyes. "Eric said he'd rather die. I should've done something—stopped him." Tears cloud Ted's eyes. "I didn't think he meant he was going to kill himself! I didn't, but I should've."

32

I'm walking out of the school to my car. The sky is blue; the sun is out. The day is prettier than my mood. All I've been able to think about today is Ted's confession. I dodge frenzied students racing to their cars, trying to get out first. *Life's not a race—it's a journey,* I want to tell them.

My phone beeps with a text. It's Matt. *Be at your house at 3:15.*

I text back, *What happened?*

His answer: *Went to the police station.*

Does this mean the detective is reopening the case? And knowing what I know now, is that good news? Is Ted making more out of what Eric said than he meant? Oh, hell, I don't know. I'm so damn confused. And scared. Scared we're reading the dreams all wrong. Scared this will wind up hurting Matt instead of helping him.

I'm not sure what I'm going to say to Matt. Ted pleaded with me not to tell. He wants to be the one to tell him.

I never promised anything. I don't know what's right or wrong.

As I drive home, I keep hearing bits and pieces of Ted's conversation. *Eric said he'd rather die than . . . than do nothing.*

I don't understand the *than do nothing* part. *What* the hell was Eric dealing with? It's like there's a missing piece to the puzzle.

I pull up in my driveway. The house looks lonely. Funny how I can tell Mom's not home.

I get out of my car and unlock the door. I miss her calling out to me, miss the cookies. Miss her asking how my day was.

I wouldn't have told her it was effing bad, but it's nice to be asked. Not that I want her to stop working. It's the last thing I want. She deserves a life.

Nothing but the house's hum fills the space.

I grab a cold Coke and go to my bedroom. I deposit my backpack on my dresser and try to shed the stress.

The pink clock on my bedside table shows the hour. Matt will be here in twenty minutes. What am I going to do? Tell him, not tell him?

I pop the top of my drink and lay back on the bed. I hold the cold can to my ear, listening to the fizz *pop-popping* in the can.

Tell him? Not tell him?

And what is he going to tell me?

My phone rings. It's Mom, checking in. We talk for about four minutes. She's already loving her job. It occurs to me again how much she gave up for me. I never want to go back there again—stealing the lives of others while losing mine.

We hang up, and I stare at the ceiling and remember my "skipping school" comment that sent Matt into a panic. How would he feel if he knew that if I accidently skipped a pill, my body would start killing Eric's heart? That I would die? Eric's heart would die?

Is it fair of me to be dating Matt? To be lying to him?

I'm not lying. I'm just not telling him everything. And I will. Just not when we're still new. Let him see how normal I can be before I tell him that I'm not.

I look at the time. I force myself to get up, change blouses, comb my hair, and am brushing my teeth when I hear the door-bell.

I rinse my mouth and run for the door. In spite of the whole to-tell-or-not-tell issue, I want to see him. Touch him. Breathe in his scent.

"Hey." I force a smile when I open the door. Then I see him. Matt's eye's almost swollen shut. I gasp.

"What happened?"

"It's just a black eye." He steps inside. Closes the door.

"Did you have a wreck?" I reach up to touch him but am afraid I'll hurt him.

While I'm staring at his eye, he moves in for a kiss. I stop him.

"No. Tell me what happened." I touch his cheek.

"Don't be mad," he pleads.

Just like that I know. "You confronted Jayden?" And I'm mad. "You promised—"

"I confronted Cassie, not him. While I was driving to the police station, I saw her walking. I followed her. I found her in a park. She got mad—was yelling at me when Jayden showed up and . . ." He holds his hands out. "And this happened."

My mind's going in circles.

"Let me get you some ice." I step back.

He grabs me. "I already iced it."

I see his swollen hand and moan. "Doesn't it hurt?"

"Less than it did before. And even less now that I'm with you. You're magic." He wraps an arm around my waist. "Detective Henderson is going to look into things. He had me write everything down. Said he'd call me when he learns more."

Hope lights up his eyes. Dare I tell him what Ted said? Risk taking away Matt's hope? It's not like Eric really said he was going to kill himself. How many times had I said that I'd die before doing something? It's a figure of speech.

"What did Cassie say?" I ask.

He sighs. "Basically what you said. It hurts to see me. And she swears Eric didn't come see her that night. But Eric told me—"

"How do you know he told you the truth? I know you think Eric didn't keep secrets. But he never told you about Jayden. Maybe he wasn't really going to Cassie's that night."

Matt frowns. "You think he was meeting Jayden? That he

didn't tell Cassie?" Matt releases me. "He might have been going to threaten him with the gun and then . . . It could have happened." Doubt resonates from his voice.

He runs a hand through his hair. "Why wouldn't he tell me that? I don't get it."

"Maybe he was embarrassed, thought it made him look bad."

"But he told John and Cory!" The hurt gives his words a deeper quality.

"Your opinion mattered more," I say, wanting to say anything to help.

He gets quiet again. "She also told me that Jayden wasn't the one Eric was pissed at."

"Who was he pissed at?" I ask.

"She wouldn't say. She just clammed up, and I know she was just protecting Jayden."

I look up at him. I sort of agree that Cassie isn't telling us everything. But I also don't believe she's lying about everything either.

He wraps his arms around me again. "You can't ever go back to Cassie's or Jayden's house. Officer Yates told Henderson he thinks we're stalking Cassie."

"Me?"

"Yeah, and the last thing I want is to get you in trouble. So stay away."

I nod.

He looks up at the ceiling as if thinking about something that's bothering him.

"What's wrong?" I ask.

"It's . . . I just wish Cassie would talk to me. If she's not behind this, and she's hurting, I think . . . I'd like to help her. What if Jayden hurts her?"

We stay there, leaning into each other, my head on his chest, his cheek on top of my hair. It's so easy to be here. To stay here. To forget everything but how this feels.

But some things have to be said. I force myself to speak. "I worry that we might never have all the answers. Will you be okay with that?"

"I'll just never stop looking." His body tenses. "I need answers."

And what if the answer isn't the one Matt wants? What if the dreams are a way for Eric to show us how scared and hopeless he felt. To make us understand why he did it.

I'm so confused now. I don't know what to believe.

I put myself in Matt's place and realize either way I'd need to know. Maybe even the wrong answer will offer Matt closure. But closure isn't pain-free. I want to protect him.

"Sooner or later we have to let bad things go." I hear my own advice, and I know I'm still working on heeding that wisdom myself. I realize that, no matter how different our issues are, we are dealing with the same thing. Death.

But not just that.

Life. Learning to live. Learning to count on tomorrow and next year. Knowing we're both still here and figuring out where to go next.

"I missed you today," he says after a long pause.

"Me too." I lift my chin and rest it on his chest.

He looks at me, swollen eye and all, and leans in for a kiss. I recognize the kind of kiss this is. One that takes us to temptation. I pull back. "We should study first."

He grins. "Why did I know you were going to say that?"

I take his left hand and lead him to the dining room to study, but I remember my backpack is in my room. I keep walking down the hall, his hand in mine.

I release his hand to grab my books. When I look back, he's leaning against the doorjamb. He's staring, his eyes wide. I remember walking into his room, liking that I was going into his space. Everything in his room reflected something about him.

My room doesn't quite offer the same. "Go ahead and say it."

I can tell he's trying not to laugh. He steps in. "It's pink." He does a slow turn and then looks up. "I don't think I've ever seen a pink polka-dot ceiling fan."

I laugh. "When I was in the hospital, Mom redid it. She likes pink."

"What matters is if you like it."

"No. What matters is she did it out of love. I don't like it. But I didn't have the heart to tell her. Not until recently anyway."

"Then redo it. I'll help you paint."

I smile. "Be careful—I might take you up on that."

"I hope you do." He walks over to my dresser and stares at the framed selfie of Brandy and me. "How long have you been friends?"

"Since she moved here in third grade."

"I can tell she cares about you."

I think about him and Ted again. "I care about her too."

He points to the jewelry box. "Is this where you keep the locket?"

I'm surprised again that he remembers stuff. "You want to see it?"

"Yeah."

I open the box; the little ballerina pops up and starts dancing to the chime of a slow love song. I pull the necklace out. It's cold to my touch. It's old, not antique, but old. The heart locket, etched with swirly designs, hangs open. I feel the sadness I felt the day I found it.

"I cleaned it. It was dirty." I hand it to him. "The clasp is broken on the locket."

He studies it. "Maybe there was a picture in it and it just fell out. Maybe it isn't a sad story."

Does he remember everything I say? "I broke it when I opened it. But it could have rotted out or something." It's kind of odd how one associates emotions with things. The locket makes me sad. Books makes me happy. Hot chocolate makes me miss Grandma.

Matt's staring at my reflection in the dresser mirror, and I swear he sees everything. My crazy emotions, my fears, my love for him. It hits me then. I love Matt Kenner. It's too soon to say it, but I know it's true.

"Maybe the girl who lost it had a happy ending. And she just lost the necklace."

"Yeah," I say, but it comes out forced.

"We're going to be okay, you know," he says. "You make me okay."

"And you me." I reach up on my tiptoes and press my lips to his. And I'm the one deepening the kiss. Oh, hell, we can study later.

I kiss and walk at the same time, moving him backward until he hits my bed. Then I give him a slight push. He falls back and laughs. I fall with him.

I smile down at him. "Gotta problem with my pink bed?"

"Not if you're in it."

We kiss.

We touch.

We dive right into temptation.

But like before, we leave the clothes on.

It still feels amazing.

We get to that point—even quicker than before—when we have to stop or we're tempting fate. Matt ends the kiss.

Yet fate has never looked so welcoming. I lift my head and take his mouth again. I run my hand under his shirt and up his chest. Our legs are a tangle, pressing in all kinds of wonderful places. I stay on that ride. Not wanting it to end.

Matt pulls back again. "We should probably . . ."

"Stop," I finish for him. "Sorry."

"Don't be." We lay there, only our hands touching and watching the pink polka-dot fan whirl above us. He leans up on his elbow.

I see his face. "Crap, I didn't hurt your eye, did I?"

"No." He sweeps a gentle finger over my lips. "This . . . it's your call."

I know what he's talking about. I nod. Part of me wants to say now. Right now.

"I have . . . protection," he says. "For when you're ready."

"Okay." No way am I going to tell him I have some too—that my mom bought them for me. Or that I'm on the pill. But I'm glad we're actually talking about it. I look over at him. *Oh, and I have a scar and I'll be wearing a sexy camisole when it goes down. I hope you don't mind.*

The words do backbends on the tip of my tongue. But I can't push them out.

"And we can go somewhere," he continues. "A nice hotel . . ."

"That would be good." Talking about sex so matter-of-factly has every nerve in my body tap-dancing. It makes it so real.

And bam, I'm suddenly curious. Has he done it before? I want to ask, but I might not like the answer. Then other crazy questions start popping in my mind. Does he sleep in the nude? Does he read before he goes to bed? Does he ever talk to himself in his sleep?

Burying my unanswered questions, I grab my backpack. We move to the dining room table and study. My curiosity fades into just . . . excitement. About him. About us. About discovering every little detail of who he is, all his habits.

This is living, I think. The electric hum I feel in my body. The obsessive need to know everything about him. The thrill of knowing love and expressing it. This is what I would have missed without Eric's heart.

———

Matt arrives home, freeing Lady from her kennel and letting her smother him in kisses. Then he ushers her outside. While she does her business, he does his. He writes a big whopping lie of a text to his mom.

Played ball. Had fun, but got elbowed in eye. Got a shiner.

He knows if she arrives home and just sees it, she'll freak. If she's forewarned, she'll still freak, but not as much. And she won't question his story so much.

She texts back.

Oh, goodness. Put ice on it. Be home in two hours. Love you.

Already iced. Love you too.

He pauses and then texts back, *Did you have fun?* She'd met her sister halfway between Dallas and had gone shopping.

Yes. Got work clothes.

Every day he sees her getting better. She's looking better too. She's taking better care of herself. He knows she's still hurting. He's not sure it will ever go away, but she's living again. Sort of like him now that Leah's in his life.

He and Lady go to his room. His mind plays back the whole scene with Cassie and Jayden, of speaking to Henderson, but quickly leaves those memories in the dust to concentrate on his time with Leah. How it felt being on top of her. Under her. Beside her. How just being with her is like a drug.

He remembers the locket he'd seen at the jewelry store. It wasn't exactly like the one she'd found. But he didn't want it to be exact. Just enough that the message was clear. She would have her happy ending. Her locket wouldn't be empty.

He grabs his phone to see if one of the pictures Leah took of them on the bench last week could work. Jumping up, he downloads the images onto his computer and prints them out. They're almost perfect.

The doorbell rings. Lady starts her high-pitched barking. When he turns into the living room, he sees Ted's car out the window. Matt's surprised to see him.

Things still feel strained between them.

When he opens the door, Ted stands there, shoulders drooped and his hands buried in his jean pockets.

"Hey." Matt opens the door for him to come in.

"Shit. What happened to your eye?"

"A scuffle . . ." Matt hesitates to say more.

"With who?"

"Cassie Chambers's boyfriend. I found out she was seeing him when Eric and her were dating."

"Crap," Ted says. "I thought she was crazy about Eric."

"I know." Matt moves into the kitchen and drops into a chair.

Ted's hands go back into his pocket. His shoulders drop lower. "I . . . need to tell you something." He pulls his hands out and sits down looking extra nervous.

"What?" Matt asks.

I'm running. A tree, a big tree, looms ahead. An oak tree. Beside it are two pine trees. Twins. Identical in size. Identical in shape. Not that it matters. Nothing matters but running.

I'm winded. Can't get enough air. My sides pinch. My legs cramp. I need to slow down. I can't. I'm going to die. All of a sudden I hear a gun explode. Everything starts moving in slow motion. I see the bullet shoot out in front of me. The bark on one of the pine trees in front of me splinters. I see where the bullet buries itself deep into the pine. But I still can't stop running.

Faster. I have to go faster.

Another sound surrounds me. Not a pop of a bullet. It's . . . it's . . .

My alarm's tone makes the dream feel less like reality. But I feel myself still running. I gasp at air and finally yank myself free of the dream. I lay in my pink room, pulling in air and not moving. I try to remember the details.

This dream was different.

For almost the last two weeks, I've had the same dream. Nothing changed.

Now it's different. Why? Does it mean anything?

I sit up; my head's pounding. I press a hand against my temple. Blink. Wait for it to go away. It always goes away. Not this time. Then it hits. This isn't Eric's pain. It's mine.

I pick up my pen and pad and write down the notes. Bullet. Twin pine trees.

A chill runs down my spine. I shiver. This isn't an I'm-scared chill, but an I've-got-a-fever chill.

No! No! No! My heart starts racing. I find the thermometer and bury it under my tongue. The pain in my head throbs with each thud of my heart. I start counting, waiting for it to beep. Waiting to be proved wrong. Twenty-three, twenty-four . . .

Finally, the tiny beep fills the silence. I pull it out. I stare. A gulp of fear forms in my gut. Effing hell!! I have a fever. 101.

I'm not positive of all the signs of rejection, but I know fever is on that list.

"You up, sweetie?" I hear my mom's voice. "I'm about to head out."

Shit! "Yeah," I say and slam back down, pretend to be half asleep.

She peeks in. "I'll see you this afternoon. Love you."

"Love you." I wave. As soon as the door closes, tears fill my eyes. It's only been this week that she stopped asking me about the temperature or blood pressure. This week that she stopped being afraid.

I can't tell her. I can't. I don't want to pull her back to rubbing her hands raw. Back to preparing herself for her only child to die.

Dad calls out his goodbyes. I respond with, "Love you." And I do. God, I love them, and I don't want to hurt them anymore!

As soon as I hear the door close, I grab my blood pressure cuff and fit it on my arm.

Even as panic turns my blood cold, I know I'm overreacting. I inhale and force myself to remember that there could be all kinds of reasons for the fever. Reasons that don't mean I'm rejecting the heart.

Reasons that don't mean I'm dying.

33

"Congratulations," Dr. Hughes says. "You have your first post-transplant cold."

"A cold?" I've never loved a diagnosis so much. But yeah, on the way here I noticed my throat hurt, but the panic had already set in. The marbles were crowding my chest and didn't allow me to think straight.

The doctor moves in. I hadn't even called her office. I'd called Brandy.

We'd been waiting at the doctor's door when the front desk clerk unlocked it.

"Just a cold," I say. My phone dings. I ignore it. Dr. Hughes has a no-phone rule. Plus, I kind of know it's from Matt. I'd texted him and told him I had a headache and wouldn't be at school.

"Your transplant book lists the kind of cold meds you can take, but I've written them down here. Because of your immune system, the cold might hang on longer than before. You need to rest, get fluids and TLC. Don't go to school as long as you're running a fever."

She tilts her head to the side and folds her hands over her chest. I know that look. "Your mom doesn't know you're here, does she?"

I shift my shoulders, trying to knock off the guilt. I'd lied to the desk clerk, but lying to my favorite doctor is harder. "She just started her job this week. I didn't want . . ."

I hear her exhale. "She's going to be furious at you for not telling her. And she's going to be livid at me for not calling her."

I get my con face on. "But I lied to you. You never knew any different. My bad."

She sighs.

"Besides, I'll take her anger over her quitting her job or something. Because she would have. You've seen her." Those damn marbles rolling around my chest get heavier. "She gave up everything to take care of me. I refuse to do that to her again."

Dr. Hughes frowns. It hurts. I don't get a lot of frowns from her. "She loves you."

"And I love her. That's why I did this." The doc's frown remains steady. "I'm going to tell her. But now I can tell her it's just a cold and you've given me your white-coat blessing."

She drops down in a chair. "How are things other than your cold? You feeling okay? School not too much for you?"

"It's great. Good."

"College plans?"

"Working on 'em."

She picks up her chart and clicks her pen. Click. Click. Click. "And the dreams?"

I consider lying, but I've already done that today. "Still having them." I vaguely recall I had one this morning.

"And you still believe these are more than dreams?"

"Yes." I wish I could lie to her. I know that's what she wants to hear.

She nods. I can't read her expression. Not sure if it's disappointment or disbelief. "There's support groups that you can join. Others who may even share your feelings."

That almost sounds as if she believes me. "I'm okay." Right then I realize I'm no longer scared of Eric. Maybe it's because I love his brother.

Maybe it's because I'm more afraid of Jayden Soprano.

When I leave, Brandy is in the waiting room, chewing on her nails. She does that when she's nervous. I didn't think about how bringing me to the doctor would worry her. I'm a terrible friend.

I walk over to her. She looks up, eyes round, cheeks pale. It's a look I haven't seen on her face in a long time. It's the oh-God-my-friend's-dying look. I hate what I've done to everyone. But at least this time it's nothing. *This time.* "I have a cold."

"You scared the shit out of me over a cold?" she says way too loud.

Then she jumps up and hugs me. The waiting-room crowd watches us.

"You're going to get my cold," I whisper.

"Don't care," she says. "I love you," she blurts out.

"I love you too," I say, and get teary-eyed. When we pull back, I see everyone is staring. But they're smiling too.

On the drive back, I text Matt, confirm it's a cold, and say I'm fine.

Brandy insists on playing nursemaid. She gets me home, runs to the store, and buys the cold medicine Dr. Hughes suggested and a couple of cans of chicken and stars soup.

I hate chicken and stars soup. But when she serves it, I eat at least half of it because she bought it. I strip down to only my old extralarge, extraworn blatant-book-geek T-shirt and panties.

We lay in bed. I still have a few marbles rolling around my

chest. But they are lighter as I listen to her talk about boys, sex, and graduation. She's scared we'll stop being friends when she goes away to Austin. She's afraid Brian will find someone else when he goes to school in Alabama.

I can't promise for Brian, but I assure her we'll still be friends when our hair's gray and our boobs hang down to our belly buttons. And that really happens. I know. I saw Grandma naked once. Not pretty.

At one o'clock, the doorbell rings and Brandy goes to see who it is. When she returns, she's not alone. Matt stops at the foot of the bed. "How sick are you?"

"Just a cold," I insist.

Brandy walks behind him. "Okay, who's going to tell me what happened to his eye?"

"I ran into a wall." Matt keeps staring at me as if worried.

"Ooookay." Brandy says with disbelief, but drops it. "He brought chicken and stars soup. I told you everyone eats it when they get a cold."

Brandy hangs out a while, then heads home. I try to get Matt to go, so I can regroup and decide how I'm gonna tell Mom. He refuses.

He lays in bed with me, and we talk about trivial stuff. His best vacation, his favorite movie, the best scenes in Harry Potter.

Then I notice the flicker of pain in his eyes. Did he have another dream? Or . . . ? "What's wrong?" I ask. "Did you hear something from Henderson?"

"No." He pauses. "Ted came by last night. He told me about Eric. He also told me that he told you."

I feel disloyal for not telling him sooner. "He begged me not to tell you. Said he should do it."

"I know. It's fine. I . . . What Eric said was just a figure of speech. He wouldn't do that. He wouldn't."

I bite down on my lip. He wants me to reassure him, and I

want to, and I believe him, mostly. But there's a part of me that worries Ted's right, not even so much about Eric but about me trying to get Matt to move on. Am I helping Matt or hurting him? If I encouraged him to stop, to let it go, would he? "Henderson is going to get to the bottom of it." That's all the encouragement I can do now.

We settle back into low-key chatting. The cold medicine must have made me sleepy, because the next thing I know, a deep loud voice is yanking me from slumber.

I pop my eyes open.

"This is not okay!" Dad's standing at my door. Matt's snuggled beside me. He's lifting his head off my pillow, staring at my dad. I must have kicked my covers off and my T-shirt rose up because my white panties are there for everyone to see.

I snatch the blanket to cover myself.

Dad points a finger at Matt. "Get out!"

Matt scrambles up. "I . . . I . . ."

"It's not what you think, Dad!" I blurt out.

"What I think is he was in your bed. Am I imagining that?"

"I'm sick. I went to the doctor. He brought me soup." I wave to the bowl of half eaten chicken and stars. The fact that Brandy brought that can doesn't matter.

Dad's anger fades faster than ice cream in August.

"What's wrong?" His fear, the familiar pain, echoes in his eyes. And smacks me right in the chest, reminding me how much I've hurt them.

"It's a cold. Just a cold. I went to see Dr. Hughes. She did bloodwork and everything." I sneeze, perfect timing.

"Why didn't your mom call me?" Dad's no longer glaring at Matt, who's now standing as far away from my bed as possible, looking eager to bolt but unable to do so because Dad's blocking the doorway.

Dad's gaze shifts to Matt. Matt shuffles his feet. "We were just talking, sir. She fell asleep. And I did too."

Dad nods but his gaze goes to my covers and I can read his mind. *Next time you have a cold and are just talking in bed with a guy who brought you chicken soup, you should be fully clothed.*

It's a week and a half later. Friday night, to be exact, and I hear the doorbell, knowing it's the pizza Mom ordered. I sit up, nervous about the dinner conversation I plan to have.

Breathing deep, I stand up, stare at my reflection in my dresser mirror, and finger-comb my hair. It took everything I had to kick that cold in the ass. Actually, I think it kicked me first. But it didn't kill me. It did increase my I-could-die anxiety.

Dr. Hughes was right about the cold lasting longer than before. She was also right about Mom being livid that I hadn't called her before I went to see Dr. Hughes. When she came home that night, she did exactly what I was afraid she'd do— had a hissy fit, started rubbing her palms on her hips, and threatened to quit her job.

I did exactly what I shouldn't have done. Something I'd never done. I blew a gasket. It wasn't pretty.

It was as if those marbles in my chest turned into golf balls, and the only way I could make them go away was to speak my mind. I told her she had to stop treating me like I was dying. Never mind that I was trying to stop doing that myself. I told Dad he had to accept I wasn't thirteen and would eventually get naked with a guy.

Thankfully, Dad, always the negotiator, although upset, played referee during my gasket blow and Mom's hissy fit.

We ended up compromising. Dad worked from home while I recovered from my cold. Mom didn't have to miss work after just going back. I apologized for not calling them when I realized I had a fever—though I wasn't really sorry about that—and for threatening to run away. Perhaps that was a tad dramatic. I didn't apologize about being in bed with Matt.

We hadn't been doing anything wrong.

I still blame the biggest part of my gasket blow on being sick. Which was a bummer. Not that the whole week sucked. I read four books. I'm up to ninety. Yes!

Brandy came over every day. So did Matt. However, the Dad-at-home part of the bargain meant Matt's visits were stressful. Not that Matt complained. And not that Dad was rude, just curt. When I apologized to Matt, he said he didn't care. Nothing was keeping him from seeing me.

We didn't make out, but we studied. And we talked. A lot. I think I know just about everything there is to know about Matt Kenner. His favorite cartoon was Pokémon. His favorite band is the Chainsmokers. He told me Eric and Matt stories.

I noticed that when he talked about Eric, he didn't clench his jaw like he had before. I think that's a good sign.

Mom calls me to dinner. I move in and sit at the table. Instead of diving into the needed conversation, I dive into the pizza. I pretend I'm not freaking out. Pretend I'm not about to lie to my parents. It's not as if I haven't lied to them before. I'm not a saint. I've lied to them plenty of times.

Just not a premeditated lie. And I've been premeditating this one to death.

"Do you really like pineapple on your pizza?" Mom asks.

"Yeah. For some reason, I've been craving sweet and salty things together." Not that I'm tasting anything right now. "It's good." To prove it, I take another bite. I'm chewing. I'm contemplating.

Oh, damn. I'm pretty sure I'm going to screw this up.

I actually consider telling them the truth. Just come out and tell them that tomorrow Matt and I will spend the night in a hotel. Telling my parents—well, at least telling Mom—should be easy. She took me for a presex exam. She bought me protection. She put me on the pill.

Yet the last thing I want to do is tell her. Because then all I'll think about tomorrow is about her thinking about me having sex. So . . . I hafta lie.

"Oh," I say around the pizza as if speaking with a mouthful makes lying easier. "I'm spending tomorrow and tomorrow night with Brandy."

Did I sound guilty? Shit shit shit! I sounded guilty!

"You're not going out with Matt?" Mom asks, wearing her concerned-Mom expression.

"She doesn't have to go out with Matt," Dad says, looking pleased. If only he knew.

"We'll probably all go to a movie." I toss out another lie and start chasing a loose mushroom around my plate. When I catch it, I fork it.

"That sounds fun," Mom says. "Your dad and I are going to the Bensons' for dinner."

I swallow, chase, and kill another mushroom. Then push my plate away. "Do I need to help clean up?"

"Nah, you did dishes last time," Mom says. "It's your dad's turn."

Dad grins. "She can clean up if she wants to."

"Wouldn't want to take that joy from you." I force a smile. Now with the lie completed, I can go to my room and start having my scheduled panic attack over me spending the night with Matt.

34

"I'm going fishing with Ted this weekend in Galveston," Matt sits down with his mom Friday night when she returns from grief counseling. Lying is always a little hard, even when he's not doing anything wrong.

Then again, it's not just the lie that has him on edge.

It's this weekend. As ready as he is, as excited as he is, he's nervous. He wants Saturday night to go perfect.

"That's nice. You haven't done that in a while."

So true. He swallows. He knows she doesn't mean what he's thinking about, but it still hits a nerve. If the saying "practice makes perfect" is true, he's in trouble. It's been eighteen months. And he wasn't so sure he had everything down then. Jamie didn't always seem to enjoy it nearly as much as he did.

And he really wants to make sure Leah enjoys this.

His mom gets up and opens the fridge. "You want a sandwich?"

"Nah, I had a hamburger." He turns the soda can in his hands. The condensation makes his palms damp. Or is that nerves?

Pushing those thoughts away, he glances up at her. "Didn't you go out and eat dinner?"

"Yeah, some people in the grief-counseling group met for dinner. But I'm usually pretty overwhelmed after the meeting and never eat more than a few bites."

Matt watches her take out the mayonnaise and lunch meat.

"But it's helping, right?"

"Yeah. I'm better than I was." She grabs a knife and starts

spreading mayonnaise on the bread. She glances back up. "Then sometimes I feel guilty because I'm better."

"I know," Matt says. He'd been dealing with that himself. There's a part of him that's walking on air when he's around or thinking about Leah; then there's the other part. "I realize I'm happy and then I feel bad for being happy."

The fact that he hasn't had the dreams lately is good because he's sleeping better. But there's still those odd times, like seeing the shake menu, when it hits him.

Detective Henderson called him yesterday with good news. He'd confirmed that Jayden did have a police record. They weren't officially opening the case yet, but they'd called to get Jayden to come down for questioning. That's when Henderson learned Jayden was in Florida with his dad. Matt flipped a little and told the detective Jayden wasn't coming back. Henderson assured Matt that he'd already called and spoken to the father.

Patience.

"The counselor says it's normal. We have to keep going," his mom says. "He promises that it'll get easier."

Matt nods and decides to just blurt it out. "Mom, I went to see Detective Henderson again."

He waits to hear her scold him, tell him that he has to let things go. Instead, she places a piece of ham on the bread, and he wonders if she heard him. He starts to repeat himself when she looks up.

"I know. Detective Henderson has kept me in the loop."

He swallows the gulp of surprise. Did she also know where he got the black eye that is only now starting to fade? "Why . . . why didn't you tell me?"

"I was trying to figure out how I feel about it." She brings the sandwich to the table and sits down. Her green eyes are round and unreadable.

"And how do you feel?" *Did he really want to know?*

"Scared," she says.

"Scared of what?" he asks.

"To believe it. I want so badly to believe that Eric didn't . . ."

"He didn't, Mom. I know."

"I hope that's true." She takes a deep breath. "But then when I think someone did this to him, I get furious. And I realize that I can't let that consume me either."

"I know," he says. Right then he remembers what Ted told him Eric said that night. It was the first time Matt really felt any doubt. But when he tried to envision Eric pulling that trigger, knowing what it would do to him and his mom, Matt kicked the doubt away. He knows that Jayden Soprano killed his brother.

When he looks up, his mom's staring at him again. She leans over and puts her hand on his. "No matter what, we have to go on living."

"I'm doing that." He takes a sip of soda.

She settles back in her chair. "I know. I see you smiling more. And I can't help but wonder if it isn't due to the elusive and mysterious Lori."

"It could be," he says, but his gut knows that's the most ridiculous understatement that's slipped off his tongue in a year. *Lori* is the biggest reason he's doing as well as he is.

"I want to meet her," his mom says.

"Yeah." That's something to worry about another day. How will his mom feel when she discovers that Leah has Eric's heart?

Saturday I drive over to Brandy's and park in her driveway. Her parents are away this weekend, making it perfect timing. Except that I know Brian is staying there.

I don't like the idea of interrupting their time. But Brandy insisted I show up at noon so we could chat before Matt arrives at one to pick me up. He hasn't told me exactly where we're going, except to Galveston.

I'm nervous as hell. Probably more about my scar than the sex. I keep hearing Brandy's gasp when she saw the scar and imagining the sound coming from Matt's lips. I hope he can handle it.

I grip the steering wheel and do some deep breathing to calm my nerves.

"You coming in?"

I jump an inch off the seat, then look at Brandy—still wearing her frumpy pajamas—standing outside my window. I wonder if that's what she wears when she sleeps with Brian. I brought some long pajama pants, but I also have some sexier tight boy shorts that will match the pink silk camisole that I plan on wearing to bed . . . and keeping on.

"Yeah." I get out of the car and go ahead and grab my bag so I don't have to get it out of my car when Matt gets here.

"You okay?" Brandy asks.

The girl reads me like a page-turner. "Fine." I realize Brian's car isn't here. "Where's Brian?"

She grins. "I asked him to leave so we could talk. I knew you'd be nervous."

"I wish you weren't right."

She drops a hand on my shoulder. "It's gonna be great."

We crash on the sofa to talk and wait on Matt. Brandy starts giving me hints on what guys enjoy in bed. It gets weird really fast. It gets funny even faster.

We end up laughing so hard I forget to be nervous. But I sure as hell remember the second the doorbell rings and I realize it's probably Matt.

Brandy gives me a best friend hang-on hug. The kind that only comes from real friends. "Don't worry."

I grab my bag and go to the door to meet Matt.

His kiss is more than just a quick hello. That's all it takes for me to know how much I want this. I love him. I know that for certain. When the sweet, almost sensual kiss ends, he notices I have my bag and takes it from me. "So you're ready?"

"Yeah." We offer quick goodbyes to Brandy and walk to his car.

When we get settled, he looks at me. "I left my phone at home. Do you mind if I swing by and get it?"

"No."

On the quick drive to his house, we talk about Lady missing him and about the math test we took yesterday.

When he pulls up in his drive, he says, "Come in. Mom's not here."

I get a strange feeling about his "Mom's not here" comment. It occurs to me that he hasn't introduced me to his mom. Not that I'm worried. It just seems . . . odd.

"Yeah, I probably should use the restroom before we take off."

I follow him inside. Lady barrels toward me, her whole body wagging. Matt heads to the kitchen and motions to the bathroom. "I thought my phone was on the table. I probably left it in my pants." He heads off on his phone search.

I head for the bathroom. Lady stands outside the door whining.

A minute later, I step out of the bathroom. That's when I hear the front door opening and closing. I freeze. A woman steps into the kitchen. Our eyes meet.

"Hi," I say. She's blond with green eyes, pretty. Doesn't look anything like Matt, yet somehow I know it's his mom.

"Matt's . . . looking for his phone."

She smiles. "I'm Matt's mom. You must be the mysterious Lori."

No. "Uhh . . ."

She drops her purse on the table and moves in. I think she's going to hug me, but at the last minute, she stops and drops her hands to her sides.

"Matt talks about you. You've been . . . good for him. I appreciate that."

I nod. "He's been good for me too."

Footsteps sound as Matt walks in. "I found . . ." His gaze shoots to his mom and then me. His eyes round with what looks like panic.

"Hi, hon. I just introduced myself to Lori."

Matt nods, his gaze shifts to me. "Yeah."

"Would you like something to drink?" his mom offers. "I have tea, Coke—"

"No," Matt's speaks up. "We're . . . I've got to drop her off and head to Ted's."

His mom looks disappointed. "Well, we'll chat another day. Soon." She shoots Matt a motherly look then turns to me. "Lori, make sure he brings you back."

I barely have time to nod when Matt takes my hand and leads me out.

"Sorry," Matt says before we even get in the car.

"For what?" I ask.

"You weren't prepared."

Huh? "What would I have to be prepared for? She seems nice." We get in the car.

"She is. She just . . . For a while, she was unpredictable."

"She seems fine now." I smile. "Although, she has my name wrong." I look at him. "Did you used to date someone named Lori?"

"No." He pulls out of the drive and looks tense.

It hasn't occurred to me that Matt might be nervous about this, us being together. I kind of like it that he is.

It's four o'clock when Matt pulls into the hotel entrance. He needs to tell Leah the truth. Why he's worried about his mom meeting her, but . . . it sounds bad, or wrong.

As he goes to get the keys, Leah waits outside. He has the fake driver's license that Eric made for them. Matt had never used it, but right now he's glad his brother got it because the legal age to rent a hotel room is eighteen, and he's a couple months shy of that date.

Matt greets the clerk and lays the license down that claims he's twenty-one, praying there's not an issue. This whole weekend would be ruined if he can't get in.

The woman smiles, welcomes him, and hands him a parking pass and keys.

He hurries back out to Leah. Climbing in the car, he smiles at her. She smiles back. He can tell she's nervous. And he hopes his plans will put her at ease. And him too.

"I thought we'd take our bags up to the room, then go to the beach. I brought a blanket."

"That sounds great." She looks across the street to the beach. "I don't think we could have gotten better weather."

"I ordered it," he says, teasing.

Ten minutes later they're sitting on the blanket listening to the sound of waves coming in. The wind is blowing, a little cold, but not uncomfortably so. They're wearing jackets, but the sun, low in the eastern sky, adds a bit of warmth.

Leah's watching the waves and he's watching her. Her dark hair is blowing in the wind. She looks so carefree. So beautiful. He pulls out his phone and snaps a picture.

She looks at him, and he snaps another. "My hair's a mess." She pulls a handful of hair back.

He takes another, then adds, "No, it's beautiful." She scoots closer to him and looks back out at the ocean.

Right then he has one of those moments that he and his mom talked about last night. Where he feels so damn happy and lucky, followed by a wave of guilt because Eric can't feel this.

Then he remembers how many times Eric told him, *"Hey, Dad wouldn't want us moping around. We gotta keep going."*

Eric wouldn't want him moping either.

When Leah looks back at him, she's smiling again.

"This is beautiful," she says. "Thank you. I haven't been to the beach in forever. I forgot how much I love it. The sound is . . . like music. The salty air. Even the sand." She runs her fingers in the loose sand.

He leans over, brushes her windblown hair from her eyes, and kisses her. "I wish it was Maui or some other famous beach. You deserve something exotic. Something picture-perfect."

"This is perfect!" She looks back to the waves. "We should have brought the metal detectors. We might have found treasure."

"I did find some," he says. "You."

She looks at him, and this time she kisses him. It's sweet but sexy, reminding him of what they have to look forward to later. When the kiss ends, they recline on the blanket. He wraps his arm around her middle, her back pressed against him, and they face the water and waves.

Her hair occasionally blows in his face. He doesn't care.

They talk about everything and nothing. Beach movies. Beach reads. The different beaches they've been to.

Above, a few pelicans and seagulls fly past. A few other waterbirds are right at the water's edge, dodging the tide each time it rolls in.

He kisses the back of her neck. "You taste salty."

"Sorry," she says.

"I like it." He kisses her neck again.

She giggles as if it tickles. It's the sweetest sound in the world. He closes his eyes and buries his face in her hair that now smells like fruit and the ocean. Emotion fills his chest. Happiness and . . . love. He loves Leah McKenzie. He's never been surer of anything. But he worries it's too soon to throw it out there. So he keeps the "L" word to himself for now.

They stay there, wrapped in each other's arms, surrounded

by sand, water, and a magical feeling that says nothing in life could go wrong. Not that Matt believes it—too much in life has already gone wrong—but this moment is perfect, and he wants to celebrate that.

Every now and then someone walks past, but it doesn't take away from the feeling that they exist in a world of their own.

Time passes but they don't move. The sun starts to set and everything feels washed in gold. They watch as the sky turns shades of pink and purple, then goes to a dark blue.

It gets colder, and they just move closer until the day fades to night.

She rolls over and faces him, touches his cheek. Emotion fills her eyes. "I'm so glad I didn't miss this. I could have . . . left and not remembered how the beach feels, smells, or sounds. I could have left without knowing what you and I feel like together."

Her words both move him and scare him. "You're not leaving. You've got the best heart in the world." And he kisses her.

After getting all sappy at the beach, Matt and I go to the restaurant beside the hotel. I concentrate on enjoying every moment, telling myself that even the nervousness is a rite of passage, like skipping school.

I realize all of the other things that should've been on my bucket list: fall in love, lay on the beach, watch the ocean for hours, skip school, and make love to the person who rocks my world.

Matt rocks my world. I love him, but I want him to say it first.

We order fried coconut shrimp, fries, and steamed vegetables. Only one order because neither of us is very hungry. But when the shrimp arrives, it's hot, crispy, and a little sweet. I eat more than I thought I would.

We walk back to the hotel holding hands. We ride up to the

eighth floor holding hands. We stand in the room that is big and feels expensive holding hands.

I was here earlier, but I feel as if I'm seeing it for the first time.

Both our bags sit on the end of the bed. A big bed. I offer to pay part of the room cost, and Matt's insulted. "I just don't want—"

He shuts me up by kissing me. When he pulls back he says he's going to shower to get the sand from his ears. He grabs a few clothes and walks in the bathroom. The click of the door closing sounds loud. I can't help but imagine him undressing.

I get my makeup bag, my sexy boy shorts, and camisole out of my small suitcase and wait for him for to finish so I can shower. Sitting on the edge of the bed, a high bed, my feet dance an inch off the carpet. I feel small.

I listen to the spraying water.

In my mind, I see him again. Water rolling down his body. Even as nervous as I am, I feel an electric kind of anticipation.

I try to not to think about my scar. Then I think about it. I panic and practice what I'll tell him when he tries to take off my shirt.

The shower cuts off. I take a few deep breaths. He walks out; a puff of steam escapes behind him. He's only wearing a pair of navy boxers. Nothing else. There's still a few droplets of water moving down his torso. His hair looks darker, his chest wider. He looks older. I suddenly feel young. Or maybe not young, just inexperienced.

I slide off the bed. "My turn."

He steps in front of me and kisses me. He's shower warm and smells like hotel soap. I kiss him back. Then I pull away.

"I should . . ."

"Yeah." He steps back. I walk into the warm bathroom with steam that smells like Matt. I shut the door and start to lock it, then don't because I'm afraid he'll hear it and interpret it to mean something. It doesn't mean anything. Except I'm afraid. Of him seeing me naked.

I feel my blood running in my veins. I strip down, step in the shower, and let the hot water hit my shoulders. Finally knowing it's time, I step out. I dry off with the fluffy white towel and slip on my pink camisole and the light blue-and-pink boy shorts.

I brush my teeth, silently sing the birthday song, comb my hair, and then I just stare at myself in the foggy mirror.

I can do this. No, I want to do this.

35

Turning to the door, I recall how confidently Matt walked out of the shower and try to do the same.

He's sitting on the bed, his back against the headboard. There's soft music playing from his phone. I feel his eyes on me. He's seeing more of me than he's ever seen. And I'm aware of every bare inch that his eyes are taking in. I'm aware of how my breasts feel in the top without a bra. I'm aware of how high the boy shorts fit on my thighs.

I get into bed and sit beside him. Our arms touch. He dips his head down and his lips brush my bare shoulder. "You're so . . . hot."

I know what he means, but I say with a tease, "The water was too warm."

He chuckles.

Then I blurt out. "I've never done this. I might not do it right."

He brushes a wet strand of hair off my cheek. "I'm nervous too. But I think we'll figure it out."

He kisses me. And in just minutes we are stretched out on the bed. I'm on my back, he's leaning on his elbow. His bare leg is against the side of my bare leg. I'm in awe of how his skin feels against mine. How good his palm feels resting against my mostly bare abdomen. How there's not an inch of him without muscle.

He kisses me; his hand moves down my forearms to my waist. "Tell me if . . . if you don't like something."

"Right now, I like it." I'm savoring every tingle, every touch.

He pushes his hand up, captures the bottom of my camisole and starts bringing it up.

I catch his hand, pull it to my lips, and kiss his palm.

He gazes up.

"I . . . I prefer to keep the top on."

His brown eyes, filled with heat, stare up at me through his dark lashes. He lifts up on his elbow and studies me as I rest on my back.

I feel butterflies in my stomach, and not the good kind. "I . . . I have a scar." I swallow. "It'll fade in time. But now it's . . . not pretty." I bite down on my lip.

He presses a finger over my lips, the touch so soft I can barely feel it. "I don't care about the scar. I care about you." His finger slides down my chin, follows my neck down, and stops on the top of my camisole, right where the scar starts.

"If it makes you feel better to keep it on, then do it."

I nod.

He keeps talking. "But I have an ugly scar on my leg where I was skateboarding and rolled onto a broken beer bottle. Should I put my sock back on?"

I know what he's trying to do, but . . . "It's different."

"No." He sits up and leans back against the headboard again. Then he bends his knee and shows it to me.

It's about nine inches long and it's zigzagged. And it's a lot more puckered than the one on my chest. He takes my hand and runs it down the marked skin. "It's just a scar." He kind of smiles. "Eric was always jealous of it. He said it looked cool. Made me look tough."

He pauses and then starts again. "Did you know in some cultures scars are looked at as badges of courage?" He hesitates. "I don't see mine like that. But yours? Yeah, that's how I see it. I've never met anyone else who's been through what you have and is so brave. The day I went to your house to tutor you, you were so . . . alive."

"I wasn't brave," I say. "I didn't have any other choice."

"We always have a choice."

I don't know if it's his words, the tender way he's looking at me, or something inside me that says for this to be right, to be perfect, I can't hold back. I can't hide.

This, being with him, is not just about removing my clothes. It's about removing my fears, vulnerabilities. It's about trust.

I sit up and reach down to pull the camisole up over my head. I feel bold and bashful at the same time. But I also feel vibrant. Like for the first time I'm living in full color. Maybe this is what growing up feels like.

Or maybe I'm letting go of Old Leah and completely embracing New Leah.

Matt draws in air, but in a good way. "You're amazing."

And there's nothing in his voice, his eyes, or his expression that says he's lying.

He eases me back on the mattress and presses his lips to the top of the scar. Slowly he kisses his way down.

I no longer feel the scar. Just the soft whisper of his lips on my skin. For the first time since I was told my heart was dying, I don't feel broken.

I feel whole. I feel beautiful. I feel normal.

———

Monday morning at school, I'm waiting by my locker for Matt. He dropped me off at Brandy's around three yesterday. We talked on the phone for about three hours last night. An amazing three hours.

I'm studying the oncoming crowd, searching for his face. Waiting to feel that jolt of joy.

I think I finally found a negative side to having sex with Matt. Being with someone in that way makes not being with them feel wrong. I missed Matt so bad last night and this morning that my bones ached.

I finally see him walking toward me, and he's smiling as big as I am. There's a spark in his eyes that I don't know if I've seen before. I wonder if everyone can just look at us and know we had sex. He wraps his arm around me and kisses me. Not a long kiss, but not a short one either.

"Good morning," he says.

"Not as good as yesterday," I say.

"Tell me about it."

Hands locked, palms touching, we walk to his locker to get his science book. I hear his phone buzz.

He reaches for it quickly and finds a spot between lockers to take the call. I start beside him and suddenly realize what today is. Monday. The day Detective Henderson is talking to Jayden Soprano.

"Hello." Matt answers, listens, and then frowns. "No, I haven't sold it yet. I already told you I won't go down that low." He pauses. "Sure. But if you're just not willing to pay my asking price, please don't waste my time."

I realize it's about the cars he's selling. When I was sick, Matt met about eight people at the police station's safety zone to show the cars and give test drives. All of them tried to talk him down on the money. He refused to sell them. I wonder if the reason is really the money. Or is it the fact that the cars belonged to his dad and brother.

"Okay." Matt squeezes my hand. "Call me when you make up your mind."

I look up at him when he hangs up. "And?"

"It's the guy from Houston. He wants to see Dad's car again—the third time. Just to make sure he's not paying too much. The car's got less than a thousand miles on it."

"Are you supposed to call Detective Henderson today, or is he calling you?"

"He said he'd call me. But if I haven't heard from him by four today, I'm calling him."

I reach over and hug him.

"I'm okay," he says, sensing my concern.

"Yeah," I say, but I know he's not. He's holding his breath to hear from Detective Henderson. Waiting for closure and justice for Eric.

Since Matt's mother is working, after school we go to his house to free Lady from her kennel and study. All three of us end up in Matt's bed. An hour later, we are just getting to studying when the doorbell rings.

Matt jumps up and puts his shirt on. I make sure my clothes are on right and follow him to the door, not wanting to get caught in his bedroom.

I sit on the sofa with our books, and Matt opens the door.

"You know something?" Matt says, and I look up and see the man at the door.

I realize it's Detective Henderson.

"Can I come in?" he asks.

"Yeah." Matt swings open the door. "I was about to call you."

The detective looks at me. "I'm Leah," I say.

"Nice to meet you." He walks in and sits in one of the chairs and then glances back at Matt as if suggesting he do the same.

That's when I know he doesn't have good news. I feel it. It's as if a dark cloud followed him inside.

My stomach knots, and I move the books to the coffee table. Matt sits next to me. I can see from the way he drops that he suspects the same thing I do.

"What do you know?" he asks.

The detective exhales. "Jayden Soprano didn't do this, Matt."

"Just because he said it! You believe him? What do you expect, for him to admit it?" Matt shoots up; his posture screams pain. My chest aches.

"No." The detective's voice is calm, direct, but still somehow caring. "He wasn't in town. He and his stepmom had gotten into a big argument and he went to New York to stay with his mom. I spoke to the mom; she confirms everything. He even got a speeding ticket on his bike the day Eric was shot."

Matt stands there, his fists tight. His spine tighter. He looks beaten, abandoned, alone.

But he's not. I'm here. I go to stand beside him. I try to slip my hand in his, but he won't take it.

"Eric did not kill himself!" he says to the detective.

Detective Henderson stands up. "I feel terrible having given you false hope. I really thought . . ."

"It's not false!" Matt says.

"Matt, I know you believe that. And hell, maybe he didn't, son, but there's not one thread of evidence that says that. And it's going to eat you alive. You promised you'd let it go."

When the detective leaves, Matt's torn up. I try to talk him into taking Lady for a walk, but he won't do it.

When I try to hug him, he pulls away and says he wants to be alone. I start to argue, but remember times when I was sick in the hospital and asked my parents to leave. Most of the time, they wouldn't do it. And I needed it.

So I squeeze his hand and I leave him.

But I don't stop hurting for him. I call him that night, but he doesn't answer. A few minutes later, he texts me, *Just need time.*

"Are you okay?" his mom asks.

Matt looks up and sees his mom standing in Eric's doorway. After Leah left, he forced himself to come in here. He's not even sure why. He needs to be as close to Eric as he can be. And in here there's not one spot in the room where he can't see him. Sitting at his desk doing his homework, laying in the bed playing his Gameboy or tossing a football up and catching it.

His mom walks in and sits beside him on the bed.

"You're early," he says.

"Detective Henderson called me."

"I can't accept it, Mom."

She puts an arm around him. He hears his own sobs before he knows he's crying. She hugs him tighter.

He pulls himself together and sits up. "Eric knew what this would do to us."

"Son, I don't want to believe it either. I swear I don't, but . . ." She takes a deep breath. "Right after your father died, I got to this mental place. It was so dark, Matt. So dark I lost connection to who I was. To the fact that I had you two boys to care for."

"But you didn't kill yourself."

She hugs him again, and he hears her breathe in. "I thought about it. And I'm sorry for that."

Matt stares at her. She speaks up again. "I hope to God you never get that depressed, but having been there, I understand how Eric could have done what he did."

Today's Friday. The past few days have been status quo. We met up after school and either went to his house or mine. I can tell

Matt's working on accepting things, but he's still hurting. I can feel it when I touch him, when he touches me. When I look into his eyes. What he's feeling is so raw and deep I can't soothe him.

Matt and I have a date tonight. But he has another appointment to show his brother's car and probably won't come over until around eight. I know even selling the car is going to be hard on him.

As I'm driving home, my stomach growls, my mouth waters, and I realize I barely ate my lunch. Suddenly I know what I'm craving. I drive past my neighborhood and head to Desai Diner for butter chicken.

I get seated in a back table and the same waiter, Ojar, comes over. I'm pretty sure he's the owner. "The usual?" he asks.

"Yes, thank you."

I pull out a book from my purse and read while I wait for my dinner. The food arrives, and I eat and read, losing myself in a story about a girl dating a guy who finds out he has cancer. It's sad, but I'm compelled to keep reading. I'm not sure if it's really that the book's good. It could be more the subject— dying—that is so relatable that it has me sucked in.

A few chapters in, emotion floods my chest. It's so strong that I stop reading. Maybe I'm not ready to read this.

I sit there and chase my chicken around my plate but don't eat any more. I drink my water, leave money on top of my bill, and go to leave. I'm almost out the door when I realize that the emotion wasn't coming from the book.

Sitting alone at the other side of the restaurant is Cassie. Considering I haven't felt this or had dreams in almost three weeks, I thought I was finished feeling Eric. Then I can't help wondering if it was Eric who brought me here now.

I watch as Ojar delivers Cassie's food. He walks off. She's looking down at her food and doesn't see me—which is a good thing since she probably already thinks Matt and I are stalking her. I start to walk off but everything inside me says it's wrong.

No, not everything. My heart says it's wrong. Eric says it's wrong.

Well, shit. How much time will I get for first-offense stalking? I walk up to the table.

She looks up. I start to introduce myself, but then her eyes widen. "Oh, great. Now you're following me too."

"No. I was here before you. But since we're both here now—"

"Just leave, okay. And stay away from Jayden. He told me what you did."

I swallow. My better judgment says I should go, and I try to: I turn, but I can't. Something inside won't let me.

I swing around and sit down on the other side of the booth.

"What is it you want?" she asks.

"Eric loved you. He still loves you," I say, because I think he wants me to say it.

She wasn't expecting that and falls back against the booth. "That's why it hurts so much." She looks around. "I've just now got to where I'm able to come back here. We came here all the time. This was his favorite restaurant."

"I know."

She sits her fork down. I see she ordered the butter chicken.

"You're eating Eric's favorite dish," I say.

She studies me. "Are you the girl he dated when we broke up?"

"No." *I'm the girl who's got his heart.* "I'm dating Matt, but . . . I feel as if I know Eric, because Matt's always talking about him."

"They were close. Sometimes I was even jealous of their relationship. He loved me, but he loved Matt more." She fiddles with the napkin. Her eyes are tearing up.

I see her pain. I feel her pain. Cassie didn't do anything to hurt Eric. But, like Matt, I suddenly think she knows something.

I hesitate. "You told Matt that Jayden wasn't the one who Eric was pissed at. Who was he angry at?"

She looks up, then down. Refusing to answer.

I don't stop. I feel it more than ever. Cassie holds the key to unraveling what happened to Eric. "Do you really believe Eric pulled that trigger?"

Her shoulders tighten. She bats a few tears off her cheeks. "The cops said he did. It was his dad's gun."

"But do you believe it? Matt can't, and like you said, they were close. Wouldn't someone that close to Eric know if he was desperate enough to take his life? Wouldn't you know? Don't you think there'd be some signs? Did you see those signs?"

She looks away and starts shaking her head. "He was upset and . . ."

"About what?" When she doesn't answer, I continue. "Matt says Eric couldn't have done that. He wasn't depressed. He wasn't going through a crisis—not one Matt knows about, anyway. What was going on that we don't know about?"

She looks down at her plate. Contemplating. Thinking. She almost looks as if she's praying. I don't know what she's doing, but my gut says to let her be.

She finally glances up but appears dazed, lost in remembering something unpleasant. Tears collect in her eyes again. "I don't want to believe it."

"Believe what?"

She swipes her tears off. "If you and Matt are right, then it's my fault."

My breath catches. "What's your fault?"

She stares down at her plate. "I told him. I should never have told him."

"Told him what?"

"I didn't have proof. But you know these things. You know them with your heart. But I still shouldn't have . . . Eric was trying to fix it."

"Fix what?" She doesn't hear me.

She closes her eyes and lets out a deep breath that sounds

like pain and regret. "Matt's right. Eric wouldn't have done that. He wouldn't have left Matt or his mom. Or me. He cared too much." Her voice shakes. "That means it's really my fault. It would have been my fault either way, but this is worse."

"What?" I lean in, wanting her to look at me, to see me. To respond to my questions. To make sense of her ramblings.

She doesn't answer. "I have to go." She gets up, grabs her keys on the table, and rushes out.

"Wait," I say, but she's out the door. Without paying for her meal. Without even getting her purse. The waiter looks over as if worried. I pull money from my wallet, grab both our purses, and run after her. She's driving off. I wave my arms, holding out her purse, but it's too late. She's driving out into traffic.

36

I head home with Cassie's purse. Freaking great. Will someone accuse me of stealing it? My mind's racing. My chest feels heavy. Do I tell Matt this? Or was Cassie talking out of her head? Did I honestly learn anything?

I get to my subdivision turnoff, but I can't just go home. I did learn something.

Turning around, I head downtown. I pull into the police department parking lot.

I have to ask around for the right office. I finally get sent to the second building. I walk up to the desk clerk.

"Is Detective Henderson available?"

The receptionists looks up. "Name?"

"Leah McKenzie. I'm here about the Kenner case."

The woman hesitates and stares at me.

"I won't take much time."

She picks up the phone. "Detective, a Leah McKenzie is here to see you." Pause. "Yes." She looks up. "Okay."

I don't think he's going to see me. She stands up. "Follow me."

She waves me into an office. Detective Henderson is sitting there. He looks up at me about the same way I used to look at needle-carrying nurses walking into my hospital room at four in the morning.

"Have a seat." I can tell he's trying to control his tone, but I still hear it. He doesn't want to talk to me.

I ease into a chair, lift up my chin, and remember my parents' taxes pay his salary. At least that's what my dad says. "Have you spoken with Cassie Chambers?"

He frowns. "Several times."

"Well, I just saw her a few minutes ago."

He shakes his head. "I thought I made this clear. You guys leave her alone."

"I was at a restaurant. She came in. I wasn't following her."

He leans back in his chair and it squeaks. He's still shaking his head.

"She said something to Matt that he didn't tell you. She said Jayden wasn't the one who Eric was pissed at. She wouldn't explain what she meant, but today when I asked her she admitted she didn't believe Eric killed himself. She knows something. And I know she's this close to spilling her guts. If you could talk to her."

He runs a hand over his mouth. "Leah, I'm sorry. I spoke to her Wednesday. Her stepfather brought her in. She swears she doesn't know anything. She swears she didn't see Eric that night. I can't keep investigating a closed case."

He puts his hand on the pile of manila folders. "I wish I

could help. You have no idea how much I wanted to prove Matt right. But it didn't play out. I have other cases."

I suddenly feel what Matt's been feeling this whole time. The answer is there and if the cops would just do their damn job they'd find it.

I know with all my heart—no, I know with Eric's heart—that he didn't kill himself, but no one's going to listen. No one's going to do a damn thing about it.

I pop up on frustrated and shaky knees. "I have Cassie's purse."

"What? Why do you have her purse?"

"She left it at the restaurant."

"Great! They'll accuse you of stealing."

"I didn't steal it!" I shoot out the door.

He calls my name, but I don't give a damn.

I'm still fuming when I get home. Storming into my bedroom, I toss my backpack and the two purses onto the bed. But I stand there. "What happened, Eric? Just tell me, already! Help Matt. He needs to move past this. Help him!"

I drop back on the bed. I see my notebook. The notebook where I wrote the dreams.

I pull it out and start reading. There's nothing there. Nothing to help. Then I turn to the last page. It's written in messy handwriting. It's the last dream I had.

I remember that was the day I woke up with a fever. I start reading. There's not a lot of detail, but then I read, *big oak tree, twin pines.*

And bam, I remember seeing the bullet going into the pine tree. I stand there. Shit shit shit! Maybe Eric did tell me something.

I grab my purse and keys. Run out to the garage and find the metal detector. If that bullet's still there, I'll find it.

322   C.C. HUNTER

Matt, driving Eric's Subaru, pulls into the police department parking lot and heads to the side lot where the exchange zone is. Damn, he doesn't want to sell the car, but his mom's right. Eric would approve of his doing it to pay for the restoration of the Mustang. He also wants to go buy the locket for Leah.

He parks in the designated spot. Thinks about seeing her tonight. Lately, he's been in such a piss-poor mood that he's surprised she even wants to go out with him. He needs to move past this. He recalls the promise he made to Detective Henderson. He's going to keep that promise. He's going to let it go. He just doesn't know how yet. He can stop digging for answers, but he's not sure his heart knows how to let go.

He scrubs a hand over his face. A lump forms in his throat. Then he forces himself to push it away and looks around for the black Chevy truck Mr. Barker said he'd be driving.

Right then, a cop car squeals to a stop right behind Eric's Subaru.

Matt watches, thinking something is about to go down, but then an officer—no, not just any officer, but a large angry-looking Officer Yates—jumps out. He storms toward the driver's side of Eric's car.

"Hands up where I can see them!" Officer Yates orders.

Matt raises his hands. He looks over his shoulder, and the man has his gun out. *Fuck!*

"Now, get out of the car! Keep your hands up."

Matt complies with his every order, because, damn it, he doesn't want to get shot.

The moment he's out, Yates rushes in and slams him against Eric's car.

"Now you're following me? I'll admit it, you got balls, kid!"

"I wasn't—"

He grabs Matt's arm and pulls it tight. Matt holds in a groan.

"I'm here to meet someone about selling this car," he says through clenched teeth.

"Don't lie to me!" Yates barks out.

"I'm not!"

Another police car pulls up. "Gotta problem, Yates?" Matt looks back at the two officers getting out of their car.

"Just a kid who thinks following a police officer around is funny."

"I wasn't following you. I told you: I'm selling a car." Matt looks back at the other officers standing beside their cars. He speaks to them, because he doesn't think Yates will listen. "Detective Henderson told me I could come here to meet up with potential buyers. Ask him! Call him."

"I smell weed on the kid." Yates pulls his arm even tighter.

"I don't have any weed!" But damn it. What's going on? Why is this guy . . .

A black Chevy truck pulls up. "That's him!" Matt yells, looking back at the other officers. "That's Mr. Barker. I put an ad in Craigslist. Ask him."

Yates slams Matt against the car. Voices sound behind him.

"He's telling the truth, Yates," one of the other officers says. Matt exhales, praying this is over.

"What's happening?" Another voice pipes up behind him, a voice Matt recognizes.

He tries to turn around to see Detective Henderson. Yates slams him against the car again. "I was meeting someone from Craigslist and he accuses me of following him."

"Let the kid go!" Henderson yells. "He's telling the truth."

Yates releases him. Matt swings around and fights the temptation to take a swing.

Officer Yates scowls at the detective. "The kid's been stalking my girlfriend's daughter. You heard her say that he practically assaulted her friend at the park."

"No." Henderson moves in and gets between Matt and Yates. "I clearly remember her saying that Jayden was the one who struck first."

"Because this piece of shit was in her face."

"She also said he wasn't hurting her. That Jayden had over-reacted."

"He followed me into the station!" Yates said. "He's stalking me now."

"That's a lie. I was here first!" Matt says.

Officer Yates takes an offensive step toward Henderson. "Why are you siding with the kid?"

"I'm not . . . I'm saying you don't have a reason to come at him."

"I won't forget this." Officer Yates takes off. So does Mr. Barker and Matt's chance of selling Eric's car.

Matt turns to Henderson. "I wasn't following him."

"I know that." Henderson stands there watching the police car pull off.

"That guy's an asshole!" Matt's fury builds remembering how the guy had slammed him into his car.

"I know that too. Now."

Matt stares at Henderson. "I can't believe he's a cop!"

Detective Henderson exhales. "We get all kinds." He sounds baffled.

"I was sitting in the car, and he came here and pulled his gun out." Matt sees the sign behind Eric's truck that says the area is under surveillance. "Check the video. You'll see!"

Detective Henderson exhales. "Give me a second." He walks over to the other cops.

"Can I leave?" Matt calls out, wanting to get the hell away from here.

"Just a minute!" Henderson sends him a wave with a frown.

Matt crosses his arms. Anger crawls on his skin like fire ants. He kicks Eric's tire just to feel better while the three cops talk.

Finally, Henderson returns. "Come on, let's go to my office and cool off."

"I just wanna go."

"No. You want to come with me. Let Yates get away from here before you start out."

I pull over in front of the roadside park. I'm still hearing Cassie say, *"Matt's right. Eric wouldn't have done that. He wouldn't have left Matt or his mom. Or me."* The second my foot crunches on the graveled path, I'm greeted by the eerie sensations that seems to say, *Hello, you've been here; you've died here.*

My heart thumps against my breastbone. Is Eric doing it, or am I just afraid? I stare into the woods. The gray cold seeps through my jacket. Most of the trees are bare of leaves, everything is brown, everything looks . . . dead. I realize it's not Eric I'm afraid of here. It's death. It lives and lingers here.

That monster got so close to me that I smelled its hideous breath.

While I won that battle, it took almost two years of my life away. I sometimes think it stole part of my soul, and I know it took some of my parents'.

But I'll be damned if I let it take anymore. And if I can stop it from taking more of Matt's, I'll do it. I grab the metal detector from the backseat. I don't have a clue where the oak or twin pine trees are, but I'm on a mission, and I'm not leaving until I find them.

I hesitate as I walk past the picnic table. It was easier to be here when I had Matt by my side. I stop, consider texting him, then decide against it.

When I find that bullet, I'll text him. I lift my chin, take a deep breath, and walk to the woods where Eric died. No, where Eric was murdered.

It's just like Matt said. I know it now more than ever. Eric didn't commit suicide.

Matt's sulking in Detective Henderson's office while the detective is asking him about Eric's car, acting as if he's actually interested in buying it. It's bullshit.

But Matt plays nice. Nice because Detective Henderson just rescued him from God only knows what. He seriously thinks that jackass might have planted weed on him.

"So it's still under warranty?" Detective Henderson asks.

"Yeah."

The detective gets quiet for a long pause. "Did Eric know Cassie when Officer Yates dated her mom?"

"Don't know. Why?"

"Nothing." He rakes a hand over his face. "What motor does that car have?"

Matt's heads swims with the change of subject. Then his phone dings with a text. He pulls it closer. It's from Leah.

Meet me at the roadside park. Now.

What's she doing there? He knows how much she hates that place.

Looking up, he interrupts Henderson talking about . . . Hell, Matt doesn't know what the man's saying because he's not listening. "Can I go now?"

Before Henderson can answer, there's noise in the hall.

"I said he was with someone!" The voice echoes.

Matt recognizes the receptionist's voice. Both his and Detective Henderson's gazes zero in on the door. Matt's not sure who's surprised more, him or Henderson, when Cassie Chambers walks through the door.

Her blond hair is tossed. Her eyes are wet and red. She looks at Matt. "You were right."

37

"Eric didn't kill himself!" Cassie wipes tears from her cheeks and stares at Matt. "I'm sorry."

Matt inhales. He thinks he's imagining it.

More tears fill her eyes. "My mother's boyfriend. Joe Yates. He . . ." She takes a deep breath. "I'm pretty sure he drugged and raped me. I'd been drinking. Mom was out of town. I came in, and I think he was drunk too. He offered me a beer. I should have said no, but I didn't. When I woke up, I was naked and had vague memories of him . . . on top of me. I confronted him. He said I was drunk and it never happened."

Detective Henderson mutters, "Oh, hell!"

"It messed me up. I broke up with Eric. When we got back together, I told him. He wanted to confront Yates. I told him no, that we didn't have proof. I told him to forget it. But it messed up Eric more than me. I . . ." Her voice shakes. "I broke up with him the second time because he wouldn't let it go."

"Did you tell anyone? Anyone besides Eric?" Detective Henderson asked.

She shakes her head.

"Not even your mom?" he asks.

"I tried. I went to her, and I didn't even get to the part where I thought he raped me, and she blew up. She said I was trying to break her up like I did with her last boyfriend. And I *had* tried to break them up, because he was using my mom. She said she finally met someone she loved and wasn't going to let me ruin her life. I knew she wouldn't believe me."

She brushes her tears off her cheeks. "I made a video. I told her everything. I was going to send it to her, but I never got the nerve."

Detective Henderson's chair squeaks as he leans forward. "Do you still have it on your computer?"

"Yeah, why?"

Henderson inhales. "It's proof you didn't make this up. Computers have time stamps."

Matt's head is swimming. "Why didn't you say any of this earlier?"

"I believed what the police said. Eric was so upset, I thought . . ." She looks at Matt. "But you kept saying that he wouldn't do it. And then I saw him all those times. Why would he go there?"

"Slow down." Henderson leans forward. "Saw who, where?"

"Yates, he goes to the roadside park where Eric was shot. When Jayden drives me home, Yates's car is there. Like almost every day. I don't know why he goes there."

"I do," Matt says. "He's looking for a bullet." He remembers. "Shit!" Matt bolts up. "Leah's there now!"

I hold the metal detector high, up against the tree, for the tenth time. Just to hear the beep, just to confirm it's really there.

The beep sounds, then is soaked up by the trees. I still smile. It's just like the dream. The oak, the twin pine trees. And I found it. Or did Eric find it? I don't care. I want to help Matt. And Eric.

I owe them. Matt lost his brother. Eric lost his life. And I got to live. There's still something that feels wrong about it. Maybe this will make it right.

I push that thought away, but another concern arrives. How will we get Detective Henderson here? Will he believe us? I remember the frustration in his voice today. Not targeted at me, more aimed at his inability to help.

I know how that feels. Before the transplant when I knew I was dying and could see what it was doing to my parents, I felt helpless. If I pretended I was brave, it seemed to break their heart. If I showed my fear, it seemed to break their heart. Ultimately, I accepted it. I was going to break their hearts anyway.

I raise the metal detector again, but my arms are tired. Where's Matt? I drop the detector and pull my hoodie tighter.

Then I pull out my phone to make sure my text went through. Reception along this street is iffy. Right now, I'm not showing any bars, but it appears my text went through.

It's getting colder. Darker. The car would be warm. But I can't take the chance of leaving here and forgetting how to get back. It's not on the path.

I notice a big pine tree with a large bulge, like a bumpy scar on its trunk, visible from the path. It's a landmark. Turn at the scarred tree. I can remember that.

I take one step and stop. I try to imagine where Eric might have run. Did he head back to the path from here, or did he go farther away? I suddenly feel what Eric might have felt. Being followed. Chased. My mind is playing tricks on me because I swear I hear the sound of feet pounding on the path. Running. Trying to escape death.

I know how that feels. And not just from the dreams.

More chills scatter across my skin. I wonder if, in the end, Eric got tired and gave up, like I did when I accepted death. Or is Matt right? Was Eric a better fighter than me?

I'm not quite to the path when I see someone walking toward me.

The low-hanging branches block most of my view, but I see enough to know it's not Matt.

Having just thought about Eric running, I get the craziest thought to do the same. I take a step back and a twig snaps. The person stops. That's when I see the uniform.

"You Leah McKenzie?" he asks.

I don't answer.

"You okay?" he asks.

"Yes."

He looks me over and nods. Then he pulls his phone out. "I got her. She's fine."

I'm fine? "What's wrong?"

"Someone was worried about you."

"Who?"

"Detective Henderson, for starters. He's on his way. Let's walk back to the road."

"I don't understand," I say. "Am I in trouble?"

"All I know is the detective wanted me to come here and see if you were here. He's on his way."

And how did he know where I was? I'm tempted to ask, but the officer looks clueless. As we move down the path, I realize how dark it is. When we step out of the woods, car lights slash across us.

The car isn't stopped when Matt bolts out of the passenger seat. He grabs me. "Why didn't you answer your phone?"

"I didn't . . . get a call."

He pulls back, pushes a hand through his hair, and releases air that seems to have been held for a long time. "Shit. The reception sucks here. I should've remembered."

Detective Henderson gets out of the same car Matt jumped out of. I look back at Matt. "What's this about? Cassie? She left her purse. I took it to give her."

"What?" he asks. He looks confused. "You saw Cassie?"

I nod.

"That's why she did it," he said.

"Did what?"

His smile takes the edge off my curiosity, because I haven't seen it in what feels like forever. "Cassie came to see Henderson. She thinks . . . Yates, her mom's boyfriend, shot Eric."

I gasp. "But he's a cop."

"A bad cop."

He runs a hand up and down my forearm. "I got the text from you and I was worried he—"

"I'm fine." Then I remember. I lean close and whisper, "I found it."

"Found what?"

"Proof."

Saturday morning, a week and one day since everything went down, my alarm rings. I wake up in my pink room, stare at my pink polka-dot fan swirling above me. Brandy and I went to the paint store and found two soft shades of gray that I want to paint my room in. We even went shopping for a new bedspread and curtains. Right now, I let myself absorb the pink. As much as I want it changed, I see it for what it is. Mom's love. She did this to make me happy.

I reach for my thermometer, stick it in my mouth, and close my eyes. It has been a hard week. I blame it on the lying. The big question was about how we found the bullets. Did we run the metal detector up and down each tree?

Thankfully, Matt and I got our heads together and came up with a believable lie before we were interrogated, since telling them about the dreams wouldn't go over well. And I've repeated it all four times I've been asked: "We just assumed the only reason Eric would have brought a gun was if someone else had one. So we'd been on a hunt for a bullet. And yes, we almost searched every tree."

Yup, it's been a hard week. Maybe it's not just the lying but because I'm grounded—from Matt. My parents are . . . Let's just say a little upset.

My thermometer beeps. I pull it out. It's normal. I grab my blood pressure cuff. I really don't have to do this every day anymore. It was required for the first seven months. Now they just suggest I do it a couple times a week. But every morning I check. I don't know why.

Or maybe I do.

Sometimes, I still feel it, that monster that took Eric—death. It's not breathing down my neck like before, but it's there. Good numbers help convince me it's not that close.

I roll over. I miss Matt. Since I'm underage, Detective Henderson had to call my parents as well as Matt's mom. Yup, Mom and Dad heard everything. About how I went to Cassie's house, called Cassie, went looking for Jayden—whom we thought was a killer—and was questioned by a cop, who turned out is now suspected of being the real killer.

My defense: *I didn't do anything wrong, so why should I be grounded?*

Their argument: *What was right about their seventeen-year-old daughter, who just had a heart transplant, trying to hunt down a murderer?*

Maybe they have a point, though I don't feel like I had any other choice.

The worst part is that they blamed Matt. I explained I did all this behind his back. It didn't matter. They pointed out that I'd never behaved like this before and it must be his influence.

That part really pissed me off.

My blood pressure machine beeps. I lift my head and look at the number. It's a little high. Ten points. Not really bad. Not good. Being without Matt isn't healthy for me. Though I have spoken with him every day at school and on the phone. It's just not enough.

He came over and apologized to them last Saturday, but instead of accepting his apology, Dad gave him a ration of shit. I'm proud of Matt; he held it together. He kept calling Daddy "sir" and apologizing.

Me, I didn't do that well. Thankfully, I didn't lose it until Matt left.

"Why did you do that?" I asked Dad.

"Me?" my dad answered. "Let me turn it back on you, young lady. Why, after we fought like hell to keep you alive, why would you put yourself in that kind of danger?"

Because the guy I was finding justice for is the guy who gave me life. It's his heart that's keeping me alive. How could I not do it for him?

I came so close to spitting it out. But then I'd end up telling them about the dreams. That would probably lead me to a psychiatrist.

So I pulled myself together and went to my room. I've spent a lot of time in my room this week. Good news is, I completed one of my bucket-list items. I finished a hundred books. Bad news is, the time alone started me worrying again. About if Matt's attraction to me isn't more about finding justice for Eric than it is about me. It doesn't help that we haven't been able to go out.

And now it's Saturday morning, and I'm about to ask if I can go out with Matt tonight. I look at my pink clock. It's three minutes after nine. I'm late. I pull myself out of bed, slip my feet into my Dumbos, and rub my temple, where the slightest headache lies.

When I get into the kitchen, Dad's holding up the newspaper and Mom's reading over his shoulder, a cup of coffee clasped in her hands.

I get the feeling it's about the case. Things I probably know about because the detective has been giving Matt and his mom updates.

I'm about to start my pill routine when Mom sees me. "Leah." Her eyes round.

My dad shuts the paper. He doesn't fold it nice and neat like usual. He sort of crunches it together as if trying to hide something.

I stand there looking at them. It seems like this is more than just about the case.

"What?" I ask.

38

"Nothing," Mom says too quickly. She can't lie worth a damn.

Dad glances back at Mom. "She's going to hear about it."

"Hear about what?" I move in.

"There's a story about you," Dad says.

"Me? About finding the bullet?"

No one answers.

And bam, I remember the article the press did on me when I got my artificial heart. I hated doing it. But Mom told me I should because it would encourage people to become donors and Old Leah didn't argue. Still, I had imagined everyone from school reading it, knowing I was dying.

"About the heart transplant?" I ask.

Mom nods, but clearly she's still hiding something. "What else?"

Dad looks up. "Were you aware that Matt's brother died the same day you got your heart?"

I catch my breath. "What . . . are they saying?"

Dad looks concerned. "They pointed out that Eric was a donor. They interviewed one of his friends. And they say you got a heart and . . . and . . . that you helped get him justice."

"It's a good article," Mom pipes up, "about people signing their donor cards. They don't say that you got the transplant the same day. We just . . ."

I stand there shaking my head. Mom moves in. "Honey, don't even go there. It's impossible. Eric would have to have had AB blood. And you know how rare—"

"No one is supposed to know!" My chest tightens, squeezes. Tighter.

I imagine everyone reading the article. Everyone knowing I have Eric's heart. I think of Matt's friends. How will they feel about me? Will they think Matt's with me because of this? And I was starting to feel almost normal at school! Now I'm back to being the freak. A freak who benefited from them losing the most popular guy in school, their quarterback, their friend.

I suddenly can't breathe.

I grab hold of the back of a chair.

"Leah, you okay?" Mom grabs me.

I lock my knees to keep from falling, nod, and pull away. I manage to move around and sit down. On my own.

"You okay?" Dad repeats Mom's question.

Tears fill my eyes. I nod and keep trying to pull oxygen into my lungs, inconspicuously, which is almost impossible.

"Honey," Dad says. "It would have to be . . . a perfect storm that you actually got his heart."

I look at him. I'm shaking inside. I'm barely getting air.

Dad stares at me. He always has been able to read me. "Shit."

Mom says, "What?"

"What type of blood does Matt have?" Dad asks.

"Why?" Mom asks.

"They're identical twins." Dad's gaze finds me again. He knows. He knows it's true.

My lungs loosen. I feed them oxygen. Air pumps blood to my brain. To my limbs. I'm able to move. I take the newspaper.

Ignoring my parents, I open it up. There's a photograph of me. It's from when I got the artificial heart. I'm wearing my back-pack.

I've got dark circles under my eyes. It was taken the day I left the hospital. I looked like I was dying. I *was* dying.

The title reads HEART TRANSPLANT RECIPIENT HELPS HEART TRANSPLANT DONOR GET JUSTICE.

I start producing fresh tears. They'll know. People aren't stupid. They'll do the math. They'll know. And they won't be like Matt. They won't understand. They'll blame me.

I get up, take the paper with me, and go to my room. Mom calls me back. I ignore her.

I get dressed, grab the paper and my purse, and walk out. Mom tries to stop me.

I look at her. "I just need to be alone. Please."

Mom says no. Dad takes her hand and nods at me.

I leave.

I don't have a clue where I'm going. But I end up at the park where Matt and I walk Lady. I get to our bench and read the ar-ticle. It's not as bad as I thought it would be. It's more about becoming a donor than about me or Eric, but I know it's enough. Enough for some people to start putting it together.

I sit there for almost fifteen minutes before I grab my phone and dial Matt. I wonder what he will say about it. Probably the right thing. He always says the right thing. I need to hear him say it won't matter. That I'm overreacting.

"Hey, beautiful," he answers the phone. "Did your parents say it was okay for you to come out tonight?"

"Uh, I didn't ask. Matt—"

"Hang on, I'm coming up to an intersection."

I pause. When he comes back I ask, "Where are you?"

"We're out of dog food. I'm running to the vet."

"I'm at the park," I say.

"Our park?" he asks.

Our park. Knowing he sees it the same way I do offers me a sense of awe. "Yeah."

"I just passed it. I'll turn around. Be right there."

"I'm at the bench," I say right before he hangs up.

In less than five minutes I hear him coming. He takes one look at me and says, "What's wrong?"

It's only then I realize I don't think I've even combed my hair. Or does he see it in my eyes?

"You haven't read it?"

He drops down, leans in, and kisses me. "Read what?"

I hold it out. "It points out that Eric was a donor." He takes it. Scans it. Then moans. "Is this in today's paper?"

I nod.

"Shit!" he says.

I bite down on my lip. "I'm scared people will start putting it together and then they'll hate me."

He runs a hand through his hair. "Who told them he was a donor?"

"It says a friend," I say.

"I should . . ." He stands up. "Mom went to show a house. I should go before . . ." He leans down to kiss me goodbye.

"She'll hate me, won't she?" I ask.

"No . . . I don't . . ." Then he exhales. "She resisted donating his organs. I . . . She's doing so good and I don't want . . ." He closes his eyes a second, then opens them. "I'll call you." He kisses me again. "It's going to be okay. You'll see."

But I don't see. Not in his expression. He's scared of his mom knowing. He's probably scared of his friends knowing too.

As he walks off, I remember something. I remember his mom calling me Lori. Did Matt tell her I was Lori just in case . . . in case she heard about a girl named Leah who got a heart transplant?

I pull my knees up to my chest and hug them. This is so messed up.

And even as I let my own issues consume me and feel slightly abandoned by Matt, I realize how selfish I'm being. I'm worried about how people will feel about me, but I'm alive. Eric isn't. And now he finally has a chance at getting justice. Isn't my privacy a small price to pay?

When Matt arrives home, his mom's car is in the drive. The newspaper isn't on the lawn. "Damn!" He walks in. She's in the kitchen, at the table. The newspaper is open.

He doesn't know how much she'll put together. She might not even recognize Leah. Leah looks really bad in the picture. He sits down beside her. He's holding his breath.

She glances up. Tears rim her eyes, and his chest knots.

"When did Leah get her heart?"

He doesn't answer.

"Does she . . . You don't think she has Eric's heart, do you?"

He could say he doesn't know. He could lie. But maybe it's time. "Yeah. That's what I think."

She swallows. It sounds painful. "How do you know?"

"The afternoon when we signed the papers, I saw her and her parents going into the hospital. I knew her. She went to my school, and I knew she was on the transplant list. I figured it out."

His mom looks back down at the paper. "I'm such a terrible person."

This isn't what he expected her to say. "No, you're not."

"I am. I didn't want to do it. And even now, when I look at her"—her voice shakes—"I think she's alive and Eric's isn't."

He rests his hand on hers. "That doesn't make you terrible." He hates admitting it, but he does. "I felt like that when I first saw her at the hospital. It's normal."

She brushes tears off her cheeks. "Do you feel him? When you're with her, do you feel Eric?"

He thinks of the dreams, the connection he feels with Leah. "There are some things. She suddenly started liking Indian food. But . . . I don't feel Eric when I'm with her. At first, I thought I would. She's her own person. But I'm proud. She's only alive because of Eric. It was his idea to sign up to be a donor, not mine."

This is the first time he said that aloud. "I only did it because he did. I even asked him, 'But don't you think the doctors might let us die just so they can sell our parts?' Eric laughed. Accused me of reading too many horror books."

She covers her mouth a second. "He wasn't afraid of anything. Both of you are like your dad."

"Eric was," Matt says. "I think I'm more like you, Mom." Too emotional. More cautious.

"I think you got more of your dad in you than you think. You found out what really happened to Eric. It took courage to look for the truth when nobody would believe you."

Be he had Leah's help and Leah believed him. "You know, I don't feel Eric when I'm with her, but in some ways I think Leah and Eric are alike. I tutored her once when she had an artificial heart. She didn't seem afraid either. I don't think she even realizes how brave she is. But she's a good person, Mom. She deserves Eric's heart."

"I'm sure she does, son. It's just going to take some getting used to."

Mom and Dad are waiting for me when I step in the door. I meet their eyes, which are loaded with questions.

Mom rushes forward. "You okay?"

"Yeah. I just . . . I didn't want people to know. Everyone loved Eric so much." I swallow the knot in my throat and again push back the feeling that it's all about me.

"But, baby," Mom says, "how can you be sure you . . . ?"

As I drove home, I'd decided not to mention the dreams. It sounded too weird. "I saw his obituary before I left the hospital. I knew he died the day I got the transplant. And I also knew that Matt had AB blood, so Eric did too."

Dad walks over. He's wearing his I'll-take-on-the-world face. The expression he wore most of the time when I was sick. "Honey, if Matt said anything ugly—"

"No! He's known. He saw us coming into the hospital that day. We talked about it before we even got together."

Dad inhales. "Then obviously, he's okay with it. If he can be—"

"It's not that easy, Dad. He's worried about his mom. She didn't want Eric to be a donor. She lost her son and she'd already lost her husband."

Mom gets tears in her eyes. "But it's not your fault."

"No, but she's going to hate me. So are his friends. To be honest I kind of hate me too. I benefited from something so terrible." I start sobbing and Dad grabs me and pulls me into his chest. It's my safe haven, but I don't feel safe right now.

In the end, Mom and Dad tell me the same thing Matt did. "Don't Worry. Everything is gonna be all right."

It's going to be all right. And for the next few days I believe it. My parents take back my grounding. Mom, Dad, and Matt survive the awkwardness of the truth being out. Awkward because Mom hugs him and thanks him. I cringe. I mean, it sounds like she's thanking him for his brother dying.

According to Matt, his mom is working on accepting that I have her son's heart. I don't ask him about why she called me Lori. But it still bothers me.

On Sunday, Matt's hanging with his friends. I curl up with a book. A few minutes later, I get a text. From Matt.

Playing ball. Ted's girl is here. Wanna come watch? I might take my shirt off.

I laugh. I'm tempted. But I'm . . . tired. I text back. *Just got into a book.*

I go back to reading.

An hour later, I'm jarred awake. "Leah? You okay?"

I wake up. Mom's standing over me. The book's on my chest. "Just fell asleep. I'm all right."

But when I go to get up, there's the slightest rumble of my heart. *Boom, boom, boom.*

I check my breathing. It's okay. When Mom leaves the room, I check my blood pressure. It's okay. I'm okay, I assure myself.

Monday comes. Teenagers obviously don't read the paper. Or so it seems, because nothing is said. A few people stare, but mostly when Matt and I are together. I think they're still trying to figure out why is Matt Kenner hanging with Leah McKenzie?

Honestly, I'm still trying to figure that out too.

Otherwise, nothing is that different.

Nothing except I'm tired.

Maybe it's the worrying over the article. And the lying the week before. As I head to my last class that afternoon, I have trouble making the long walk between my classes. I have trouble catching my breath when I get there. I'm okay, I assure myself. And when I do a second check, my breathing is fine.

Matt and I skip school on Tuesday. We go to a bookstore. We each choose a book. Then we pick out a book for each other. We eat pizza with gooey cheese for lunch, go to my house, and make love in my pink bed.

Cuddled up in each other's arms, I'm loving life. Loving Matt. Enjoying every second of skipping school. I want to start writing things down on my bucket list and marking them off.

Matt talks about working on the Mustang. There's something slightly different about his voice now. It's lost more of the grief. Listening, I fall asleep. When he kisses me awake, I'm embarrassed.

That afternoon, before he leaves, Henderson calls Matt. We learn Officer Yates cratered and admitted he shot Eric. He claims it was self-defense. Claims Eric came at him with his dad's gun, they wrestled, and the gun went off. Matt puts his phone on speaker, and I hear Detective Henderson say, "Don't worry. He's going to have a very hard time making any court believe it. Especially since his bullet in the tree shows he most likely fired first. And we have testimony from Cassie's mom that indicates Yates was the aggressor, so we have a very strong case."

We hug and dance around the room. Then I drop on my bed. I feel my heart pounding. Happy pounds.

I hear that Bob Marley song that was in *The Little Mermaid*, about everything's gonna be all right. It sounds like a promise. One that's so easy to believe. But I know *The Little Mermaid* is a fairy tale. In fairy tales people don't get viruses that kill their hearts. In fairy tales, there are no transplants.

And if they did have a transplant, it would never be rejected.

I decide to check my vitals that night, and I plan to do it again in the morning. Everything is going to be all right. Only the next morning, I almost don't have time. I'm so tired. Mom has to come into my room and poke me awake. "You okay, lazybones?" she asks.

"Yeah." The song lyrics "don't worry . . . every little thing gonna be all right" are stuck in my head, but on Friday I know it's a lie when I pick up my backpack to go to my last class and I can't catch my breath. It's not the good kind of breathlessness that I get when Matt kisses me or when we make love. This is the kind of breathlessness that reminds me of monsters. Of pain. Not even my pain, but others. Of the people who care about me.

I go to the nurse's office. Check my temperature and blood pressure. It's fine. It's okay.

But I know it's not. I felt like this a month before I was diagnosed with a deadly virus. A week before my life got sucked down the toilet. Before I lost everything. My dignity. My sense of self. My belief in a future.

I leave the nurse's office, but instead of going to history class, I go to the bathroom and google "symptoms of heart rejection." Feeling tired or weak is symptom number one. Number two: heart palpitations. Number three: breathlessness.

I remember the times I thought the shit had hit the fan and then realized I was just panicking. Am I doing it again?

That thought keeps me from calling Mom. Keeps me at school.

Matt shows up at my locker before last period talking about us going to the college after school. He says I agreed to it on Tuesday. I don't remember. Probably when I was half asleep in bed with him. But I don't say anything.

I wait until after school. Hoping the Friday buzz will revive me. And I'll feel silly. I'll feel like New Leah again.

39

Leaving school, I don't feel the Friday buzz. Just the Friday busted.

Matt meets me at my car. He kisses me. I want to forget everything. I want to go back to the beach, listen to the waves. I crave the happy silence from that day. The way it felt to have his arms around me. To be about to make love for the first time.

He ends the kiss. "I think you missed me today."

And bam, the thought hits. I'm going to miss him for the rest of my life. I swallow.

"You want to take one car to the college?"

"How about let's do that next week," I say.

"Don't," he says.

"Don't what?" I ask.

"Start the one-day-at-a-time crap. I told you: it scares me."

It does me too. But I own this. Not him.

"I can't handle it, remember?" he says.

"Yeah, I remember." It's why he bailed the first time. It's why I have to do this.

I tilt my chin up. "You lied to your mother, didn't you?"

"What?" he asks.

"You told her my name was Lori." I use it, because in truth it kind of hurt.

Guilt flashes in his eyes. "I was afraid she . . ."

"Couldn't handle it. Runs in the family, doesn't it?" It's such a low blow, but I use it, because, damn it, it hurt me too.

You couldn't pay me to hurt Matt, but I just don't want him to have to see it. Of all the things I've experienced in this life, he's the best.

Let's say I'm imagining it. Let's say I've become a paranoid sick kid and I'm not rejecting the heart now. It still could happen.

If not today, tomorrow. If not this week, the next. If not this year . . .

I will never be able to live in years. I'll always be looking over my shoulder for that monster. And Matt can't handle it. He shouldn't have to handle it.

Nobody should have to handle this.

"Whoa. What . . . ?" he asks. "What's going on, Leah?"

I swallow my tears. No. No. No. Can't let him see me cry. "Maybe we were just supposed to find out the truth about Eric together. And we did."

He looks slapped. I feel slapped. I feel sapped. I feel sick.

I take a step to my car.

He catches my arm.

"Wait!" he says. He's getting mad—or, I should say, frustrated. Matt doesn't get so much mad as he does hurt. But this is going to hurt him much less now than if he has to watch me lose Eric's heart.

He lost his dad.

He lost Eric.

Now he'll lose me. And Eric again.

"What are you saying? What did I do? If I did something wrong, or said something . . . wrong, I'm sorry."

"You lied. And you didn't call me back."

"When did I not call you back?"

"The first time," I say. "You kissed me and then you wouldn't even call me. I can't trust you."

He holds his arms out, as if he wants to pull the world back to him. "I apologized for that. I was in a bad place. But this isn't . . . What's really going on?"

Pain. I see it in his eyes, hear it in his voice. Marbles, big old gnarly knots of hurt form in my chest. I need to leave.

Now.

I pull away.

"Leah," he says my name.

I get in my car. Before I pull out of the school parking lot, I turn my phone off and my heater on. It's warm outside, and yet I'm cold. A chill spiders up my spine.

Symptom number four: fever.

When I get home, I confirm symptom number four with my thermometer. It's 101.

I check my blood pressure. This time it's low. Too low.

Symptom number five: low blood pressure.

I sit on my bed, my phone in my hands. I think about what this call is going to do to my mom. To my dad. I think about what it will do to Brandy and to Matt. Even Matt's mom, who still hasn't accepted that I have Eric's heart. But I know she's not all bad. She raised Matt and he's good. So I know sooner or later she'll hurt. It'll be like losing Eric again for her too.

Mom answers her phone on the first ring. "Everything okay?"

Her tone, that hint of fear in her voice, disturbs me. Maybe she's never really gotten over me being sick. Maybe it's a mother's intuition. I can almost see her rubbing her free hand down the side of her hip. I remember how raw her hands were for so long. I remember when she had to put Band-Aids on them. And I'm doing it to her again.

"I've got a fever."

"Sore throat?" she asks.

"No."

"Blood pressure?"

"Ninety over sixty."

I hear that sound. The way her breath catches. It's so small. But it's so loud. I recognize it. It's pain. It's fear. It's her losing another piece of her soul.

I close my eyes. I'm sorry, I want to say. I'm so sorry.

"Where are you?" she asks.

"Home."

"I'm on my way."

I hang up. A chill runs down my spine. I pull my pink covers up and over me. I start shivering. I'm alone. I'm scared. I'm going to die.

My fever is up to 103 when Mom gets there. She starts freaking out.

"Mom," I tell her. "It's gonna be all right." But I know it isn't.

She calls my dad and I hear them talking, trying to decide if she should take me to the closest hospital or the bigger one. The transplant hospital.

They decide on the transplant hospital. Dad's meeting us

there. I get in her car. I take my blanket and my phone with me. But my phone is off. I'll keep it off.

Mom almost pushes me out the door. I have a hard time buckling the seat belt. Mom does it for me.

She's leaning over. It clicks locked. Her scared round green eyes lift and meet mine. "I love my pink blanket," I say.

She does one of those laughs that sounds like a cry. And I think it's both.

I lean against the window and watch the world go past. I kind of remember doing this when I went in for the transplant.

We don't talk. Except every five minute when she asks, "Okay?"

And I lie. "Okay." But in truth, it's getting hard to breathe.

I close my eyes and think about the ocean.

And I think about the locket in my jewelry box. And I wonder, did the girl who owned it push everyone away to protect them? Was that why it was empty? To save someone from being hurt?

If that was it, then it's not as sad as I thought it was. Then at least she loved someone. Like I loved Matt. And maybe that's enough.

Mom won't let me even try to get out of the car. She blows the horn and runs in. I can hear her shouting. I shut my eyes tighter, as if that will keep me from hearing.

Almost immediately, a gurney is rolled out. They get me out of my car. I try to hold on to my blanket, but they won't let me.

The second I'm rolled into the emergency room, I see Dad. Then I see Dr. Hughes. Dad probably called her.

From across the room, her gaze meets mine. I see it. Disappointment. Even a little fear. She really, really, really wanted to give me those years. I hope I get a chance to tell her I'm not sorry. She only gave me months, but they were good months. The best months of my life.

Dad rushes over. He takes my hand. He's wearing that I'm-gonna-take-on-the-world face. He's trembling. Or am I?

Maybe it's me. I keep trying to pull in more air.

They push me into a room. I hear Dr. Hughes tell my parents to stay out.

Four people surround me. I realize I must look really bad, because they don't ask me to take off my clothes. Instead, they start cutting them off of me. I try to tell them to stop. I've got on my good bra, but my teeth are chattering too much. Yet when the cold metal scissors touch my skin, I cry out.

I want my pink blanket back. I want to go back to the beach. I want to be able to breathe.

A nurse is putting the electrode sensors on my chest. Someone else is holding my arm down and trying to get a needle in my vein. I feel the needle go in. Go out. Go in.

Dr. Hughes comes and stands over me. She starts spouting out different tests she wants done. Medicines she wants pushed and how fast she wants them pushed.

"I can't get the IV in!" the nurse screams.

"Damn it," Dr. Hughes spouts out. "We need it in now! Is the heart monitor even plugged in?" she yells. "Come on, people. We can't fuck this up!"

I've never heard her cuss before.

Her eyes meet mine briefly. They have tears in them. She touches my face. I can't hear her, but I think she said she was sorry.

And everything goes foggy.

"You can't do this," I hear Matt say.

I turn around until I see him. "Can't do what?"

"Be here. You gotta go back."

"Where are . . . we?" I look around and gasp when I see the ocean. But Galveston has never looked so perfect. The water is the prettiest color, not quite green, not quite blue. The waves reach up

and peak, capping off in white foam as it falls forward. It looks like a poem sounds. It's so pure. The sand is so white.

"Did you hear me?" he says again. "Go back."

I turn around and look at him. "It's so beautiful, Matt."

He laughs. "Please . . . I'm the better-looking twin."

Voices ring in my mind. "Leah! Stay with us. You hear me, stay with us!"

I look back at Matt, no Eric. I know because his hair isn't curled at the ends. Then I gaze back at the ocean. I sit down on the sand. It's soft, fine, and I run my fingers through it. I want to stay here.

40

Something is wrong. Matt feels it. He knows it. Knew it since Friday night.

And he's waited long enough. Matt steps up to the front porch and knocks. He finally hears footsteps. A woman answers. She's wearing a robe. He's guessing it's Brandy's mom.

"Is Brandy here?"

She blinks and tightens the robe. "It's not even seven o'clock and it's Sunday."

Yeah, but he's sat outside in his car for the last two hours. "I'm sorry, but this is important. It's about Leah McKenzie."

The mother makes a face. "Is she sick again?"

He nods. But he prays he's wrong. Unfortunately, that's the only damn answer he can think of. She wasn't herself and then . . .

He called her. Dozens of times. Finally, last night, when he couldn't sleep, he went to her house. It was midnight. There were lights on. Leah's car was in the driveway.

He walked around to the back, climbed the fence, quietly, expecting any minute for Mr. McKenzie to come out with a shotgun. No one came out. He got to Leah's window. Her light was on. Her bed empty. She wasn't there.

It was midnight, for God's sake.

Then he went around to the front of the house, and that's when he noticed the front door was ajar.

He still knocked. When no one answered, he rang the doorbell. No one came to the door. He walked in. Fear turned his stomach to acid. He worried there had been some kind of home invasion.

But no one was there. And the house didn't look burglarized. It just looked like no one was home. Like someone had left in a hurry and forgot to shut the door. An emergency.

Brandy's mom finally backs up and lets him come in. "Let me get her."

Matt waits in the living room.

Brandy walks out wearing pajamas. "What's wrong?"

"Have you spoken with Leah?" he asks.

"No. I tried to call her yesterday. It went straight to voicemail. "Why? What's wrong?"

"She's not at home. Neither are her parents. The front door was open."

"Someone broke in?" Panic sounds in her tone.

"No, it didn't look like it. Do you have her mom's phone number?"

"Yeah, let me get my phone."

When she returns, she touches her phone. "Let me try Leah first."

He stands there gripping his hands. She frowns and looks up. "It's going to voicemail." She hangs up and touches her phone again. He guesses she's calling Leah's mom. He waits. She frowns. "It's going to voicemail too."

She drops down on the sofa. "Hi, Mrs. McKenzie. This is Brandy. I'm just kind of worried. I can't get in touch with Leah. Can you call me back?"

She hangs up and pulls her hair back. "Are you sure they aren't home? In bed?"

"I went through the whole house. No one's home."

He clasps his hand behind his head and squeezes. "I'm really worried."

"I considered calling the hospital, but . . ."

Brandy frowns. "If Leah's sick, she's in the Medical Center."

"Houston?" he asks, remembering seeing her at the hospital.

"Yeah. They make her go there. It's where they know how to take care of transplant patients."

He nods and turns to leave.

"What are you going to do?" Brandy asks.

"I'm going there."

"Why don't you call first?"

He doesn't wait to call. He already knows they won't tell him. He'd called several times the night Eric died. No one told him shit. *Please God, don't let it be like that.*

But he feels it. He feels that same overwhelming loneliness he felt the night Eric died.

"Leah?"

I hear my name. I try to open my eyes. They feel glued shut and gritty. I kind of remember a beach. But what's that smell?

"She's awake," I hear my mom say. I finally get my eyes to open.

The first thing I do is try to swallow. I really don't want there to be anything down my throat. I don't want my chest to have been cracked open again.

My throat is empty. I don't know about my chest.

I blink. Mom looks exhausted. Dad's right there with her. His eyes are red. Mom's hair is all over the place. Dad's is sticking straight up. "You two look like shit."

Mom does one of her laugh-cries. Dad squeezes my hand. I breathe, get another whiff of something nasty, and realize it's my breath. I make a face and cover my mouth.

My mind's fighting cobwebs, trying to remember things. Then most it comes back. I hear the beeping of a machine keeping time with my heart. I look around. I'm in the ICU. I recognize the serious medical décor.

I look at Mom. "I'm rejecting the heart," I say.

Mom blinks. "You were. But you're doing better now. The fever is coming down. Your blood pressure is up. Dr. Hughes says that's good."

"How long have I been here?"

"Two days," Mom says.

I try to moisten my lips, but my tongue is so dry. I see again my mom's bloodshot eyes. "You need sleep."

"We're fine." Mom smiles. She takes my hand. I feel her palms. They feel red and raw.

"You don't look fine," I say.

"What?" Dad asks. "You don't like my new hairdo?" He runs a hand though his hair, and it sticks up higher.

I try to smile but can't do it. "Water?"

"Ice chips. They brought it just in case you wake up." Mom puts one on my tongue. It's wet and it's wonderful. I look down and see something hanging from my chest. "What did they do?"

"A heart cath, just to check."

Great. Another scar.

I open my mouth and feel like a baby bird. But I don't have enough energy to do anything else.

Mom spoons another sliver of ice on my tongue. "Matt and Brandy are here."

I nod, and then I remember. I look up. "Make them leave."

"What?" Mom asks.

"Tell them to go away. I don't need them here."

"Honey."

"I'm serious." I knock the spoon out of my mom's hands. It hits the tile floor with a big cling. "I don't want them here. They shouldn't have to go through this."

"Go through what?" Mom says.

"This!" I hiss out, because my throat hurts. My heart hurts. My soul hurts.

Dad moves in. "Calm down, baby."

Mom sets the ice down. "Hon', they care about you."

I look at Dad. "Make them go, Dad. Please." I start crying. "It's bad enough that you two have to see it. Please make them go!" I hear my heart monitor beeping faster.

"Honey, don't cry," Mom says.

"I'll make them go," Dad says. "You calm down. Okay. I'm sending them away. I promise." He backs out.

I roll over, close my eyes, and beg to fall back into oblivion.

I hear a *click*, *click*, *click*. I recognize it.

I open my eyes and Dr. Hughes is standing there staring at me. "I asked your mom to bring Donald and Dumbo back up."

I try to sit up.

She drops her pen and pad. "Let me help you," she says. The electronic hum of my bed moving fills the tiny ICU space.

Only when I'm up do I try to speak. "It's not your fault."

"What's not my fault?" she asks.

"You apologized when I was in the ER. And you were cussing like a sailor."

She grins. "I'm sure you imagined that."

I try to smile back, but can't quite pull one out of my holster. "Am I losing the heart?"

"It doesn't look like it," she says. "Yes, you were rejecting it. It stopped beating properly, causing pulmonary edema, which means fluid started building up in your lungs. But we took care of that, and you seem to be responding to the antibiotics and prednisone. We've put you on a different immune suppressant."

"And?" I ask.

She just lifts a brow.

"There's always an 'and,'" I say.

She crosses her arms. "Why am I picking up a woe-is-me vibe?"

"You say it as if I don't deserve it," I say. "Haven't I earned it?"

A frown tightens her eyes. "I'm just saying it's not like you. But here's the 'and,' you wanted," she says. "I'm going to run some tests to see if there was any damage." She picks up her pen, starts clicking it, then smiles. "I don't want to be too optimistic, but I have to tell you, your blood pressure now and even in the right heart cath, it looked good. Your heart appears strong right now. Surprisingly strong."

"It's not mine," I say.

She lifts another brow. "Haven't you heard that possession is nine-tenths of the law?" She touches my shoulder. "I hate to ruin your bad mood here, but I'm feeling very positive."

She pulls out her stethoscope and has me breathe. When she pulls back, she asks, "What's bothering you?"

I almost don't answer. Then I give in. "I'm tired of hurting people. Sucking the life out of them."

"Who are you hurting?"

"My mom and dad. Brandy and . . . Matt." I swallow and look up at her. "You. And don't deny it. Your mask slipped in the ER. I saw it in your eyes."

She drops her stethoscope back in her pocket and grabs her pen to make more notes on her chart. "Damn masks."

She mutters. Then she looks up. "Unfortunately, it's part of the human condition. Caring. I wish I could offer you some words of wisdom. But the best I can do is . . . tell you to get used to it. People aren't going to stop caring, Leah."

I feel a tear roll down my cheek, and I swipe it away.

"Well, I take that back," she says. "You could start being a miserable person. Bitch about everything. Throw your food at the nurses and doctors. We hate that. But I've gotta tell you, I don't see that in you."

I look up at her. "It hurts. Seeing them. Knowing what I'm doing to them."

"Yeah. But you know what you haven't seen? The ones that lose their children. Or their friends. Or their girlfriends. That's the worst pain, Leah."

She stands straighter. "You didn't die. You gave us all a scare, but, much to my surprise, your prognosis looks good. Remember, I told you things like this could happen? Sometimes the body's immune system picks up and sees the heart as something that doesn't belong. I'm going to keep you in the hospital for a while, a long while. Do tests every few days. I'm not sending you home until I know your heart is fine. But I think you're going to be okay."

"Until next time," I say. "Or until I get cancer because of the immune suppressant drugs, or when these drugs stop working and I kill this heart for good."

Her gray eyes tighten and meet mine. "You're right. I can't promise you that there's not going to be a next time. Or a next. I can't promise you that you're not going to get cancer. But what you do with the time between all those next times is what makes a difference. Because that's life, Leah. No promises. No guarantees. But if you're lucky, you might use that time to make a few dreams come true."

She gives my shoulder a squeeze and walks out. I know

356 C. C. HUNTER

there's comfort to be found buried in her words, but I'm not in the mood to go mining for comfort right now. I'm hurting people who love me. I don't deserve comfort.

They move me to the transplant unit. Mom asks if I'm up for company. I tell her, shit no! And remind her of Dad's promise.

Days pass. I don't keep track. I read until I finish a book—day or night—then sleep, and repeat. Works for me.

Mom and Dad are there around the clock. They try to encourage me to get on a schedule. I try to explain that I hate schedules and reading makes me sleepy. More than that. It makes me forget.

Still, I'm not a happy camper. Mom and Dad aren't happy campers. When Dr. Hughes comes in that afternoon, she isn't a happy camper either.

She clicks her pen and looks at me. "There's this very dirty word I hate, and I'm wondering if you've heard it," she says.

I look at her. "I think I've heard them all. But I'm a word person, and I'm always eager to learn another one."

"Depression," she says.

I almost tell her it's her fault, or the transplant team's fault for letting me have a heart from someone from my own town. But right before the words spill out of my mouth, I stop myself.

I do it because to say it would imply I was sorry I got Eric's heart. And I'm not. I'm not sorry I helped Matt find out who killed his brother. I'm not sorry I fell in love with Matt. Or that we had sex, or that we laid on a beach and watched it for more than two hours.

But neither am I sorry that I broke up with him. It was the right thing to do.

"How about let's go for a walk in the halls?" she suggests. "I'll go with you."

I say I don't feel like it, insist that going to the bathroom is more exercise than she realizes. Then I bury my nose in a book. It's rude. But at least I didn't throw my food at her.

Mom and Dad get to the point they are making lame jokes. It's really sad. And their jokes are really bad. I try to cheer up, for them, but hey . . . my heart's broken and in more ways than one.

I make a deal with Mom. If she goes back to work, I'll try to smile more.

She counters with, "If you'll take a bath, walk the halls the way the nurses tell you to, sleep regular hours, and smile more, I'll go back to work three days a week."

I counter. "I'll smile more."

As pathetic as it sounds, it works. Mom goes back to work three days a week. But I notice Dad is taking time off. Parents are sneaky like that.

I finally give in and have a bath.

But baths are still optional in my world. My IV comes out. The central line, dangling from chest, stays in.

Every day one of my parents brings me a little gift. In the beginning it was always a new book. Yesterday it was a new pair of slippers. I got Minnie Mouse. To mix things up, I wore one Mickey and one Minnie. And when I cross my feet, I swear it looks like they are screwing. I do laugh a couple of times at that.

Mom keeps trying to get me in the shower. "Later," I say and put my nose back in a book. The deeper it's in there, the less I smell myself.

Parents love you no matter how you look. Or smell. And I'm not trying to impress anyone else. I'm sure Dr. Hughes has seen worse. Though you wouldn't know it from her expression.

Yesterday Dad brought me an "Oh shit" button. I press it and each time it gives me a little different version of my favorite catch phrase. "Crappers. Bull Shit. This is a pile of stinky poo. This is S. H. I. T." It was a great gift. It helps me keep my promise to my mom to smile more. But I miss Matt so much my nose hairs hurt.

Not that I want him here. He said it himself. He can't handle it. And the more I think about it, I think his bond to me was always solving his brother's murder. That and I have his brother's heart. But, like Dr. Hughes said, possession is nine-tenths of the law.

I miss Brandy too. I almost crater and tell Mom to let her come up, but then I remember the look on her face the day she took me to see Dr. Hughes for the cold. What kind of friend would I be to make her feel that way again? And again. And again. I'm never going to be normal.

Besides, dangling from my chest is still the central line that looks like a tampon, where they inject my medicines. And Brandy would pass out if she saw it.

It's the right thing to do, I tell myself. And honestly, I don't need friends. Books are my friends.

That night, I ask Dad to go down to the hospital library and get me some more friends. He tells me that I should walk down to the library myself. "The walk would do you some good."

When Mom gets in, I ask her the same thing. "A walk to the library might do you good." That's when I know there's a conspiracy, but I'm not that easy to manipulate.

"That's okay," I say in a pissy tone and start reading the book I wasn't thrilled about. The next morning, or maybe it's night—I think it's my twelfth day/night here—I finish that book.

A nurse walks in, and I actually smile at her. "Uh, can you take a quick trip to the library on your break and bring me some books? I'm a blatant book geek, so I'm not picky."

"How about you take a walk down there yourself? I'll show you where it is."

Damn! So the nurses are in on it too.

I frown. "I can't." I motion to my haven't-showered-in-two-days—wait, three-days—self.

"Wow, that's a good idea. Why don't you take a shower?" She leaves before I can tell her no. When she comes back, I tell her no, but she doesn't listen. She has the stuff to wrap my central line so it won't get wet, and she starts doing it. Then she unplugs the electrodes reading my heart.

"You want me to help you in the shower?"

"No." I hate bullies.

"You need a shower," she says.

"Yeah, but I think I'll take a nap first." I lay back and turn away from her.

Bathing is overrated. Besides, in the historical novel I finished—which was mediocre at best—they took monthly baths.

I hear her walk out. I lay there and realize it's been twenty-four hours since I read. I'm getting jittery. Having withdrawals. I might actually have to go take a shower. Or . . . I might just go down to the library stinking, wearing a gown I've worn for three days.

After a three-hour boredom nap, I wake up to find another gift sitting beside my half-eaten lunch on the table. A small package. I'm a little miffed that it's not a book.

I look down at the front of my pajamas and notice that half of my lunch is still on there. I brush some taco meat off my boobs. See, I do have some self-pride left.

Then I realize it wasn't today I had tacos. Ugh. I run my tongue over my teeth. I'm not a complete slob. I'm still brushing my teeth. Or did I do it last night?

Dropping back on the mattress, I look back at the gift.

This one is wrapped.

I should wait until Mom or Dad are here. It's the polite thing to do, but . . . I'm bored. I don't have a book. And people who haven't showered in days aren't really known for their politeness. So I open it.

My breath catches when I see the locket. It's . . . it's not the

one I found, but it's close. I open it. And when I see the pictures,
I instantly tear up.

It's not from Mom and Dad.

On each heart side of the locket is a picture. One of me and
Matt and the other of Lady and Matt.

41

Damn. "Shit shit shit," I bellow out. They should add that to
my shit button.

Mom picks the worst time to walk in. I'm crying. I'm hurt.
I'm angry. I need someone to throw my emotion at, and she's
just big enough I can't miss.

"I don't want this. I thought Dad promised to keep him
away. If I can't count on him to keep that promise, what can I
count on?"

Her mouth thins, her eyes tighten, and she shakes her head
and slips her hand on her hip. Not to rub it like she does when
she's nervous, but to prop it there like a statement. A statement
I haven't seen her make in a long time. But I recognize it.

Mama's about to have a hissy fit.

And that's fine. We can have one together.

"Dad promised!" I repeat.

"He tried," Mom snaps. "But Matt wouldn't go. That boy
has been here every day, Leah. Every day he sits in that waiting room. And every day he asks to be able to see you. It's breaking my heart."

"Then make him leave. Tell him I died or something." My chest is quacking.

Mom's other hand finds her hip. Her eyes tighten. Through the tight slits, I swear they turn a neon color, like vampires do in some of my favorite books.

"I can't force you to be his friend," she hisses.

I've never heard my mom hiss.

She takes a step closer to my bed. "I would never force you to start dating him again. But I didn't raise you to be rude. And he deserves a thank-you for that gift. So I'm going to walk out of here and tell him he can come in. If he's brave enough! Because, believe me, what he's about to see isn't pretty!"

She starts out, then swings back around. She points a finger at me. "I recommend you comb your hair and brush off what's left of your breakfast and lunch from your dirty pajama top."

"No, Mom," I yell. "I don't want . . ."

She walks out. I slam my hand on my "oh shit" button and it belts out, "Now that's a pile of crap!"

I hear voices in the hall. I bolt out of bed. Right before I get to the bathroom I hear the door open. Well, hell, Mom was right. What Matt saw wasn't pretty. Yup, I'm certain he got a nice view of my ass hanging out of the hospital gown.

I slam the door, drop on the toilet, and cry.

I'm in there for a good ten minutes before I realize the tampon dangling from my chest is still wrapped. And a clean gown is hanging on a hook.

I crater. I shower.

Dressed, hair soaking wet, I listen at the door to see if I hear anyone. There are no voices. I ease the door open. I don't see anyone, but I can't see the chair against the wall. I grab the back of my gown together and walk out.

Good thing I did. Matt's there.

He looks good. But he looks tired too. Not haggard like Mom and Dad look sometimes, but just tired.

My heart goes to hurting.

I crawl into bed and don't say anything.

"I know why you did it," he says.

"Did what?" I ask.

"Pushed me away. You're trying to protect me."

I don't say anything.

"Problem is, I don't want to be protected. And it chaps my ass that you did it. Because that hurt!"

I look up. My throat's so tight I'm not sure I can speak, but I do it anyway. "Welcome to my world." My vision blurs. "You said you couldn't take it. Do you know how long I pretended I was normal for you?"

I grip the sheets in my fists. "I'm sick, Matt. I have to take medicine every day, twice a day. If something is uncooked and it's not one hundred percent clean, it could kill me. But then again, so could the medicine. It's known to cause cancer. Yet if I don't take it, my heart—Eric's heart—will die. Because my body really wants to kill it. I'm never going to be normal. I can't have kids. I don't know if I'll even be able to think in years."

He's staring at me. There are tears in his eyes.

"I'm sucking out everyone's soul that cares about me. And I can't help it. So go, Matt. Believe me, you don't want this! And I don't want to see it happening to you." I point to the door.

He tilts his chin up. "I never asked you to pretend. You kept it from me."

"Yeah. So you wouldn't leave me again. Don't you see?" I ask, and tears are running down my face. "Please, just go."

"I said I was sorry. I told you that first day. Do you think I didn't regret it? You said you forgave me, but you lied. You didn't even give me a chance! You gave up on me!"

I put my hand over my mouth. "You've already lost too much."

He gets up and walks to my bed. He even sits on the bottom edge of it. His leg is touching mine. I'm hurting. I'm hurting so damn bad.

"Yeah, I have lost a lot," he says. "But do you think if someone told me that I would lose my dad that I would have said I didn't want him in my life? Do you think I would have said I didn't want to be a twin? To know Eric? To love him? I want to be a part of your life, Leah."

"Why?" I ask. "Why would you want this?"

He moves up. He's sitting at my waist now. I can smell him. I've missed that smell. He reaches out and touches my hand. It's electric. It sends bolts of want, need, and love into me.

When he doesn't answer my question, I ask again. "Why? Is being close to me your way of staying close to Eric?"

He shakes his head. "You are the stupidest smart person I've ever known. I don't want to be a part of your life because you have Eric's heart." He puts his hand over my chest, over his brother's heart. Then he leans down; his lips are so close. "I want to be a part of your life, because you have my heart, Leah McKenzie."

He kisses me. Then he kisses me again. And again.

"I love my locket," I say.

"Good." He kisses me again.

"And I love you, too," I say.

"Good."

The next thing I know, we're making out on a hospital bed. I look at him. "It's not going to be easy."

"Who wants easy?" he says. "I love you."

He shifts. His foot hits the bedside table. Something falls to the floor and we hear, "Now that's a pile of shit." We both laugh, the kind of laugh that makes life feel sweet. And it is . . . sweet.

epilogue

MAY 28TH

"You ready?" Principal Burns asks me.

Hell, no! Why did I agree to this? Oh, yeah, Matt and I had Chinese food the night before Burns called me into his office and asked me to do it. I'd have said no if my fortune cookie hadn't read: "Take the next challenge offered you."

Lesson learned. Give up Chinese food.

I hear my name over the loud speaker. Mom and Dad give me the thumbs-up and a proud-of-you hug. There's so much happiness in their expressions that I almost start crying. Which really wouldn't be good right now.

I nod, straighten my graduation hat, and walk the green mile to the podium.

"Hi," I say to the auditorium holding over a thousand people.

My palms are sweaty. My stomach's a racetrack for butterflies. "Well, you know my name. You should also know that the only reason I'm up here tonight is because our mayor, who was scheduled to speak, got caught up in something."

Everyone laughs, because, thanks to the news, everyone knows what he got caught up in was a lady of the evening. Never mind it was daylight, in a car, parked in front of the courthouse, with photographers nearby and he exposed tattoos no one knew he had.

I take a breath. "Desperate, Mr. Burns asked if I'd fill in. He seems to thinks I'm qualified, probably because . . . I'm working on my third heart. And because, as yet, I'm tattooless." More laughter echoes, and I feel better.

"In all seriousness, a virus called myocarditis killed my first heart. The doctors gave me an artificial one. But it's like a spare tire: it's doesn't promise you a lot of miles. Then some brave person and his family gave me his heart when he died. And I'll talk more about that in a minute." I swallow the emotion threatening to take out my tonsils.

"Some of you may have noticed we changed the motto for graduation. It was Live for the Day. The only way I'd agree to speak was if I was allowed to change it. Our new motto is The Art of Making Tomorrows."

I look up, and a banner with the motto unfolds above us. People clap. I stand up a little taller. "I decided to talk about a few lessons I picked up while going through my first two hearts.

"So often we are told not to live in yesterday. And there's some sound advice in that. If we aren't careful, yesterday can steal our todays and tomorrows. But we can't forget yesterday either. It's part of the map of how we got to today. Yesterday holds secrets, good memories, great memories, and really bad ones. It holds our mistakes. Someone said that our mistakes really just mean we're trying. But it can also mean we need to try in a different way.

"So if we forget our yesterdays, we'll lose the lessons we learned from our mistakes. We'd lose some cherished memories. For all of us graduating, it would mean we'd forget high school. We'd forget how awful it was and how freaking fantastic it was. We'd forget those stolen kisses in the hall, the lunchroom tuna casserole, and how it felt to ace a test. We'd forget how we learned to stand up for ourselves. And I don't know about you, but I need to remember those lessons, to apply them as I move forward. And I already have applied them. I have committed myself to never eating tuna casserole ever again."

I breathe in when they laugh. "Then there's that old motto Live for the Day. That's really good advice. Living in the present means we're taking in more, caring more, enjoying more. Regretting less. And that's a win-win, but only if we remember our journey doesn't end here. We've probably all heard the song, 'Live Like You Were Dying.' I'm here to tell you, it's not all it's cracked up to be.

"Personally, the tomorrow lesson is the one I had the most trouble with, because . . . it felt like myocarditis stamped an expiration date on my butt.

"I was too scared to count on tomorrow. Not just for me, but for those people who cared about me. Every time I looked at them I knew I was letting them down by leaving them too soon. A very smart doctor told me that caring is part of the human condition and you can't stop people from doing it. But I still thought if I didn't count on tomorrow, they wouldn't be so disappointed if I didn't get it.

"When I stopped thinking of tomorrow, I also stopped hoping, wanting, and dreaming. I wasn't thinking about college. I wasn't planning my future, because I didn't think I had one. But not thinking about tomorrow is as bad as being stuck in yesterday.

"To plan for our futures, we must remember yesterday, live for today, but dream for tomorrow. Just three weeks ago I signed up for college. I want to get an English degree and become a published author one day.

"I'd never have enrolled or felt the thrill of living my dreams if someone hadn't signed the donor card. I'd never have known what it's like to fall in love or graduate high school. I'd never have seen the pride on my parents' faces today when I put on this cap and gown." I look out into the crowd and I see my mom crying and hugging Dad. "Look at them. Look at their happiness and you'll know that the heart I got wasn't just a gift for me, but for them. All you parents out there should be able to relate.

"So, please, prove my doctor right. Prove that caring is a human condition. Sign up to be a donor so others out there can experience the art of making tomorrow. And while you're at it, get creative with your own life. You only get one. Make it matter. Live, not like you're dying, but like tomorrow is a promise."

I tip my hat and then move off the stage. I hear clapping. It goes on for a long while. Matt and Brandy are at the other side of the stage. Brandy, tears in her eyes, yells, "You rocked it!" Matt picks me up and twirls me around.

I'm not sure I rocked it, but I'm glad I took the challenge. Maybe I won't give up Chinese food.

They start calling everyone's names to receive their diplomas. Afterward lots of people come up and thank me for the talk. When the crowd starts to clear and I see someone starting to approach, I almost gasp.

"You came," I say. I'd sent her an invitation, but I really didn't think she'd come. "Of course I came," Dr. Hughes, with tears in her eyes, says. "And just so you know, I don't think I've ever been prouder of my work than tonight. You are amazing."

I hug her hard. When she moves on, I see who's behind her. My stomach goes instantly tight. Mrs. Kenner walks up closer. I can't read her expression.

"Matt's right. There is no one I'd rather have my son's heart. And I guess I could say that about both my sons."

"Thank you." We hug, and it's then, right then, that I feel my new heart making itself at home in my chest. I needed that hug. Eric needed that hug.

It's then that the last shadows of guilt I've felt about being alive fades. It's then that I finally feel comfortable in my own skin, comfortable with being New Leah. It's then I realize I'm really ready. Ready for my future. Ready to see where this crazy new life is going to lead me.

Dear Reader,

It was thirty-five years ago. A cute, curly-haired man with a twinkle in his blue eyes, whom I'd dated all of three times, told me we needed to have a serious talk. Sitting on a sofa that night, he told me he had polycystic kidney disease and there was a good chance that his later years would be difficult. He'd been told that by the time he was forty, he would be on dialysis. He told me he was falling for me and thought it was only fair that I knew this up front.

I remember looking at him and saying, "Why the heck didn't you tell me this on our first date?" Because, dad-blast it, I was already half in love with him. Less than a year later, I married him for better or worse.

Because he took such good care of himself, he didn't need dialysis until he was fifty-three. We did what we were supposed to do: got on the transplant list. His blood type was one that took longer to find a match. Soon the dialysis took its toll, and it wasn't just his kidney disease trying to steal him from me, but his heart.

There wasn't a day that passed that I didn't pray for a miracle. Not a day that I didn't wonder how I would survive without his love, his sense of humor, and that damn twinkle in his eye.

Like Leah, I got that miracle when someone chose to donate their organs, and my husband got a second chance at life.

As I write this, I'm reminded of how often I'm asked, "What's the book of your heart?" I always used to spout out the book I was working on, because it felt closer to me. I can't do that anymore. While this story is fiction, the emotion on the page came directly from my and my husband's hearts, from our pain, our fear, and from the miracle we experienced.

And while my husband is one who seldom ever remembers his dreams, when he woke up from that transplant, he started having a reoccurring dream. A short, succinct dream where he woke up to find an old man with his face right in my husband's, staring at him.

When we discovered it was a kidney from a sixty-five-year-old man, it gave us goose bumps. The doctors assured us that the medications he was on could cause those vivid dreams. And maybe that was it. Or maybe it wasn't. Either way, the experience gave me the plot thread in *This Heart of Mine*.

I hope you enjoyed the story. I hope it inspires you to live your life to the fullest. To write your bucket list now and start fulfilling it. I hope you might even decide to become a donor to help someone else get their second chance at life.

If you are interested in becoming a donor or helping out in some other way, please go to https://www.donatelife.net/.

Thank you,
CC

TURN THE PAGE FOR A SNEAK PEEK AT
C. C. HUNTER'S NEXT NOVEL

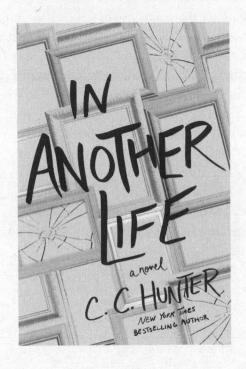

AVAILABLE MARCH 2019

1

"What are you doing?" I ask when Dad pulls over at a con-venience store only a mile from where Mom and I are now living. My voice sounds rusty after not talking during the five-hour ride. But I was afraid that if I said anything, it would all spill out: My anger. My hurt. My disappointment in the man who used to be my superhero.

"I need gas and a bathroom," he says.

"Bathroom? So you can't even come in to see Mom when you drop me off?" My heart crinkles up like a used piece of aluminum foil.

He meets my eyes, ignores my questions, and says, "You want anything?"

"Yeah. My freaking life back!" I jump out of the car and slam the door so hard, the sound of the metal hitting metal cracks in the hot Texas air. I haul ass across the parking lot, watching my white sandals eat up the pavement, hiding the sheen of tears in my eyes.

"Chloe," Dad calls out. I move faster.

Eyes still down, I yank open the door, bolt inside the store, and smack right into someone. Like, my boobs smash against someone's chest.

"Crap," a deep voice growls.

A Styrofoam cup hits the ground. Frozen red slushie explodes all over my white sandals. The cup lands on its side, bleeding red on the white tile.

I swallow the lump in my throat and jerk back, removing my B cup boobs from some guy's chest.

"Sorry," he mutters, even though it's my fault.

I force myself to look up, seeing first his wide chest, then his eyes and the jet-black hair scattered across his brow. *Great! Why couldn't he be some old fart?*

I return to his bright green eyes and watch as they shift from apologetic to shocked, then to angry.

I should say something—like, add my own apology—but the lump in my throat returns with a vengeance.

"Shit." The word sneaks through his frown.

Yeah, all of this is shit! I hear Dad call my name again from outside.

My throat closes tighter and tears sting my eyes. Embarrassed to cry in front of a stranger, I snatch off my sandals and dart to a cooler.

Opening the glass door, I stick my head in needing a cooldown. I swat a few stray tears off my cheeks. Then I feel someone next to me. Dad's not letting this go.

"Just admit you screwed up!" I look over and am swallowed by those same angry light green eyes from a minute ago. "I thought you were . . . Sorry," I say, knowing it's late for an apology. His look is unsettling.

He continues to glare. An all-in-my-face kind of glare. As if this is more than a spilled slushie to him.

"I'll pay for it." When he doesn't even blink, I add another, "I'm sorry."

His question seethes out. "Why are you here?"

"What? Do I *know* you?" I know I was rude, but—hotness aside—this guy is freaking me out.

His eyes flash anger. "What do you want?" His tone carries an accusation I don't understand.

"What do you mean?" I counter.

"Whatever you're trying to pull, don't do it."

He's still staring me down. And I feel like I'm shrinking in his glare.

"I'm not . . . You must have me mixed up with someone else." I shake my head, unsure if this guy's as crazy as he is sexy. "I don't know what you're talking about. But I said I'm sorry." I grab a canned drink and barefoot, carrying sticky sandals, hurry to the front of the store.

Dad walks in, scowling.

"Careful," a cashier says to Dad while mopping up the slushie just inside the door.

"Sorry," I mutter to the worker, then point to Dad. "He's paying for my Dr Pepper! And for that slushie."

I storm off to the car, get in, and hold the cold Diet Dr Pepper can to my forehead. The hair on the back of my neck starts dancing. I look around, and the weird hot guy is standing outside the store, staring at me again.

Whatever you're trying to pull, don't do it.

Yup, crazy. I look away to escape his gaze. Dad climbs back in the car. He doesn't start it, just sits there, eyeballing me. "You know this isn't easy for me either."

"Right." *So why did you leave?*

He starts the car, but before we drive off, I look around again and see the dark-haired boy standing in the parking lot, writing on the palm of his hand.

Is he writing down Dad's license plate number? He's a freak. I almost say something to Dad but remember I'm pissed at him.

Dad pulls away. I focus on the rearview mirror. The hot guy stays there, eyes glued on Dad's car, and I stay glued on him until he's nothing but a speck in the mirror.

"I know this is hard," Dad says. "I think about you every day."

I nod, but don't speak.

Minutes later, Dad pulls over in front of our mailbox. Or rather Mom's and mine. Dad's home isn't with us anymore. "I'll call you tomorrow to see how your first day of school was."

My gut knots into a pretzel with the reminder that I'll be starting as a senior at a new school. I stare out at the old house, in the old neighborhood. This house once belonged to my grandmother. Mom's been renting it to an elderly couple for years. Now we live here. In a house that smells like old people . . . and sadness.

"Is she home?" Dad asks.

In the dusk of sunset, our house is dark. Gold light leaks out of next door, Lindsey's house—she's the one and only person I know my own age in town.

"Mom's probably resting," I answer.

There's a pause. "How's she doing?"

You finally ask? I look at him gripping the wheel and staring at the house. "Fine." I open the car door, not wanting to draw out the goodbye. It hurts too much.

"Hey." He smiles. "At least give me a hug?"

I don't want to, but for some reason—because under all this anger, I still love him—I lean over the console and hug him. He doesn't even smell like my dad. He's wearing cologne that Darlene probably bought him. Tears sting my eyes.

"Bye." I get one slushie-dyed foot out the car.

Before my butt's off the seat, he says, "Is she going back to work soon?"

I swing around. "Is that why you asked about her? Because of money?"

"No." But the lie is so clear in his voice, it hangs in the air.

Who is this man? He dyes the silver at his temples. He's sporting a spiky haircut and wearing a T-shirt with the name of a band he didn't even know existed until Darlene.

Before I can stop myself, the words trip off my tongue. "Why? Does your girlfriend need a new pair of Jimmy Choos?"

"Don't, Chloe," he says sternly. "You sound like your mom."

That hurt now knots in my throat. "Pleeease. If I sounded like my mom, I'd say, 'Does the whore bitch need a new pair of Jimmy Choos!'" I swing back to the door.

He catches my arm. "Look, young lady, I can't ask you to love her like I do, but I expect you to respect her."

"Respect her? You have to earn respect, Dad! If I wore the clothes she wears, you'd ground me. In fact, I don't even respect you anymore! You screwed up my life. You screwed up Mom's life. And now you're screwing someone eighteen years younger than yourself." I bolt out and get halfway to the house when I hear his car door open and slam.

"Chloe. Your stuff." He sounds angry, but he can just join the crowd, because I'm more than mad—I'm hurt.

If I weren't afraid he'd follow me into the house all pissed off and start an argument with Mom, I'd just keep going. But I don't have it in me to hear them fight again. And I'm not sure Mom's up to it either. I don't have an option but to do the right thing. It sucks when you're the only person in the family acting like an adult.

I swing around, swat at my tears, and head back to the curb.

He's standing beside his car, my backpack in one hand

and a huge shopping bag with the new school clothes he bought me in the other. Great. Now I feel like an ungrateful bitch.

When I get to him, I mutter, "Thanks for the clothes."

He says, "Why are you so mad at me?"

So many reasons. Which one do I pick? "You let Darlene turn my room into a gym."

He shakes his head. "We moved your stuff into the other bedroom."

"But that was my room, Dad."

"Is that really why you're mad or . . . ? He pauses. "It's not my fault that your mom got—"

"Keep thinking that," I snap. "One of these days, you might even believe it!"

Hands full, chest heavy, I leave my onetime superhero and my broken heart scattered on the sidewalk. My tears are falling fast and hot by the time I shut the front door behind me.

Buttercup, a medium-sized yellow mutt of a dog, greets me with a wagging tail and a whimper. I ignore him. I drop my backpack, my shopping bag, and dart into the bathroom. Felix, my red tabby cat, darts in with me.

I attempt to shut the door in a normal way instead of an I'm-totally-pissed way. If Mom sees me like this, it'll upset her. Even worse, it'll fuel her anger.

"Chloe?" Mom calls. "Is that you?"

"Yeah. I'm in the bathroom." I hope I don't sound as emotionally ripped as I feel.

I drop down on the toilet seat, press the backs of my hands against my forehead, and try to breathe.

Mom's steps creak across the old wood floors. Her voice sounds behind the door. "You okay, hon?"

Felix is purring, rubbing his face on my leg. "Yeah. My stomach's . . . I think the meat loaf I had at Dad's was bad."

"Did Darlene fix it?" Her tone's rolled and deep-fried in hate.

I grit my teeth. "Yeah."

"Please tell me your dad ate a second helping."

I close my eyes, when what I really want to do is scream, *Stop it!* I get why Mom's so angry. I get that my dad's a piece of shit. I get that he refuses to take any blame, and that makes it worse. I get what she's been through. I get all of it. But does she have a clue how much it hurts me to listen to her take potshots at someone I still sort of love?

"I'm going to sit out on the patio," she says. "When you're out, join me."

"Uh-huh," I say.

Mom's steps creak away.

I stay seated and try not to think about what all hurts, and instead I pet Felix. His eyes, so green, take me back to the boy in the store. *Whatever you're trying to pull, don't do it.*

What the heck did he mean?

I leave the bathroom, but before I open the back door, I stare out the living room window at Mom reclined on a lawn chair. The sun's setting and she's bathed in gold light. Her eyes are closed, her chest moves up and down in slow breaths. She's so thin. Too thin.

Her faded blue bandanna has slipped off her head. All I see is baldness. And—*bam!*—I'm mad at Dad again.

Maybe Dad's right. Maybe I do blame him for Mom's cancer.

It doesn't even help to remember that three weeks ago, the doctor ruled her cancer-free. In fact, her breast cancer was found so early that the doctors insisted it was just a bump in the road.

I hate bumps.

My gaze shifts to her head again. The doctor claimed the short rounds of chemo were to make sure there weren't any cancer cells floating around in her body. But until I see her hair grown back, and stop seeing her ribs, I won't stop being afraid of losing her.

When she was diagnosed, I thought Dad would come back, that he'd realize he still loved her. What's sad is that I think Mom thought he would, too. It didn't happen.

Mom's eyes open, she adjusts her bandanna, then stands up with open arms. "Come here. I missed you."

"I was only gone three days," I say. But it's the first time I left her overnight since she got cancer. And I missed her, too.

We walk into each other's arms. Her hugs started lasting longer since she and Dad separated. Mine got tighter when the big C stained our lives.

I pull out of her embrace. Buttercup is at my feet, his wagging tail hitting my leg.

"Has she redecorated the house?" Her tone is casual, but still loaded with animosity.

Just my room. Going for a conversational U-turn, I ask, "What did you do while I was gone?"

"I read two books." She grins.

"You didn't pull up your manuscript and try to write?" Before Mom and Dad's problems, Mom spent every free moment working on a book. She called it her passion. I suppose Dad killed that, too.

"No. Not feeling it," she says. "Oh, look." She pulls her bandanna off. "I got peach fuzz. I hear women pay big bucks to get this look."

I laugh, not because it's funny, but because she's laughing. I don't remember the last time Mom laughed. Are things getting better?

She moves over to the swing. "Sit down."

It sinks with her weight. Mom's shoulder bumps into mine.

She looks at me, really looks at me. Is she seeing my just-cried puffiness? "What's wrong, baby?"

The concern in her voice, the love in her eyes, they remind me of when I could go to her with my problems. When I didn't weigh every word to make sure it wouldn't hurt her. Because she already has way too much hurt.

"Nothing," I say.

Her mouth thins. "Did your dad upset you?"

"No," I lie.

Her gaze stays locked on me as if she knows I'm not being honest. I throw something out there: "It's Alex."

"Did you see him while you were there?"

Another lump lodges in my throat—I guess this subject is too tender to touch on, too. "He came by and we talked in his car."

"And?"

"And nothing." I bundle up that pain for another time. "I told you he's seeing someone else."

"I'm sorry, baby. Do you hate me for moving you here?"

Duh, you can't hate someone who has cancer. But now that the cancer is gone . . . ? Tempting, but I can't. Just like I can't hate Dad.

"I don't hate you, Mom."

"But you hate it here?" Guilt adds a sad note to her voice. It's the first time she's considered my feelings about this. I tried my damnedest to talk her out of moving—I even begged—but she didn't give. So I gave. I've done a lot of giving.

My vision blurs with tears. "It's just hard."

My phone dings with a text. I don't want to check it, thinking it's Dad texting to say he's sorry, and Mom might see it, then I'd have to explain. *He is sorry, isn't he?* I want to believe he realized giving my room to Darlene was a mistake.

"Who's that?" Mom asks.

"Don't know." My phone remains in my pocket.

It dings again. *Shit!*

"You can check it," Mom says.

I pull it out and hold it close. It's not Dad. And now that stings, too.

"It's Lindsey." I read her text. *Come over when you can.*

"She called earlier to see if you were home. Why don't you go see her? I'll fix dinner."

"I'll just text her," I say, knowing Lindsey will ask about my trip, and I don't know her well enough to dump on her.

"Okay." Mom pats my arm. "What do you want for dinner?"

"Pizza." I'm starving. I barely touched my lunch before leaving Dad's.

"Pizza? On an iffy stomach," Mom says. "How about tomato soup and grilled cheese?"

I hate tomato soup. It's sick food. Cancer food. We ate that every night of chemo. Then again, I suppose that's what I get for lying. "Sure."

Soup, a sandwich, and two sitcoms later, I hug Mom goodnight and head to bed. Both Buttercup and Felix follow me into my room. Or rather, the room I sleep in. *My* room doesn't exist anymore.

I grab my phone to see if any of my old friends, or maybe Alex, has texted me. Nothing's there except a message from Lindsey, reminding me to text her when I'm ready to leave for school.

I flop on my bed. Felix jumps up, snuggles beside me, and starts purring. Buttercup leaps up and lies at my feet. Phone still in hand, I swipe the screen to the selfies I took of me, Cara, and Sandy this weekend. We're all smiling, but not that big, natural kind of smile. All of us look sort of posed. Like we're faking something. Fake smiling. Faking friendship.

My finger keeps swiping until I find the older selfies with Cara and Sandy. We aren't posed, or phony looking. We're having fun. It shows in our expressions, our real smiles.

I keep going until I get to one of me and Alex. He's kissing my cheek. His blue eyes are cut to the camera, and I can tell he's laughing. I remember when it was taken. The first night we slept together. Tears fill my eyes, and my finger swipes faster. Images, snapshots of my life become nothing more than smears of color flying across my phone's screen.

I wonder if that's all life really is, just smears of color. A collage of sweeping moments in different shades and hues of emotions. Times when you're happy, sad, angry, scared, and when you're just faking it.

I toss my phone to the end of my bed and stare at the ceiling fan going around and round, and my emotions do the same. My eyes grow heavy, then—*bam!*—I'm not there staring at a fan. I'm trapped in a memory almost as old as I am.

I'm sitting on a brown sofa. My feet, buckled up in black patent leather shoes, dangle above dirty carpet. I'm wearing a pink frilly princess dress, but I'm not a happy princess. Deep heartfelt sobs, my sobs, echo around me. I'm a fish out of water. I can't breathe.

I sit up so fast, Felix bolts off the bed.

It's the only memory I have from before I became Chloe Holden. A few months before my third birthday. Before I was adopted.

Lately, the memory has jumped out at me. Haunting me, in a way. I know why, too. It's the sensation. The one of being plucked out of my world and planted somewhere else.

Not that it didn't work out. Back then, I lucked out and

was adopted into perfection. I had a mom, a dad, got a cat I named Felix, and eventually we got a dog named Buttercup. We lived in a three-bedroom white brick house filled with lots of laughter. And love. I had friends I grew up with. A boyfriend I'd given my virginity to.

I had a life. I was happy. I smiled real smiles in photos.

Then came Dad working late.

Mom and Dad fighting.

Dad's affair.

Mom's depression.

The divorce.

The cancer.

And then the move from El Paso to Joyful, Texas. Which, by the way, isn't joyful.

And here I am. Plucked again. So *plucked*.

But this time, I'm not feeling so lucky.